PRAISE FOR
CURSE OF THE COLORING BOOK

A Novel Inspired by a True Story

"The author depicts clearly that even in the darkest of times, life is something to be cherished. Though there's pain and chaos, life still has its own tenderness. I served in combat in the Vietnam War, and this thoughtful story, with well-developed characters, had a deep impact on me, bringing back memories, some of which I didn't want to remember. Fortunately, humor is balanced with the ills of war throughout the book, coming at just the right times."

—Sam N. Torres
Vietnam Veteran

"First-time novelist Howard L. Hibbard carries the reader along on his journey as a naive frat boy who leaves his "coloring books" behind to enlist as a combat infantry lieutenant headed for Vietnam. Flashbacks to his unforgettable war experiences along the Cambodian border plague the protagonist, who is now an attorney, as he defends himself against a malpractice suit. The story is artfully woven together with colorful vignettes that poignantly portray the harsh realities of war while reminding us of the humanity and the consequences of surviving. This is a liberating story that will foster both empathy and understanding of our Post-Traumatic Stress Disorder vets. It is a book you will not soon forget and a must-read if you love a vet who is struggling with PTSD."

—Elizabeth B. Williams
Attorney

"*Curse of the Coloring Book* tells one man's story, beginning with when he went into the Army, and of leading a platoon of men known as the Wolfhounds at a time when the war was at its worst. The reader will get an inside look at life in the theater of combat as each man tries to figure out how to make it through one more day. Although the characters are given fictitious names, I recognized many of the men I served with in the second platoon. I served in the platoon in 1968–69 and left Vietnam just as Howard was coming in. Reading the book helped me to remember the great Wolfhounds I served with. Our motto, *Nec Aspera Terrent* (No Fear On Earth), reflected our commitment to serve with distinction and always having our brothers' back."

—Staff Sergeant John "Big John" Quintrell
2/27th Wolfhounds, C Company, 2nd Platoon
Vietnam Veteran

"Howard L. Hibbard crafts an engaging story around his own service in Vietnam and coming to grips with PTSD after returning home. His realistic story telling about an infantry lieutenant's tour of duty rivals that in other classic Vietnam War novels, but goes well beyond the battlefield. A unique twist is weaving the lasting impact of his combat experience into the fabric of his future life as a struggling lawyer. Action-packed battle scenes and courtroom drama combine to make *Curse of the Coloring Book* a must-read."

—Dave Mandelkern
Tech & Health Care Entrepreneur

"I thoroughly enjoyed *Curse of the Coloring Book* and recommend that anyone who served in Vietnam read it. The story is very authentic; I know because I served with the Wolfhounds in 1969. The novel brought back memories I've suppressed for forty-plus years. It also realistically portrays how we dealt with life when we returned home."

—James "Jim" L. Brandau
Staff Sergeant, 2/27th Wolfhounds, C Company, 2nd Platoon
Vietnam Veteran

"A terrifying and humorous account of a combat soldier's ordeal in Vietnam. Terrifying because it's based on a true story. Humorous for the wild, funny characters and crazy stories."

—Dr. Douglas Gauvreau
Army Captain, 82nd Airborne Division Veteran

"I served in combat in Vietnam, and *Curse of the Coloring Book* puts the reader inside the head of the main character; through his eyes we all see the hard reality of leadership and its effect. I've read hundreds of books by Vietnam Veterans, and this one book covers it all, from Vietnam to civilian life."

—Tommy Clack
Captain RET, Forward Artillery Observer
2/27th Wolfhounds, C Company
Vietnam Veteran
Wounded 5/29/69

"Takes you inside the heart, soul and emotions of the Vietnam War era. If you don't understand how or why PTSD exists, or what our brave young service people went through, you will after reading *Curse of the Coloring Book*."

—Susan Uccelli

"*Curse of the Coloring Book* describes the very human experience of surviving a year in an infantry unit in Vietnam, and then trying to hide it in some internal box so that it doesn't destroy the rest of one's life after the war. We learn through the main character, Herald Lloyd, that his life after the war, his marriage and law practice, are influenced by underlying trauma from his combat experience. Fortunately, he never loses his sense of humor about the human condition in general and his own life in particular. In spite of it all, Herald never takes himself too seriously, and we get to ride along with him as he delves into his two worlds.

"Mr. Hibbard's mainly autobiographical story of war, and the subsequent attempt to adjust to a civilian world, is one most Americans have no understanding of. It is one of the reasons that this book is so compelling. It's a story that must be told again and again until society develops some equation between the decision to go to war in some remote part of the world, and the life-altering devastation it leaves behind in the soldiers who participate."

—Thomas Bailey
　　Lieutenant Colonel, Vietnam Veteran
　　Retired Attorney

Curse of the
COLORING
BOOK

Curse of the
COLORING
BOOK

A Novel Inspired by a True Story

Howard L. Hibbard

Ghost Dog Enterprises, Inc., Daly City, CA

Curse of the Coloring Book: A Novel Inspired by a True Story
Howard L. Hibbard

Permission Rights to Reprint Lawrence Ferlinghetti Poems

"The world is a beautiful place to be born into" (excerpt of 11 lines)
CREDIT LINE: By Lawrence Ferlinghetti, from A CONEY ISLAND OF THE MIND, Copyright ©1955
    by Lawrence Ferlinghetti. Reprinted by permission of New Directions Publishing Corp.
SALES TERRITORY: U.S., its territories, and Canadian rights only.

"And that's the way it always is and that's the way" (excerpt of 8 lines)
"Cast up the heart flops over"
"Christ Climbed Down" (excerpt of 11 lines)
"Don't let that horse eat that violin"
"In Goya's greatest scenes we seem to see" (excerpt of 31 lines)
"Johnny Nolan has a patch on his ass"
"'One of those paintings that would not die'"
"See it was like this when"
CREDIT LINE: By Lawrence Ferlinghetti, from A CONEY ISLAND OF THE MIND, Copyright ©1958
    by Lawrence Ferlinghetti. Reprinted by permission of New Directions Publishing Corp.
SALES TERRITORY: U.S., its territories, and Canadian rights only.

Library of Congress Control Number: 2016957950

Publisher's Cataloging-In-Publication Data
(Prepared by The Donohue Group, Inc.)
Names: Hibbard, Howard L., 1947–
Title: Curse of the coloring book : a novel inspired by a true story / Howard L. Hibbard.
Description: Daly City, CA : Ghost Dog Enterprises, Inc., [2016]
Identifiers: LCCN 2016957950 | ISBN 978-0-9856344-6-9 (paperback) |
    ISBN 978-0-9856344-7-6 (ebook)
Subjects: LCSH: Lawyers--California--San Francisco--Fiction. | Vietnam War,
    1961-1975--Veterans--United States--Fiction. | Vietnam War, 1961-1975--Psychological
    aspects--Fiction. | Post-traumatic stress disorder--Fiction. | LCGFT: Historical fiction. |
    War fiction. | BISAC: FICTION / Historical. | FICTION / War & Military.
Classification: LCC PS3608.I333 C87 2016 (print) | LCC PS3608.I333 (ebook) | DDC
    813/.6--dc23

To those lost souls of the Vietnam War
my respect and compassion
to the survivors
living with unexpected adversities

CONTENTS

CHAPTER I
GETTING TO KNOW YOU

HOW HAS IT COME TO THIS? Herald Lloyd wondered as he laid on the horn of his 1969 VW van, swerving around a stalled, brand-new 1988 station wagon. If he did not make it to court in the next thirty-five minutes, his life as he knew it—not to mention his wife's and daughters' lives—would take the old plunge down the crapper. All he had to do was convince a judge he should be forgiven for a clerical mistake on a legally binding document. The situation was considerably more complicated, but that was it in a nutshell.

To keep his brain from locking up with fear, Herald thought back to how this had all begun, starting on what seemed like an ordinary morning just thirty-seven days ago.

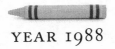

YEAR 1988

THE BLUE NORTHERN CALIFORNIA sky called for a glance upward, but as Herald complied, the sun's rays seared his forty-one-year-old eyes, bloodshot from another night of excess. Shading his eyes from the unwelcome glare, he climbed the five steps to the 1908 vintage Queen

1

Anne Victorian house that now served as his office. He had acquired the building in 1987 and renovated it to showcase his legal practice. The building satisfied his great love of finely crafted, turn-of-the-century architecture. It was an inviting place to conduct legal business. The office desks and file cabinets, arranged in an artful way, gave a dignified look to the dark wood-paneled rooms. His clients would often comment that though they did not like having to visit an attorney, they enjoyed the charm and warmth his office offered. To them most law firms were cold and formal, devised to make already nervous clients feel even more intimidated.

The hangover throbbing in Herald's head from the prior night's Jack Daniel's excesses thundered like Indian war drums at Custer's Last Stand. Yet the drums were preferable to the pounding coming from deep inside his psyche, where he had attempted to incarcerate the torment of his hidden combat horrors.

After his tour of duty as a combat officer in Vietnam in 1969–1970, Herald pledged to lock up all his wartime experiences in an imaginary steel crypt in the lower recesses of his brain. To maintain this memory tomb, he planned to use the mental control he'd forged to keep himself composed while leading his men through rice-paddy conflicts in Vietnam. With these distractions now buried, he could focus his energies on civilian life.

Eighteen years later the doors of Herald's mental catacomb had become rusted and warped. The pressure of his war memories clamoring for resolution, combined with the day-to-day stress of running his law practice, was taking its toll. More and more he'd begun to rely on alcohol to dilute his past and present anxieties, the dependence causing physical damage and clouding his judgment. To friends who questioned his drinking, his temper was quick, insisting he needed no help from the VA or anyone else. He snapped, *"I can handle any Vietnam post-traumatic crap by myself."*

But that was then. This was now.

Hungover, he opened the large mahogany door to his office and allowed himself a moment's appreciation of the cool, dim room. Shutting the door, he walked to Deborah's desk to see if anything important had come in yesterday's mail delivery. Deborah, his chief legal secretary, kept the mail at her desk and disapproved of his opening it in her absence. However, since he usually arrived at 7:00 a.m., long before she arrived and before the telephones began ringing, he believed it was more efficient for him to open the mail from the day before and perform his research and dictation early, before his legal world erupted with distractions.

Noticing a thin, nonthreatening envelope he hadn't seen earlier, Herald picked it up and pulled out a single sheet of paper. He concentrated his blurred vision on the document until his throbbing eyes cleared and he was able to focus on the large block of words typed in a threatening upper case:

REQUEST FOR HEARING ON DEFAULT.

There was his client's name on the same line as the default damages—*demanding $2.4 million!*

Herald shook his head and blinked hard several times to make sure what he was seeing was not a product of last night's hard drinking.

"Holy shit!" he cried out, seconds before retching black bile into a nearby trash can.

Eight months earlier a homeowner association, claiming construction defects arising from his client's geotechnical report, had taken defaults against both his client's civil engineering corporation, Thall, Rogers & Associates, *and* his client individually, Norman Thall. An agreement had been reached with opposing counsel to relieve both from default. In layman's terms this REQUEST FOR HEARING ON DEFAULT meant that somehow the default against Thall had not been relieved; therefore his client had, in the court's view, ignored the court order to respond to the plaintiff. By letting this happen, Herald had committed legal malpractice in the career-ending sum of $2.4 million.

Dropping the rest of the mail, Herald hurried to the file room, a cloud of black doom starting to form around him. He whipped open the drawer in the heavy, fireproof cabinet that held the case file. Coughing sporadically to clear his throat, he grabbed the pertinent folder and pulled out the agreement.

"Oh my God," he whispered, face flushed. His breathing became labored, and the palms of his hands went damp as he asked himself, *How could I have been so goddamn stupid?*

The correspondence listed both parties, but as he scrutinized the formal document for relief from default that he'd filed with the court, he saw that only his client's *corporation* was named. Norman Thall as an *individual* was not named on the legal document. This was malpractice.

Memories of his Vietnam experiences began clouding his brain and confusing his concentration. He began feeling haunted, fearing this legal error was punishment for his oft-relived sense of failure in not living up to a promise to call the parents of his platoon sergeant as soon as he was discharged, to tell them their son had been killed in action alongside him, a solemn pact the two comrades had made during the war.

An attorney should at least be sure both of his clients' names are on the critical document. This was an open-and-shut case against him. The six-month time period for seeking relief from this mistake had passed. The only way to obtain relief now was to file a motion with the court, requiring a much more difficult—if not impossible—burden of proof. To make matters worse, the motion had to be heard by the court within thirty-seven days.

Herald's dream of running a mass-production law firm that would handle complex cases at the lowest possible cost to his clients by using standardized procedures and computers was at death's door. His lack of malpractice insurance would be the fatal blow if his motion to be relieved from default failed. His client Norman Thall, a man who made no pretense in displaying his aversion to lawyers, would have an airtight case for malpractice against Herald, a lawyer whose briefcase was *not* bulging with money.

Squeezing his temples with the heels of his hands, Herald pressed his sweaty forehead against the cold steel of the filing cabinet. His pre-programmed reflex made him reach over and open the file drawer marked

"W." Groping for relief behind the files, he grabbed the emergency half-pint of whiskey and, with a practiced hand, spun the top off using just his thumb. He took a deep swig. It seared all the way down.

This malpractice bomb had ignited his liquor-soaked emotions, leaving him burned out and with little energy to keep the metal doors of his psychological vault sealed against the clamoring, horrific war memories. The powerful Vietnam experiences fought back to escape the mental prison he had erected around them. He'd had this feeling before, but never with this intensity and never during the day. He took another gulp from the bottle.

I can handle this!

Up until now memories of Vietnam had intruded only in his nighttime dreams. The last war nightmare had occurred just two weeks ago: a Viet Cong soldier had jumped into Herald's bunker and shoved a bayonet at his throat before Herald could reach for his rifle. He woke from the dream and realized his workday stress had triggered this flashback.

Herald's mental control, honed in Vietnam by the looming specter of death, was in jeopardy. This was daytime. True, he was under intense stress, but he was fierce about keeping his war memories locked up.

Through a miniscule crack in the seal of the dungeon doors he had formed in his psyche, Herald felt a sinister neurosis gain fluid form and ooze out like blackened mercury. Looking for a way out, the dark fluid slithered its way up from his lower brain using any available blood vessels and aimed for his right ear.

Fighting against the incursion, Herald stooped, moved to the wall behind him and clapped his hands over his ears, a maneuver meant to block the murky fluid's movement to either ear and arrest his first daytime nightmare. As he mustered all his mental focus to drive the surging demon back, the fluid changed its course from his right ear and centered on his nasal passages.

Before Herald could pinch his nose closed, he visualized the fluid shooting from his nostrils and gathering shape in the corner of the room. Drawing its energy from Herald's anxieties, the black blob began to shape-shift, rising, growing and assuming the form of a Tyrannosaurus Rex.

The upper portion of the beast's head took on the aspect of a Viet Cong soldier's face, but the menacing mouth was all T-Rex, with a wide expanse of six-inch, dagger-like teeth. The prehistoric horror, now wearing the black pajamas of a Viet Cong soldier, charged at him.

Herald's imagination placed him on an expansive, flat rice paddy with no cover in sight. He groped for his weapon but found nothing. He did not panic; this dream was a rerun. It was the same nightmare that had paralyzed his mind when he'd first come under enemy gunfire in Vietnam. This dinosaur manifestation had exhausted its ability to cripple Herald.

There is always a catch in catastrophic nightmares; a tear in the fabric of credibility brings the dreamer's consciousness back from the edge. This was the apparition's second appearance and Herald was ready.

His earlier antidote to the fearsome dream rose in his consciousness: *How did the Viet Cong obtain black pajamas big enough to fit a T-Rex?* This amusing thought brought him back to reality.

Not this time, Mr. Hysteria. You've already played the dino card.

Herald crimped a smile. His war angst was growing stronger, but by locking the steel doors of his mental dungeon with his hard-earned combat control, he could still hold the line.

Sure, he could handle this. He raised the half-pint to his lips and finished it. The dinosaur vanished, leaving the inner passages of Herald's nostrils raw.

Regaining control of his breathing, Herald shuddered at the prospect of malpractice consequences. The possibilities produced the same dreaded acidic feeling in his stomach he had known so often in Vietnam, when terror was so close he could taste it all the way down his throat. Despair gripped his heart as he envisioned the worst consequences. He knew they could destroy the treasured post-war life he'd worked so hard to create.

The question of whether to disclose the mistake to Thall passed through his mind. He could manufacture some excuse. But he knew the battle commander's basic rule: in the face of disaster, retain your presence of mind and composure. Lose that and you lose everything. This mistake was bad enough to wipe out everything he and his wife and law partner Thea had

built up economically over the past nine years. The bad press and humiliation would be horrible. For any chance to correct the mistake, he had to
take the blame.

Herald squinted his eyes and lowered his head, thinking back to when
he and Thea had started their law firm. At the time, many other attorneys
had laughed at them, pointing out that San Mateo County was a closed
shop, already having too many established law firms.

Undaunted, they found a small office with three rooms in an older
building with a low rental rate. The upstairs back room had been rented
previously by a heroin-addicted silkscreen artist. He'd trashed the place
upon vacating, leaving used hypodermic needles stuck in the walls.

Herald and Thea had refurbished the hardwood fir floors, painted
the walls, installed ceiling fans, and hung old lithographs inherited from
his grandmother. The space took on the air of a charming 1930s office.
In appreciation the landlord gave them a reduced rent of $90 per month.

Herald and Thea launched the first legal clinic in the county dedicated
to helping people with large legal problems and small bank accounts. The
two of them worked hard, with Herald carrying a huge caseload and Thea
carrying a smaller load plus managing the law-office books and typing all
the legal proceedings and letters.

Those first years of keeping their business afloat involved cutting out
all unnecessary expenses. This translated to such unheard-of sacrifices as
no home telephone or TV, but the dream of running their own business,
having children, and buying a home made the frugal budget palatable.

Herald chuckled, remembering that a night of good entertainment in
those days was going to the grocery store. He recalled a trick he used to
play on Thea. When they went grocery shopping, he would sneak in a silly
purchase. One time it was 100 chopsticks; another time, two pizza pans.
Thea would scold him when they unpacked the purchases at home, but they
always got a good laugh at the silly game.

Now they played the blame game. It was not easy taking blame, especially since he had been getting so much of it lately from Thea. She was

on his case about his drinking, as he was drinking all the time. No way to escape that one.

This legal emergency made Herald realize he needed to apply one of the many rules he'd learned in Vietnam: be willing to take the responsibility—this is the important first step in regaining control of a situation. He owed it to Thea to step up on this one and make it right for the business and family.

The responsibility he felt for his client and family, just like his loyalty to his men in Vietnam, filled Herald with resolve. He pledged to find a passable route through the legal labyrinth.

Despite this resolution, anxiety and stress overwhelmed him. Perspiration beaded on his face and arms; his breathing became labored and shallow. This physical response revived memories of the sunny day in March 1970 when he was discharged from the Army, a mere twenty-two hours after leaving Vietnam.

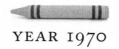

YEAR 1970

HERALD ENVISIONED HIMSELF leaving the out-processing clinic at Travis Air Force Base located halfway between San Francisco and Sacramento. He strolled, with the casual air of a person a-b-s-o-lutely no longer on an Army timetable, to the middle of a shabby parade field.

He likened his swift discharge to the perfect cherry atop an imaginary ice cream sundae made inedible by a frothy layer of the curdled whipped cream of social betrayal.

Herald removed his uniform shirt and slacks and, clad only in underwear and socks, gathered the uniform into a pile at his feet. Dropping to one knee, he removed a plastic resealable bag from the front breast pocket of his crumpled shirt. The bag contained a few books of matches sporting the bright red worn logo of Rick's Café Américain, Taipei, Taiwan. Herald pulled out one water-stained match and struck it.

Previous exposure to moisture in the Vietnam tropics caused the match tip to crumble and flare out in a tiny, burning, spiral arc. Removing two more matches, Herald struck them together. They lit slowly, each helping the other to ignite. When the matches were burning together, he touched their flaming tips to the worn elbow of the shirt on the ground and used his free hand to shelter the flame from the afternoon breeze.

The thin fabric was perfect tinder; the shirt quickly caught fire, and he fed his slacks to the eager flames. The blaze seemed to disappear in the bright sunshine and was visible only as a black flowing wave of smoke over the folds of the garments.

Jolted from his incendiary task, Herald was now laughing at the Army doctor, a short, overweight captain who had discharged him half an hour earlier, panting as he rushed down the three wooden steps descending from his office and screaming, "Hey, soldier! Earth calling, *Eaarrth caallling!* What the hell are you doing running around in your underwear and burning your uniform?"

The clinic was one of many old buildings surrounding the parade field that had been slapped together in record time to fill the urgent, growing demand during WWII for housing, food, and administration for a training brigade. In better times the walkway had been bordered by the decoration of small, roundish, irregular-shaped rocks, painted white, leading to the parade field. The rock border was now irregular due to rocks long gone. Only flakes of white paint remained in their absence, and the landscaping was dead. Overgrown weeds surrounding the buildings captured and held large scraps of white paint that had peeled from building walls. The dilapidated complex had been reopened for the out-processing and discharge of Vietnam returnees.

The doctor was coming down an overgrown path toward Herald. Bald and in poor physical condition for a thirty-something, Medical Captain Remph approached Herald with his stethoscope bobbing to and fro off his large belly. He looked like an uncoordinated circus juggler. His heaving chest struggled to bring oxygen to his exercise-starved lungs.

Shaking his head as he came within hearing range of Herald, he spit out his thoughts. "The Army is crazy to discharge soldiers directly off an airplane from a war zone without any concern for readjustment to society. This job of out-processing the Army's human refuse gets me no respect."

Remph was carrying a blanket, the end slowly flapping in the arid wind under the glare of a hot California noonday sun. Ripples of oven-temperature heat hovered about the doctor as he approached the almost-naked Herald, standing in the middle of the unkempt parade field.

As the doctor approached, Herald eyed the years of overgrown dead weeds, their condition signaling there was no popular interest in celebrations for Vietnam returnees.

Parades down Times Square in New York City are only for winners, he mused bitterly.

He'd overheard the doctor scolding himself for yelling his "Earth calling" insult in what could be an explosive situation, with the fuse beckoning to be lit. He watched as sweat dripped from the doctor's forehead down his nose onto the blanket; then he defiantly jerked his head to "attention" and stiffened his upper body.

Noticing this, Remph slowed his approach. For him it was easy to see the physical difference between those soldiers who'd walked the war and those who'd stayed in the large base camps. To him Herald appeared mesomorphic, like a weight-lifting gym rat; his back was an oversized "V" shape, with an overly muscular posterior for a man five-feet-nine.

Herald, remembering he was no longer in Vietnam, loosened up. When the doctor saw Herald's body relax, he picked up his pace. Symptoms of muscle tension and stiffening of posture could possibly lead to aggressive behavior. In the clinic, after the short time needed to adjust to the doctor and the medical surroundings, most uptight soldiers would relax, signaling the doctor could continue with his examination.

The doctor's job was to discharge returning soldiers from Vietnam, not to address their mental problems. But he knew some of these boys who served in the infantry needed special attention, having sloshed through the filth of war at its most basic level. He wondered if there was any easy prescription to help these young soldiers make the leap from survival mode in a combat zone to reassimilation as a civilian back in the U.S.—all within the blink of an airplane ride.

Herald glanced at his flaming uniform, turned his expressionless sun-burned face toward the doctor, and made direct eye contact. "Been dreaming of this for a long time, doc." He did not feel the heat from the sun or the blazing uniform. He was numb.

The doctor pondered what was behind those strange hazel eyes: a combination of confusion, anger, disappointment and who knew what else. The frown on the doctor's face softened and, wiping the sweat off his brow with the blanket, he asked, "Been dreaming of what—being without your clothes?"

The peaceful moment ended abruptly when the familiar *whurrr* of the propeller and sound of the piston engine on an Air Force ground attack plane passing overhead caught Herald's ear and spun him back to Vietnam.

The about-face change—being freed suddenly from his combat line-officer responsibilities—caused Herald's mind to burst into a swirling plasma of nerve impulses, like the mental equivalent of a fierce solar storm. Sweat immediately broke out on his face, gathered into rivulets, and dripped off his chin. His breathing became labored and shallow, as the memory of the physical effort to breathe Vietnam's humid 100-degree air returned. Without looking at the aircraft, he was back on patrol in Vietnam, when fire of another sort tore at the landscape.

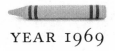

YEAR 1969

HERALD'S PLATOON WAS BREAKING through a thick bamboo hedge one kilometer east of the Cambodian border. The hedge surrounded a system of rice paddies about ten acres square. As he stepped out of the bamboo hedge, a thin bamboo shoot, trampled down earlier by the point man's boot, popped back up and slapped him in the face. He lowered his rifle, rubbing his stinging eyes and face with his free hand.

A hot breeze across the dry rice fields raised a musky dust, smelling of dried human and buffalo feces used to fertilize rice—adding another layer of grime to Herald's face and filling his nose.

Remind me again why I love this country ... ?

As Herald entered the rice paddy the *snap-snap* of rifle fire from a Russian-made AK-47 echoed overhead. With the first report he dove for the safety of ground, yelling "SHIT!" His entire platoon hit the dirt. Any one of those snaps could end a human life.

Three men in black pajamas about 100 yards away jumped up and ran to the back of the field, where two thick bamboo hedges met at a 90-degree corner. Two newbies in the platoon jumped up yelling, "Hey, LT, let's go get 'em!" The rest of the soldiers tensed and rose up to one knee, waiting for orders.

"Stop right there," Herald hollered at the newbies, "or I'll put a bullet in you myself! This is a trap called the 'bloody nose.' At the opposite corner of this field is a Viet Cong ambush just waiting for you stupid GIs to run into it, thinking you have Charlie on the run!" The fresh recruits stopped in their tracks, turned, and moved back to their assigned position at the rear of the platoon.

After three minutes or so, when the VC calculated the platoon was not going to run headlong into their ambush, they opened up with a 51 caliber heavy machine gun from the corner of the bamboo hedge. This weapon fired an inch-long, half-inch wide bullet at supersonic speed that could blast off a human arm or leg. Green tracers, which appeared to be the size of bricks, were discharged trailing every fifth bullet, confirming to the shooter their line of fire. Whistling overhead with the 51 caliber were more snaps of AK-47 fire—too numerous to count—from the same direction. The platoon remained on the ground.

Grabbing the radio, Herald snarled, "Baker One to Baker King, fire mission, ambush at grid 2044, any air support available? Over."

"It's your lucky day, Baker One. Just happen to have a FAC on deck. Call sign Air One. Over."

"Roger that. What's the frequency? Over."

"44.44. Out."

Changing the frequency, Herald keyed the mic on the radio hook and yelled into it, "Baker One to Air One, fire mission, Charles at opposite corner of field, need support. Popping a yellow smoke grenade now at grid 2044, watch out for the golden BB, over."

The reply carried the growl of a light observation plane engine in the background with the words jumping, "Got your smoke, and the green tracers coming your way. This is your Vegas jackpot. I'm just overhead, and 51-cal *a-a-ain't* no golden BB. A BB is at most a lucky AK-47 round. Two Sky Raiders inbound. It's going to get really hot, so get really small."

A mere forty seconds later, the *ROAAAAaaar* of the two Air Force attack planes resounded in the platoon's ears. As the planes' silver bodies flashed overhead, the soldiers could feel the ground pressure from their wings as the engine noise reverberated in their chests. The soldiers married their bodies to the ground and only then turned their curious heads sideways toward the corner of the field.

Four shiny aluminum napalm bombs, two per plane, left the aircraft just above the hidden platoon, giving off a low *whooosh*. The firebombs tumbled end over end, igniting and creating a blanket of fire on both sides of the field's corner.

Announcing the napalm's arrival was the impact of high-velocity, 20 mm cannon fire at 700 rounds per minute, four guns per plane. The pilots maneuvered their planes so the machine gun tracer fire sprayed back and forth over both sides of the rice paddy corner, penetrating through bunker walls and trees and removing any body part hit.

As the planes passed overhead, spent shell casings pelted down around the platoon, forming a hot brass carpet. The casings bruised exposed skin and clinked as they ricocheted off the soldiers' helmets. Two shell casings bounced off Herald's back—and they hurt like hell.

Never shoulda pulled that joke of having my frat brothers color pictures in that 'GI Joe Coloring Book' as a send-off to my joining the Army!

Even from 400 yards away, the overlapping sound of four 500-pound napalm bombs with 2,000 pounds of jellied gasoline igniting, *WO-VOOOOOM, WO-VOO, WO-VOO, WO-VOOOOOOOM,* sucked air out of his lungs, and the heat from the napalm nearly singed his hair.

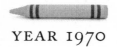

YEAR 1970

"OUCH!" HERALD BLURTED, yanking his hand back as scorching flames rose from his fiery uniform and snapped him out of his flashback. He stepped aside and succumbed to the hypnotic effect of the flames as they ebbed. The name tag on his uniform shirt was the last thing to yield to the fire's dark wave.

The whip-stitched edging of the tag blackened and transferred its heat inward until the letters were lost in gray cinders. The last evidence of the event was a thin trail of black smoke vanishing into the sky.

Keeping one eye on the doctor, Herald peered past him for possible threats coming from behind; then looking to the heavens, he recited to all those marginalized to just a number in the armed forces, "OK, comrades in arms, I'm discharged back into the real world. Far from feeling the joy we took for granted, I feel only an emptiness and slight nausea."

"What is your name, soldier?" the doctor asked in a cautious but authoritative tone.

"First Lieutenant Herald Lloyd."

"How old are you?"

"Twenty-two—twenty-three next month."

The doctor stared at Herald. The slight droop of Herald's eyebrows, age wrinkles beginning around the corners of his eyes and mouth, and gray hair at his temples belied Herald's age.

"Not to interrupt the sacred nature of your speech and uniform burning," the doctor added, "but Lieutenant Lloyd, what the hell does it mean?"

What the hell does what *mean?*

Then Herald remembered, as his attention returned to the burnt uniform. Rubbing his singed hand, he asked, "See my burnt uniform? This ceremony is akin to my old college SAE fraternity symbol, the Phoenix. The Phoenix, if you remember your Egyptian history, was a legendary bird that lived for 500 years and was reborn from the ashes of its own funeral pyre. Burning my uniform is my rebirth from the Army. I intend to bury all my war memories in the back of my mind and move on with a good attitude—no matter what."

"I see. Well, we have a problem, 'Mr.' Lloyd. As you recall, I'm the doctor who out-processed you this morning. The memo I read from Command this very morning regarding combat stress reaction requires me to report 'any divergent psychotic conduct—in triplicate.' You did seem just a bit edgy during our debriefing period, definitely distant, but wholly conscious of your surroundings. I could overlook this 'bird-based' uniform burning as a childish gesture, or I could report it. That, by the way," he added with a snicker, "would cause me to lose my rendezvous with a certain nurse of dubious reputation. Considering the options, I want nothing to do with putting a psycho hold on any discharged soldier harboring a mythological bird fetish."

Herald had to chuckle at that, as the doctor continued.

"Let me make a few more inquiries before we agree to drop this entire matter. Now, what does the Phoenix have to do with your discharge?"

Herald smiled. "Once back in the world, I promised myself two things: one, I would burn my uniform in a private little ceremony; and two, I would always maintain a good attitude and composure, both of which I learned as a combat officer." Looking to the ground, he pointed at the shadow encircling his feet. "See that? It nearly got me killed."

The doctor rolled his eyes, a gesture confirming the only threat this individual posed was terminal boredom. He cocked his head, narrowed his eyes, and with a patronizing smile inquired, "What thing nearly got you killed?"

Flinging a gesture at the sliver of shade surrounding him, Herald exclaimed, "My shadow!"

The doctor looked to the sky and sighed. "You and your shadow won't get far without clothes. You may think you are done with the past, but the past may not be done with you. I suggest your next step toward civilian life be to take this blanket and move your posterior off this base to a climate less hostile to your personal symbols. To put it another way, burning a uniform could be misinterpreted as an anti-American gesture, which could result in two possible and equally unpleasant scenarios: one, I place you on a seventy-two-hour psycho hold; or, two, I announce on the Travis Air Force Base loudspeaker system that a naked anti-war protester was found burning a uniform torn off a crippled vet. It should not take a lad with your grasp of philosophy any time to assess your options and make the correct choice. Take the blanket and move on."

Herald smiled and scratched his head. "Thank you for your kindness and your suggestion to clear out forthwith. I have a promised telephone call to make and a bus ride to take. Accomplishing those two simple tasks will take all my strength."

He reached over with his right hand, removed the blanket from the doctor's outstretched arm, flipped it open, and wrapped it around his body. Turning, he headed for the bachelor officers' quarters, kicking up dead weeds and dust that swirled in the afternoon breeze and clung to his body and blanket like an old friend.

"Ta-ta, my lost friend," groaned the doctor. "Take your shadow and good attitude with you." He turned back to his clinic to finish the daily process of releasing a mass of damaged humanity. After all, he really was only in the business of recycling soldiers back to civilian life.

Arriving at the officers' quarters, Herald mounted the outside steps and entered the front door. The building foundation, slapped together in record time to fill the enormous, growing demand for military housing in WWII, had settled quite a bit. The entire building tilted at a slight angle to the right. Herald moved down the hall, adjusting his stride to compensate for the angle. His odd gait gave him the appearance of a cripple.

After forcing open the ill-fitting door to the designated room, Herald walked into the cell-like space and dropped the blanket. His small duffel bag, stored for a year back at the company headquarters in Vietnam, had been transferred from his flight home to the single cot.

A stale whiff of dried mold overwhelmed Herald as he unzipped the bag. Pulling out his military and civilian clothes, he shook each piece and laid them on the bed, with the sunshine filtering through the dirt-streaked window. A roll of quarters fell to the floor, and the moldy paper wrapper holding them together split open. Quarters flew everywhere.

He'd stored the quarters with his civilian clothes, making sure they'd be ready to use as soon as he got back; they were an absolute necessity for placing long-distance calls from a phone booth. Herald pulled on the blue jeans and blue work shirt he had worn in college; then he knelt on the floor. One by one he picked up the quarters, his eyes misting as he put them in his pocket.

Standing up, he paused for a moment to smile faintly at the sunlight filtering through the dirty window; then he stepped out into the common hallway. He hesitated, turned, and eyed the pay telephone at the end of the hall. Adjusting his gait to the sloped floor, he walked to the phone, pulled out a small piece of paper from his pocket, read the familiar number, dropped in a quarter, and dialed the operator. After two rings the operator answered, "AT&T, may I help you?"

"Yes, I want to call Boston, Massachusetts; the Pearlman residence at 617-555-7881."

"Please deposit sixteen quarters for the first three minutes."

Shifting the receiver from his hand to his left shoulder, Herald cupped the plastic crescent against his ear. He pulled out a handful of quarters with his right hand and poured them into his left; then he selected a couple and inserted the first into the telephone slot. As the coin fell, a tinny ring chimed through the receiver.

Gray shadows of guilt began to stir within him. How was he going to answer *the big question*?

With the second, third, and fourth quarters, the ring tone took on an ominous sound, like a small church bell, and he felt his stomach gurgle as the guilt lurking in the back of his mind grew.

As the fifth, sixth, and seventh quarters magnified the tinny Ma Bell tone to a large church bell's gong, Herald's stomach acid bubbled. He asked himself over and over: *What are you going to say to Pearlman's parents 'bout the question?*

The eighth, ninth, and tenth quarters sounded with the resonance of a large cathedral bell. *GONG. GONG. GONG.*

Herald's gastric acid, now boiling, was burning his throat. Sweat beaded his face.

Clinks from the eleventh, twelfth, thirteenth, and fourteenth quarters resonated as if Herald were standing in the bell tower of Paris's great Notre Dame Cathedral. The deafening gongs vibrated through his body. More sweat gathered on his forehead.

The sweat collecting on Herald's temples and forehead dripped off his brow with the fifteenth quarter's *GONNNG*. Rubbing his glistening brow with his right hand, he moistened the last quarter. It stuck to his sweaty fingers and he missed the slot. The coin dropped to the floor.

Crouching, he groped for the quarter his teary eyes could not locate. Finding it, his large fingers fumbled at the edges of the sweaty coin to break its moisture seal on the smooth linoleum floor.

Maneuvering the quarter off the floor, he stood up and popped it into the slot with a huge sigh.

The quarter seemed to hover in the coin slot before dropping in with a final *GONNNG* that reverberated like an echo in the cavern of Herald's mind. He put his left hand on the wall to steady himself, leaned to the left of the telephone, and spit stomach bile on the floor.

With the last quarter inserted, there was a pause, several click-click-clicks, another pause, and then the telephone rang. On the first ring, Herald's breathing became heavier and more labored. His mind was running in circles.

Question, question, goddamn question!

At the second ring sweat ran freely down over his face and neck to his chest. The third ring accompanied sweat dripping off his face onto the receiver.

His shirt became soggy at each armpit and the small of his back. With a gurgle, he spit more stomach acid on the floor, still thinking: *Question, question.* The word ran through his mind to the tune of a nursery rhyme.

Ring around the rosie, a pocket full of posies. Question! Question! We all fall down!

After the third ring, Herald wanted to hang up but held on. He was not going to break his combat promise to call Pearlman's parents not more than one hour after he was discharged. He fought back guilt and called upon his willpower and motor control.

On the fourth ring, the guilt won; it seized control of his mind and constricted his throat so he couldn't speak. Herald slammed the receiver back in its cradle, turned, pushed himself against the barrack wall for support, but slowly slid to the floor. With the call incomplete, all sixteen quarters clanged and tumbled noisily down to the coin return like he'd won a jackpot, but he could only pant as his brain exploded in concentric rings of emotional disappointment. The gray *question* appeared in his mind like large electronic letters flowing on a huge billboard: *Why did my son die? Why did you live?*

Survivor's guilt consumed Herald.

Adding to this burden, Herald believed he had done something bad—something very, very bad. He had offended humanity by going to Vietnam.

His mind took sanctuary—brief, blessed sanctuary—as he remembered when he quit college and this whole catastrophe started. Back when quitting school seemed like a great idea. The promised telephone call to Pearlman's parents would have to wait until he had an answer to *the question*.

That important interrogative took a merciful back seat as the memory of the day he quit college came to mind.

CHAPTER 2
THE COLORING BOOK

YEAR 1967

IT WAS FALL of 1967. Herald parked his old, white VW Bug in front of his fraternity house at the University of Vermont. It was the beginning of his sophomore year and the beginning of something even bigger: the day he went to the Army recruiting office and signed his name on the dotted line.

He would be free of his grandmother's disappointment in him. His perceived lack of accomplishment—compared to his father's outstanding educational achievements and meteoric rise in his career—wouldn't matter. His father, who'd graduated first in his class from Massachusetts Institute of Technology, cast a giant shadow. At age thirty-two, he had been named president of a chemical engineering company—and had met his untimely death in a plane crash. Herald was ten years old.

Herald exited his car and stood surveying the front of his Sigma Alpha Epsilon fraternity house. The building suffered from architectural schizophrenia. It had two distinct parts. One side was classic English Tudor. The old brick walls were lined with English ivy. Wide wooden trim followed the roofline, featuring carvings of spiraling vines and flowers. A pitched, green slate roof covered with moss completed the classic design. Attached to this was the new addition. Turning to the right, Herald grimaced at the industrial-looking add-on with gray cement-block walls, flat roof, thinly framed narrow aluminum windows, and gray steel doors. It was as if an architectural cancer had infected the old classic home and grown a huge square tumor.

Herald turned back to his car and reached through the passenger window to retrieve his enlistment papers from the glove compartment. Folding and placing them in his back pocket, he reached down to the floor to pick up a large brown paper bag holding his prized purchases from Woolworth's and the state liquor store, along with an item from his breakfast at Denny's, and walked to the house. Standing in the front doorway, left open as usual, he bellowed, "Hey, Tom-Tom, where the hell are you?" His voice echoed throughout the fraternity house like a foghorn, with a resonance that disturbed anyone and everyone within reach.

Crossing the entryway to the main staircase, Herald yelled again, "Tom-Tom, where are you, man?"

Tom, five feet nine and about 165 pounds, had curly, jet-black hair and blue eyes that lit up when he was excited. Right now he was annoyed. He grimaced at the ceiling of his room and yelled back, "Upstairs in my room, you stupid bastard, trying to engage in an activity you should try sometime: studying! Why do you think I had to pick a different roommate this year? So I could stay in school, party animal!"

Laughing, Herald started up the elaborately carved walnut stairs and shouted, "Goddamn, book learning will rot your brain, Tom-Tom … at least what's left of it." The old stairs creaked in protest as Herald jumped two to three steps at a time. Halfway up he added, "Hey, asshole, are you ready for my revelation of the week? I have decided to quit school. *Color my ass gone.*"

Tom slapped his hand on his desk and raised his eyes to the ceiling in amazement. "To my knowledge, 'gone' is not a color, so cut the crap. Does insanity run in your family, or gallop? If you quit school, you'll be drafted inside a month … and off to fight in Vietnam!" He spun around in his swivel desk chair and narrowed his eyes as Herald entered the room.

"Hey!" Herald leaned toward Tom, "Just ... cannot ... do ... the school ... thing ... any ... more. When I sit down to read, my mind scampers out the back door. I just don't have the heart for it. It's going to become embarrassing. What I need is an adventure that offers an unquestionable test of my mettle. The Army is a good place for that. The experience should carve a cornerstone to build my life."

"Ri-i-ight," Tom groaned as he rocked back in his chair and gazed again at the ceiling. "OK, cut the crap. There's another reason. What?"

Herald laughed, extended his right arm, thumb up and index finger pointed at Tom like a pistol and boasted, "I want to be a gunfighter. Yeah, a gunfighter. That, *O Studious One,* is the reason."

"Oh please," Tom snorted, "tell me you did not say 'gunfighter.' You can't even spell it!"

"*G–U–N* ... "

"No, asshole, not spell in the sense of reciting alphabet letters, the sense of what size balls it takes to be one. Forget cornerstone; the only stone you'll get out of going into the Army is a *tomb*stone. Look, *O Moronic One,* with your history of alcoholic excess and attention span of a small rodent, the only certain result of your military experience will be your demise. Leaving college for the Army is suicide!"

Laughing, Herald looked up to mock Tom's ceiling-gazing habit. "With a choice between living a rich doctor's wealthy, empty life or experiencing the excitement of a war, I'll take war. I think I can make it—and I'll be a better person for it. I will have something no one can take away and something my father never accomplished."

Tom smiled. "Oh. So that's what this is about? Well, speaking of fathers, read this."

Herald placed the large paper bag he'd been holding on the floor, stepped forward, leaned down, and grasped the folded sheet of paper from Tom's hand. Straightening up, he smoothed out the letter and with a blank stare read the typed text. Only the movement of his eyes and periodic rising of eyebrows indicated his reaction to the content. After finishing he looked into Tom's blue eyes with the same blank stare, which begged the question, *What am I missing?* Herald had no clue as to why Tom requested he read a personal letter from his father. "Looks very much like a letter from your father."

Tom did a 'thumbs up' and sneered. "Correct-a-dumbo, Mr. Holmes. And did you not notice anything odd about the letter from my dear parent?" He spun his chair a full 360 degrees.

Herald reread the letter. "Well, your father is still upset about the usual laundry list that irritates all fathers. Let's see here, hmmm ... first, the outrageous sums of money you have spent so far this semester, versus the heroic way he lived on air alone in medical school after being a pilot in the Marines in World War II. Second, the reminder you wrecked several vehicles in high school, the result being the extra expense to send you away to a private school. Third, you'd better get over a 3.0 grade point average or he will cut you off.

"All in all, it appears a pretty standard parent letter." Puzzled, he raised his eyes from the page to look at Tom.

Tom slapped the desk. "Look, lamebrain, have you ever received *a typed letter* from your stepfather?"

"Yes," Herald answered while staring out the open window, "my stepfather has written to me ... but not all that often. Remember the letter I showed you last month where he responded to my telling him I'd experimented with marijuana last summer? He was pretty pissed off." Scratching his head, Herald turned from the window and looked back at Tom.

"Well, the letter ... was it typed or handwritten?" Tom asked as he stood up, grabbed his father's letter from Herald, and crushed it in his right hand.

Herald flinched and moved back. "It was handwritten ... and in a rather hostile tone, if I remember correctly." He took a second step back to avoid Tom, in case his buddy went berserk and tried to strike him with the crushed letter in his hand.

"My point," Tom insisted, "is your stepfather's letter was handwritten. What pissed-off parent writes to his son by dictating an angry letter to his secretary?" Agitated, Tom paced about the room, slam-dunked the balled-up letter into the trash can, and plopped into his chair, rotating it 180 degrees to look out the window.

Herald stepped forward, knelt down on one knee, and started singing off-key the first bar of The Animals song, "We Gotta Get Out of This Place." Picking up and opening the top of the paper bag he'd placed on the floor earlier, he announced in an even, unemotional tone that verged on the comic, "On a happier note, as a celebration of my freedom from the tyranny of higher education, I have purchased this worthy vessel of one of our favorite beverages, a half-gallon of Heaven Hill bourbon. *And* I also bring you an official *GI Joe Coloring Book*, plus, ahem, children's crayons 'obtained' from Denny's Restaurant."

Herald looked around the cluttered room and found a small, unclaimed spot to set the bag down, reached in with his right hand, and pulled out the bottle of bourbon by its long neck. With his left, he removed the brightly covered coloring book and the small pack of crayons. Waving the flimsy book over his head, he caused the pages to give off an ominous sound, like a bird fleeing a predator.

Tom, still looking out the window, spoke over his shoulder. "Herald, I enjoyed our little tête-à-tête, but, absent completing this assignment, I will also be leaving school—by flunking out! Medical school requires a minimum 3.0, which as you might guess, requires my attention. My military experience, if any, will be in the Medical Corps, as far away from you, my Teddy-Roosevelt-Rough-Rider-Charge-Up-San-Juan-Hill-John-Wayne-destined friend, as possible."

Herald smirked. "You, my future-head-reflectored-grab-your-nurse's-ass friend, are consigning yourself to a lifetime of menial medical slavery. Furthermore, unless you have some fun in your life, you will be an empty, successful, wealthy eye doctor. An optometrist on the golf course of life muttering, 'Rosebud, Rosebud, where is my damn little red golf cart sled?'"

Tom, diverted by the chattering gray squirrel that inhabited the lush maple tree just outside the window, pondered the observation. "For the life of me, Herald, I don't know how you think this stuff up. I've had more intelligent conversations with the squirrels outside my window ... that one, for instance. The world is what the world is. Accept it and move on. Whatever led you to believe you are entitled to more? Even if you are right, which I doubt, what else is there to do? I'm not going to live in a cave to protest the system."

Herald snorted. "Your observation is like trying to persuade me that a lawn mower has fun when it mows. Well, the least you could do as a future doctor is empathize with the gravity of my decision and help me cope with what you, in a hostile fashion, believe to be a mortally jeopardizing move. You may not realize it now, but when I'm gone, you will miss me. Who else is worried about your soul—and what about my sterling personality?"

Shaking his head, Tom looked to the ceiling again and surrendered. "All right. A-a-all right. If I don't join in the festivities, you will most likely start to threaten members of my family. Upon further reflection, it *is* five o'clock Sunday night. I've completed most of my studying and ... yeah, a drink or two always helps me concentrate, right? And lastly, my retarded one, the *GI Joe Coloring Book* has piqued my curiosity. What immoral scheme have you thought up now? Is it a new angle to excite the interest of the babes? Do we get to color on the girls?"

Herald looked at Tom and lowered his voice. "This is my school yearbook. At the end of every year in prep school or high school, did you not buy a yearbook? And did you not engage in the stupid custom of having as many people as possible sign it? God, what did we do that for? Was it a validation of our popularity, based on the number of classmates who inscribed their names? Anyway, this 'magic' *GI Joe Coloring Book* will be my college yearbook. I will have everyone color a page to celebrate my departure."

"Herald, you've got to stop drinking! You weren't given an overly large dose of intelligence to begin with, and if you continue to let alcohol slough away your brain cells, soon you won't have the mentality of a dried cranberry. Picture the response of the masses when you ask them to color in a kiddie war book as a going-away gesture. *HELLO?* What the hell are you thinking? Everyone here is terrified of Vietnam; they're all antiwar, and you make a joke of it? I will not only drink to, but participate in, this carnival of horror. Hand me the ceremonial spirits. To truly take part in this bizarre scene, one must get in the mood, no? Yes! By the way, what are you going to do when 9,000 screaming Viet Cong want to hang your head on the wall and you are out of ammo?"

Herald laughed and kicked Tom's chair. "Simple: I shall call upon one of the guaranteed wishes from my certified magical coloring book to protect me."

"'Simple' is right: simple-*minded!* You make my head spin!"

Tom turned in his chair and surveyed his desk. Peeking out from under the centerfold of a *Playboy Magazine* was a stolen eight-ounce cafeteria water glass with some brownish yellow liquid in the bottom. In one smooth movement Tom picked up the glass, swirled the liquid clockwise and sloshed it out the window. The quick motion alarmed a squirrel and caused it to retreat, chattering in protest.

Pulling his arm back inside, Tom raised the glass and swiveled his chair to face Herald, who stepped forward and timed handing the bourbon to Tom just as his chair brought them face to face. Bourbon in hand, Tom twisted the sealed cap off with his teeth, spit it onto his desk, and, with the practiced skill of a chemist, poured the bourbon into the glass to midlevel; about four shots.

As though deeply absorbed in a vital diagnosis, he looked through the amber liquid to Herald, whose image was distorted by the dirty glass and tinted bourbon.

"Go to the refrigerator," Tom said in a semi-reverent tone, "and pull out the ice tray and lemonade mix. Bourbon straight, this early, is too much for my stomach."

Herald turned, smiled, and began singing on his way to the buzzing, rust-streaked, ancient refrigerator. "We gotta get out of this place, if it's the last thing we ever do."

As he opened the refrigerator, the sickening aroma of stale beer, unidentified piles of mold, and rotting anchovy pizza invaded his nose. He hid his face behind the refrigerator door to avoid the horrid smell. "Christ, Tom-Tom, is this some type of medical experiment in decay?"

Herald kept his nose as far away from the refrigerator door as possible to avoid the lethal vapors. Holding his breath, he glanced over the door for a moment, reached around, and grabbed the open can of lemonade mix with his left hand. With his right, he reached over the top of the door to the freezer inside and flipped opened its door to grab the ice-cube tray. Tray in hand, he used his foot to tap the refrigerator door closed with a thump.

As the door was closing, the necessity of a drinking glass entered his mind. He looked up and spied another dirty cafeteria glass on top of the refrigerator. Left with the concept that a third hand could actually be useful to mankind, he placed the ice-cube tray on top of the fridge and used his free hand to grab and seat the streaked glass on the tray. With the satisfied grin of someone who had just met and conquered a problem that had plagued mankind for centuries, he walked over to the desk and placed the ice tray on Tom's chemistry book and the lemonade on his yellow notepad.

"Thank God the bourbon will kill any germs still residing in the glass," Tom kidded.

"Your first medical opinion?"

"I surely hope so, or I'm a dead man. But on a more interesting note, have you told your parents yet of your bright idea to go get your ass shot off? I'm sure your mother will be charmed," Tom said, as he lifted the can of thawed lemonade and poured some into the glass, leaving room for ice.

"Not exactly," Herald replied, raising the stained glass and turning it to estimate the amount of chalky debris in the bottom. Taking the bourbon bottle from Tom, he poured just a touch into his glass, swirled it around and tossed the gross liquid into an overflowing trash can to his left, confident the paper would absorb the discharge. He then poured the glass half-full, put the bottle down, seized the lemonade from Tom's hand, and poured it into his own glass, leaving room for ice. Grabbing four loose ice cubes from the tray, he slid two into Tom's glass with a soft clink and the same into his glass.

"Well, since I have already enlisted, there's not much my parents can do about it," Herald said in a thoughtful tone, spinning his drink counter-clockwise and raising it to eye level as if examining a fine wine. Eyeing the leftover swirling lemon flakes in the bourbon, he began thinking aloud. "I wonder … below the equator in Vietnam, when you flush a toilet does the water rotate clockwise or counterclockwise?"

Tom smacked his hand on his desk, scattering his lab experiment papers, and cried, "Who cares which way toilet water rotates anywhere in the world when you flush? As a matter of fact, Herald, this entire crayon-book crap has the stench of low grades and fear of failure, eh?"

"Tom-Tom, I hafta go. Hafta. Not doing well, here. Just going to get worse. I need to get out from under my dead father's MIT shadow. My mind just shuts off when I open a book; forget about remembering what I read. The Army is my only way out. Even my mother is disappointed I'm not in a better college.

"I know it's the same stupidity as the moth drawn to the flame. The flame may burn the moth, but he doesn't seem to care … and don't *you* bug me about it." Herald looked up and laughed. "'Bug me.' Damn, how very pun-ish of me! Or am I *going* to be punished? After all Vietnam is not even a real war, just some sort of dumb border conflict, right?"

Herald looked to the floor, cocked his head, and with his right little fingernail, dislodged an errant lemon flake from one of his front teeth onto his tongue. He spit the flake onto Tom's study lamp. "So there you have it. I'm retarded, and you're not. Odd, how in your heightened mental aware-ness, you were so affected by your father's typed letter. No, you are *right!* You're clean, clean as an Irish whistle. No-o-o emotional problems for you."

Tom smiled, looked toward the wall and laughed. "Yeah, no father problems for me. HA! I could never equal my father being a fighter pilot in World War II and going to medical school afterward. I choose to be an optometrist, with just a dash of the Army Medical Corps. Fifty years from now, I still want to be *alive*, to sit in my rocking chair and wonder why you went and got yourself killed—coloring-book witchcraft or not. Hey, stop spitting lemon flakes on my lamp."

Tom jumped from his chair, and the effect of the bourbon hit hard. He stumbled against Herald. After steadying Tom, Herald knelt down and picked up the coloring book and crayons. They left Tom's room and paused at the top of the stairs to prepare for the descent. Clutching arm in arm as if going to a fancy ball, they stumbled down the steps, bouncing off the walls and banister, taxing the structural integrity of the old stairs that creaked loudly in protest.

At last they hit the oak-floor landing at the bottom, with Herald dropping to one knee for a moment until, with Tom's assistance, he regained his balance to stand up and continue walking. The landing opened to the elegant living room, with its high ceiling elaborately carved with a medallion design and old-world molding. They crossed the shiny hardwood floor and ascended metal stairs leading to the cheap tile floor of the great room in the "architectural cancer" section of the building.

The great room was furnished with secondhand, cloth-covered couches, and chairs of various and questionable styles and origins. The furnishings, grouped into three sections, allowed the various social cliques to dominate a section and establish their spheres of influence.

The cinder-block walls, painted lime green, were crowned by a white, acoustical drop ceiling bearing numerous holes. Beer and shrapnel-like shards of broken beer bottles had stained and scarred the ceiling tiles, a telling history of the frat brothers' enthusiastic parties.

Spotting the reigning fraternity brother social director, Herald prodded Tom. "Hey, Tom-Tom, I spy Brother Coyote holding court on yon far side of the room with the fair Calysta."

Tom raised his hand to his eyebrows in an "Indian scout" pose and looked to the far end of the room. "Indeed, you are correct, Kemosabe. I am unable to think of anyone more suited than Coyote to launch the coloring-book send-off program. Brother Coyote sets the social standard in this house."

Coyote was a tall, good-looking chick magnet with a large bank account. His ride was a 1965 fire-engine-red convertible Pontiac GTO, and he had a morbid fear not only of war but of ever holding a legitimate job.

Smiling at Tom, Herald teased, "If your parents were brain surgeons who just happened to invest in twenty oil wells as a tax-loss haven, but instead—*surprise!*—they all struck oil, maybe you would be more sympathetic to Coyote's frailties."

"Awww ... poor Coyote," Tom kidded back, shaking his head and lowering his line of sight to the floor in a false gesture of mourning. He looked back up at Herald and grinned. "Only if he stops using every damn British cliché he heard during his summer trip to Great Britain could I begin to cut him some slack. It still gives me the creeps when he calls all us guys and every girl he meets 'Love.'"

Passing the second furniture cluster, Herald tripped over a foot sticking out near the end of a couch. It was attached to Brother Prol, who was lying on the floor in front of the couch.

Prol was from a small Vermont town that bordered Canada and boasted a population of 300 people, more or less, but less in winter. His parents, members of a fanatical religious sect, had controlled every second of his life until college. Thrust into the world without religious parental supervision, Prol succumbed to the untested demons of his youth and the allure of alcohol. He traded his white shirt and black suit for tattered jeans, no socks and a dirty t-shirt.

Catching himself from the stumble, Herald looked back to identify the owner of the size-12 obstruction. "Ah! Prol! So, how goes the Brooklyn Booze Diet?"

Prol, twisting around a bit to address the origin of the sound, rose up on his elbow and rested his head on his hand. Yellowish drool pooled on the floor where his cheek had been resting. Blinking his bloodshot eyes hard he slurred, "Scored over two gallons of beer from discarded cups this morning after last night's party. Only had to remove two cigarette butts. Finished off the keg by 11:00 a.m. Did you know cigarette ashes are good for the digestion? And ... the small flakes of tobacco add a rare smo— quality. How long have I been out on the floor here?"

"We're not usually our brother's keeper, Prol," Herald answered. "However, we were witness to your attempt to climb the stairs just as the party was breaking up, at about 2:00 a.m. I use the word 'attempt,' as you lost your balance on the second landing. You leaned to the rear to catch yourself and did a back flip descending three stairs—with an exciting one-point impact on the first landing—on your head. Before we could check your pulse for signs of life, you started crawling to the great room and up onto the very couch you now repose in front of, on the floor. You obviously revived yourself this morning for your beer-recycling repast."

"Yes," Tom chimed in, "the judges gave you a nine, eight, and ten for difficulty on your back flip, but only a four, five, and four for artistic ability. The judges' consensus was that your routine had rhythm but was hard to dance to."

Prol fractured a smile and replied, "Well, Tom, if I'm so out of it, how come my 4.0 grade point average is way better than your puny 3.2?"

Herald and Tom looked at each other, smiled, and nodded. They acknowledged the improbability of Prol's alleged perfect grade point average, considering his alcohol intake. They continued on their way. Prol dropped his head to the floor with a sigh. His cheek resumed its original position next to the dried drool.

Coyote held court as social director on a worn, beer-stained couch in the last section of seating. This was where the fraternity officers and future protégés sat during meetings. As soon as Coyote spied Herald and Tom approaching, he edged closer to his current prized female toy for the month. He even risked a rare public display of affection by draping one arm over her shoulder to signal his territory.

Herald and Tom weaved over and stopped next to the last furniture enclave. Herald, giving the faux-Brit Coyote a stern, challenging look, inquired, "Brother Coyote, do you consider 'sharing' an important concept?"

Coyote, attempting to short circuit what he knew were loaded questions, wrinkled his brow and darted his eyes left and right. Coming up with a vague enough answer, he responded, "Yes, by Jove, sharing is an important concept; but," he added as he winked at Calysta, "it jolly well should never be overdone, eh, Love?"

Herald continued baiting him. "Ahah. Then, Coyote, do you think it is important for brothers to help each other in social development?"

"Right-o," Coyote agreed again, nodding at Herald. He knew the punch line was just down the road.

"Very well," Herald grinned. "Since you agree sharing is an important concept, you won't mind sharing Calysta with Tom-Tom and me, would you? We promise to return her to you, only slightly worn."

Coyote stood up and bellowed, "Right. There is no bloody way I would *ever* share my girlfriend with you blokes. Just being in the same pub with you should require we update our shot records to protect ourselves from all the little nasties you guys have in your bodily fluids."

Hearing Coyote's response, the brothers in the room laughed at the answer to another of Herald's unanswerable questions.

Herald held out the coloring book. "OK, you can't blame us for shooting for the moon, but how about letting the fair Calysta color in my going-away, enchanted *GI Joe Coloring Book*?"

Coyote grabbed the book and quickly reviewed it to make sure there were no tricks involved. Looking up he replied, "Right-o, but only if the fair lady wishes to be troubled with you ruffians." He handed the book back to Herald, who gave it and the crayons to Tom.

Herald looked into Calysta's blue eyes, knelt on one knee, and implored, "Fair Princess, I am but Sir Herald the Humble, a knight in your Lord Coyote The Usurper's service. My squire, Tom-Tom of Maine, bears what will be my amulet in battle, a *GI Joe Coloring Book*. I would be ever so honored and humbled if you would be so kind as to pick any page your fair heart desires and color it. A page colored by you would be my lady's mark of favor that would inspire me in the trying days to come."

Sensing a prank, Coyote grabbed the coloring book from Tom, rolled it into a tube, and shook it at Herald. "Look, old sport, what kind of sick puppy are you to take liberties with the honor of British Knighthood to gain favor with a lady? I wager this is just a jolly good show. Going away? Where to? Another college, I hope! What proof can you offer this is not a bloody joke?"

Herald reached into his back pocket, pulled out a piece of paper and unfolded it. He gave it to Coyote, who read the page and shouted, "Bloody hell, you are one stupid bloke to leave the safety of college to join the Army!"

Herald looked over to Calysta and thought, *What a fine piece of real estate, five-feet-four, blond hair, blue eyes, 34-24-32.*

Calysta, a sweet person gifted with good looks and possessing a Vermonter's practical sensibility with an added sense of humor, was attempting to circumnavigate the college environment while preserving her dignity. She looked at Herald, smiled, and said, "I would be happy to color a page in your enchanted book, Sir Herald, as a proper send-off."

Herald stood up and guffawed, a typical sound from him, but one everyone dreaded, as it would fire spittle in every direction. Assuming the demeanor of a true herald, he proclaimed, "Squire Tom-Tom shall obtain the scripture from Lord Coyote and deliver it to the fair princess with yon cache of crayons so she may complete her mark of favor."

Turning to Coyote, he continued, "The compromise you make to stay in college, Dark Lord Coyote, rather than face your fear of war and work, is a ticket to brain death. Maybe *you* will be happy as a millionaire zombie. As for *me*, give me liberty or give me death!"

Tom handed the book and crayons to Calysta, took one step back, and in an intoxicated but ominous voice, boomed, "For leaning on clichés twice before 6:00 p.m., twenty lashes!" Whereupon he grabbed Herald and proceeded to beat him on his back, a torment creating loud, hollow thumping noises but little damage. The commotion caused a small group to gather about, curious about the disturbance. Lord Coyote, sensing he was losing control but wishing to avoid a confrontation wherein he did not understand the concepts, was careful to keep one arm draped over Calysta.

The coloring book was simple enough, made up of outlined military action pictures for children to color with crayons. There was a soldier hurling a grenade in the thick of battle, and a frogman diver on a secret mission swimming with dynamite through an underwater minefield. Games were in the book, too: the "Air Strike Game," again with a picture to color, was for taking turns with friends, dropping marbles aimed at targets, such as an airstrip, oil refinery or cargo-ship supply train; and educational games, one teaching how to decode a semaphore message.

One of the most benign pages illustrated a sailor mopping a deck on a battleship. Calysta stopped there and glanced for permission from Coyote, who thought, *What could be wrong with coloring this page for a brother's swan song?* He nodded approval.

Calysta put the coloring book on her lap and paused to view the logo of Denny's Restaurant as she opened the flap of the tiny crayon box. Counting the crayons, she remarked, "Herald, you only have four crayons. There are more colors in the spectrum than the primary colors."

Herald looked deep into Calysta's eyes, and in his most mysterious voice said, "These are wizardry primary colors. Take these divining crayons and do the best you can to speed me on my quest."

The use of the word "quest" sparked Calysta's motivation. She pulled a blue crayon from the box, lowered her head, and began to color intently. Her long blond hair fell from her shoulder, over her eyes, and onto the page. With delicate grace, she flipped her head, the gentle motion causing her tresses to caress her perfect bare shoulder and cascade down her back.

The clingy leotard top she was wearing had only one shoulder strap, and its scooped neck molded to her perfect 34C breasts.

Ohhhh, my, thought Herald as he let his gaze wander over the enticing sight. This was the only aspect of the letter "C" in the academic grading system that Herald fully embraced as being a perfect "A." In a surge of testosterone-fueled frustration, Herald turned and, out of earshot of Calysta, whispered in Tom's ear, "Why do they do that to us?"

"Do what?" whispered Tom, as he, too, was eyeballing Calysta's cleavage.

"Leave one shoulder bare to taunt us! What I would give just to lick her shoulder for only one minute; really, just lick lightly, one second, perhaps.

How could it matter to a princess? A lick is but a minor intrusion to her, a life-shattering event for us peons. We are but subservient minions to her beauty, ripe to be used and abused. Worse, we are boringly predictable due to our inability to control the one-eyed *him*."

Tom smiled and noted, "I should point out that her current selection, Dark Lord Coyote, has great wealth. This places him in a league to which we are not even invited. However, it was a bonus he lacked the common sense to forbid you to drive his new, red GTO convertible. He should have known better than to listen to your hollow promise you would never peel out in all four gears."

Undaunted, Herald turned and laid down The Rule in an elevated tone to the fair Calysta: "Neatness counts in the coloring competition."

With this admonition, Calysta pulled out the three other crayons and tossed the box on the coffee table. She bent even lower in keen concentration to keep precise within the lines of the sailor's image, exposing even more soft round cleavage.

To the onlookers' regret, Calysta completed the coloring assignment, well supervised by Lord Coyote.

Coyote then took possession of the coloring book and crayons and began thumbing through it looking for a page to color. He selected a scene of a soldier crouched in the jungle ready for a bayonet charge. After he completed coloring, Princess Calysta retrieved the book and returned it to Sir Herald, who smiled and said, "May Allah be merciful."

With Brother Coyote and the fair Calysta having colored the first pictures, Herald had accomplished his goal of group social acceptance. The compulsory herd behavior of adolescent males would ensure an adequate following of the whole fraternity.

Prol rose up on one arm yelling, "Bring me the sacred text."

Herald walked over, knelt down, and handed the book and crayons to him. Prol grabbed the book with his grubby paw, spread it on the floor, and leaned on one elbow to choose an image. Thumbing through the pages, he paused on a figure of a soldier in a bayonet charge. After completing the coloring-in of the soldier in green, he improvised drawing a red, comet-looking explosion in the sky, with yellow rays emanating in all directions and the word, "BOOM!" Next he drew a yellow line representing a ricocheted bullet, emphasizing with the word, "ZING!" Yellow spittle drooled onto his creation, and before Prol could finish his drawing, another brother walked over, leaned down, and snatched the book from his hand. Collecting the crayons, this brother wiped the sputum off on Prol's shoulder. He parked himself on the couch and leafed through the pages; he spied the image of a soldier on one knee, firing a flare gun. Using only blue, he pressed the long side of the crayon, making messy, wide strokes, with no respect for the illustration's borders. Picking up a yellow crayon, he drew at the soldier's pelvis, a man's dripping genitalia to complement the illustration's caption, "Firing a gun."

When he was done, another brother seized the book and crayons, plopped on the couch directly above the floor where Prol was still lying on his stomach, propped his feet on Prol's back, and perused the book. Finding an image of a soldier scanning a battlefield with binoculars, his muse inspired him to write the caption, "Scouting for a woman," rather than referencing a military purpose. Brother after brother took turns degrading the *GI Joe Coloring Book's* images to pornographic lampoons of war.

When the coloring book was laid to rest on a coffee table, Herald clutched his farewell memento and walked to the near side of the room. Feeling dizzy, he braced his body against the waist-high wall heater. Perhaps it was the bourbon on an empty stomach, but the room began tilting thirty degrees, slanting to the right. Herald slid past the heater to the floor with a dull thud.

Color my ass a goner for mocking war!

Had he launched his own heroic Greek tragedy? His imagination spun and blurred until he was one of the soldiers in the *GI Joe Coloring Book*: he'd entered the coloring book's Pandora's portal and become one of the cartoon action figures. Herald imagined himself gliding between pages into the different scenes of the coloring book. He moved freely, lifting his arms and legs, picking up weapons, dodging bullets, hearing the cries of wounded men …

CHAPTER 3
BACK ON THE HORSE

YEAR 1988

THE EFFICIENT BUSTLE of his secretary entering the office snapped him back to the present. Glancing at the clock, he recalled that his presence was required at a 10:00 a.m. court appearance, sixty miles away in Martinez. No time to agonize about his malpractice now. He threw the empty pint into the trash can and grabbed his file. As he passed Deborah, he said, "Good morning, gotta run, see you later." Herald hurried down the steps to his van, jumped in, and drove off. He made it to the court on time.

Malpractice dominated Herald's thoughts on the long drive back from Martinez, generating the feeling he was a rat in a psychological experiment being electrically prodded to run a maze. The sensation nauseated him, causing him to perspire all over; his mind was boiling over from his mistake. His growing anxiety caused phlegm to rise in his throat, giving him the urge to spit. The more he thought about it, the more he was convinced that his failure to call Pearlman's parents was linked to a curse—a curse that had caused this legal error.

He stopped at a liquor store, picked up a pint of bourbon and took three sips to ease the pain. As Herald left the store, his mind seized on an idea to alleviate his angst. Why not treat this malpractice problem as a military operation? His military maneuvers had been successful in the Army; he could just transfer his military mind-set to his law practice.

Military actions always have an acronym. He decided assigning one to this situation would help him maintain his cool.

Let's see, I discovered the malpractice earlier today. I have thirty-seven more days until the motion is to be heard: "Malpractice Doomsday." That makes today Malpractice Doomsday 38 ... "MD 38." Every day after today will be a countdown to MD Zero.

Satisfied, he tucked the half-empty pint into the glove compartment.

Arriving at his office around 1:00 p.m., he reached over to the passenger seat and grabbed the black leather briefcase given to him by his staff. Carrying the Martinez client's fate in his hands, he walked past the white picket fence and turned up the red flagstone walkway that curled in a lazy "S" pattern toward the office entrance. Just before he climbed the five steps to the porch level, he surveyed his office, a two-story Victorian built originally to house a prosperous Bay Area family.

The building filled a prestigious corner lot. A porch extended around the two sides facing the street and ended with a large turret on the right. Thea's office was there. The daylilies along the side border of the house were in full bloom, their orange blossoms waving in the warm afternoon breeze.

Mounting the stairs covered with rust-colored outdoor carpeting, he admired the brass sign: Lloyd and Lloyd, Attorneys at Law; yet he wondered how long he'd be able to keep the building if he were unable to correct the malpractice issue. But just having decided to organize his defense with the MD designation, he now was in good spirits.

He turned the brass knob on the huge mahogany door and swung it open to a large foyer with multiple openings to the other rooms of the spacious house. Walking into the foyer, he turned right into the living room that was his secretary Deborah's office and dropped his briefcase at the door just before entering.

Deborah controlled the administrative functions of the law firm. She had been a gymnast in junior high school and still had very muscular arms and legs, but puberty had robbed her of a gymnastic career when her body filled out. She was a tough, buxom, good-looking gal from Chicago.

At the rear of Deborah's office was the sunroom where Cricket, the file clerk, worked. It contained the copy machine, mailing materials, Cricket's desk, and an enormous closet the length of the wall housing six fireproof filing cabinets. Cricket, a teenager whose sensuality permeated the office, was only five feet tall, but had curves in all the right places and the smile of the "girl next door." She attempted to look taller by wearing four-inch high-heel shoes and one-and-a-half-inch long fingernails painted bright red with an appliqué of ballet dancers on each nail.

In the back, attached to the former dining room, was Herald's working office, known as "The Parrot Room." At the time the house had been built, the room had been part of the open porch and, like Cricket's office, had been enclosed. The office had been dubbed "The Parrot Room" due to evidence of extensive damage from chewing: the former owner had imprisoned a large, angry parrot in this room, and the strong-beaked bird had sought revenge on the wooden trim.

This was Herald's room to "organize" as he saw fit. To designate different stages of work completed, he would spread files on the floor and label them with Post-It notes. Other documents and research books were strewn on the desk. He called it "organization." His wife called it chaos.

The original house plans called for the floor of the porch to slant downward from the building in order to keep rainwater from seeping into the house. The inclined floor had to be corrected and leveled in Cricket's office for the copier machine. In the Parrot Room, the angled floor gave the place a surreal effect that Herald enjoyed; however, it also caused minor equilibrium problems for others rising from a seated position.

The staff loved the concept that Herald's room had a slanted floor and formerly housed a chewing bird, the joke being that both he and the former winged occupant had "diminished mental capacities." At least Herald did not chew the woodwork. Instead, the staff teased, this was where he chewed out all the legal angles. The only desk in the room was a large flat table. Month by month, and sometimes even day by day over the past year, his office had been getting messier and messier.

The former small kitchen was the domain of Sarah, the word-processing queen. All the appliances and cabinets had been removed to make room for Sarah's big desk supporting the mammoth word-processing station and printer.

At one time, Sarah, at five feet eight, had been a real beauty with long, blond hair. Now her hair was stringy and unwashed. She still had the body of a Miss America; however, excessive drugs, alcohol, and cigarettes had taken their toll on her thirty-five-year-old face. This was most evident around her mouth and eyes, which were surrounded by a complex roadmap of interlocking deep creases, wrinkles, and dry, flaking skin. Her current paramour, with whom she resided, was an abusive, drug-addicted biker.

Sarah had the amazing ability to type more than 100 words per minute accurately, even when totally drunk, totally stoned or any combination thereof, a feat that amazed the entire staff. Deborah was convinced Sarah's daily morning coffee breaks, when no one was looking, were actually coke breaks involving a ritual of snorting cocaine and washing it down with cheap-tequila-laced coffee. Post-break she always emerged from the bathroom acting particularly cheerful, talking faster, typing faster, and enveloping anyone near her with dragon breath. Yes, Sarah gave new meaning to a midmorning pick-me-up.

Well, Herald thought, feeling sorry for her, *as long as she does her job, gets along with the other staff, and keeps her excesses to herself, why not give her a break?*

After all, the firm had gone through many other word processors. Anyone who could handle Herald's freeway-speed dictation was worth her weight in gold, quirks and all.

Sarah always wore tight blouses, accentuating her bust, and very short skirts. When Herald was in the dictation room, she made sure he could view her exquisite long legs. He always wondered what it would be like to have sex with her, but he knew crossing that line with an employee could lead to disaster. Herald had heard a rumor from an attorney at Sarah's last employer that Sarah had exploited sexual contact with her boss to gain leverage over him.

Herald's head was still pounding from his hangover, and though the day's booze had taken the edge off a bit, he approached Deborah's desk and jived, "Hola! How goes the office war?"

Deborah looked up, tightened her jaw muscles, and adopted a sarcastic tone. "Well, aren't we quite the study in contrast today?"

Drawing on his comic reserves of naïveté and theatrics, he arched his brows and teased, "Contrast? Moi?"

"Your bloodshot eyes contradict your devotion to always looking perfect. You stand here before me in your perfectly tailored suit, starched cotton shirt, Italian silk tie, and polished penny loafers—and come off like a dyed-in-the-wool New Englander."

"Curses!" he groaned, twisting an imaginary moustache. "Foiled again!"

"And with all the time you spend at the gym, it seems you're interested in taking care of yourself. So once again, I smell alcohol on your breath. If you don't mind my asking … why do you overdrink at lunch?"

Herald reflected on that for a moment and replied. "The people I admired most in the Army were the hard-drinking infantry airborne officers. They'd get drunk every night and, no matter how hungover they were, led the five-mile run at 6:00 a.m. in tailored fatigues and spit-shined boots. They'd be so hungover, sometimes they would vomit on the run. They made it appear they were just spitting, hiding that their stomachs were convulsing and filling their mouths with vomit. They carried on— never whined or quit running."

Deborah grimaced. "That's very inspiring. And did you get the license number of the truck that hit you last night?"

"Huh? What truck?"

"The whiskey truck that ran you over last night, Army boy!"

She laughed and shook her head; then she continued. "As for me, I've had it for today! Cricket's boyfriend deserted her to move in with a divorced waitress and her baby. Surprise! It might be his. Cricket, as could be expected, is a basket case. She refuses to come out of her office or even talk about the mail. The only noise I've heard all day is her muffled sobbing."

Herald moved to interrupt, but Deborah beat him to the punch.

"Ah, but wait ... there's more! Sarah finished her dictation and declared an informal holiday by passing out cold on her desk. I thought she must have killed herself when I heard her head hit the keyboard, but her partying last night apparently included sufficient recreational drugs to anesthetize her from the impact. The keyboard may not have survived the attack, but I do not want to violate the first rule of first aid and move her. And for your dining and dancing pleasure, there's no blood in sight."

Herald again tried to get a word in edgewise, but Deborah barreled ahead.

"In the client category, Erik Swallows, God's gift to himself and the women of the world, just left another phone message. He's outraged that the law protects only those people who don't pay their rent ... and by the way, he attempted to hustle me for a date while holding me personally responsible for rushing his eviction case along! To put it bluntly, Perry Mason, we simply have *too many cases* for the number of staff in the office. Your efficiency methods and use of paralegals to process cases on a mass-production volume and give clients the biggest bang for their legal buck is going to catch up with us if we don't get more employees. Even *you* can't continue at this pace. *Warning, Will Robinson, Warning! Mistakes are going to be made!*"

Her harangue having reached its wham-bam climax, she sat back and took a deep breath.

Herald, head pounding and eyes practically crossing from the strain, looked at her and spoke in a cool, flat tone. "You have no idea how right you are. My business plan to provide the best legal bang for my clients' bucks may have already caught up with me. What are my messages?"

"Glad you asked. Here they are, all twenty-two of 'em. You need another paralegal just to keep up with your telephone calls. And, oh, by the way, Indie Gupta called to say he'll be stopping by to thank you personally for retrieving his $90,000 real estate commission. You're on a roll; this is your third grateful client this month." With a smirk, she added, "Are you *paying* these people to say something nice about you?"

Herald smiled and nodded his head at her lunch, still uneaten on her desktop. "Is that a Kaiser or sourdough roll? Hey, don't you realize client compliments are good public relations? Well worth the fifty dollars each one costs. Oops! Disregard that last remark."

Deborah laughed as she replied, "As a matter of fact, I hear Indie's footsteps on the stairs now. Why don't you go and meet him? Make it brief, please; we have a lot to do today."

Herald nodded, turned, and walked back to the foyer to meet his client. He opened the front door just as Indie reached for the knob. This shocked Indie, who jumped back and said in his best English, "Mr. Herald, Mr. Herald, I want thank you for getting my commission. I just cashed check this morning. I feel betrayed by my own kind when *my* Indian clients refused to close escrow. Later, when I found out they opened new escrow and closed sale behind my back to steal commission, I had no one to turn to. A friend told me about you. I hear terrible stories about what attorneys do to immigrants. He said you help anyone in need and charge reasonable fee. You had to drag my clients to court, but they paid. You saved my family! It was my only deal so far this year! Now I no longer afraid. When they want me sign something, I know I don't have to. I wait and show it to you before I sign. I don't have to worry anymore. It feels good to know I have attorney if I being pushed around."

"I'm glad to help, Indie. It's always sad when immigrants from the same country band together to help one another but then take advantage of each other. Remember, you have that other matter with the Bank of America loan on your friend's store. You need to make a decision before the bank forecloses."

"Yes, Mr. Herald, we should have new loan in next two weeks so not worry. Thanks again for help."

Offering a friendly handshake, Herald responded, "You're certainly welcome." He opened the door for the happy client to leave. "I appreciate the compliment, but I have to get busy; I have others to help. Thanks again and have a good day."

Indie walked out the door and down the steps. Halfway to the gate, he turned, waved, and shouted, "Thank you, again, Mr. Herald, I tell my friends."

Herald waved back and closed the door. It did feel good to right a wrong, but now back to Deborah; he returned to her desk.

She reached for the pertinent documents and resumed her "to do" recital: "The settlement conference is confirmed for Monday in *Dunn v. Patterson*. The client will meet you at eight forty-five Monday morning in the basement cafeteria at the Redwood City Superior Courthouse. The trial judge called about the Johnson case and said the trial will continue to Monday afternoon in Martinez as another matter had to be calendared for the morning. Good thing, too, as even *you* can't be in two places simultaneously. Let's see … Nope, looks like that's everything."

Looking up from her papers, she took a closer look at Herald. "Are you aware your hand that's holding the messages is shaking?"

Herald massaged his aching head with his free hand and argued, "Look, drinking keeps the Vietnam demons under control. I do not need you to amplify Thea's request that I go to counseling at the VA. I can manage this myself. Did anything nice happen while I was enjoying my drive from Martinez?"

"Oh yes, how could I forget? My favorite television lunch soap, *All My Children*, was bounced for a baseball game. Losing my TV show really iced my cake. I physically threw out my boyfriend after we fought last night. Then this morning the manager of the apartment house calls to tell me he is worried maybe he shouldn't have let him back in my apartment after I left for work, as he has absconded with most of my furniture. Mind you, this would be for his move to Arizona! I would have brought it up to you earlier, but everyone else was busy having their own mental breakdowns. Looks like if I want support from this group, I need to put it on the calendar to ensure priority!"

"Ha! Remind me to return to the office only when it is deserted. Speaking of your mental health, how is your post-breakup brain?"

"Engaging in the famous boxing technique of 'bob and weave,' between 'How could I throw him out?' and 'Thank God I did!'"

"Well, it's not like there were no indications of underlying problems in your relationship. You have to admit, as you noted on many occasions, anyone who begins every day at 5:30 a.m. by lifting weights at a gym with the sole intent of compensating for being five-feet-two is a little weird. He needs to supplement his physical goals with a step up from his career as kitchen help. The raw-egg diet, in the mode of the original *Rocky* movie, never sat well with me, either—and I'm not yoking," grinned Herald.

"I could deal with the raw eggs, even your silly puns, Herald, but for him to leave me after he begged, pleaded, and pouted me into leaving Chicago is too much," Deborah declared as she gazed out her window. "Know any sane eligible bachelors who are interested in an amply endowed, both mentally and physically, legal secretary, who recently entered the singles market?"

"Personal foul," Herald quipped while making the gestures of a football referee grabbing a facemask. "Fifteen yards and cleaning the coffee pot for two days for the implication that any bachelor *I* know is sane." Turning on his heel as if still in the military, he walked toward the Parrot Room to deal with the natives, the sounds of legal malpractice war drums in his head.

Just then Thea walked out of her office and met Herald in the foyer. She now worked part-time running the law office and maintaining only her own cases, to spend more time with their two children. But she remained very businesslike, disguising her statuesque figure in tailored suits and keeping her blond hair in a blunt, shoulder-length cut. Her manner was always coolly aloof.

Herald admitted to himself that as his partner and office manager— forget wife—she needed to hear about *the mistake*. Giving her his "little bad boy" smile he said, "I need to talk to you in private," took her arm, escorted her back into her office, and closed the door. He sat down in one of the two client chairs in front of her desk.

Thea tossed her head to flip her hair back from her face, a habit that usually indicated she was nervous or just about to get angry, and sat down.

"And what is this about?"

Christ … here we go. Herald began envisioning Bette Davis about to say her famous "Fasten your seatbelts" line.

He leaned forward, buried his face in his hands, and in a low apologetic tone, began. "I was … I was checking the mail this morning. It appears that … that I have committed malpractice … to the tune of 2.4 million dollars." He lifted his eyes to see if his mistake warranted a full hair flip.

"HOLY SHIT!" Thea cried out as she jumped up, her hands involuntarily rushing to her face. After a few seconds, seeming more like an hour to Herald, she regained her customary decorum and lowered herself back into her chair.

If she flips her hair again, I'm toast!

True to form, Thea flipped her hair.

Marmalade, anyone?

She clasped her hands together on her desk and, teary eyed, said, "I would really appreciate a better explanation than that, if possible."

I am in it so-o-o-o deep …

He lowered his face into his hands again, thought better of it, and faced her squarely, to explain the lack of the client's name on the stipulation.

Thea clenched her hands into two hard fists on the desk and flipped her hair as she raised her voice. "Well, you've really done it this time. For the last three years, I've watched you drink more and more and more. You're out late at night doing God knows what. You have nightmares and won't seek any type of help. The combination of files scattered everywhere and your excessive drinking every night was malpractice looking for a place to happen."

Taking a brief pause to collect herself, she asked, "Do we have any legal way out?"

"There is a Motion for Relief From Default. But as you remember from your civil procedure in law school, there is a six-month limitation, so we're over the deadline. However, there are several very narrow interpretations which do allow for relief from default. I believe our case falls in one of those limited exceptions. It's … it's a very long shot."

Thea stared at him and punctuated her unspoken thoughts with another flip of her hair. After taking a minute to regain her perspective, she decreed, "I want you to call in another attorney to help you. With your drinking and the mess this office is in, I'm not sure you have the ability to handle the day-to-day legal work, much less this malpractice problem."

Indignant, Herald stood up and gave his rebuttal. "We barely have the cash flow to keep the office running. We are overextended to the extreme, with home and office mortgages and the cost of raising the children. You talk about hiring more people, but you have not been carrying your load. You have divorce clients you should bill and two probates you could close. What about that?"

Thea frowned and flipped her hair one last time. "Look, our deal is, I work half days and help the kids at school. Remember? *Remember?* Billing and closing probates takes a huge amount of time. I've had it with this entire lifestyle. I'm tired of your antics—and there appears to be no end in sight. If you do not change your behavior, malpractice or worse will keep occurring. We could lose everything. *I never bargained for this!*"

Getting more upset, Herald shouted back, "I don't need any help, either legal or psychological. I can manage this myself, thank you. I'm going to the law library to do research on the motion. Thanks for your vote of confidence!"

With that, he rushed to the door, opened it, and slammed it on the way out, chafing from his legal-eagle spouse's reprimand.

CHAPTER 4
MARLIN FISHING IN SOUTHEAST ASIA

IT WAS A HOT SATURDAY, MD 34, and Herald was at home, relaxing in shorts and a t-shirt. He had just finished his three-Budweiser lunch. Raising his hands straight out in front of his eyes, he could see that his hangover shakes had settled down.

Nothing like a Bud to calm down the nerves and hands.

It was time to go looking for cracks in the foundation of his home in San Carlos. In addition to handling the multitude of cases stacked up at his law office and confronting his career-threatening legal mistake, Herald was trying to establish a case against the former owners of his house.

He had discovered what appeared to be cracks in the exterior walls. The former owners had not only failed to disclose extensive cracking in the exterior stucco, they had concealed it by applying flexible caulking and a thick coat of new, yellow paint to mask the foundation failures. This constituted fraud.

Armed with a flashlight, Herald ventured to the backyard and jerked open the old access door to the dark, cool space beneath the house. The rusted door hinges squeaked in protest. The first real issue Herald encountered was a sheet of spider webs. Ten years of cobwebs were matted together, layer upon layer, thick with dust, and hung as a foreboding wall blocking the entrance. His fear of spiders had developed in Vietnam, where they were everywhere—some of them poisonous. Herald had never gotten used to sharing his bunker with a variety of spiders, along with venomous centipedes and scorpions. But then again, the dugout was *their* domain and Herald the invader.

Rethinking his first tactic, he walked back to the garage, retrieved a broom, returned to the entry, and, using the broom handle, attacked the ornate webs blocking the opening, rooting out the little buggers suspended to catch their next meal.

Still attached to their silk threads, the unlucky arachnids were captured in their own trap and dragged into the daylight for certain death under Herald's gym shoes in a "Death of the Spider" dance.

Kneeling down to peer into the web-free crawlspace, Herald noted the foundation footings seemed straight. He crawled in, allowing his eyes to adjust to the darkness. The clay floor was cool on his hands and bare knees. There was a subterranean quiet, long forgotten.

Thoughts of his malpractice suit began creeping in. To change his focus, he reached up to stretch his left hand across his forehead and squeeze his temples hard between his thumb and forefingers. Stomach cramps grabbed at his abdomen. The fear of losing his law practice, home, and family overwhelmed him, and he knew the physical impact of stress. The thumping from his Vietnam-memory crypt reverberated through his entire body.

His breathing became labored; sweat broke on his face; his chest muscles knotted up. It felt like a heart attack. He lay flat on his stomach and placed his forehead onto the damp clay floor to cool himself. Suffocating in his fear of losing everything, he forced himself to focus on remembering a happy moment. True to his desperate mental request, a happy memory filled his mind's eye. It was good—except it took him back to Vietnam.

YEAR 1969

"REEL HIM IN SLOWLY—*ack*—steady pressure on the line. He may just be taking a short—*ack*—rest before he makes another run," suggested Buck Sergeant "AckMan" in a quiet, steady tone. AckMan had a habit of peppering his speech with a strange involuntary cough when he was under stress. It sounded like "*ack*," but the tone and volume would vary, depending upon the situation. At the moment, AckMan was chatting with Platoon Sergeant John Pearlman, "Johnny" to his family, about fishing in the Song Vom Co Dong, a river about a klick from their Area of Operations, or AO. They were playing their imaginary game of fly-fishing.

Pearlman, assigned temporary platoon leader, had been running the platoon for the past three months, after their former lieutenant had been killed in an ambush. Five-feet-ten, thin, with deep blue eyes, straight black hair grown long, showing it had been nine months since his initial Army buzz cut, and a prominent nose and high cheekbones, Pearlman had the regal bearing of a Roman emperor. A nonpracticing Jew from Boston, he was also an only child whose parents, both Harvard-educated doctors, held high expectations for him.

Safe behind the earthen protective berm surrounding Firebase Jackson, Pearlman was holding his imaginary deep-sea fishing rod and sitting on a worn Sears & Roebuck aluminum lawn chair with red and green plaid plastic webbing for the seat and back. Strips of the chair's webbing were worn through; shreds of it waved back and forth with his movements—a memory that made Herald smile.

"'*Pesce d'aprile*,' dere-a 'e go, or is-a dat-a 'dar-a she blow'?" shouted the one-rank-above-private, Specialist 4 Ferlinghetti, standing to one side of the lawn chair—and speaking in his not-quite-English-not-quite-Italian way. At just five-feet-two, he was the smallest squad leader of the platoon, but his squad members trusted his criminal instincts to keep them alive. No one, neither friend nor foe, was going to be sneaking up on old Ferlin.

Yessiree, Ferlin—aka, "It Won't Be Pretty, Weasel"—would get them back, long before any of his college-educated platoon cohorts.

"Remind me why Sarge always gets to—*ack*—fish first? We never get to—*ack*—fish first," AckMan challenged from the other side of the lawn chair.

"*Chi detta la moda, chi lancia 'na moda.* 'e's-a da Sarge-a, no? 'e's da one 'o save all-a our ass-a many-a time, no?" nodded Ferlinghetti, explaining that Sarge was the one to dictate or launch a trend—not AckMan.

One of the oddest members of the platoon was nicknamed "Dog," who communicated solely by barking; he refused to speak English. Dog would elongate his lower jaw and put his lips together like a dog getting ready to bark, look to the sky, and utter a "Ruff," nodding his head "yes" to a good cast while watching an imaginary fishing line arc through the sky into the barbed wire surrounding the berm.

Sergeant Jones was sitting on the sandbag roof of an interior bunker, watching the fishing with avid interest. He nibbled at the soil-stained fingernails of his left hand while writing down every word said in his notebook.

Pearlman wiped the sweat from his face and furrowed his brow, absorbing Ferlinghetti and AckMan's instructions on how to cast his line. This was the only time he could go fishing. After an all-night ambush, the platoon was kept in reserve; it was only then that a soldier could enjoy a peaceful morning of angling in the wire.

Pearlman raised his left hand to shade his eyes and surveyed the area where his imaginary fishing line disappeared into the rolling waves of barbed wire that circled the firebase. This was his big chance to catch the great white one, once and for all, and he was not about to blow it. At just the right moment, he jerked the imaginary rod hard with both hands while rising to a standing position. When Pearlman stood up, the lawn chair upended and fell behind him with a soft clank of aluminum hitting the dirt.

"Wow!" Pearlman exclaimed, as his imaginary giant marlin crested the barbed wire and disappeared back into the rolling metal waves.

"*Soooeeee!*" Ferlinghetti shouted. "Is-a da biggest-a *pesce* I ever see!"

"You callin' Pearlman's fish—*ack*—a pig? Pigs go 'sooee,' not—*ack*—fish!" Ferlinghetti smiled and jumped up. "Tu' mamma go 'sooee,' no?"

"Mama, my—*ack*—ass! I'll show you my mama, you—*ack*—little wopsucker!" And with that, AckMan jumped onto the berm shrieking with laughter and leaping on Ferlinghetti's back. The two rolled around in the dirt punching each other, laughing and arguing about who was going to get on top first.

Pearlman glanced over his shoulder at the commotion. "AckMan, Ferlinghetti, it's tough enough to fish these dangerous waters without you two scaring the damn fish with your roughhousing." With a deft move of his right foot, he flipped the tattered lawn chair upright. When he sat down, the movement made a small cloud of red dust rise from the fine, dry clay soil and hover above the chair legs.

Pearlman … AckMan … Jones … Ferlinghetti … Dog … the most important people in Herald's Vietnam life. Ferlinghetti, an Italian who had survived the street wars of Newark, New Jersey, was offered the choice of jail or the Army after his criminal conviction at eighteen years of age. He had the deep-set, shifty eyes of a thief. Jones, five-feet-ten and checking in at 195 pounds, was a dropout from Duke University who constantly gnawed on his fingernails. AckMan, balding at twenty-two and from Ohio, was a high school dropout, but after joining the Army, he passed the GED and applied to Ohio State just before being assigned to Vietnam. Dog, who had given up speaking English for barking, was a simple, lanky, Southern boy from Fort Smith, Arkansas. With his drooping eyes, large ears, and head and face covered with blond hair, he resembled a bloodhound.

Herald, still half asleep, was curled up five feet below ground under his camouflage poncho liner on the dusty red-clay floor of his interior bunker. The last remnants of the cool, damp night air hung in the lower part of the bunker. The heat and dust, signaling the new day, filtered into the dark bowels of the bunker along with a deep, oily odor of burning human waste. The disgusting stench filled Herald's nose, causing him to wake up with a start and rub his offended nostrils.

To manage the sewage of hundreds of soldiers in the firebase, empty fifty-five-gallon gasoline drums were cut in half and placed under the seats in the latrines. Early each morning, the waste-filled drums were dragged out, the contents doused with liberal amounts of diesel fuel and set on fire. This became a practical, sanitary way to dispose of human sewage when the high water table prohibited trenches in the ground. However, the odor was exactly what one would expect from burning human feces with diesel fuel: putrid. The incomplete burning of the diesel fuel and waste created a dark, sticky smoke that clung to the insides of soldiers' nostrils.

As Herald rubbed his nose to get the smell out, his ears picked up the sounds of deep-sea sport fishing terminology, shouts of "your mama," and the wrestling noises of the boys scuffling and rolling in the dirt with one another. A faint whiff of marijuana smoke was also in the air—a peculiar odor when combined with burning diesel fuel and feces.

Better check on the lads. Idle hands, the devil and all ...

He rose to one knee and put his right hand on the top of his head. This careful act of prevention, almost second nature to him now, was to make sure he wouldn't bash his head on the metal engineering stakes or wooden planks latticed to support the ceiling of two layers of sandbags. With his bunker not quite tall enough for him to stand up in, he'd learned this protective measure the hard way.

What were those old folktales that held your fortune could be read by the number of bumps on your head? Right. I should be so lucky! Besides, we're a long way from Kansas now, coloring book moron. How's that for good luck?

Herald began stretching and massaging his right arm, still tingling from having slept on it. He'd taken a nap after being awake all night on ambush patrol. Now disrupted, it carried both mental and physical costs. He felt a general nausea, and when his muscles moved, they hesitated, as if not in sync with his mind. He felt as though he'd suffered an electric shock. His mind was clouded and unable to focus. Whatever coated his tongue left a sour taste. The overall physical effect was very much like a bad hangover—without the fun of drinking. Herald's head, spinning from lack of sleep, forced him to lie back down on his poncho liner.

When his dizziness cleared and he'd established the parameters of the bunker, Herald turned onto his side, propped his head up on one elbow, and looked at the cut shovel patterns of the damp, red-clay wall facing him. He thought about the huge amount of time he had spent in Army schooling, trudging through various military regimes.

Two years! Two years to get ready for what, to find myself scared, aching, sick, and staring at a damp clay wall? Talk about irony!

The Army prepared America's youth for Vietnam first with eight weeks of Basic Training, focusing on weapons use, physical conditioning, following orders, and the creation of a military mind-set. Next came eight weeks of Advanced Infantry Training, or AIT, with instruction on all infantry weapons, squad tactics and map reading, plus basic Vietnam War rules to live by. Then came six months in Officer Candidate School with its memorization of detailed schematics of Army weapons; studying small-unit tactics combined with use of artillery and air support; learning specific Vietnam tactics and how to command platoon-sized maneuvers. These lessons were taught in Georgia during the summer months, when heat sirens signaled temperatures exceeding 100 degrees; the oppressive humidity went unmeasured.

Herald and his fellow OCS students referred to the program as "Officer Cantaloupe School." It was fun to compare their institution to a fruit farm. He smiled to himself as he remembered that underground slogan and what he and his comrades used to say: "I cannot spell 'lieutenant' but now I is one."

After OCS came eight weeks in Motor Officer School, in Louisville, Kentucky, where Herald learned about the maintenance of all motorized vehicles, from tanks to jeeps, and the required paperwork. Louisville was fun; as an officer with all the attendant privileges, he went to the Kentucky Derby.

Officers were not required to be in their barracks at any specific time; they could leave the base at their leisure, without the necessity of a pass. This was Herald's first taste of freedom in the military.

His first assignment was to Germany, where he commanded a mechanized platoon of four armored personnel carriers. The APCs were a type of fighting vehicle designed to transport infantry to the battlefield, a kind of "battle taxi."

Preparing for Vietnam, the twenty-one-year-old read every guerrilla-war book he could get his hands on. These books explained guerrilla tactics used in Malaysia and the Philippines, such as the "bloody nose," the "ambush counterattack," and the "sniper drill." The overriding concept proved to be invaluable mental ammunition: never be baited into anything, because losing one's cool means losing one's life.

The primary fear of male college students in the latter part of the 1960s was being drafted. At its worst, the draft meant death or dismemberment in a misunderstood war. During his assignment in Germany, Herald came to realize his odds of being injured or killed as an infantry lieutenant in Vietnam did not look good. The military statistics in one of the manuals he'd read estimated the life span of a lieutenant to be thirty seconds from the first enemy shot fired, and Viet Cong guerrillas would target command-and-control first.

So, the buck stops on my ass? They didn't show that *picture in the coloring book!*

Academic book learning is just book learning: a nonthreatening, intellectual exploration—*no* personal risk. If things get out of hand, one just puts the book down. Firsthand experience is the great qualifier when the first bullet snaps over a soldier's head.

Why does the Army spend so much time on schooling? Didn't I quit college to get away from school?

Yet he found himself learning more every day. The culmination of his practical military education came from Sergeant Pearlman, who coached him in the day-to-day cautious way of life required in Vietnam to stay alive. This part of his education spanned from directing formations for patrol to what C-rations to blend for a good meal.

The end result of all this effort was Herald lying five feet underground on a dusty, clay bunker floor looking at a damp clay wall. And scared. Maybe he should have followed his father's path; at least it would have been less dangerous to his life and limb.

This is entirely that evil coloring book's fault. It has to be destroyed! Herald thought, as he sat up and pounded on his thigh. *Other people could fall under its curse. It has to be destroyed in a manner befitting the abuse it's inflicting on me!*

Torture came to mind as he rubbed his chin.

Burn one page ... toss another into a freezer for days ... tape ten pages to the railroad tracks ... toss another ten off a freeway bridge at rush hour in the rain ...

His mind reeled at all the possible methods of destruction. He had to save others who might be seduced by the temptations of war as glorified by the nasty book.

In his rage toward the book, Herald forgot the Golden Bunker Rule and jumped up. His head hit a supporting steel roof stake. The pain flashed blinding red through his mind. He dropped to one knee and rubbed the red flame from his consciousness. As the searing pain subsided, a single thought emerged, overwhelming all other thoughts.

Wait! I can't take revenge on the coloring book. I'm in *the goddamn thing!*

Standing again—and this time remembering to place his right hand on top of his head—he massaged the pain and shook his head left and right, in disbelief he'd been so stupid to forget the Golden Bunker Rule.

Turning to face the exit, he walked toward it and paused to look at a calendar tacked on the rough wood frame of the door. Beneath the obligatory smiling *Playboy* model, the bottom half of the calendar, with the days framed in squares, had specific dates marked off with wide black slashes from the top-right to the bottom-left corner of each square. The marking stopped at September 14, 1969, with the words "OUTTA HERE!" in large red letters. Herald had no idea how many days had passed since that lucky soldier had gotten "outta here." He just knew he—Herald—had been the bunker's main resident for a very long time. In Vietnam everyone loses track of what day it is, as days of the week are meaningless, with a three-day workweek and no weekends.

In his mind, he reviewed an infantry line officer's week in Vietnam. Day one: daytime patrol. Day two: off all day; all-night ambush patrol. Day three: off until midnight; after that, in reserve only if trouble came up.

Then, if one were lucky still to be alive, back to Day One. It never occurred to Herald before Vietnam that a three-day workweek could be a bad thing. With more than nine months to go, counting off remaining days would not be an option. Too depressing.

At the bottom of the stairs from his underground nest, Herald was stunned as the sun's harsh brightness blinded his sleep-deprived eyes. He wasn't doing well on a night of no sleep and a morning of little rest. He paused again on the second step, still shaded by the bunker roof, to adjust to the harsh morning light two inches in front of his nose. After a few moments, he moved through the shimmering heat barrier to the top step, placed his arms on the bunker wall to steady himself, and scanned the firebase. As his eyes adjusted to the light, the bleakness of his gray-sandbag-and-barbed-wire world came into focus.

Hmm ... Another day in "paradise."

The morning after an all-night patrol was the only time a soldier could relax; the all-night unit was the last that would be mobilized in case of an emergency. This would be the time, if a soldier were so inclined, to partake in the herb that refreshes. While smoking marijuana was illegal for the troops and could be grounds for a court martial, most of the platoon leaders cut a deal with their men.

To outlaw recreation of any sort was to invite a dangerous situation. Marijuana grew wild everywhere. It was all the men had, outside of a few beers, to ease their anxiety and raise their morale. A total ban would only force those who were going to smoke to do so at potentially dangerous times; smoking on guard or on patrol exposed everyone to danger.

The large number of booby traps in the area forced everyone to be alert anytime they were outside the protective rolling waves of wire forming the perimeter of their compound. Being stoned equaled being careless. Carelessness was a fast trip to the dusty morgue, as recent history had pointed out: his company alone had lost sixty men to booby traps in the last four months.

Pot smoking was tolerated at specific times so casualties would not occur. Strange behavior might be witnessed those mornings when the boys were allowed a visit with "Herb." When high, every soldier's uncontrolled imagination took flight. A large number of Herald's platoon would talk to Herb on these mornings, passing several joints around the group before "going fishing."

Before Herald could fully acclimate to the light and heat, Lieutenant Chump walked over to reintroduce himself.

"Lieutenant Lloyd, I just wanted to say hello since we're both assigned to the same company. I haven't seen you since Wolfhound orientation."

Herald glanced over his shoulder to look at Chump. The orientation he spoke of was a one-week training camp in the center of a large, safe base in Cu Chi, where a few veterans screened and trained the newbies.

These instructors drilled the newbies by making them chant important strategic pointers over and over. It was akin to children memorizing a rhyme. For instance, the response to *"WHAT'S THE WORD?"* was shouted back in percussive rhythm:

Do not kick or pick up things
   'less you plan to meet your king.
When you hear a muzzle blast
   hit the dirt or lose your ass.
Do not linger or look around
   'til you're married to the ground.

Such instructions were drilled into each soldier and expected to be filed in his brain's IMMEDIATE ATTENTION category of automatic reflex. This is the most important first response for survival: the GET REAL CAREFUL OR DIE theme of the training. Everybody passed. Surprise!

Herald was graduated from OCS and transferred to Vietnam two weeks before Chump; therefore, he had "time in grade" on him. Time in grade controlled who had higher rank among soldiers of the same rank. Chump previously served and claimed to have been in the Green Berets. An antiguerrilla unit, the Green Berets' primary job was to train the indigenous people of any country in the throes of fighting an insurgency where the U.S. had political interests. Green Beret units of twelve to fourteen men acted alone, beyond the control of any large military unit. Insurgencies were plentiful in the 1960s.

Chump seemed to confuse being a Green Beret, where one acted almost entirely independently, with being a platoon member, just a small cog in a big machine. He was first to remind everyone of his experience and importance. His brash demeanor concealed the question his experience could not answer: would he be a good commander under fire?

Nodding a hello, Herald inquired, "How goes the war?"

"Great! I have a plan to trap Sir Charles in the water. I'll place my platoon on an all-night ambush next to the river and wait until he crosses. Once in the water, he'll be easy pickin's."

"Chump, it appears you fail to comprehend that the U.S. Navy patrol boats control the river and have a free-fire zone on any life form next to the river. They tend to be a bit jumpy, as Sir Charles constantly ambushes them. I suggest you reevaluate your plan. You and your men could become part of the landscape if a patrol boat spots you and opens fire."

Chump, sweat dripping off his nose, shifted his five-foot-five body from foot to foot and reassured Herald. "I have a pencil flare I got from an Air Force pilot. They use them to signal the Navy if they're down and need help. Not to worry."

"Wrong, Chump. One, our orders are never to set an all-night ambush close to the river; two, Charles uses flares to signal an ambush to open fire; so, our river patrol would interpret your flare as the beginning of a Charles ambush, not as a 'Help!' signal from a downed pilot; and three, those patrol boats have twin 50-cal machine guns, one automatic 40 mm grenade launcher and two M-60 machine guns—and they do *not* ask questions. Yours is a very bad and dangerous idea."

"With your lack of imagination, we'll never win this war," Chump huffed as he turned and stomped back toward his bunker.

"And with your lack of understanding the reason for orders, Chump 'old buddy,' you will just be another casualty of this war, along with a lot of your men," Herald yelled over his shoulder as he focused on his troops at the perimeter. He thanked God for Pearlman and all his experience to guide him as he grew into a combat officer.

Herald languished outside his bunker as a company orderly walked over, burdened with a heavy, two-foot-square cardboard box under his right arm, and large satchel of mail hanging off his left shoulder. With a grunt, he hoisted the box onto a nearby bunker's roof and dropped the satchel next to it; then, he mounted the bunker roof, pulled a couple handfuls of mail from the satchel, and yelled, "Second Platoon, mail call!" The squad leaders left Pearlman to his fishing and headed for the bunker post office, nodding to Herald as they passed.

The rest of the platoon, responding to the mail call like subterranean animals, crept out of their bunkers in the hope someone from home remembered them.

After about twenty had gathered, along with Herald, the orderly yelled the names of those lucky few who had received something.

"FERLINGHETTI: Two more last notices from AA Jewelers. The warning stamped on the envelope says they'll be sending the matter to their attorneys soon. One last notice from OK Auto Sales. But relax—the police are not looking for you here; you're already in prison. If they came to get you, they might get shot by Charles, who don't like any Americans, cops or not.

"JONES: Three requests—count 'em—for money from the Duke University Alumni Association.
"ACKMAN: Looks like you made it into Ohio State.
"HENRY, a.k.a. DOG: Four issues of the Fort Smith, Arkansas *Democrat-Gazette*.
"JACOB: *Ummm*, smells like love.
"LLOYD: Nice handwriting ... and again perfume. That is all."

Each man stepped forward as his name was read, picked up his letter, and walked away for a bit of privacy. Jones picked up Herald's letter, admired the elegant cursive handwriting, and ran the letter under his nose, smelling the fragrance of good perfume. He handed it over with a smirk.

The remaining soldiers sat silently, empty looks on their faces. LeMaire, a hairy, hulking, 260-pound French-Canadian Maine machine gunner, cursed, *"Mon Dieu, merde,"* and wandered off, his steps kicking up small clouds of red-clay dust. Back and chest hair protruded over the collar of his t-shirt like a cheap fur scarf.

The orderly picked up the unopened cardboard box and threw it down to the ground. "Here's a box from some women's club in Montana. I'm supposed to give one box to each platoon. Enjoy."

The abandoned soldiers jumped on the box and tore at the sides. It split open, and paperback books flooded the air in all directions.

"What's wrong with our country?" one mail-less soldier yelled. "Don't they get we need something edible, not bulky or heavy to carry? Christ! *Books!* We are all alone here, boys!" He kicked one small book almost to the berm as he walked away, exploding clay dust into the air with each step.

Ferlinghetti was walking back to the fishing party and eyeing his bills, not the ground. His right foot caught on the thin book that had been the focus of the frustrated kick. It tripped him just enough to set him off balance. He stumbled twice in an attempt to recover, but it was too late. His left foot locked behind his right, and he hit the ground with a heavy thud, sending a cloud of dust rising over his head and body. Spitting out the dust his mouth had captured, he swore. *"Figlio di puttana!"* He grabbed the thin book and was about to throw it at the closest bunker when his eyes focused on the book cover. There, in big letters, was *A Coney Island of the Mind*, by Lawrence Ferlinghetti. *"Mamma mia!"* he yelped. "Look-a, guys, I write-a da book-a! I write-a da book of-a … of-a … *la poesia?! Ma che …* "

Pearlman, still in his chair, brushed his long black hair back over his head with his left hand. He straightened, laughed, and yelled over his shoulder, "Who are you kidding, Ferlin? The only way you would be found with a book is if you stole it."

Ferlinghetti yelled as he opened the book, "'ey, 'arvard-a, I did-a pretty good in-a school-a until-a my papá 'e run off-a, den I have-a to work. Madonna! I 'ave-a my own gang until-a we get-a bust-a and I'm-a chose-a da Army over da jail-a!"

Jones stopped writing, took his nail-bitten index finger out of his mouth, and addressed Pearlman. "Hey, Sarge, Ferlinghetti is pretty smart for no formal schooling. I've been reading some novels with him, and the little Italian is getting it. He's got a knack for literature. His diction needs improvement, but he's got a pretty good brain. Poetry'd be a good way to keep him busy—and you know we all want to keep Ferlinghetti busy."

Pearlman, still trying to focus on his imaginary fishing, smiled, smacked his forehead with his hand, and replied, "Who woulda thunk it?"

Ferlinghetti glanced to his left and right, as was his custom to avoid the police, and confronted Pearlman: *"Rompicoglioni, tu! Romperò palle tuo!"* He brushed the dust from the book and read several pages while standing in the burning sun. Closing the book, he walked over to Herald, his uniform still covered with dust from the fall in his bunker and earlier tussle with AckMan. "Ciao, LT. I read una poema, OK?"

Herald looked at Ferlinghetti, the Italian thief from the Rosewood West Ward suburb of Newark, New Jersey, who had not graduated from high school. He rubbed the sleep out of his eyes and said, "Poem? You did say, 'poem,' right? OK, everything else is weird, so why not a poem in 'Nam."

"Ah, si! You bet-a you ass-a!" Ferlinghetti glanced left and right again, opened the book to a random page, and, in carefully placed—and surprisingly understandable—diction, began.

Johnny Nolan has a patch on his ass

Kids chase him
          thru screendoor summers

Thru the back streets
          of all my memories

Somewhere a man laments
          upon a violin

A doorstep baby cries
          and cries again
      like
      a
        ball
          bounced
            down steps

Which helps the afternoon arise again
to a moment of remembered hysteria

Johnny Nolan has a patch on his ass

Kids chase him

(A Coney Island of the Mind: Poems, page 37)

"W'at-a you t'ink-a, LT?"

Herald looked to the sky and rubbed his chin. He found it difficult to react to a poetry quiz when he was barely awake. "This is a type of free-flowing poetry of the mind. These are the author's memories of long-past summers of his youth. And you know what else? This was one of my favorite poetry books in prep school."

"*Accidenti!* Wow! Questa poema take-a me back-a to Newark-a summer … chase-a da Spics off-a my turf-a."

Herald smiled and scratched his head. "Well, there you go. You got it. Keep reading; you may find more to interest you."

"You 'elp-a w'it-a da words, LT?"

"Absolutely!" Herald agreed as he rolled his eyes. "I honestly can't think of a *better* place for poetry than Vietnam! But first I have to check on the boys and get some chow," he added, moving toward the fishing party.

On the bulldozed berm forming the perimeter of the camp was the most important man in his world, Platoon Sergeant Pearlman, sitting in the tattered lawn chair.

"How're they biting today?" Herald inquired, wiping away a yawn with his right hand.

"Not bad, LT. Lost two, but one is a whopper! Look, I've still got 'im on the line," Pearlman answered, over his shoulder, as he went jerking back and forth in the chair. Then, imagining the marlin jumping high into the air, he stood and shouted, "Look at the size of that one!"

"Ride 'em, cowboy!" Herald shot back.

"Just imagine how it would look on the wall of my family room, at the head of the pool table."

"Yep," Herald agreed, nodding and applauding, "truly a trophy-sized catch for the man with the imagination and skill to land him."

Dog lifted his head like a coyote baying at the moon, pushed his lips together, looked to the sky, and gave a long, exaggerated, "Rr-rr-*ruff!*" of approval.

Herald turned to his squad leader Jones, the perpetual scribbler, still sitting on the sandbag roof. "Good morning, Jones. And what are we writing about, now?" There were blood spatters all over the pages of Jones's log. The pressure of Jones holding a pen between his fingers caused his rough-chewed fingernails to bleed. The blood-splattered pages made Herald sick to his stomach.

Jones smiled. "At Duke I wanted to experience enough of life to write a book. I've got plenty of material here, 'cept no one's gonna believe it. Always behave in Vietnam, LT, as if you're a wanted man, 'cause you are. Oh, and good morning, LT."

"Good morning to you, and best of luck with the book. I wouldn't believe it, either."

Herald turned and walked back to Pearlman. "Since I'm the newest member of the platoon and haven't ever been shot at, I'd like to ask you a few questions. Mind? This can wait until after fishing, if you prefer."

Smiling, Pearlman replied, "No. Go ahead, shoot."

Herald hesitated. Then, looking at the ground, he inquired, "How do you keep your cool under fire?"

Pearlman stroked his hair and stood up for a deliberate, give-me-a-moment-to-think stretch; then, he sat back down. "OK, it's like this: I make the chaos of war my personal mental hurricane. I place myself in the center of my hurricane's eye, a place where things are calm. You still see the madness and death swirling all around outside. But inside the eye, you have created a calm place that allows you to think."

He cleared his throat, to take a brief pause, and continued. "If you stay in the eye and ride out the storm, you will be doing all you can to create some semblance of control, allowing for stillness and calm to think inside the great hurricane of chaotic and infinite fatal possibilities. *So-o-o*," he smiled, "just keep saying to yourself, 'Ride the eye of the storm, ride the eye ... ' and you should be able to keep your cool."

Herald thought about the concept. Never having been in a situation where he was faced with ultimate turmoil, he could only store this advice in a safe place for later use. Thinking further about the eventuality of it all, and his mates, he asked, "What about the platoon?"

Pearlman rocked back in his chair and, with his eyes trained on the barbed-wire waves, replied, "I wondered when you would settle down enough to want to understand your platoon members better. Congrats. After one month, you are right on schedule. Fire away."

Herald scratched his chin for a moment and started. "What's the story with LeMaire?"

Pearlman looked around to see if anybody was listening; then, he grinned. "LeMaire is more orangutan than human ... but ... watch out: he's a true killer in every sense of the term. Efficient, keeps his ammo clean, no talk, all business, very hairy, wide, prehistoric face like a Neanderthal. Be as smart about protecting him as you would your favorite son. He is fearless, a quality to be revered 'in the shit.' When it hits the fan, he will hold the line. Just avoid sharing his bunker."

Herald chuckled, scratched the back of his head, looked to the sky for a moment, and questioned, "Why not share his bunker?"

Pearlman laughed so hard it caused him to choke for a moment. Shaking his head back and forth, he explained, "LeMaire's nightly routine, just before bed, is chanting over and over in his super-low bass tones, *'Veee got to geeht out of di-i-iss place!'* While chanting, he twists the long black hair on his forearms into little inch-high tepees, spaced every two inches up his arms in a long column, three columns to each forearm. It takes over an hour. After twisting his arm hair into tepees, he laughs with this very dark, low tone and sets one of them on fire. He ignites the blaze with a Zippo lighter his father passed down from his time in the Korean War. After the skin under the tepee starts to bubble, LeMaire snuffs out the flames and dismantles the remaining tepees by sweeping his free hand rapidly over his entire forearm. Then he wipes down the tepees on his other arm."

By this time, Herald's jaw was at his knees. Pearlman continued.

"I've seen it just twice. It gave me the creeps both times. His burning hair gives off a pungent, sickly sweet smell, like an animal electrocuted on a high-voltage fence. I've been told that after he finishes burning all available hair on one forearm, he starts on the other one. His hair grows so fast, by the time all the tepees on one forearm have been incinerated, the hair on the other arm is back.

"Somebody heard him say the habit is for mosquito abatement, but the smell is beyond human olfactory tolerance. He always has plenty of space in his bunker—nobody can stand it—except for Dog!"

Shaking his head in disgust, Herald inquired further. "So, what's the story with Dog? Why is it he only barks and refuses to speak?"

Pearlman lowered his voice and looked far out past the waves of barbed-wire rolls. "Dog has chosen to walk point his entire tour and not speak English until he rotates home. As you now know, point is the person who is first in line and first to be killed by Charles. You and the radioman are next on the hit parade, by the way. Dog's best friend tripped a booby trap and was killed when we were all taking turns on point. He blames himself for his friend's death and vowed to walk point until he goes home.

"Dog's dad had a string of bloodhounds out of Fort Smith, Arkansas. He hunted armed convicts all over the South. Dog grew up hunting dangerous men. He came to me and requested to walk point and further said he was not speaking English anymore until he leaves. I told him nobody else wants point, so OK. He nodded and barked, 'Roh-RAH,' meaning, OK."

Herald nodded and smiled. With sweat dripping off his chin, and looking out over the rows and rows of wire, blinking his eyes to cope with the fierce sun, he admitted, "I'm only now beginning to understand the nuances of Dog's barking."

Pearlman shuffled his posterior back and forth in the old Sears & Roebuck chair, its worn aluminum joints squeaking in protest under his weight. The movement of the chair's legs on the parched soil gave rise to a cloud of clay dust that spread all around the chair like a translucent, ancient red fabric supporting a Viking warrior's throne.

Laughing to the sky, he advised, "Follow the tone of his barks. They'll make more sense than words from those who purport to speak English. Since he has chosen to walk point, I'm not going to argue with him. We have *stranger* people in the platoon."

Herald smiled at the bond between the platoon sergeant and his men. He focused his eyes on Pearlman and asked, "What about the '*ack*' of AckMan?"

Pearlman smiled, coughed gently, and tilted his head a bit to the left as he replied. "He's the one you should choose to replace me, if I catch one. Don't be put off by his '*ack*.' It's just his way of dealing with the shit. Finding someone who is cool under fire is hard enough. Add that he has already earned the respect of his men, not just for holding on under fire but for maintaining *command* under fire. He should be on your short list of people to keep your ass alive. You find someone better who *doesn't* '*ack*?' ... hire *him*."

Raising his right hand to shield his eyes from the sun, Pearlman leaned forward to survey the rows of dusty concertina wire surrounding the firebase. Running the palm of his hand over his forehead to collect the large amount of sweat beaded there, he whipped it off with a flick of his wrist. The whipping motion accelerated the beads of sweat off his hand; they hit the ground, making little dust clouds rise.

In a slow, low, unemotional tone, he continued. "Platoon leader is actually a misnomer. It should be 'gripe leader.' Before you arrived, I was platoon leader and got complaints from the officers and squawks from the lower ranks. My two biggest pet piss-me-offs are the officers' endless grumbling about everything and the grunts' sniveling when I picked someone to walk point. Point, walking point, is the issue here. 'Point,' to place it in Vietnam terms, is the same as 'slow torture.' Everyone who walks point reacts to the stress. The anxiety comes from the reality that most firefights in 'Nam are fought within thirty feet of Charles. Bonus point to Charles—he gets the first shot. So this brings me back to Dog's offer.

"Dog's offer was twofold: yes to walking point; no to speaking English. Oh, my God, no more bellyaching from Dog, the know-it-all criminal tracker from the South who always knows better. With anyone else in the platoon, the heat and fear of being shot or blown up causes sweat to seep off their head like water oozing out of a small fissure in the top of a rock cliff. Their energy drains with every step. You can usually see it in a point man's face; his brain is ablaze with fear. His mind is screaming, '*LEAD FACIAL, LEAD FACIAL!*' thinking of bullets streaking toward his face. In the first hour on patrol, the tension manifests itself as small, involuntary muscular movements: a short jerk of the arm, tight twists of the neck and chest. The next hour, in addition to the physical reactions, audible '*urps*' are heard, as the pressure of possibly catching a bullet at close range takes the form of an involuntary vocal response.

"Dog could care less; he's just huntin'. I remember only one conversation with Dog. I asked how he could walk point and be cool. His reply was short: 'Them crim-in-als al-ways had guns just like Charles. Everyone being armed keeps it even.'

"All these assholes seem to forget that, as platoon leader, you walk right behind the point man, within arm's reach of a goddamn radio. I—now it's you—might as well have a neon sign on your ass flashing 'Shoot Me.' We get to experience the same danger and the same physical symptoms as the man on point but have no one to bitch to. Shi-i-it!"

Pearlman leaned to the right and spit as he continued. "So, let me reflect back on Dog's offer. He volunteered to walk point and not speak English. Then he clinches the deal: he says he will walk point for the duration of his tour."

Pearlman scanned the base to be sure no one was listening, rocked back in his chair, and laughed. "Well, strike me dead. Not having to fight over who walks point is every platoon sergeant's dream! I'm going to take Dog home and marry the mother-*F*-er. He will have my child, maybe even twins—or a litter! I don't mind having puppies. No expense sending them to college."

Both he and Herald burst into laughter at the thought. Then Pearlman took a resealable bag from his breast pocket, opened it, pulled out a spiral notepad and flipped it open. Herald heard a *zzi-i-i-ip* as the first page of the notebook was torn out. Pearlman handed it up above his left shoulder to where Herald was standing.

"What's all this?" Herald asked, as he grabbed the paper and scanned it.

Pearlman placed the notebook back in the bag, sealed it, and returned the bag to his pocket. "This is a Dog-to-English dictionary. You're ready for it now."

"Are you kidding me? A translation guide?"
Herald raised the paper to his eyes and read:
DOG TO ENGLISH
Grrh = Disgusting
GRRrrrr = This could be dangerous
Hur-roh = Hello
Rah-ROU! = Careful!

Rah-TA-RATH = Serves you right
Rarh = Yeah
Rarh-re-ROOH = Here we go
Roh-RAH = OK
Roh-ra-Roh! = Oh My God!
Rooh-rooh-rooh = Crying
Ror—ro—*RRH*! = Make Room
ROUH-rah-HA-HA = Laughing
RrrrOH! = Wow!
Rr-rr-*ruff* = Absolutely
Ruff = Approval
RUGGH = Gross
RUH-Roh = Uh-oh
Ur Rat = You're right
WRRRrr Rot! = Immediate danger!
Yipping = Nervous

Herald lowered the paper, pursed his lips, emitted a long, slow whistle, and then laughed out loud. "You've got to be kidding me!"

A quiet voice behind him inquired, "Lt. Lloyd, who is kidding whom?"

Herald spun on his heel at attention; he was facing an older man of about fifty, a colonel but wearing no rank. Herald responded, "The lads thought a spot of imaginary fishing would be a nice way to forget the rigors of life here. Care to join in the festivities, sir?"

"No, no, deep-sea fishing is a sport best left to the young, don't you think?" He walked away and another soldier, whom Herald knew to be the Executive Officer, second in command of the battalion, approached the group. Herald greeted the XO without saluting. This was to avoid distinguishing another officer in case a sniper was watching. Snipers were always a possibility in this enchanting land.

The XO looked at the scene and then commented to Herald, "A lively group, Lieutenant. Do they belong to you?"

"Yes, sir, and they're good soldiers where it counts."

"Admirable attribute, loyalty. Save it for the court-martial, Lieutenant. Do you know who the older man was, the one who witnessed the fishing hubbub?"

"Not to be rude, sir, but this is the only time the men may engage in frivolous behavior. And no, who was that man?"

"The colonel," responded the XO as he made for the command tent through the swirling heat and dust—the trademark of this country's every season.

"Well," Herald called after him, "it beats the men coloring in books with crayons."

The XO looked back, shook his head, and kept walking while speaking over his shoulder. "It's a sad day when line officers are discussing children's coloring books as a stress reliever and tolerating fictional sport fishing for marlin. I should have stayed in Korea."

YEAR 1988

BAM! SUDDENLY THE LIGHT from the crawl space opening went dark as the door closed with a raucous *sque-e-eak*. Herald heard fading laughter as Katherine and Elizabeth, his eight- and five-year-old daughters, ran back to the safety of their mother after trapping their father under the house. The childish prank did nothing to help control his fear of losing everything due to his legal mistake. The law library closed at 4:00 p.m. on Saturdays.

Damn! I gotta get going!

Understanding his mind needed a change of scenery to regain his objectivity, Herald spent Sunday, MD 33, watching nothing in particular on TV and drinking beer. Yet even the copious amount of beer he'd downed could not drown the persistent memories that cried for attention from his mental dungeon.

CHAPTER 5
SHUFFLE OFF TO BUFFALO DUNG

DRIVING BACK FROM MARTINEZ on Monday, MD 32, Herald exercised his mind by running it through the different arguments he could make for his motion to be relieved from malpractice. Dwelling on it succeeded only in twisting his chest muscles into a knot and jabbing a more intense pain into his left shoulder. Route 4 narrowed from four lanes to two, and traffic slowed. Tooling along at the reduced pace, he noticed several homemade memorials on the side of the road—tributes to those who had perished in traffic accidents. They spooked him; it was an omen. Now he was sure the source of his legal mistake was the Pearlman telephone curse.

Crosses with pictures and other small trinkets mourners felt important in memory of the deceased came into focus. Plastic rosary beads, dead and fake flowers, a weathered baseball glove, a plastic doll, a faded photo, all hung on small, aged crosses, marking where a human life had ended.

Well, at least it's something. Better than what we got when we came back from 'Nam.

The drumming from behind the doors of his subconscious war-memory tomb resumed, crescendoing from a murmur to an intense pitch.

To help his chest muscles relax, Herald opened the VW's glove compartment and reached for the half-consumed pint of Jack Daniel's he'd stashed earlier. He grabbed the bottle, whirled the top off with his thumb, and, ignoring the cap flying onto the floor, took a sip.

Just for medicinal purposes ... don't need help ... I can handle this myself.

The doors of his memory opened to the day one of his troops shot down an American helicopter. A conversation from long ago flooded his mind.

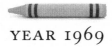

YEAR 1969

"LT, LEMAIRE IS CLEANING his machine gun in a really weird way. Is he all right?"

It was Billy Boyd, the platoon's newest member, asking Herald the question as he whisked sweat from his dirt-streaked face.

"Hello, Billy," Herald responded, as he rose from the sunbath he'd been enjoying. "And how do *you* like being in the shit? Have you discussed your concerns with your squad leader or Pearlman?"

"No," he whispered and shrugged, scuffing his foot and raising a small, reddish puff of dust.

"If you trust your squad leader or sergeant's work ethics, you should check with them first. Don't you think it's important to check in with one of them before coming to me?"

Boyd started to move away. "You're right, LT, I guess I should check with AckMan or Sergeant Pearlman first."

Herald caught Boyd's arm and turned him so they faced each other. "As our newest member, what is THE WORD?"

Boyd looked down and responded, "Yeah, I know it."

"OK, then say it," Herald demanded.

Boyd raised his head high and droned,

Do not kick or pick up things
   'less you plan to meet your king.
When you hear a muzzle blast
   hit the dirt or lose your ass.
Do not linger or look around
   'til you're married to the ground.

"OK. Good. Now I'll tell *you* something: *everything* LeMaire does is weird. Talk to me when he is not doing something weird. *That* would be weird." Herald ran the cleaning rod back and forth in the barrel of his M16 and looked down the barrel. Even at 8:00 a.m. it was already so hot sweat ran off his cheek and neck onto his shirt.

"LT," Boyd continued, his tone of voice becoming dubious, "y'know, I've been hunting in Vermont and handling weapons since I was ten, and I *never* saw anyone put their tongue in the breech of a weapon to clean it. Is this when LeMaire is *not* doing something weird?"

"Hmmm," Herald nodded, raising his sweaty brow and looking up from cleaning his own rifle. "LeMaire put his tongue in the breech?"

"Yessir, and he cuddled the weapon in his arms and kept mumbling something that sounded like, '*Vooleevoo kooshay avikmwa cesswa,*' and the look on his face was real creepy. Do you know what that means?"

Herald scratched his chin. "It all depends on whether LeMaire is putting his tongue in the feed side or the ejection side of the breech of his gun. If it's the feed side, we ignore it; if it's the ejection side, we must be concerned for hygiene purposes. Look, LeMaire is just fooling with you. No one cares if he is using his tongue as a cleaning aid or if it's just to taunt you into questioning me. Pretty much anything short of causing bodily injury to others is considered normal for LeMaire.

"However, if you must know, I do have one serious concern. It's when LeMaire is ready to rotate out of Vietnam and won't be allowed to take Bridget, his machine gun 'wife,' home with him. Even with my limited French, I believe the words he muttered to his gun mean, 'Do you want to go to bed with me tonight?' Yup, come the day LeMaire and his Bridget are to be parted, he just may take it *real* personal in a violent way. The quartermaster staff back at the base that issued Bridget is not prepared to face fear, back in the rear, when it comes to separating LeMaire from his gear." Herald chuckled at his clever, spontaneous rhyme.

"For now try to think of LeMaire as your eccentric, large uncle looking out for your ass. His firepower alone could turn the tide of an ambush and place you back on even footing. That footing could give you time to regroup and figure your way out of the kill zone."

Herald put the barrel of his M16 down alongside the other rifle parts arranged on a towel he had spread on his bunker's sandbag roof. Perspiring from his sunbath, he blotted his sweaty lower back using his already-damp shirt. Turning to Boyd he continued, "However, the ability to turn the tide of a firefight carries a heavy burden. Once LeMaire opens up with his Bridget at 550 rounds per minute to give *you* time to regroup and survive, his life span becomes very short. Short because every Mr. Charles will stop and fire on LeMaire to shut down his goddamn machine gun. So he may be weird, but he is our favorite kind of weird. Finish cleaning your weapon and relax. It's going to be a *lonnng* war."

Boyd turned, his shoulders slumped, and started back toward his bunker, his clay-stained boots exploding small clouds of dust with each step. Stopping in his tracks, he turned back to face Herald and, a bit embarrassed to ask but overcoming his shyness, inquired, "Hey, LT, why is it I just can't seem to make friends with anyone in the platoon? I mean, *really* get to be buddies, like my schoolmates back home?"

Herald smiled, pulled up the bottom-left side of the towel always hanging around his neck, and wiped more sweat off his face. "Well, Boyd, 'Nam is not back home. Many guys in the platoon have zipped up their friends in body bags after they have been shot, blown up, or dismembered. It's an experience you do not want to remember. You can't afford to get attached. Lose your concentration over a buddy's death and you may be next.

"It's the same for me. Don't you think I would love to understand why AckMan '*ack*s,' why LeMaire burns his arm hair, or why Dog refuses to speak English? It takes deep emotional damage to support strange behavior patterns like those. However, in 'Nam, those emotions need to be kept hidden. Nobody wants to know about me, and vice versa. Hell, everyone even refuses to learn my name. At least the *platoon* knows your name. All I get called is 'LT.' Yes, it's lonely; but protecting yourself from the pain of seeing your friends die is a full-time job. Nobody wants to leave here with any more psychological damage than necessary."

Boyd looked down at his feet, sighed, and shuffled away.

Herald took a deep breath as he sat down to reassemble his M16. He picked up the stock and interlocked it with the barrel assembly; then he pushed the locking pin until he heard the telltale click announce it was secured. Finished, he stood up, grabbed his weapon, placed his hand on his head, and took the three steps down into his dark bunker. Spying the sandbag he'd used as a pillow the night before, he kicked it over to the rear corner of the bunker to position himself facing the door. He leaned his weapon against the clay wall and plopped down on the bag, pulling his knees up to his chest and folding his arms over his knees. Sweat dripped from his face as he lowered his forehead to his arms, allowing himself a moment to relax.

He absorbed the cool darkness of the bunker's earth, fifteen to twenty degrees cooler than the 105 temperature out in the sun. His childish college image of war, as illustrated in the *GI Joe Coloring Book*, was now replaced by Vietnam's sweltering, stinking, dangerous reality. What a change from a college fraternity room to a hole in the dirt, eight-by-eight feet square, five-feet-five inches deep, with small firing portholes for windows. If he ever survived this nightmare, that coloring book was toast!

Leaning over, he pulled his rucksack closer and reached in. After shifting the contents, he pulled out a resealable plastic bag and removed a pad of airmail paper. The humidity made it necessary to keep all paper in plastic to keep it dry. Grabbing the pen from his vest pocket, he put the pad on his knee and began to write.

"October 10, 1969. Dear Mom and George, Everything is going great here. I was assigned to a supply unit in the rear. Life is pretty boring back in the rear. We have an officer's club and pool to while away the hours.

"Hope all is well back in Litchfield and you are all in good health. I also hope the haying season will be good, but must confess I don't miss stacking 4,000 bales of hay and shoveling endless tons of manure! Honestly, the hardest work I've ever done was on your dairy farm every summer. It gave me great respect for what hard labor really means. Stay in touch and do not worry. I am safe here. Your Son, Herald."

The thin, light-blue airmail paper had preprinted blank squares on the back for the delivery and return addresses. He filled in the boxes and folded the paper along the dotted lines as instructed, to make it into an envelope the size of a standard postcard. No stamp needed; postage was on Uncle Sam. He placed the letter in his pocket, returned the writing pad to the plastic bag, and put it in his rucksack; then, he slid his pen into his vest pocket and secured it with the clip. Placing his right hand on his head to avoid banging his head again, he stood up and started putting on his gear.

Kneeling back down in the dry red clay, he pulled up the webbing of his rucksack, disturbing the fine dust on the ground. He slid his right arm through one strap and then struggled to get his left arm through the other. Shrugging both shoulders, he shifted the web gear enough to settle the bag on the center of his back so he could buckle his belt.

The rucksack carried his entire world. He never imagined in his wildest dreams that his total personal effects would consist of what he was wearing: shirt; pants; socks; no underwear—it was too hot for that little nicety; boots; and a towel around his neck; along with the few items in his rucksack. Stored in the rucksack was a second inventory: a poncho liner used as a blanket; a few toilet and hygiene products, including cream for jock rot; a roll of green surgical tape to secure grenade-trigger levers and for other practical purposes; and hard candy. Preserved in a resealable lunch bag were an airmail pad, and a picture and letter from Pamela, his girlfriend back home.

Readjusting the straps and pack for comfort, he checked the three grenades in the metal webbing loops at the front of his shoulder straps to ensure the surgical tape was still securing the grenade levers and the grenades themselves. He lifted the cloth strap of the claymore mine pouch over his head and hung it on his left shoulder, raised two bandoleers of M16 ammunition over his head to his right shoulder, and shook both shoulders to achieve balance. Picking up his helmet and rifle with his left hand and placing his right on top of his head again, he stood up until the back of his hand made contact with the ceiling.

He took two squatting strides toward the three sandbag steps leading to ground level. Climbing the first step, he flinched as the blast of heat from outside hit his face. On the second step, the roof shade ended with a line of light that oscillated with heat. The light was so bright at the crest of the stairs it was like the viewing hole of a steel blast furnace. He paused for a moment to appreciate that in Vietnam, even this early—9:30 a.m.—it was already a scorcher.

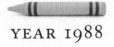

YEAR 1988

BACK FROM HIS DAY DREAM for a moment, nearly eighteen years later, perspiration beaded on Herald's forehead; a physical response to his memory of that scorching day. He wiped the sweat off his brow with his hand and continued his drive from Martinez while drifting back again to Vietnam.

YEAR 1969

THE LONG-FORGOTTEN WORLD of Firebase Jackson ignited in Herald's memory. He was back again circling the base in a helicopter. Below him was a bulldozed, circular, earthen berm about five feet high with a perimeter approximately half a mile in diameter. Bunkers were evenly spaced every fifty yards, with the interior bunkers dug between the perimeter bunkers for fire support and command. Herald saw the six 105 mm artillery on a raised berm, along with a pit of three 4.2-inch heavy mortars and 82 mm mortars. All the artillery was to support the soldiers' retreat from a patrol or to defend the base if Mr. Charles came for a visit.

Landing, Herald approached the three bunkers his platoon occupied on the perimeter. "Pearlman, AckMan, Jones, Ferlingetti, and Dog, time for a pow-wow-wow—now!" He spotted Hollywood, his radioman, lying on his back sunning. "Hollywood, stop tanning! Bring your ass and your radio."

After Platoon Sergeant Pearlman, the three squad leaders, and Dog arrived, he spread out the comics topographical map on the bunker roof. He had met with the company commander the evening before and plotted a route on it with a red erasable crayon. The battalion intelligence officer, in his unarmed light observation helicopter, LOH, was to accompany them.

"OK, guys, I met with the CC," Herald said, while pointing at the map, "today's event: bait time. Where? 'Over the river and through the woods' to the border of Cambodia we go. The objective is to get close enough to taunt Mr. Charles out for a party in daylight. Every man is to carry extra ammunition, grenades, and at least one claymore mine. Any questions?"

Pearlman, the Harvard dropout, shook his head no. As his blue eyes rose up from the map to look at Herald, a little bead of sweat dropped off his nose onto it. In his Bostonian accent he quipped, "Guess we lucked out again, eh, LT? How long until we blast off? And bring extra *wa-a-ater*, right?"

Herald looked up at Pearlman. With a sweeping motion of his right arm, he wiped the moisture from his eyebrows with his sleeve and replied, "About thirty minutes. But first I want all of you to look over the map in case I catch one and you guys are all on your own. We will stay about one klick in from the river in a half-moon shape, with the river always on our right. The battalion intelligence officer will link up with us in an LOH to supervise our progress, so we have to do this one by the numbers."

It all sounds like a game, except it's my ass *taunting Charles out! Should have stayed in school, fool, and left the coloring book for art class.*

The company mail clerk walked up, climbed on a bunker, and yelled, "Mail call!"

The squad leaders looked to Herald for an OK. "Go ahead," he allowed, "but be quick."

They gathered around the bunker where the mail clerk was standing above the other platoon members.

Curious, Herald looked up from the map and gazed at his platoon sergeant. "Pearlman, why do you never go to mail call?"

"When I quit Harvard and said I was joining the Army, my family disowned me. I haven't received a letter from home since I left two years ago. Not only did my family leave me, my supposed girlfriend starting dating my college 'Jody' roommate—something about better prospects. You know the term 'Jody,' right? He's the guy who gets your girlfriend while you're away."

"Nothing for two years? Isn't that kind of hard to deal with?"

"Yes and no. Some arrive here and cling to the mail as their only hope, only to see hope betrayed. When I get back to the world, it'll be a fresh start with no illusions about permanence. I'll take it as it comes."

Pearlman turned when the mail clerk was through and yelled, "OK, everyone cut the crap and get your gear. It's party time!"

A feeling of dread always descended on the soldiers as they cleared the last rolls of the concertina wire gate and stepped out of the firebase. The platoon filed out through the coils of wire; then broke into two parallel lines, to enter the open country, each line and man spaced three to five meters apart. The distance of separation was to avoid losing more than one man to the killing zone of a grenade, mortar round, booby trap, or burst of automatic-weapons fire.

"LT," groaned AckMan, moving up to his left, "they're sending us over the river—*ack!* One platoon isn't enough men. We're ... we're so screwed, man! Mr. Charles is going to—*ack*—jump out just long enough to make us a permanent part of the landscape. Even LeMaire is acting—*ack*—spooked. He told me a story. In his clearest attempt at English yet—*ack*—he said, and I am attempting to quote, 'River, merde, like ocean.' LeMaire was rolling—*ack*—dice or bones like an Indian warrior in a movie he—*ack*—saw, a movie about men hunting a huge white whale that ate the captain's leg and sank their ship. The Indian rolled—*ack*—bones to ask the gods his future. The gods gave him a death sign for all—*ack*—aboard the ship, save one. LeMaire rolled snake eyes, and we are not—*ack*—coming back. *Au revoir!*"

Still concealed in the foliage just short of the river's edge, Herald stopped walking. With his back to the platoon of twenty-one souls, he signaled for them to freeze in their tracks by raising his arm halfway in the traditional "Stop!" gesture but with clenched fist. After checking the area for any possible danger, with a forceful movement, he dropped his arm with clenched fist to signal all to "get small." The platoon shifted from a marching lineup to a staggered formation, as if in a choreographed GI ballet, with each man dropping to one knee and alternating the angle of his body and weapon to face either left or right, opposite the direction of the soldier in front of him; maneuvering to prevent a sniper from taking out a whole lineup of soldiers with one directed blast, and providing equal coverage on both sides of the platoon.

Herald, turning to face AckMan and the platoon, dropped to one knee himself. Using the only dry spot left on his sweat-stained right sleeve, he mopped the moisture from his brow. "AckMan, AckMan, only a juicy target is enough to draw Mr. Charles out for a dance in the open daylight. I say again—*daylight*. Remember, we rule the day; they rule the night. Look, this is just going to be a long, hot walk in the sun. We'll have a whale of a party and be back for dinner. Now is not the time for squad leaders to be starting rumors about anything that sparks fear."

Hollywood shifted the radio on his sweat-soaked back. "Hey, man, easy for you Louies to be calm. Try and run with a radio on your back, plus your gear and weapon. This radio weighs more than my surfboard!" Hollywood removed his helmet and wiped his forehead with his towel, which had turned brown from his smuggled tanning cream, and jostled his shoulders to shift the radio from side to side to relieve his back. He had huge sweat stains under his arms and around his neck. From just behind Herald, he continued, "Man, I'm a two-digit midget with less than twenty days 'in country.' I could be … I could be killed … killed out there, *killed!*"

Herald turned to Hollywood and yelled, "Take off those goddamn California beach sunglasses. It would be just like you to trip the trigger wire of a booby trap because your sunglasses block the clear fishing line from sight. And since you're always within four feet of me so I can reach the radio, we'd both be in the kill zone. TAKE THEM OFF!"

Looking past Hollywood to check on the spacing between the men, Herald noted the unique markings on each trooper's fatigues. It was hard to believe they'd all started with the same basic jungle utilities uniform.

LeMaire's was the most decorative. He sported a large, pink-ink peace symbol on the front of his helmet; a Marilyn Monroe picture pin on his front left pocket; a patch with a paratrooper slogan of 'Death From Above' on the right pocket, even though he was never a paratrooper; a French Foreign Legion airborne badge on his right shoulder, and a 'Free Huey Newton' pin on the left. The entire ensemble was accented by a red silk scarf around his neck.

The others had little decorative pins on their helmet covers with symbols drawn in indelible magic marker of everything from "Black Death" to their girlfriends' names. All of them had something different to advertise what was left of their identity.

"LT, where do we meet the boat?" Pearlman asked as he approached from the rear of the platoon, wiping his forehead on his shirt sleeve.

"Right over there," replied Herald, pointing to a log in the mud that would support the boat's landing ramp.

Just then, the *chug-chug-chug* of an old WWII landing craft's diesel motor echoed around the bend of the river.

Pearlman pointed to the west and smirked. "I just love Cambodia this time of year. Will we be visiting Grandma or hunting the Big Bad Wolf?"

"Hopefully, only Grandma, in the form of the battalion intelligence officer, who is going to supervise us by LOH to ensure we do not nap."

In an exaggerated deep southern drawl, Pearlman joked to Herald, "Nobody be nappin' ovuh de ribbuh, Massah. It be on'y half a klick to de Cambodian bo'duh an' Massuh Charles' base. Do we be habbin' any uthuh bodacious frien's to he'p, if'n dat ol' big bad wolf hr decide to come a-eat'n po' ol' Gramma?"

"Negatron, li'l young 'un," Herald joked back in kind. "Dat'd give us a fightin' chance: bait don't be gittin' no fightin' chance. Dat ain't no good bait. Gib de worm a weapon while he be a-fishin', an' de fish be findin' somet'in' e'se to feed on—an' dat be de trut'!"

The boat drawing nearer reminded Herald of war movies he'd watched as a child; it filled him with apprehension. He recalled what had happened to those soldiers landing on beaches in the Higgins boat, the Navy's primary amphibious landing craft to ferry troops over the ocean to land on beaches.

The Higgins was never intended as a riverboat. It had a front ramp that, when dropped, allowed soldiers a fast way out of the vessel but also exposed the entire inside of the craft. Only the driver was protected behind a steel barrier in the rear. WWII movies loved to depict the landings at Normandy, the front ramp dropping and German machine guns riddling all the exposed troops with thousands of bullets. In Vietnam the reality was when the gate dropped, it gave Charles a closed killing zone surrounded by metal on three sides. The metal sides gave the bullets a second or even third chance for a ricochet hit on all the men inside.

Whenever Herald was aboard a Higgins, if he heard any *tink-tink* sounds before the gate dropped, he'd make sure the Navy did not drop the gate; those *tinks* were the impact of small-arms fire on the steel door—bad news for the soldiers on board.

To lighten the moment, Herald turned to Pearlman and pointed to the landing craft. "Hey, I got a Higgins boat 'Knock-knock' joke for you."

Pearlman half smiled. "Yeah?"

"Knock, knock."

"Who's there?"

"I tink."

"I tink who?"

"I tink you're dead if you drop this ramp."

"OK for a war joke—but don't quit your day job."

As the platoon stood on the riverbank waiting for the landing craft, sweat glistened on every face. The skin around their eyes and mouths tightened.

AckMan was driving everyone crazy with his infernal *acking*. This was considered a bad omen. He was believed to have a gift of prophecy. When he *"ack"*ed, everyone's nerves went on edge as there was a good possibility, far above Las Vegas odds, that they were in Sir Charles's gun sights. With each *"ack,"* LeMaire caressed his machine gun; a behavior pattern causing everyone to lower their heads and fear the worst. Their response was to eject the magazines from their M16s, tap them on their helmets to make sure the cartridges were properly seated, and reinsert them with a distinct click.

The river's treacherous, muddy water raced past them at hyper speed, the currents bubbling up everywhere. It was the monsoon season.

Ah, yes, fall into the water laden with your equipment and you get a short lesson in drowning!

The ugly current also brought to Herald's mind the mythical Greek River Styx. Staring at the murky water, Herald could almost see Charon's skeleton in his black robe ferrying the souls of the dead to Hades for small coin.

As the boat approached the pickup point, Herald signaled to direct the Navy captain to the log where the boat could drop its front ramp. Right on target the ramp splashed onto the log near the muddy bank and several other downed trees.

The Navy crew of five was restless, displaying the customary irritation the Navy had for the Army, combined with their own angst at being so far inland. The Navy boys jeered as the platoon approached the antiquated landing craft. "Glad to be having you boys on this cruise," one of them teased. "Too bad you are too late for the morning buffet, but the shuffleboard tournament is just starting!"

"Ho-o-okay," Herald muttered, as he looked down and stepped on one of the downed trees to reach the ramp with as little contact with the mud as possible. Riverbank mud was deceptive; it could be several feet deep. He boarded and moved to the right side of the boat as the platoon stepped with caution on the tree trunks and onto the ramp of the rocking craft.

This was no pleasure cruise. In addition to being a vulnerable target out there in the middle of the river, each soldier had more than 100 pounds of weapons and ammo attached to his body. This equaled a double death warrant: if the Higgins boat—a very high-value target by itself—were sunk in this swiftly flowing river, the men would drown before they could remove their gear and swim to safety. Being prepared for a gunfight was incompatible with swimming.

The craft pulled back from the shore in a cloud of black diesel smoke; the tremendous noise unnerved everyone. The boat chugged upriver, and, within fifteen minutes, Herald and the boat captain spied a landing spot next to open ground with a short, steep bank, where they hoped the mud would not be too deep.

As the craft turned to shore, Herald took off his helmet, seeking some relief from the heat to no avail, and called out, "Lock and load, boys. It's show time. Dog, point. LeMaire, go second just in case Charles plans a surprise party. Move out about twenty feet and set up. Watch out for trip wires strung along the bank. AckMan, fill in with your squad after they set up. Any questions?"

"Yes, LT," AckMan responded, "In OCS I heard the—ack—motto was 'Follow Me.' If so, why are you—ack—staying in the boat?"

Herald smiled and stroked his chin. "AckMan, you simply misunderstood the slogan. The words are 'Follow Ye.' 'Ye' is the old English term for 'you.' After you set up a base of fire, I will be there to call in the world if we get into trouble."

The bank looked firm: but when Dog took his first step, the mud sucked him in up to his waist just as a large black snake zipped past his arm. Three men from AckMan's squad knelt down on the ramp to grab him, but by some miracle, Dog, with a "Ror—ro—*RRH!*" leapt back up into the boat.

AckMan laughed, slapped his leg, and pointed at the drenched Dog. "Did you see the look on his face—*ack*—when he went past knee level? He looked like—*ack*—he'd been dropped in a sewage pit. And when he saw that snake—*ack*—he leapt into the boat like he had wings; and if that wasn't the biggest doggie yelp I ever heard … *Hahaha!*"

Grinning, Herald nodded and addressed the skipper. "Well, it looks like we better find another location. Mr. Snake owns this mud bath, and I rather fancy to let him keep it. Move over there, and we'll try again."

With a roar and another cloud of smoke, the boat pulled off the muddy bank, moved down sixty feet and docked again. This time Dog lowered his head, bared his teeth, and gave a "GRRrrrr" as he reached out and tested the mud with one foot. He was still spooked about nearly drowning in muck. Who could blame him? Convinced it would not hold his weight, he experimented by stepping into the mud with his left foot and leaping forward on his right. It sank a bit but held firm on the incline of the river-bank. He then sprung his left foot onto the grassy bank, looked back and gave a loud "*RARH!*"

Hot on his swampy heels were LeMaire and AckMan, the latter bringing his four-man squad. Just as they gathered in a semicircle wiping the sweat off their heads, the LOH with the battalion intelligence officer on board swept up the river at sixty knots and blew by all of them, the burnt jet fuel from the copter filling the air around the platoon like a fine, black mist.

Hollywood's radio crackled. "Ranger One to Rover One, you boys are late. We have several likely locations I need you to check out, so move it now. Over."

Herald grabbed the hook Hollywood handed him and keyed the mic. "Rover to Ranger, my boys were enjoying the mud spa downriver which slowed us up, but we are good to go. Over."

"Rover, if I want stupid excuses, I'll be sure to look you up. And no joking on the radio," yelled the West Point major with no combat-line experience. He continued, "Watch where I pop smoke and follow with your unit as fast as possible. Out."

"Rover to Ranger, these fields are a foot deep in mud during the wet season and lined with booby traps. We will follow your orders, but safely. This unit has lost sixty boys to booby traps over the last year, and we do not need any more casualties because of speed, unless necessary. Over."

"Rover, you will never make captain with that attitude, soldier. Move out now! Out," yelled the major as his chopper circled the platoon, the deafening high-pitched whine from the turbine engine blasting in everyone's ears. The major was clueless about advertising their position—and his—to Charles, who was a scant kilometer away in Cambodia.

The major flew half a kilometer, popped smoke to identify a location he wanted them to check out, and dashed off to another location. The platoon slogged through to the smoke-marked destination and found no evidence of Charles, weapons storage, tunnels, or any logical reason for them to be there. After investigating three more smoke markers over two kilometers of wet clay ground, the entire platoon was exhausted and in danger of dehydration. Each man was already overloaded with equipment, so hiking in the clay mud was like tying an extra twenty-five pounds of dead weight to each foot.

YEAR 1988

HERALD'S MIND REFOCUSED to 1988 California, where he scowled and lifted his left foot involuntarily from the VW van floor, remembering the quicksand-like suction of the clay mud in the abandoned Vietnam rice fields. Without warning, the thick goo would grab one's foot and hold it as if locked in a vise. Extra suction was created when a foot slipped into deeper sludge. As a body shifted to step forward, its weight plus the extra equipment locked the rear foot in the mud. The body, already well into the step forward, continued its travel, leaving the soldier off balance and in danger of falling face first into the mud. To save oneself, it was necessary to do a fast two-step to redistribute weight and regain balance.

Herald laughed, remembering they called that awkward, jerky movement the "paddy two-step." "Mr. Momentum" would always get the best of the situation and *everyone* fell into the goop. With luck, a person could catch himself on one knee and avoid the full facial mud bath. The running wager was who would take the first total mud facial if he weren't fast enough to stop the fall by landing on his forward knee. Herald's laughter faded as the memory gained steam.

YEAR 1969

THE PLATOON WAS MOVING through several interconnected rice-paddy fields, which had low mud berms separating them for irrigation control. Surrounding the complex of paddies was a wide, thick hedge of trees and other plants, making a perfect cover and firing position for Charles.

If Charles were to attack during the day, he would do so only if in a superior position since he lacked the resources to call in air strikes. He made up for this with his extraordinary planning and patience, such as planting concealed booby traps below the waterline in rice paddies and waiting for American patrols to stumble into his kill zone. Herald's men could forget finding cover in the paddy; they were forced to hold their faces above the waterline to keep from drowning, making each head a perfect little target. Charles had only to spray bullets in their general direction to get the soldiers to scramble from fire and set off the booby traps. His attacks during the day were always fierce and brief so he could escape Army artillery or airstrike support.

Herald radioed, "Rover to Ranger, we need a break after the next smoke rendezvous. The midday heat and mud are exhausting the men. Over."

"Rover, we will never win the war with that attitude, soldier. Request for rest denied. Move on to the smoke grenade at the tree line to your left, possible tunnels. Out." The platoon moved out to the fifth location, where, again, there was nothing.

Finally, on the sixth smoke grenade location, after about fifteen kilometers of walking in the gluey clay and just as the major's chopper was to dip behind a tree line, LeMaire had had enough. Perhaps it was the sizzling sun, the humidity that made the air so dense gills would have helped to breathe, the fifteen-kilometer hike in the mud, or paranoia that a sniper had him in his sights all day. Or maybe LeMaire was just being his playful self. He turned, wiped the sweat from his eyes with his red kerchief, and lined up the American helicopter's engine in his sights. Without hesitation he fired a small five-round burst.

The muzzle blast only three feet away terrified and sparked everyone to dive full face into the red goo. The chopper took the hits on its engine turbines. Black smoke spat from the exhaust and, with a crunching metal noise of bullet-shattered turbine blades, the hated chopper fluttered to the ground a safe distance behind the tree line.

Herald pulled himself from the mud, wiped his face with the only part of his towel not drenched in slop, and saw all the other members of his platoon were mud puppies—except for LeMaire, who was standing with a wry smile on his face and cradling his machine gun in his giant arms while a small whitish puff of smoke rose from its barrel.

It didn't take half a second to conclude the machine gun bullets were friendly fire. Herald was in disbelief but was not about to lose his best machine gunner. Grabbing the radio hook, he wiped the mud off and keyed the mic. "Rover to Ranger, sniper fire off to the right. What's your situation? Over."

"Ranger to Rover, 'sniper,' my ass! Those tracers were red, not green, and seemed to come from your direction. Over," snapped the major, as his helicopter squatted in the mud, the rotor blade spinning slower and slower, and a small cloud of black smoke curling skyward from the rear exhaust pipe of the engine.

"Negatron, Ranger," Herald shouted. "The rounds came over us also. We are moving to investigate. Stay put. One squad is on its way over to secure your position. The rest of the unit will move on the sniper now. Call home for a retrieval action, as it will be getting dark soon. Over."

Herald dropped to his right knee as the entire platoon struggled from their prone positions in the mud up to one knee. Turning toward LeMaire, he motioned him to squat down to one knee. Maintaining his cool and speaking in a gentle but firm manner so as not to further upset the still raving LeMaire, he asked, "Why in the world would you shoot down an American helicopter? Yes, the major is an asshole running us all over 'Nam for no reason, but firing on an American aircraft is not in the cards. At least he's all right, but I have a bad feeling we are going to spend the night looking for the mythical sniper bird. Could you play the hell along and not take matters into your own hands anymore?"

"*Salaud major! Imbécile! Merde!* Piss LeMaire off," he grunted in his barely understandable French-Canadian Maine accent.

"'Merde, piss LeMaire off' or not, mind your manners or it is le beeg, au revoir court-martial in *le* sky for you. Leavenworth Military Prison is not in vogue this year."

Herald then recorded in bold print in his personal mental log: *DO NOT PISS LEMAIRE OFF!*

"Ranger to Rover. Over," the radio crackled. It was that *"salaud"* major again.

"Rover, over," Herald answered, still cleaning mud off his face.

"Rover, set up a perimeter around the chopper for the night, as insufficient time to recover the bird. Another LOH is picking up the pilot and me." Ending with a sarcastic chuckle, he said, "Out."

Herald gave the hook back to Hollywood and turned to Pearlman. "OK, we've been ordered to keep security for the helicopter. It appears the recovery copter is not available until tomorrow. Move to the bird, and we'll set up a night ambush."

Pearlman shook his head no and mumbled, "Great, just great, right on Charles's doorstep … and now it will be night—his time! Worse, we'll be bait guarding bigger, better, helicopter bait. I should have stayed at Harvard."

Just as he finished talking, another LOH screamed overhead, leaving only the smell of burnt jet fuel in the air. It hovered for a moment over the downed chopper, dropped below the tree line to snatch the pilot and the major, and then streaked back to the safety of the base, its high-pitched whine receding as it disappeared from view.

"OK," Herald yelled, "let's move it out and maintain formation."

The platoon formed two lines and squished through the goop toward the helicopter. Leery of booby traps, they took great care in cutting through the thick hedge of vegetation to where the chopper sat—right in the middle of a flooded, abandoned rice paddy.

Herald surveyed the area. The only cover was the large rice-paddy hedge they had just cut through. It was too far away to provide security. They were going to have a p.m. pool party. He turned to Pearlman at the rear of the platoon and ordered, "Set 'em up for the night."

Pearlman sighed and yelled, "Ferlinghetti, take the far berm; Jones, the left; and AckMan, the right. LT, LeMaire, Hollywood, and I will hold the berm facing Cambodia. Dog, act as spotter and ammo feeder for LeMaire. Any questions?"

LeMaire sat in the water with a squish, unfolded Bridget's tripod legs, set her up on the mud berm, and muttered to himself, "Mon Dieu, muddy merde!"

Dog gave a low growling agreement, "Roh-RAH."

"Ack— Are we going to—ack—lie in the water all night, Sarge?"

Pearlman spit into the water and moved his left arm in a wide oval gesture above his head pointing to the sky. "AckMan, do you see any other cover? If not, try to remember it's only for one night."

"Well, it's one thing to sit in paddy water—*ack*—and another to fight off *mosquitoes and leeches!*" He balanced his rifle on the paddy dike and began to tighten his boots and belt as securely as he could.

Jones ran the dirty index fingernail of his right hand back and forth on his lower lip and grated, "Leeches. Man, I do not do leeches." He pulled out his note pad and scribbled a leech memo. *Nobody would believe this back at Duke.*

The soldiers crouched on the dike and shoved their pants' hems inside their boots. Boots tightly knotted, they unfastened their belts to smooth and tuck in their shirts. Determined to form the best possible barrier against the leeches, they all strained, pulling their belts tight until they turned red in the face from the pressure. As the men filed off the dike to take up their assigned positions, their boots squished noisily in the muddy water.

Herald picked up the horn and keyed the mic to the company commander. "Rider One, this is Rover. Over."

The reply squawked back, "Rover, this is Rider. Over."

"Rider, I need to plot support fire. We are here for the night. Over."

"Rover, OK to plot. The 105s are waiting, call sign Bright Two. Over."

Herald wiped the sweat off his face on his shirt sleeve. As he verified their location on the comics, he said, "Rider, out. Rover to Bright Two. Over."

"Rover, Bright Two. Over."

"Bright, fire mission." Looking at the comics, Herald gave the grid coordinates in the fading light and instructed, "First round, Willie Peter with an air burst to establish position. Over." *Gotta love the way white phosphorus burns when exposed to oxygen.*

Bright Two, in a serious voice, responded, "One WP on the way. And don't be touching or let them embers touch you. Over."

Good advice, but Herald already knew the only way to keep from being incinerated by white phosphorus if it landed on his skin was to cut it out with his bayonet.

Within two minutes, Firebase Jackson fired the artillery, and Herald heard the whine of the shell as it screamed overhead. Phosphorus popped about 500 feet in the air and 300 yards out, establishing a firing grid between Herald's platoon and Cambodia in case Charles came looking for a pajama party.

The white burning embers wafted down to the surface. Their languid descent gave the men time to run if Herald's coordinates were off.

The cumulus of white smoke verified Herald's coordinates were correct. The falling embers died in the water with a bubbling, steamy hiss.

Grateful he was not underneath the explosion, Herald instructed, "Rover to Bright Two, coordinates confirmed; plot a full 300-meter grid to the north, south, and west, with the base point coordinates you just fired. Out."

With correct coordinates established, Herald and his men could settle in for the night knowing if Charles encroached within their protective veil of 300 yards out in any direction, Herald could call the base for artillery high-explosive strikes before Charlie reached them in the rice paddies.

He sat on the berm and carefully balanced his weapon on the narrow dike's head, peeled off the shoulder straps that held the claymore mine and M16 ammunition bandoleers, and placed them on the berm beside his weapon. Unbuckling his web belt, he spread out the webbing with the rucksack on the berm. The rest of the platoon followed suit. *It's going to be a long, wet night.*

With the sun nudging the horizon, flickering swarms of mosquitoes emerged from the hedge and clung to the growing shadows of the dikes in eager preparation for their nightly feeding.

Ferlinghetti narrowed his eyes, looked to the left and right, shrugged off his rucksack, and placed it on the berm. He pulled his poetry book from the rucksack, carefully laid it on the berm, and sat down in the paddy water with a squish. The brown water rose to just below his beltline. Opening up the book, he yelled, "*Sediamo nella merda!* 'ey, guys, w'at-a you know? First-a poema I joost-a open-a book-a to. Wan'-a to 'ear?"

Pearlman laughed. "What the hell? Why not poetry in the paddy? How alliterative, 'poetry and paddy.' Yes, yes, a reading! Hear, hear!"

Jones slowly stroked his upper lip with the dark-brown fingernails of his left hand, removed his pad and started writing.

Ferlinghetti, once again in his attempt at scholarly diction, read aloud.

The world is a beautiful place
                    to be born into
if you don't mind happiness
                    not always being
                              so very much fun
        if you don't mind a touch of hell
                              now and then
            just when everything is fine
                              because even in heaven
                    they don't sing
                              all the time …

(A Coney Island of the Mind: Poems, page 88)

"So, w'at-a you t'ink-a, Sarge?" Ferlinghetti asked, looking up with a smile.

Giving Ferlinghetti a crooked grin and nodding, Pearlman admitted, "Well, we *are* in for a little touch of watery *hell* tonight. It's just us, the helicopter, the mosquitoes, and the leeches. Isn't life beau—ti—ful?" He sat down in the paddy water with a small splash.

AckMan jumped up from the water and yelled, *"Ack*—I just felt one of those damn leeches sneaking into my boot and up my pant leg. Oh God, I hate—*ack*—them suckers. I just know what—*ack*—they're going for. I hope I can still have children. One thing I know, 'Nam mosquitoes are—*ack*—wimps. In the U.S., down South, they're bigger … and *meaner.* What d'you think, Dog?"

Dog extended his jaw, pushed his lips together, looked to the sky, and gave a "Ruff!"

AckMan kicked the water and sat on the muddy dike, positioning his legs evenly apart and easing himself down its steep, muddy side. As his body settled into the liquid red goop with a squish, he muttered, "Goddamn—*ack*—leech bait."

The entire platoon obsessed on the leeches—their hungry, thin, wavy bodies gliding in the water, smiling at their good fortune to have an entire cafeteria of people to suck on for an entire night. Everyone knew that leeches searched with infinite patience for just the smallest crease to slip through for a dinner party. They would always find a way in.

Once back at the base, after every patrol involving waist-deep water, the platoon members would check each other for leeches. It must have looked odd to witness a line of soldiers inspecting each other's nude bodies for leeches, perhaps resembling a bizarre, gay bath party, hunting over each other's bodies and inspecting their own.

YEAR 1988

EIGHTEEN YEARS LATER, Herald was reliving the feeling of lying in muddy water with leeches slinking their inevitable way inside his uniform pants, no matter how tightly he'd fastened his boots and belt. The very thought of the leeches interrupted his 'Nam flashback for a moment. He gritted his teeth, beat a fist on the steering wheel, and scuffed his left foot involuntarily on the floor of the van. The moment passed, and Herald was back in the mud.

YEAR 1969

"I CAN'T DO IT anymore! Leeches in my pants crawling for my insides! I can't do it anymore! Christ! I'm outta here!"

Billy Boyd, the newbie, struggling to jump up and down, was screaming at the top of his lungs. Muddy water cascaded off his uniform as he jumped toward the berm. But the mud held his feet in its soggy grasp and prevented his full ascent. Rather than clearing the berm, he ended up sprawled on top of it, his upper body reflecting the light of the rising moon.

Jones, Billy's squad leader, expecting someone to panic, shot up from the murky water and snared the raving Boyd off the berm, pulling him out of the moon's gleam with a gentle squish back into the shadowed sanctuary of slimy water.

Herald, watching Jones grab Boyd, thought it was like witnessing a great white shark snapping a sleeping seal off an ice shelf, something he'd seen once on a Sunday night *Wild Kingdom* TV show.

But this scene had a far gentler finale. In a calming low voice, Jones whispered, "It's OK, it's OK. I've been through this before. The leeches go for just the first layer of skin. I've never had one make it to my insides, so quiet down. Charles is the danger here, and you are telling him where you are. Shhhh. We'll get the little bastards in the morning with insect repellent. Just a little drop of repellent on their heads makes them run in their own leech way. After the head is out, feel free to take revenge as you see fit on all your leech captives. My favorite means of destruction is to marinate the little buggers in lighter fluid, then give them a blazing finale; but feel free to improvise—and be sure to keep their ears." Boyd's taut face lightened up and he laughed at the idea of keeping leeches' ears. He sloshed to his position and sat down with a squish.

Herald was also observing Pearlman's continued fury at LeMaire for shooting down the American helicopter. The water around Pearlman vibrated as he made low, hissing sounds mixed with a whispered angry chant: "Goddamn leech bait."

Pearlman's hissing was offset by the hum of the masses of mosquitoes clouding around everyone's head. Everyone was swearing at them, yet what could one do but lie there and let them suck away? The troops were left with only one option: tolerate as many stings of those barbed tongues piercing their exposed skin as possible, and tally the stings, the result being an unorthodox morale booster—keeping an accurate tally and comparing totals.

When the pain was unbearable, a soldier would cup his hand and, with a slow, deliberate sweep of his hand across his skin, crush as many of the evil suckers as possible.

Herald whispered to Pearlman, "Well, the good news is, we'll finally be able to use our mosquito repellent when we get back to base tomorrow morning for leech-removal patrol. Too bad we can't use it now, but Charles has a nose for it in the night air. Here's to ample leech hunting in the morning!

"As for leech patrol, we're all like baboons in Africa grooming each other. Never had a full quota of over ten yet, have you?" Herald gave a low "Hah" and looked up to see if Pearlman at least was cracking a smile. He wasn't.

The bobbing movement of a round, dried piece of water-buffalo dung caught Herald's eye. Using his index finger, he interrupted its course and towed it over. Reaching into his breast pocket for his ever-present plastic bag, he opened it and removed a pencil and square piece of writing paper. Inserting the pencil through the top and bottom edges of the paper, he created a tiny, square sail, and stuck the pencil point into the dung.

Watching Pearlman staring into the black night, he broke his spell, whispering, "Pearlman, do you enjoy sailing?"

Pearlman turned onto his side in the water with a soft squish, spied the makeshift fecal craft, and smiled. "Yes. At Harvard, I was on the crew and sailing team. I always loved the water. Why, LT, where did you ever find such a worthy vessel here in this country? We should take her for a spin, eh? You'd love blue-water sailing, the sea spray in your face and all."

"Avast, matey, man the topsail," Herald whispered back, as he blew on the sail and sent the craft bobbing toward Pearlman. "Yo-ho, yo-ho, blow the man down."

Pearlman puffed on the sail. The craft sailed back to Herald. "Anchors aweigh, my boys, anchors aweigh," he hummed, as he pondered why in the world he'd left Harvard to pilot a dung boat in a rice paddy. The night passed in a boring fashion, but the little boat kept sailing back and forth, with each man dreaming of a clean, blue ocean and a dry life back home.

"Did I ever tell you why I quit college?" Herald asked.

"No. I just figured you'd tell me when you were ready, for the same reason I appreciate your never inquiring why I quit Harvard."

Herald looked down at the floating dung, removed the pencil sail, took his index finger, and tapped the spoor gently, causing it to bob up and down. He began to spin the dung around in a circle until it gained momentum. When Herald lifted his finger off, the dung danced in the dirty water. He looked at Pearlman and started in a soft voice, "My father was super intelligent, a real MIT boy. You went to Harvard, so you understand. And at the ripe old age of thirty-two, he died in an airplane crash on the way to a party celebrating his promotion as president of a chemical engineering company. Pretty ironic, huh?

"MIT or Harvard would likely not even let me do their janitorial work," Herald continued. "And ... well ... I saw my college degree leading to a future in a long, boring, middle-management, commuter-train existence. I had this fear of never getting beyond my father's shadow. The only thing he never accomplished was going into the Army; he had asthma. It was my only chance to move out on my own. As I sit here in these mucky surroundings, I now appreciate that the shade of his shadow wouldn't be so bad."

Pearlman looked up from the bobbing buffalo dung, brushed his black hair back over his head with his left hand, and smiled. "Amen, brother, I will honestly admit to a few of those regrets myself, maybe even more than a few. My resentment of being forced, for all my childhood, to go to Harvard caused me to trash my parents' hopes, an impulsive act that now sticks in my throat when I think of home," he sighed, looking at the paddy wall, picking off little dirt clods and letting them fall into the water. "Hope I live through this to finish up at Harvard. It's OK by me now if my life and their expectations coincide. LT, may we both enjoy getting back on the horse we jumped off of. One thing's for sure: there's no shadow of your father or bright expectations of my parents to worry about in this black Southeast Asia night."

Herald smiled back, extended his arm straight forward with fingers spread, and observed, "God, even in the half-moon's light, I can barely see two fingers, let alone any shadow."

Pearlman's expression was barely detectable. He replied, "On a cloudy night, with no moon or starlight, it is so shit-black you can't see your hand two inches in front of your damn face. Even Charles wouldn't move when the blackness goes to void."

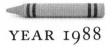

YEAR 1988

HERALD PULLED UP in front of his office and parked his VW. Taking a last sip of bourbon, he put the bottle back in the glove compartment and exited the van. He walked into the office just in time to hear seventeen-year-old Cricket yell, "What an asshole! I gave him the best years of my life!"

CHAPTER 6
PARTY TIME

HERALD WAS SITTING in the Parrot Room, Tuesday, MD 31, working on his motion to escape his legal mistake. Perspiration beaded on his brow, and the stress of having everything in his life on the line was gnawing at him when the telltale *whop-whop* of a Huey helicopter passing overhead caught his ear. That loud beat of helicopter blades slicing through the air was the hallmark sound of the war in Vietnam. The deep whopping resonated in the room and down into his chest. But the bourbon in his coffee gave him a warm feeling and quieted his fear.

Looking out the window, he searched for the helicopter, using the source of the sound as a compass. In his haste, he shoved a legal file off the end of his worktable, and the sound of flying paper masked the helicopter whopping for a second. *Must be the California National Guard on maneuvers,* he thought, pushing back his chair to pick up the file.

After gathering the scattered papers, he looked out at the exotic, spindly leaves of a pepper tree growing on the grass strip next to the street. His malpractice anxiety was tearing away at the doors of his Vietnam mental crypt.

Herald's thoughts shifted to his surreal, yet very real, experiences in Vietnam, where the *whop-whop* intruded into his consciousness many times a day. The memory of a party with another lieutenant brought a smile to his face.

YEAR 1970

SITTING IN HIS BUNKER on his sandbag pillow, he was fascinated by the mathematical precision of the shovel marks left by whoever had dug the bunker's interior walls. The only decoration on the walls, the concentric shovel marks resembled cascading patterns of waves in a clay waterfall.

Close to the upper-right edge, a former occupant had cut into the moist clay, "SP4 Peter Townsend, Little Rock, Arkansas, April 1969." Reading the inscription, Herald imagined this wall on display at the American Museum of Natural History in New York City. Archeologists had cut out his bunker wall and shipped it to the museum, where it was mounted on a white display. The title below the reverent exhibit would read, "Interior American Defensive Bunker Wall, Vietnam circa 1969."

Just as he laughed to himself about his bunker wall being displayed in a museum, his ear caught the Huey's unmistakable *whop-whop*. The sound increased, indicating the chopper might be landing for fuel.

Might as well catch this bird back to the base for a boys' night out with Grate.

First Lieutenant Plimpton R. Grate III was another line officer serving in Herald's battalion. Back in 1969 they had ridden together on the Huey from Cu Chi base camp to Tan Son Nhut Air Base, to catch a freedom-bird jet for a week of Christmastime rest and recuperation. He pulled Taiwan; Grate got Australia. The two had struck up a friendship as they waited to catch their respective rides out of Vietnam.

They found it funny: both were lieutenants in the same battalion but, until that day, hadn't met. With the Vietnam War, infantrymen were isolated within their own companies. There was little camaraderie between officers; no two companies were ever in the same location at the same time.

Herald and Grate had been promoted off-line after six months. Off-line jobs kept soldiers on base, where the danger was less than the day-to-day patrol outside base camp. Six months was the normal time for a lieutenant to be a platoon leader in the field. Both men had been assigned to S-4, the unit that supervised the resupply of all the line companies. Herald was out in the "boonies" at Firebase Jackson, and Grate was assigned to the main base at Cu Chi, because he had more time in grade, promoted to first lieutenant before Herald.

Every Friday they would go club hopping together at Cu Chi, Herald catching a ride on one of the numerous helicopters that ferried material between the main base and the outlying smaller firebases. On this particular day the *whop-whop* was emanating from a Huey stopping for fuel.

One of Herald's duties as battalion supply officer was to construct a forward helicopter-refueling station. The station was located in between the numerous rows of rolled barbed wire surrounding the base.

Herald referred to his refueling station as "Air-Wolf," nicknaming it after his unit, the Wolfhounds, the legendary, heroic 27th Infantry Regiment founded in 1901 and proudly bearing the motto, *Nec Aspera Terrent*: No Fear on Earth. "Yep," Herald would jest, "just color me 'Fearless.'" The "Air-Wolf" epithet referred to a painting created by a sergeant drafted after flunking art school. The painting, a fair rendition of a snarling wolf with oversized white fangs and golden wings, had been done on two four-by-six-foot plywood flats joined together. The panel was hung on two eight-foot two-by-fours buried two feet deep. The shifting clay at the base made it impossible for the men to get the sign completely level or totally upright.

Everyone at Firebase Jackson was excited to have the forward refueling station. Helicopter pilots loved Firebase Jackson as it was the only refueling station between the main bases. In the event of an emergency or to sustain a mission, they could refuel there instead of being required to fly forty-five minutes back to Cu Chi to refuel before setting out again. The pilots had no idea what would happen if their choppers were caught on the ground in the event of an attack.

As far as the defenders of Firebase Jackson were concerned, the real benefit of the refueling station was the additional protection of the

500-gallon jet fuel bladders that could be detonated outside the earthen berm shielding the firebase. The raging fire would prevent Charles from attacking that side of the base—leaving one very cooked helicopter. Herald was not about to dampen the pilots' enthusiasm for the refueling station by explaining to them what he and his men considered the real purpose of the fuel bladders.

Today Herald refueled the Huey and put away the equipment. After refueling, the turbine engine coughed with a dark puff of smoke and slowly whined back to life. As it did, the large top rotor blades started to turn. The *whop-whop* of the chopper grew louder and faster as its blades cut through the air—the chilling sound symbolizing 'Nam, forever frozen in the minds of all who were there.

There was something about the unique noise of increased air pressure when the helicopter blades' angle was set and the big bird clawed at the sky. The angle of the blades would slice the air, compressing it to lift the airborne war machine. The whopping sound was the audible protest of the air to the blades.

After the engine was fully warmed up and the craft checked out, Herald approached the pilot's open window in the access door and pointed to the bay, the loading space of the craft. This was the standard way to ask for a ride, since words could not be heard over the noise of the blades and the scream of the turbine engine. The pilot nodded, granting the request. The bay was a six-by-six-foot square where "human cattle" sat on the floor and equipment was carried. The pilot lifted the Huey off the ramp, and away they flew to the circus called Cu Chi. Herald was wearing his "overnight kit": a toothbrush in his shirt pocket.

Helicopter movements are slow. The choppers do not lift straight up; instead, they lift, tilt forward, and move ahead to build up momentum before being able to gain altitude, making liftoff and landing the most dangerous phases of a helicopter ride in a war zone.

As a machine with large, whirling blades and loaded with jet fuel, what it seriously lacked was armor, something to protect it from even the smallest arms fire. And to make matters worse, if it was hit in the right place, it would become a flying bomb spewing shards of metal and spraying lit fuel everywhere. All the men were aware of the danger and cringed at the ugly truth of it all.

A month earlier a Chinook twin-rotor helicopter—a huge target at liftoff—had been downed by AK-47 small-arms fire that tore holes through the main hydraulic lines. A Chinook, the largest rotary-wing aircraft used in Vietnam, could transport up to forty-five men at a time. To be sure, those first fragile moments after liftoff over Charles' turf were always a concern for the soldiers.

Now, this afternoon, the Huey transporting Herald circled the camp until the pilot reached a safe altitude and speed, and then headed for Cu Chi.

It was the dry season, and the square rice fields below looked peaceful, filled with golden, mature rice, ready to harvest. The road to Firebase Jackson flashed beneath, filled with a myriad of vehicles, animals, and humanity crowding its red dusty path.

Herald laughed, spying a vehicle known as a "cyclo." Basically a motorized rickshaw, the cyclo had an enclosed motorcycle front cab with a single seat for the driver; behind him, a small truck bed mounted on two wheels. The truck's metal bed was sometimes open, sometimes covered with a canvas top on metal tube supports raised high enough for people to ride in the back, crowded together and standing up. It was a common mode of transportation in Vietnam.

Cyclos were almost always packed and stacked beyond capacity with people, goods, animals, and everything else imaginable. The abuse those little motorcycle trucks withstood was a tribute to the Japanese engineers who built them. From the air, they looked like ants dragging large tin cans. The cans were loaded with lots of other smaller human insects, with more junk hanging off.

Flying at about 1,000 feet in the air, pilots and their passengers always noted several checkpoints en route. If the chopper went down, they had better know where the hell they were.

An abandoned, bombed, and shelled church signaled the village of Trang Bang. Years later, near the war's end, this village was made infamous by *Life Magazine* photos that showed civilian children running down the road ripping flaming, napalm-saturated clothes from their skinny bodies. The last checkpoint was a rubber-tree plantation on the west side of Cu Chi. The trees were barren of leaves, thanks to the U.S. spraying them with the defoliant Agent Orange.

He always tried to leave Firebase Jackson by 2:00 p.m. Unless he started early, he couldn't be sure of catching a helicopter ride. After a forty-five-minute flight, the helicopter landed, and Herald signaled a "thank you" to the pilot and jumped off, the noise level of the engine precluding all but physical gestures.

Walking to his rendezvous with Grate took Herald past the various support companies for the helicopter battalion: fuel, mechanics, command and control.

Cu Chi was big enough to be a small city. The brass insisted on military neatness in the larger, more civilized bases. Walkways from the main road to individual units were lined with the familiar adornment of rough stones painted white. Similar stones outlined real flowerbeds in front of the buildings. The buildings were decorated with symbols or logos involving some military-advertising concept of the company's function, lending a surreal aspect to the war and being a parody of corporate logos back home. The buildings were mostly wooden, slapped together, and on the verge of disrepair, as if to signal the approaching end of this conflict.

Herald laughed as he recalled three basic military rules for noncombat zones: if it moves, salute it; if it is movable, pick it up; if it is immovable, paint it.

The route to the bar brought him to the outside perimeter and gave him a good look at a major base's defenses: a six-foot-high, sandbag-covered berm with large twenty-by-twenty-foot bunkers spaced evenly around the base. The eight-by-eight foot bunkers at Firebase Jackson paled in comparison.

Wave upon wave of coiled concertina wire created a shimmering maze in front of the bunkers extending out to more than 400 yards and laid in predetermined rows, deliberately channeling any attacker into killing zones, areas where machine-gun fire could be concentrated.

The Viet Cong understood this and cut, tunneled, or crawled under the wire: a smart move, as the strength of American firepower would doom Charles' wire-channeled frontal attack. The bad news was, the boredom of watching the vacant wire night after night caused many perimeter guards to fall asleep, allowing Mr. Charles to breach the wire.

The view from the berm surrounding the base was a sea of mottled, coiled wire. Some of the coils were round, bright, and shiny; others were drooped and rusted dark brown. Constant moisture from the humidity and rain required that the wire be frequently replaced. Corrosion and the abuse of machine-gun and 40 mm grenade-launcher fire transformed the fierce coils of barbed wire, folding them in irregular patterns slumped toward the earth. The wire in its various states of disrepair symbolized the idea that the U.S. occupation was temporary.

Herald's first destination was the Division Artillery Club, known as Div-Arty. The club was just off the main road, which ran parallel to the outside perimeter.

He took a left down a dirt road, raised above deep drainage ditches on both sides, to the large gravel pad supporting the club's structure. Drainage was very important in this country's wet season.

The club, a red-painted wooden building, sported typical Wild West "batwing" saloon doors that swung freely in either direction, and closed in the middle. But to keep the heat out and air conditioning inside, these particular doors were full length and solid. The interior walls revealed the unfinished face of run-of-the-mill exterior plywood siding. Several old movie and travel posters were nailed to the walls for decoration. Lighting was provided by six 100-watt bulbs capped with dusty, faded-red Japanese paper lanterns.

This was Herald's target destination and the antithesis of the furnace-like bunker he now called "home." Air conditioning and a clean wooden bench to lie on represented a resort, compared to the heat and humidity of his bunker. All he wanted was a nap in a cool, safe space. Cu Chi's defenses provided enough security to afford small but adequate warnings. This gave the soldiers the luxury of rest, reminiscent of that enjoyed back home—a rare opportunity seldom appreciated until it is lost.

Shoving a $20 bill over to the bartender as he passed by, Herald nodded and winked at him. The bartender returned the nod, indicating Herald would not be disturbed.

Locating his favorite bench and using his baseball cap as a makeshift pillow, he promptly fell into deep slumber—awakened ninety minutes later by the sweat dripping down his forehead. One of the many oddities of the Vietnam experience was the unexplained adjustment from intense heat and humidity to air conditioning, often provoking such a physical response.

Promptly at 1800 hours, the doors to the club flew open. Grate's voice slowly boomed, "Fee, fi, fo, fum, I smell the sweat of an ... infantrymun!"

Herald sat up, rubbing his eyes. "Hola, my Jolly Green Giant friend. How goes the war?"

In the relaxed cadence of a Georgia plantation owner, Grate replied, "It's my birthday, and I feel an intense dryness in my ... throat. Perhaps a libation, to *e-e-ease* this country boy into the evening, is in order."

"Yes, indeedy," Herald agreed, lifting himself off the bench and moving with his friend toward the bar.

The bartender had already poured their favorite drinks: Johnnie Walker Black Label for Grate, Jack Daniel's for Herald, both on the rocks.

Three stiff drinks later—and feeling little pain—they gave each other a "Yes, indeedy!" nod and headed for the door: time for a trip to the Hospital Club for dinner, where there was always the possibility of eyeing a nurse—a prospect that intrigued every male on the base.

As they left the coolness of the air-conditioned bar, the night air, heavy with moisture and heat, began overcoming them.

Herald, his breathing becoming labored, stumbled on the pebble-lined walkway the instant the hellish-hot, moisture-soaked air attacked his senses. "Christ, you never get used to the heat, no matter how long you've been here!"

Grate, also struggling to breathe and steadying himself, agreed. "I may be a slow-talkin', country boy from western ... Pennsylvania ... but no wonder the heat hits you like a baseball bat ... moron! You leave your earthen-furnace-bunker home, with its crummy little fan ... get here ... take a nap for a couple of hours in a super air-conditioned ... room ... wake up ... start drinking like a fish ... and then wonder why the effect of the outside air is a little ... oppressive? God knows how your body ... copes! The temperature transition would *kill* most ... people!"

"Grate, you drawling Looney-Tunes," Herald laughed as he spoke, "with your speech pattern, are you sure you aren't from the Deep South ... of *Pennsylvania*? Look, getting my nap, after living in my earthen furnace, is one of the high points of my week. I admit enduring the unabated heat all week and suddenly joining the polar bear club is a lethal combination; add 'Mr. Daniels,' and that's why I do it only once a week. Let's get the Jeep and see if there are any round-eyes in need of a little companion-crap."

"Companion-*ship*, not ... companion-guano," Grate said, smiling.

"No, I have the right word. Allow me a little poetic license, as long as my word abstractions stay within the boundaries of the 'Jabberwocky.' Look, what western women would look twice at anyone in the infantry? The only decent women here are nurses. Don't you think it'd be hard for a nurse to be attracted to a class of people for whom she spends most of the day changing bedpans or zipping into body bags? Nay, nay, my apparently unenlightened friend, a western, round-eyed woman here has her choice of men. Higher-ranking officers, doctors, pilots, and others with better prospects are more than available—and begging to be in her company. Why would such a woman get involved with a man who has one foot in the grave and can't remain in one place long enough to even *begin* to learn her name? To put it bluntly, my dear Pennsylvanian hillbilly, we are *doomed*, not only for being relegated to perform the most heinous jobs with the most horrific risks but also for being socially ostracized as sexually repressed barbarians."

Grate smiled. Nodding his head side to side, he replied in his lazy language stride, "The dreaded double ... whammy. What ... sex? No, I remember, sort ... of. With sexual frustration being the only possible ... result, why do we even go where there are women? Are we now adding masochism to our other less endearing ... qualities?"

Straightening his body and pointing to the stars, Herald stated his dictum: "To remember the dream, and to pledge that no matter what the civilian road back home brings, to always make the best of our existence."

Grate nodded his head. Raising his right hand in the air, he slurred a pledge. "Amen, Brother ... Herald. I will never be a bad boy again; no ... never. Why, I'll be so 'good,' they'll define 'good' by my ... actions. I will go to law school and work ... hard. Why, 'Good' will be my middle name, yes, sir, good, ditty-good, ditty-good, good-good ... good."

Weaving their booze-laced way to the parking area at the supply office and locating their Jeep, Grate continued. "Why, I spy our trusty ... steed. Let us mount her and proceed to yon ... tavern."

"Agreed, fine sir, and allow me to chauffeur your fine posterior to the land of the fabled round-eye. Why, just last week I heard one was actually spotted!"

"Surely you ... jest. It is so early in the migratory ... season. Is this just another vicious rumor, spread by commies, to undermine our already depleted ... morale?"

The Jeep churned over several times before it started. In this climate, moisture and heat, combined with dust from the dirt roads, created a maintenance nightmare.

Herald let the vehicle idle and began singing "We Gotta Get Out of This Place," the unofficial theme song for Americans in 'Nam. Grate, in a fine, deep voice, joined in. Putting the Jeep in gear, the pair lurched down the road. Together they boomed into the pitch-black night, belting The Animals' song.

"We gotta get out of this place,
If it's the last thing we ever do,
We gotta get out of this place,
Grate, there's a better life for me and you."

During the short ride to the club, Herald continued singing at the top of his voice—until he realized Grate's voice was not harmonizing along.

"OK, Grateey-boy, where *a-a-are you-u-u*? Playing hood ornament? Hiding in the back?"

Eyeballing the hood and then the back seat by moving the rearview mirror, he realized Grate was missing in action. Jamming on the brakes and skidding ten feet, he began looking around in the dark, searching in all directions.

Jesus Christ, where is he?

Grate, gone missing on a short Jeep ride, was unusual even by 'Nam standards. He never wandered off without a goodbye.

Gunning the engine, Herald spun the Jeep around and started back down the road, driving about 200 yards, where at last the headlights illuminated a prone figure in the gravel on the side of the road. Herald stopped the Jeep and jumped out. "Jeez, man! Are ... are ... are you all right?"

"Never ... better," Grate replied, looking up with a woozy grin.

"What the hell are you doing jumping from a Jeep at thirty-five miles an hour?"

"Ah, but ... wait. Is this ... Heaven? The Promised ... Land? Why, of course ... not. I ... see Herald ... is here. Did anyone get the license number of that ... truck?"

Grate shook his head and hauled himself up. Like a man taking physical inventory of all his body parts, he checked himself out to make sure all were in good working order. He began crossing the road, his rumpled body spotlighted in the Jeep's headlights.

Herald told Grate to stop so he could check him out. Grate protested at first, but had to agree; after all, he had fallen from a speeding vehicle. Even though he felt only a little bruised, it wouldn't hurt to be safe—considering he'd been anesthetized by Johnnie Walker.

The way Grate had fallen was unique: Jeeps have no doors; their sides are open at seat-cushion level. By crossing his legs left over right, propping them on the rearview mirror, and stretching his body out, hands behind head and using the back of his neck as an anchoring point to raise his body off the seat back, Grate had made himself vulnerable to unsteady motion. Raising his stretched body had resulted in forming an arch similar to that of a high-wire acrobat dangling over a free-fall between two tiny points. The bouncing of the vehicle on the uneven road surface, combined with his arched body, had caused Grate to flip off the seat, fly out of the Jeep, and land square on his back on the flat clay surface—sliding like a surfboard for a short distance.

The yellow-red clay had smeared Grate's green uniform on all sides, forming a curious pattern. It was as if a yellow-gold ribbon, six inches wide, had been wrapped lengthwise along the sides of his entire body. His front side, including his face, chest, and legs, was clean, with no marks. The resulting clay outline gave his body an aura of a head-to-toe golden halo.

Laughing out loud at the thought of a halo being the last thing Grate would ever be wearing, Herald shouted, "Oh, man, I wish you could see yourself! You look like a Christmas present minus a bow on top of your head. And remember that painting of the Virgin Mary, where she had a full-body halo? You look like you've been similarly blessed ... except not so clean. OK, turn around, so I can see what you look like from the rear."

The back of Grate's dusty uniform revealed skid marks and long, thin tears at the buttocks and shoulders where his body had absorbed the majority of the impact and skid. Minor bloodstains dotted his back.

"Yeah, your back's all messed up, too. Well, perhaps, my good fellow, we should retire to the shower to regroup and clean up before hitting the club?"

Grate frowned as he moved his tongue inside his mouth to inventory his teeth. Turning his head to the right, he spit out some dust; then, grimacing at Herald, he slurred, "Fuck you ... asshole. We got this far, 'Virgin Mary halo' or ... not. And I need a ... drink ... so ... you drive, and I shall attempt to regain my sense of ... humor. Let's ... 'didi,' as the natives say for 'hurry up.'"

Grate jumped back into the Jeep, rocking it as he bounded in, and sulked all the way to the club.

"Right now, Herald, I feel unhinged … a strong wave of hatred for this stupid war."

Herald tried cheering him up en route by joking, even to the point of creating a baseball analogy about a great slide into home, but Grate would have none of it. He prayed that the nightclub would be tranqil, so as not to further incite his friend. Grate, never a paragon for the advancement of humor, constituted a danger to all mankind, regardless of race, color or creed.

Rather like LeMaire, Herald thought, citing a typical LeMaire-ism, *"Just don't piss me off!"*   .

Reaching the club, Grate hopped off the Jeep before it came to a full stop, shaking out each of his limbs one at a time, to reassure himself he was still up to the evening's events. In need of additional libation and walking in stiff, jerky movements, his body exhibiting the effects of the fall, he stopped at the door to the club and gave himself a final twist of his chest. Catching up at a run, Herald bowed low like a gentleman and held the door open for his buddy.

The club's dimensions were typical: a thirty-by-forty-foot shanty slapped together, with a plywood-topped, varnished bar along one side. There was the normal array of helicopter pilots grouped at one end of the bar. Doctors, nurses, and a smattering of other officers from other branches of the service were seated at two of the six tables. Except for the doctors, everyone was there just to see the nurses.

The helicopter pilots harbored a grudge against the infantry officers, believing the infantry was getting all the glory and relegating them to the thankless status of "stage hands" supporting the stars on stage. Needless to say, the boys who lived in the mud could have done with a lot less glory—slogging through booby-trapped fields and carrying 100 pounds of equipment in 100-plus-degree heat with 100 percent humidity.

But as the pilots sat all day in their helicopters, slept on beds, and drank all night, while the infantry walked, the soldiers were in much better physical shape. In addition, the infantrymen, having little relief from all the "fun in the sun," had developed meaner dispositions, and the antagonistic attitudes between the pilots and infantry would occasionally lead to brawls at the club.

A Vietnamese waitress calling herself "Marilyn," after an old American movie she'd seen on base, wore the usual short skirt, high heels, and a tight top looking as though it had been painted on. That was the good news. The bad? Her pockmarked face, wide gaps in her semi-toothless smile, and three broad, dark, lateral tribal scars on her left cheek easily qualified her for the title "Miss Double Coyote Ugly." Chan, manning the bar, looked like a sinister character out of an old Charlie Chan movie. Five-foot-five, bald, and built like a rock; his duties, in addition to tending bar, included maintaining physical control—his little bulk helped to handle his bouncer responsibilities.

Marilyn and Chan saw the boys entering and, with a classic Oriental bow, signaled them toward a table. In their culture, this gesture conveyed respect, but now it was a cliché barely masking their loathing of the U.S. occupation in their country.

"Why you no bathe, GI, before you come here?" the waitress asked. "Your body has a dust edging like you have been out sliding in dirt. You *dinky dau*."

Grate checked out his left arm and flicked off the dust with quick strokes of his right hand. "This dust trim," he drawled, "is an intentional … accessory to my formal … attire." Bending over to brush the dust from his left knee, he continued. "This fashion statement took a great deal of time and effort to … apply. Dust edging is considered … *très* … *chic*."

Marilyn and Chan recognized Grate and Herald as good tippers, so they went out of their way to be gracious, even if Grate had odd habits. The two officers just wanted to drink, socialize, and not be harassed. Laying down a "money carpet" was a good way to ensure a no-interference policy from the management.

Both soldiers harbored a fear of using the local population as workers on base during a guerrilla war; granting nonmilitary personnel access to the base was always dangerous. Historically it had proven fatal for colonial

armies of occupation who had trusted unskilled work to the native population. There was no way of knowing for sure if a native was agreeable to
the U.S.'s intervention or was waiting to take advantage of an opportune
moment to sweep the aggressor from his land, and Herald had no intention of becoming a statistic in a book entitled, "How to Be Sure NOT to
Come Home from a Guerrilla War." Even when dealing with the Chieu
Hoi Program, for VCs who had surrendered and now were fighting with
the U.S., Herald wanted them always up front, where he could watch them.
Moreover, a loyal Vietnamese worker was subject to coercion under the
right circumstances, for instance, when his family was being held hostage
by Charles.

But there was no reason to spoil a night of frivolity with security issues.
These fleeting moments of recreation were crucial to maintaining perspective. Ignoring the waitress's invitation to be seated at one of the remaining
tables, the boys stumbled up to the bar and ordered their favorite whiskies.

Herald, his head bobbing and eyes glassy, turned to Grate and, trying
not to sound too sloshed, asked, "Diiid I everrr tell you why I quit college?"

Grate, smiling groggily and scratching some of the coagulated blood
off his lower back, took a long, slow sip of his drink.

"No," he answered. "I assumed it had to be for some insane ... reason.
You could still be in school instead of being here with yours ... truly. But
I do have a foggy memory of our meeting the night before we went on
R&R at Ton Se Nute ... Air Base ... something about a *GI Joe Coloring
Book* and eating ... crow? In your inebriated ... state, you failed to close the
gap between the black bird and a *GI Joe Coloring ... Book*. I recall also you
noted eating crow would not be so bad if they would remove the burnt ...
feathers. However, you failed to identify who *they* ... were."

Looking at the ceiling, Herald smiled. "Yeah, I used 'eating crow,' as
defined in *Webster's College Dictionary:* 'to undergo the humiliation of having to retract a statement or admit an error.' In contrast, *crow au gratin*, or
topped with breadcrumbs and melted cheese, could be quite delightful, as
the feathers give the dish a slightly crunchy flavor. My personal favorite is

barbequed crow *en croute*, where most of the feathers have been charcoaled off and the bird is wrapped in pastry and baked. It would've been a nice touch to escape the shadow of my father by not brazenly quitting school and going into the Army. The icing on my psycho-cake was having my peer group color war pictures in a *GI Joe Coloring Book* that I bought as a joke."

Grate placed one elbow on the bar and tilted his head to the left. Looking at Herald through bloodshot, squinty eyes, he mumbled, "One of these ... days, when we are not so drunk as to prohibit connecting two thoughts ... together, you will kindly explain how a *GI Joe Coloring Book* caused you to quit your father's shadow ... school."

"Yeah, be sure to explain it to me, also," Herald said as he raised his drink, drained it, and dropped his hand with the glass on the bar with a *"tink."* The *tinking* sound was Chan's notice to do his thing and pour another.

Travel posters, always an easy, cheap decoration, lined the walls of the bar. Dusty with age, some were torn by patrons stroking a favored destination, remembered or dreamed.

Remembering Wild Bill Hickok's first rule to stay alive, Herald kept his back to the bar. After eyeing the group of loud, gesturing helicopter pilots, he moved to a table opposite them and sat down with his chair against the wall. This also served to remedy the problem of declining vertical stability due to alcohol consumption.

Grate, weaving slightly to the left and right, and looking for a missing Herald to bounce off of, attracted the attention of a frustrated helicopter pilot who spied weakness in his prey, to say nothing of the dirt or alcohol content. Straightening up on his chair, the pilot was ready to have fun remedying past misconceptions of who actually ran the show, the infantry or pilots.

Rising from his table, the vengeful—but, alas, naïve—pilot stalked Grate, a man not only of superior strength but one who also relished a threat from an inexperienced source, such as the approaching, clueless pilot. Into the valley of mirth he walked, and once within shouting distance blared, "You assholes in the infantry suck! You guys think you *are* the war! You all think you're 'Golden Boys.' Ha! Yeah, 'golden,' all right! Take a good look at yourself, asshole! There's a golden halo of *dirt* around you! When did you last take a bath, you shit-for-brains?"

Grate eyed the pilot and, in a slow, modulated tone—that anyone in his right mind would have feared—both greeted and sized up his victim. "Greetings, my good ... man. Delightful evening for a good thrashing, don't you ... think?"

As Grate uttered the word "thrashing," the pilot threw a long, slow, drunken sidewinder punch.

Grate squatted down. The punch went over his head. Maintaining eye contact with his quarry, he warned again, "'Gold,' my good man, is where you find ... it. And my particular golden aura is readily available from the local terra ... firma." His voice transforming into religious fervor, he decreed, "By the will of the gods ... I ... will show you where to reap your own golden ... harvest."

Grate grabbed the pilot by his belt and shirt collar. Picking him up over his head, the pilot's arms and legs dangling, Grate walked seven paces to the nearest wall and threw his victim through one of the rarest of commodities in Vietnam, a plate glass picture window—revered as a local treasure, the only one of its size. The rest of the pilots, sensing an excuse to release their own anxiety, leapt at the weaving Grate, who staggered to the left enough to evade the second attacker.

Jumping to Grate's defense, Herald stepped in front of the remainder of the advancing group and addressed the aggressors. "Don't we have enough crap to go around already? What, you don't get enough during the day? Your boy went after my friend, begging for the response he gave. Let us, as civilized people, go forward, focused toward the ...." He never finished his statement: he had to duck a roundhouse punch.

The bar exploded. The physical conditioning of the contingency from the land, with its rigors of heat endurance and walking in clay, proved to be the undoing of the contingency from the sky. To be sure, the infantry lads took their share of hits but were thrilled to release their anxiety in an all-American fistfight, a real out-and-out barroom brawl. John Wayne would have been proud. Both sides left bloodied but alive, a stark contrast to the slaughter outside the wire.

The boys counted coup on five pilots—who would think twice before exercising their prerogatives again, unless they were on their own turf: the air. The smoke cleared, and, upon examination, the bar furniture of early cave-dweller chic had suffered little damage.

Herald hurried over to Chan and hauled out a wad of military script, money printed for use in 'Nam; dollars were prohibited. As a bonus he also handed over a few prized all-American greenbacks. Chan, jabbering on the phone to the Military Police while eyeing the cash, put down the receiver. The base policy required any altercation, especially one involving infantry personnel, to be reported as a danger to others. Fighting among normal base personnel might fit within some of society's boundaries, but these ground-pounder infantry guys would all too often go for the jugular.

The crisis averted, Chan grinned at the loot and then at Herald. "You Numbah One! I no call police. You go now, take friend, please. Police come soon."

Herald grabbed Grate, helped him outside and into the passenger seat of the Jeep, ran around to the other side, jumped into the driver's side, and started the vehicle. Feeling pain in his right hand as he gripped the steering wheel, he looked and saw the knuckles were bruised; one was cut and bleeding. Lifting the hand from the steering wheel to his face, he put his mouth over the one knuckle to stop the bleeding. The odd taste of his blood made him wonder, *Why does blood taste metallic?* Moving his hand from his mouth and shifting gears, he asked Grate, "Why does blood taste metallic?"

Grate, now resuming his easy manner, was massaging his jaw and recalling the evening. "Something about the iron in our blood. Hey, that will teach those guys to make me fall out of the … Jeep."

Herald laughed and countered, "Non sequitur, Grate. Those poor lads were just the first targets of opportunity to get in your way. They were not even near the Jeep, and you know it. It's your mean streak surfacing when you're in a bad mood, instigated in this case by your flying out of the Jeep. You ought to be ashamed of yourself, especially the way you threw the lad through the window. You knew full well there wasn't any gold out in the driveway ... to say nothing of destroying a picture window!"

"Gold is where you find it, my ... friend. In this case, the gold was the psychological release I needed to deal with our world next ... week. This was an exercise in anxiety reduction on my ... part. Think of how much more of a balanced and understanding lad I will be next ... week. Those boys benefited ... too. Did you see the smile on the one lad after he landed one on your ... jaw?"

"Short lived at best when he sucked on the chair you clubbed him with. Amazing how, in the movies, the chair always breaks, but in real life, the people buckle instead."

The next morning, Grate was sitting on his bunk, rubbing his stomach, groaning. Herald woke up, saw his condition, and asked, "You OK, Grate? I'd hate for you to be sick on your birthday."

"I will never be OK in this country, thank you very ... much. Birthday or not, the scotch seems to be visiting me again with extreme ... protest."

"You know, when I feel that way, I have a Coke or 7-UP. The carbonation seems to settle my stomach."

"The very last thing I need is carbonation in this ... stomach. I'm sure if I drank anything now, it would be rotated immediately back. Neither Coke nor 7-UP is reputed to be better the second time ... around."

"Nonsense," Herald sneered, walking toward the end of the barracks to the soda machine, where he was rewarded when a light cool-green 7-UP popped out. He walked back to Grate. "Try just a little sip. It will do you good, I promise."

Grate's usual slow pace of speech increased in speed and volume, "Herald, get the soda away from me before I hurt ... you. I know of no country recipe for an upset stomach that requires ingestion of ... 7-UP. Take your stupid cures away from … me! The smell, just from here, is making me … ill. Get that crap away from … me."

"Look, how much is one sip going to hurt you? The carbonation will do your stomach good. Here, just one sip." He handed the soda to Grate, who hesitated and eased the can to his lips. Pausing, he looked to Herald, who nodded approval, and then took a long draught.

Grate was right. His face grossly contorting, he jumped up. Soda spewed from his mouth as he ran to the barrack's porch at the front of the building. Leaving a trail of soda and other liquids of various vivid hues on the floor, Grate leaned over the railing and retched violently. His body recoiled several times, as everything his stomach and intestines could grab and expel was thrown out. It was as if his entire digestive tract had turned into a wild creature bent on his destruction.

Herald laughed until he fell to the floor. Looking up at Grate, he gloated: "Now you know why they call it 7-UP. You drink it, and it comes up, over and over. And now, as it's your 'very special day,' howzabout a little serenade? 'Happy barf day to you … happy barf day to you … happy barf day with lions and tigers and monkeys like you … happy barf day to you!'"

A combat boot whistled over Herald's head. Dodging it, he ran back into the barracks and waited for Grate's vomiting seizure to finish. After the retching noises died down, Herald returned to the front porch, where Grate was sprawled in a lawn chair. Spying the drool on Grate's cheek, Herald solicitously inquired, "Don't you feel better now?"

"NO! And if I ever regain my strength, you are in big … trouble. Why did you do this to an easy-going country … boy?"

"It always worked for me. But at least your stomach must feel better jettisoning the black and reddish barf."

"Just wait a minute until I cram my digestive tract back down my … throat. When I am ready … we will play a fun game of 'Large Blunt Instrument With Your Name on … It!'"

Herald waved a goodbye as he started to leave. "I would love to stay and play 'Large Blunt Instrument With My Name on It!' Sounds like an intriguing game, but I have to get back to my own playground. Ciao."

YEAR 1988

RETURNING HIS MIND to his law office, Herald laughed and rocked back in his chair at the thought of playing any game entitled "Large Blunt Instrument With Your Name on It."

He took a swig of his strong, bourbon-laced coffee and grimaced as reality struck: it was a large, blunt, *legal* instrument with his name on it that he now faced. The thought nauseated him, so he substituted another, more pleasant idea. *I'll just hit that dive bar a block down the street.*

Rising from his chair, he left the office vowing, *I won't let those damn 'Nam demons get control. I can handle this. I don't need any help!*

Perhaps not, but now he began to realize his Vietnam memories were becoming a safe haven from his legal problems.

CHAPTER 7
A WALK IN THE PARK WITH A TOURIST

HERALD PARKED HIS VW VAN in the office driveway at about 10:00 a.m. on Sunday, MD 26. He now worked twelve- to thirteen-hour days, focusing on his motion to maneuver out of his legal mistake. For a minute after he shut off the engine, he could not move.

A sharp pain stabbed his chest, making him grab and massage the left side of his chest with his right hand and clench the steering wheel with the other. He was dizzy and short of breath. After five long minutes, Herald felt like moving; he opened his van door and walked to the office.

Sunday was Herald's maintenance day at the office. It started with a splash of Mr. Bourbon in his coffee, just to quiet his psyche's thumping on his mental cage. With himself and the mower gassed up, he mowed the lawn. After the lawn was finished, the lawyer-cum-janitor vacuumed the floors and cleaned the bathrooms.

In OCS, he had become very efficient at cleaning bathrooms. His officer-candidate platoon had the barracks chores broken down into groups. One group spit-shined the floors, a two-hour job. Another group spit-shined the stairways, another two hours. Herald's group cleaned the latrine, twenty minutes. Other groups fought to take over this job that, at first, no one wanted.

After completing the gardening and janitorial duties, he sat down and consulted with Mr. Bourbon and Coke. Knocking off his drink, he drove to the public law library to continue his extensive research on reasons why the court should relieve him of his mistake. When the library closed, he drove home.

Making his customary grand entrance, Herald smiled and announced, "Well, I've always wanted to work for a large company … and here we have it: I am Lloyd Janitorial, Lloyd Gardening, and Lloyd and Lloyd Law Office."

Thea, looking up from the couch where she was seated with Katherine, and seeing how exhausted Herald was, offered a solution. "We both need to do something other than legal work and taking care of the kids and house and family chores. When I was a child back in Vermont, taking walks in the woods next to my house was an important part of my life. Why don't we all take a walk in the park? I know a great one in Woodside."

"That," Herald beamed, "is a *great* idea. *Anything* to get my mind off my problems."

Katherine, who'd been finishing up her homework with her mother's help, rose from the couch and, toting her schoolbooks, skipped off to her bedroom.

As Katherine disappeared into her bedroom, Thea reminded her husband of an as yet unresolved issue. "Herald, you keep telling me about imprisoning your war demons in a closet. For someone who preaches to all his clients to face their fears, you are not facing Vietnam and its effect on you. I know I'm beginning to sound like a broken record, but other vets go to counseling when they have continual flashbacks."

Frustrated as she watched, yet again, Herald's eyes glazing over, she started heading out the back door to rally their young daughter from her backyard adventures. Once more resigning herself to the situation, she sighed. "I can see you tuning me out. I'll go get the kids. Give me ten minutes to get them ready, and then we can go for our walk in the park."

The words "walk in the park" gave Herald pause. Those exact words flashed in his mind like a ten-story-high title on a movie screen, and memories of a Vietnam experience began to engulf him. Sweat erupted on his forehead. His chest felt heavy. His breathing became quick and shallow. Dizzy, he put his right hand on the wall to steady himself and wondered if maybe these recurring daydreams were a sign he was starting to lose it. Sergeant Pearlman's voice, out of Vietnam history, came echoing into his mind.

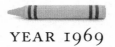

YEAR 1969

"RISE AND SHINE, LT. It's a be-e-autiful day for a walk in the park." Pearlman's sing-songy voice was lilting as he took two steps down into Herald's bunker. Placing his right hand on the "Heads Up" sign nailed to the bunker entrance's low wooden header, he jostled the roof beam just enough to start two dust trails filtering between his fingers.

Leaning over, he slowly ran his palm over his forehead, cupping the gathered sweat and flicking it to the ground. Then, with the index finger of his left hand pushing on the point of his chin and cocking his head in the fashion of a British maid, he continued in the same sing-songy fashion. "Time for all good officers to go to see the CC and find out where we're going today."

Herald, propping himself up on one elbow from his dusty bed on the clay floor of the bunker and laughing to himself, thought, *How could the gods be so angry they would allow an obnoxious platoon sergeant to make noises like this in the morning?* Sitting up and rubbing his face with his right hand and grabbing his poncho liner with his left, he threw it off his legs, looked up at the sergeant, and kidded, "Pearlman, don't you recall my asking you to call me anything but 'LT?' And now, here you are—once Harvard bound—a winner in the slow-learner department."

Picking up on Herald's playful sarcasm, Pearlman sneered at him. "Well, if you officers could last a wee bit more than just thirty seconds in a firefight, it might be interesting to get to know you. However, the responsibility of the radio and the platoon seem to be the worst combination possible for an organic life form."

"What?" Herald shot back, jerking himself to full sitting attention and staring at Pearlman. "How dare you call me organic! It's not my fault I'm so popular with Sir Charles. I clean up real good! And Charles finds the man closest to the horn irresistible in the first few minutes of any contact." Rolling over onto the dirt floor and rising to one knee, Herald continued. "Just remember, before I arrived, you had the radio as platoon sergeant because there was no LT. Upon my untimely demise, you will have the radio again, so be nice." Placing a protective hand on his head, he rose until the back of his hand touched the low ceiling.

Pearlman sneered again. "See, I told you. Hit your head on a bunker ceiling enough times, and you will adapt. Congrats."

Rubbing his head and nodding, Herald joked back, "Well, at the rate I was going, it was either death by head trauma or bumpy-headed fortune teller's bonanza. OK, I'm awake and moving my ass to talk to the CC and discuss today's dance card. Grab me some of whatever's on the menu for breakfast so we can pull out on time. The battalion commander, just in from Korea, ordered our CC to have all patrols leave at the same time every day. Our CC is worried somehow our late starts in the morning translate into 'Club 'Nam,' rather than a combat outfit. From my reading of guerrilla warfare manuals, I offered the opinion that the first rule in guerrilla war is to be unpredictable—never operate on a regular timetable; for example, patrols should never leave at the same time. I even volunteered to leave last. Any type of pattern gives Charles an advantage. But no, the CC feels we're just lazy, and this operation needs to be on a bank's schedule."

Grabbing the comics, he moved past Pearlman up two of the three steps to ground level, pausing only to adjust to the fierce sunlight and heat. After the pause, he took the third step and looked over the drab, sandbag-fortified base for a minute and then headed toward the CC's bunker.

Just as he cleared the last step, Ferlinghetti, always dropping "h's" in his usual, not-quite-English, Italian accent, called out, "Ciao, LT. I 'ave una poema to read-a, OK? Dog, 'e wan'-a to 'ear-a, too."

Herald rubbed his eyes, still adjusting to the blinding sun and heat. Looking to his left, he saw Ferlinghetti and Dog sitting on the side of his bunker.

"OK, read it, but make it fast." *This poetry shit is just too weird to be believed, but as long as it makes him happy, what the hell.*

Ferlinghetti, smiling and switching diction gears to his more studious side, began to recite.

    See
        it was like this when
                we waltz into this place
    a couple of Papish cats
             is doing an Aztec two-step
    And I says
           Dad let's cut
    but then this dame
             comes up behind me see
                and says
           You and me could really exist
    Wow I says
           Only the next day
           she has bad teeth
             and really hates
                  poetry

(A Coney Island of the Mind: Poems, page 22)

"So w'at-a you t'ink-a, LT?"

"Rarh," Dog added in approval.

"Well, guys, at first hearing, it seems to be a story about the poet getting drunk in a bar and meeting a girl. He takes her home. In the cruel light of morning, he discovers the alcohol has deceived him. She is coyote ugly and hates poetry."

"'Ey," Ferlinghetti piped up, "rememba dat-a time-a wit'-a my amichi doin'-a shots in-a bar off-a da 'ickory an'-a Freeway Drive, eh? Una bimba, sexy, no? She come-a over. She seem-a very beautiful … molto bella, sai?, so … facciamo l'amore: we make-a love, sai? My friends-a, dey laugh. I'm-a not-a know why. Next-a morning, I'm-a greet-a by La Signorina Faccia di Pepperoni Pizza! I'm-a creep outta da place-a wit'-a my cloze an'-a go dress in-a 'allway. Even after I'm-a shower, I'm-a no feel-a clean. Allora, is-a dat-a w'at-a dees-a poema about?"

"Couldn't have put it better myself, Ferlinghetti. Keep reading. You may have found a new profession," Herald quipped as he continued walking to the command bunker.

After a twenty-minute consultation with the CC, he walked back to his bunker, spread the comics on the roof, and motioned to Pearlman, who in turn yelled for the squad leaders and Dog. The men, emerging from the darkness of their bunkers like depressed workers going to a hated, repetitive factory job, gathered around Herald's bunker, where he began presenting the agenda.

"Today's selection is not bad on the shit-factor meter. Briefly, to the west of the firebase is the river and Cambodia, where Mr. Charles is known to take personal offense if we trespass. To the south and north are two Charles parks with intensive areas of booby traps in overgrown bamboo groves with flooded rice fields in between. Our route is to the lucky east. The rice fields at this time of year are cleared and dry, with a village and road system. There are some bamboo hedges, but not too bad, as they are not interconnected and offer little cover for Charles. All these areas are the least likely place to meet Charles, a veritable 'walk in the park,' as Sergeant Pearlman would put it."

Pearlman looked to the squad leaders and ordered, "We leave in five minutes. Full canteens, light ammunition load. Move it!"

"*So-o-o-e-e-e!*" AckMan yelped as he went to gather his squad, "we—*ack*—lucked into a walk in the—*ack*—park."

Dog lowered his head, bared his teeth, and gave a low warning, "GRRrrrr," seeming to take offense that any patrol would be a walk in the park. Jones, smiling, picked at the chewed nails of his left hand with his right incisor, nodded to Dog, and scribbled in his notebook.

Five minutes after the squad leaders disappeared into their bunkers like subterranean animals to retrieve needed supplies, the twenty-two members, well-adapted to life underground, poked their sweaty heads out of their dens, emerged from the earth, formed up, laid their gear at their feet, and rubbed their eyes, waiting to hear about the day's fun in the sun.

After Pearlman's head count, they all wiped the sweat from their brows and prepared to leave; each man picking up his gear, his buddy helping seat the webbing on his back and checking the other's grenades. Then they lined up in formation—two spaced columns, four men to a squad, each soldier six feet apart, each squad ten to fifteen feet from the next—and headed for the coiled barbed wire gate.

As the squads approached the gate, the guards bounced the concertina wire gates open.

And then it began: fear stole into the soldiers' guts with every step away from the camp. Most soldiers under intense stress feel their anxiety physically; it steals into their neck and shoulder muscles, tightening with every step, until it feels as if their collarbones will snap from the pressure of their upper arms and shoulders pulling up to their ears.

One good omen that day was the arrival of the local refreshment brigade, which was milling around outside of the wire. This was another of the surrealistic aspects of 'Nam. When things were safe, Vietnamese children would follow patrols, walking with their bicycles, loaded with two five-gallon utility cans strapped over each side of the rear tire. In each can was a block of ice and American canned sodas for the young ones to sell to the soldiers. With them present, the men felt like they were in a sort of safety zone. Gun battles or booby traps that killed children were bad publicity for the Viet Cong.

The truth was the VC got the children to tag after the patrols to ensure the platoon did not surprise Charlie.

Herald could never get used to this sort of surreal situation.

Television at the firebase and a cold Coca-Cola on patrol? Why not?

Outside the perimeter, he gave the order to lock and load weapons, an order hardly necessary: they all knew the drill. Dog moved to the point. The patrol walked west as a diversion for half a klick and then doubled back to the southeast of the village, trailing two stealthy bicycle "soda kids."

Vietnam had two seasons: one dry, the other wet—and both hot. The dry season was unbearably hot and filled with dust. Heat was an enemy all by itself. It sucked all energy from the men, leaving them fatigued, mentally and physically, around the clock. Vietnam never cooled off at night. The overheated mind was challenged to think. Even eyesight was affected as the heat waves radiated off the ground, blurring vision.

Not that the rainy season was much cooler, but at least the monsoon rains brought *some* relief. Perhaps relief was an illusion. When it was wet, the humidity was higher, making the lower heat, in the eighties to nineties, seem overbearing—but at least it was wet.

Herald's route, as planned by the CC, was directly down the middle of several large, flat, harvested rice-field complexes surrounded by thick bamboo hedges on all sides. The center of a dry rice field was a perfect killing zone. If troops were in the middle of a rice paddy, Charles, from the comfort of his tree-lined camouflage, could fire on them from all four sides. It was considered bad form to be caught in a perfect killing zone, orders or not.

The CC just wanted to get the job done. It mattered little to him who was in the killing zone, as long as *he* wasn't. This entire area of operations consisted of open fields, about ten acres square and interconnected for irrigation purposes, each surrounded by thick hedgerows of bamboo and palm trees—making any shortcut a safe place for Charles to ambush the soldiers.

Vietnam had wildly divergent topography and land use. The north was mountains and jungle. The coastline, like the Cambodian border, was flat, with rice fields cultivated on a massive scale. In the south was the Mekong River delta, with its intricate and expansive network of waterways.

Herald and his platoon hugged the bamboo hedges surrounding the fields. It was a somewhat longer route, but they'd have cover if they were fired upon from three sides or a close assault, if Charles attacked from the hedge side. The methodology was to charge the ambusher and get clear of the kill zone. Then, after passing through his line, turn and flank the ambusher.

The classic ambush formation was usually only one line of men deep to achieve maximum firepower on the kill zone, making it easy to penetrate. This was the guerrilla warfare manual's answer to, "How do you survive an ambush kill zone?" Everyone prayed never to have to put the answer to the acid test.

With every stride, the men experienced the fear of not knowing when they could be shot, the thought ringing paramount in their minds. Besides considering the possibility of being shot, they had to stay alert for any easy-to-miss, clear-plastic fishing lines connected to something unhealthy, like booby traps. In addition, if the men touched or kicked anything, this, too, could trigger a lethal device. The men remembered never to step on patches of leaves, brush or anything normal looking on the ground in Vietnam; they knew it could very well conceal a pit of upright, sharpened bamboo stakes covered with human feces. There was only one response to the orientation instructor's question, "WHAT'S THE WORD?"

An hour of walking in the heat, while intensely scrutinizing the terrain and eyesight blurring from exposure, strained the platoon's ability to stay focused.

Dog, with his background in hunting armed criminals in the South, proved perfect for the job. He thrived in the heat and humidity and never seemed to lose his cool outside the wire. Dog's hyper-attentiveness was driven by his perceived responsibility for his friend's death.

Herald, stopping after two kilometers and scanning the terrain, dropped to one knee and, from a dry throat, croaked, "Circle; light 'em if you have 'em; ten minutes," the standard OK for everyone to take a break, face outward and, if they smoked, light a cigarette.

Herald took a drink from his canteen and again scanned the fields. He saw nothing except dust, dry clay fields, and dark bamboo hedges looking back at him.

"What is the—*ack*—purpose of this little trip?" inquired AckMan, whose *acks* were less frequent than usual today.

"Routine patrols to keep the day ours and leave the night to them," Herald responded. "If we really wanted to get it right, we should be patrolling at night and let the helicopters have the day. However, our lives would be a lot more exciting if we walked around in the night, with the definitive drawback being that the U.S. Army did not train or equip us for night combat. So, if you want to finish this patrol sometime during this day, saddle up—it's playtime."

Having hit the southernmost checkpoint, Herald radioed in. He took a new compass bearing and headed north to meet the next landmark or the main road to Ta Ninh.

When the patrol was about a football field from the road, Herald saw a convoy of trucks on it. One, a deuce-and-a-half, otherwise known as a two-and-a-half ton truck, stopped, and a lone, unarmed figure jumped out, waved to him, turned, and waved a goodbye-thanks to the driver, and started walking toward the soldiers.

Herald looked around in disbelief that an unknown person would wave to him here and now.

Is this guy insane? He's walking as if he's crossing a cornfield in Kansas on a hot summer day. Where the hell does this Mr. La-di-da think he is?

Being off the main road, this clueless person was unaware of the threat of booby traps—or anything else, for that matter.

Jones walked over to Herald and knelt down, grabbing his notebook from his breast pocket. He sensed this conversation would be unforgettable.

Herald raised his hand to halt the platoon and circled his arm. The men automatically formed a defensive perimeter and knelt down.

As the stranger came within voice range, he spoke. "Hey, guys, I was wondering if I could walk with your patrol back to camp. I have some cigarettes in my bag." He began to fumble with a small green backpack. Jones laughed and continued to write, leaving blood spots from his chewed thumbnail on the note paper.

"Who are you!?" Herald demanded, "and what are you doing here?"

"My name is Peter Paul, and I'm in ROTC at Penn State. After my six weeks in ROTC boot camp next summer, I intend to volunteer for combat. This is my summer break, and I decided to visit Vietnam to see what's in store for me."

Herald coughed, his neck and facial muscles screwing tight. "Are you actually telling me you are not on active duty and came here as a goddamn tourist? This is not an academic exercise, buddy!"

Before Paul could answer, what looked to be a small pile of discarded rice straw located approximately in the middle of the resting platoon went flying up in the air. A Charles, while remaining deep in his spider hole, fired scattershot twenty rounds with his AK-47, the bullets shooting straight up—but neither dampening the effect nor the response of Herald and his platoon. Charles must have panicked, being in the middle of an American patrol in conversation with the tourist.

The entire patrol instantly flopped over from their kneeling position to caress Mother Earth. LeMaire, prone on the ground, set out the tripod of his M60 machine gun. Seeing half the platoon in his gun sights, he yelled in his Maine accent, "*Sacré bleu*, get your ass out my-uh kill zone!"

Another burst of AK-47 fire scratched the sky, but Charles stayed at the bottom of his hole, firing blindly into the air.

Dog gave a "WRRRrr Rot!" and rolled over the nearest rice-paddy wall.

Ferlinghetti's book went flying through the air, and he rolled after Dog, yelling, "*Trombare!*"

Jones rolled on his right shoulder and flipped over the rear paddy berm, sending his notebook into the air, while Pearlman started crawling away from the hole, yelling for everyone to do the same.

LeMaire grumbled, "*Stupide salaud*," grabbed his machine gun, and rolled over the dirt berm with a speed belying someone five-foot-ten and carrying a hairy 260 pounds.

This gook is in the middle of the platoon, Herald thought. *If anyone opens fire, we will kill each other.* Then he yelled, "Nobody open fire, nobody open fire! This is a direct order! Crawl away, crawl away now! If you fire, we will kill each other! Keep crawling! AckMan only—again, AckMan only—throw a grenade, but do not open fire, or you will kill each other!"

AckMan, who was closest to the hole, fumbled to remove a grenade from his vest. All grenades had to be secured with duct tape to prevent accidents. His shaking fingers fumbled at the tape. It would not let go or tear, and he fumbled again without success.

Alternating looking at the grenade and waiting for Charles to jump up to chest height, giving him free range of motion to level his weapon point blank, he unhooked his web belt and pulled the shoulder webbing to his mouth. Tears in his eyes, sweat pouring off his head and soaking the grenade, he tore at the tape with his teeth. At last the grenade came free, and AckMan pulled the grenade safety lever off the steel loop on his shoulder webbing. Hands shaking, he pulled the safety pin. The safety lever pinging off, he threw the grenade and, following the movement of his arm, buried his face in the dirt.

The grenade hit the edge of the hole and bounced in. Just as fast as it went in, it flew out, landing just behind a rice-paddy-berm corner, which, out of sheer luck, shielded the platoon as it detonated with a roar, shaking the ground and sending a cloud of dust twenty feet into the air.

"AckMan, you idiot," Herald yelled, "hold the grenade for two seconds so Charles does not use it to kill us—just as I hope they taught you in basic training!" Herald's ears were ringing, as though someone had plopped a 55-gallon drum over his head and was pounding it with a baseball bat.

AckMan's teeth ripped the tape off a second grenade. Pulling the safety lever off his shoulder webbing's steel loop, he yelled, "*ACK—soooeeee!*" and pulled the pin. The safety lever flipped off with a ping and, with sweat pouring down his face like a waterfall, AckMan counted to two. At two, his trembling hand lobbed the second grenade. As luck would have it, the grenade bounced off the back edge and popped into the hole. Charles was occupied with firing yet another blind burst of AK-47 fire into the air and missed the throw-back option on the grenade. The blast was deafening.

AckMan crawled to the hole, peeked in, and shook his head. *"What is that smell?"* He paused, identifying the source, laughed, and announced, "Chop gook suey, very—*ack*—overcooked."

Jones reached over the berm to grab his notebook, laughed, and wrote, "Chop gook suey. *Jeeez*us, AckMan, you are one sick bastard, comparing the death of a human being to Chinese food." Finishing his journal entry, he closed his notebook, put it back in his pocket, and went over to the hole for a peek.

The smell invaded Jones's nose, causing him to draw back quickly and scowl. Rubbing his nose and sitting on the nearest paddy berm, turning a little green, he belched up some stomach acid and spit the taste out. Dog went by, looked in, and only barked, "Grrh."

As cautious as could be, everyone else rose to one knee and checked the area for other piles of rice straw or anything else that might have been concealing another spider hole. After feeling somewhat secure, they each did a quick body-part inventory.

"ACK—LT, I never thought for a moment a sniper was hidden—*ack*—under that small patch of dried straw. I thought out here in the open we were reasonably safe. By the way, where is the tourist?"

Everyone in the patrol looked around and saw that the only part of the tourist remaining was his small backpack on the ground. The rest of him was a dark spot, running for all he was worth back to the truck; the only distinct body parts were his ass and elbows.

From the vantage point of a helicopter over the sniper hole, the scene would have looked bizarre. The simultaneous diving of twenty heavily armed men in a circle around a central point would have resembled some sort of Olympic synchronized swimming routine—artistic enough to include a dust-cloud stream, like the tail of a capital letter "Q" streaking toward the road—magnificent—scoring tens all around.

"Well, I never saw anything like it—*ack*. The boy changed from human to big-ass—*ack*—bird in flight in record time. *Sooeee!*" AckMan howled as he brushed the dust from his chest and legs.

"Well, I guess he found out what's in store for him next year," Pearlman added, smiling and brushing dust off his shoulder and hip. "Bet he's no longer excited about his upcoming trip to Vietnam."

Dog, pushing his lips together, lowered his head, looked to his right, and gave a "Ruff" in agreement as he brushed himself off. Jones, smiling, made another entry in his fingernail-blood-smeared log about preparing Chinese food using hand grenades.

Ferlinghetti, looking to his left and right, picked up his book and brushed it off. "*Stronzo maiale*," he grumbled, calling the gook a pig turd.

Herald, staying on one knee, shook his head. "This entire place is nothing but weird. It's bizarre enough we watch *Mission Impossible* on a battery-operated TV before we go out on night ambush. If you get shot, there's a good possibility you may see it on the nightly news. But this takes the cake—*a tourist in 'Nam*? Now I've seen everything. Or maybe not. But one thing *is* for sure; if the word gets out, there's going to be a sharp drop in the number of tourists."

Just as he spoke those words, the stupidity of the *GI Joe Coloring Book* flooded his mind: *he* had been a naïve coloring book *tourist* back in college—but at least he had enough brains not to spend part of his summer vacation in a war zone.

The patrol headed back to base camp. As they walked in silence, everyone was thinking the same thing: *Why was Mr. Charles in the middle of a field all alone? Why?*

Herald, sensing the puzzlement of it all, broke the silence. "In guerrilla war manuals about Malaysia and the Philippines, the guerrillas will post one observer to keep an eye on all roads to track troop movements. Charles must have gotten spooked when we were hanging around his observation position in conversation with the tourist."

The lads were still feeling jumpy, so Herald let them feel free to pop off a round at every little thing that spooked them. The fear of the *bullet with their name on it* coming out of nowhere kept consuming everyone's mind. The tourist conversation had taken the entire platoon off guard; Charles, with his uncanny ability to wait until their guard was down, possessed the infinite patience to seize a moment when their focus slipped and take advantage of the situation.

But in this case, good luck had been on their side: being caught off guard had not resulted in the platoon's demise. If the gook had not panicked, he might have been capable of taking them all down—the ultimate nightmare: Charles firing at will at a platoon incapable of defense. Usually, a slip-up like that would mean certain death.

Back at base, the little band unloaded their equipment and, without order, came together to discuss the strange events of the day.

As they arrived, Lt. Chump stopped by to talk to Herald as his own platoon filed by on their way out to an all-night ambush. "Lt. Lloyd, there's a spot I'm going to tag Sir Charles where it will really hurt him: when he is swimming across the river."

"Chump, let me remind you again … our river-patrol boats have a night patrol. When they are on night patrol, they are free to fire on anything for any reason. Do not be next to the river, or you will be sorry."

"Lieutenant, your combat experience is limited. When I was in the Green Berets, we would go wherever the enemy was, not hide where he could slip by."

"Green Berets or not, you are part of a team. This part of the team is to stay away from the river at night unless the river boys are notified."

"It takes too much time to get approval. When the brass sees the results, they will promote me. You just wish you had the idea first."

Self-satisfied with having berated Herald, Chump turned his back on him and continued following his platoon.

One of the physical tolls of being on patrol was the chronic pain from fear creeping into the men's bodies, tension targeting their shoulders, creating knots so severe it felt as if their shoulders were touching their ears. The only way to loosen the muscles and prevent a monstrous headache was by massage.

Almost everyone in the platoon would take turns massaging each other's shoulders. Many times the discomfort of the massage would be so painful, sitting soldiers would bolt upright yelling, "Stop, for God's sake, stop!" running to escape the masseur's infliction of searing agony.

It was quite the sight to see AckMan being dragged behind Pearlman for twenty yards, still hanging with a death grip on Pearlman's shoulders. Pearlman, like all the men, could stand the pain for only so long. With his mind flashing red with agony, his only thought was to flee AckMan's massage. Strange wars breed strange problems and strange solutions.

Just as massage time was winding down and before *Mission Impossible* came on TV, several nearby explosions shattered the quiet. Herald turned to see what seemed like a million tracers shooting up from the river. Sending himself sprawling, he yelled, "Everyone down!" Hardly a necessary command: it was an instinctive reaction. The platoon hit the ground, and food, toothbrushes, and whatever else they had in their hands at the time went flipping into the air. The Wolfhounds' answer to the question, "What's The Word?" went through everyone's mind.

All the support fire teams dropped everything and ran to their stations. This included the 4.2-inch and 82 mm mortar men, or about twenty-five soldiers, as well as the twenty men assigned to the six 105 mm artillery platoon. Simultaneously, the entire base population, nerves on edge, grabbed their weapons and jumped to their posts. They all knew it was out of character for Charles to start an attack before nightfall, while everyone was still awake. After the battalion siren sounded "All Clear," everyone went back to their normal activities, though still a bit on edge.

Herald, by now in the CC's bunker, knelt down and asked, "What the hell was that all about?"

"That idiot Chump!" the CC was raving. "On his own Green Beret bullshit, he went to the river to set his night ambush! He failed to obtain permission from battalion or alert the river-patrol boys. The patrol boats, with their twin 50-calibers, two M60s, and one automatic grenade launcher came up the river early. Chump, the moron, instead of staying low, fired one of the stupid pencil flares he'd bought from a Navy pilot when he was with the Green Berets.

"Well, it just so happens there were no downed Navy pilots in the area, and Charles's signal to start an ambush on the river-patrol boats just happens to *be* a small flare! Chump is lucky he suffered only one killed and two wounded. How *anyone* survived with all the patrol boat's massive firepower is beyond me. Those boys must have really sucked river mud to avoid being massacred. The worst is, Chump survived, and the battalion commander already told me Chump will not be relieved of command. The BC is as full of crap as Chump is! Chump should be court-martialed for direct disobedience of the standing order not to go near the river at night! To compound the felony, as a direct result of Chump's actions, our company suffered one killed and two wounded to *friendly fire*. It makes me wonder if Chump is working for Charles instead of us. How the hell does it make me look?"

"Yeah, CC," Herald agreed as he stood up to leave, "one soldier's poor judgment is bad for all of us." He made a beeline for his section of the firebase, knowing it was going to be a bit hot for anyone unlucky enough to have to hang with the CC tonight.

As he was walking back to his bunker, he noticed LeMaire rearranging sandbags on the side of his bunker steps and arguing with himself. *"Merde!* Sandbaghs not correct to blahk mor'tar shrapht."

Just as Herald passed LeMaire's doorway, a slender, seven-inch green snake came out of the crease between two sandbags. "Bonjour, Monsieur S*naa*ke," cooed LeMaire, as he reached down to touch it. The snake was having none of it. It reared back and spread its neck.

Herald, seeing the snake spreading its neck flange, recognized it was not a harmless green snake, like those in LeMaire's state of Maine, but a baby King Cobra. He grabbed LeMaire by his huge left shoulder muscle, pulled him back and shouted, *"Cobra!"*

LeMaire jumped back and grabbed a steel-head garden rake. Fingering the twelve steel tines, he addressed Herald, "Merci, LT, permisthion to rakgh Monsieur S*naa*ke salaud?"

"Permission to rake granted," Herald nodded back.

LeMaire took the rake and, in a rapid motion, punched the rake teeth into the snake's body over and over again, spitting out the death sentence: *"Acka–acka–acka–acka, au revoir."*

LeMaire struck one last time, taking care to pierce the snake at three points, raised its carcass into the sky, and drove the handle of the rake into the ground over the entry to his bunker. Pulling a black Magic Marker from his pocket, he wrote on half of a cardboard C-ration case lid, "Mauvais Snake," and wired the sign so the head and tail of the snake would dangle over the edges of the cardboard.

Herald put his hand on LeMaire's giant shoulder and confided, "There is something about this country. Everything is so primeval. Today, for instance, as were having lunch, I happened to have an extra piece of chocolate from my C-ration. I saw an ant on the ground and put a piece of chocolate on my finger. The ant moved up my finger and, in the way ants do, appeared to sniff the chocolate. It moved over the choco-late, paused for a moment, then sank its fangs into my finger. I rubbed him out between my thumb and finger very slowly from his tail to his head, to let his death be long and deliberate. The moral is: in this country, even the most benign creature is fixed on blood. What a place to fight a war."

LeMaire, a simple backwoods boy at heart, grunted and saluted his snake. "Welth, très bien, merci, if they wanth to play thath wayh." His sole joy at being assigned the twenty-five-pound machine gun was to announce, "Bonjour, Monsieur Charles, *mangez le* machine gun. *Au revoir, fils de pute.*" As the youngest of his family, he had been assigned the hand-me-down, oldest chain saw, which weighed twice as much as his brothers' chain saws but still weighed less than his machine gun.

Ferlinghetti walked over to admire the snake hanging from the rake and announced, "LT, I 'av' una poema to read-a. OK?"

"Sure, why not? Might as well finish a weird tourist day in the shade of a dead snake with a poem." *This better be good or I will have to kill him.*

Ferlinghetti began to recite.

Don't let that horse
                    eat that violin

cried Chagall's mother

                    But he
        kept right on
                    painting

And became famous

And kept on painting
                    The Horse With Violin In Mouth

And when he finally finished it
he jumped up upon the horse
                    and rode away
        waving the violin

And then with a low bow gave it
to the first naked nude he ran across

And there were no strings
                    attached

(A Coney Island of the Mind: Poems, page 29)

"W'at-a you t'ink-a, LT?"

Herald paused, rubbed his head, and smiled. "I have no idea, but the poem's play on words is fun to ponder. Poetry is the poet's thoughts and the unique way they are put to words. What was the tourist from Penn State thinking to come here on vacation and not understand, in a war zone, there are always strings attached? These strings are with or without giving a violin to the first nude you come across."

"Must-a t'ink-a." Turning to another page in *A Coney Island of the Mind*, written by his namesake, Ferlinghetti slowly walked to his bunker, ever careful to keep one eye on the lookout for police, even in Vietnam.

Jones, after observing the snake body dangling over LeMaire's sign and hearing the poem, smirked and, picking at his canines with the soiled fingernail of his little finger, began writing in his notebook.

YEAR 1988

THEA RETURNED FROM preparing the children for the walk in the park and noticed Herald staring at the wall. Realizing he was lost in a daydream, she crept up behind him, put her mouth close to his ear, and yelled, "Lieutenant, incoming!" Herald jumped. Thea walked away giggling. They held a long tradition where Herald would sneak up and scare her. She would try to return the favor but usually never got him. Today she did.

"OK, OK," he said, a chuckle in his voice, "I'll be ready to leave in two minutes, as long as this trip is short and uneventful. However, let's not use the phrase, 'a walk in the park.' How about something less evocative? 'A family outing in the woods?'"

CHAPTER 8
THE HOME FRONT

HERALD WAS BACK IN HIS LAW OFFICE after a long day in court, Monday, MD 25. Placing his briefcase on the foyer table, he attempted to creep past Deborah's open office door. He got as far as one step when Deborah yelled, "Hey, are you really trying to sneak by me? Get over here. We have lots to talk about."

Curses! Foiled again?

Herald slunk to her desk. Deborah asked three questions on a new client's corporate minutes and gave Herald his telephone messages. She continued talking and gestured for him to reach out his hand to her. He thought this was a signal to hand over some other messages or mail and extended his hand.

Deborah surprised him by grabbing his arm and stapling a yellow post-it note to his shirt sleeve. "Thea begged me to keep reminding you to leave early tonight. You need to attend the March of Dimes Fundraiser; so, rather than staple the note to your forehead … "

Herald gave her a big grin and disappeared into his office.

Later, finishing up his work for the day, he drove the ten-minute commute from the office in Redwood City to his home in San Carlos, singing along to the radio and flicking the note reading "7:30 p.m., March of Dimes

Fundraiser" stapled to his shirt sleeve, kidding himself about being glad it hadn't been stapled to his forehead—or other parts unknown.

The VW van groaned as it climbed the steep incline to his home in the hills. He parked on the one-way street in front of his house, being sure to turn the wheels in toward the curb against the downhill slope.

The house was only 1,200 square feet but designed in a manner reflecting California suburban living: small interior living space with large outdoor playing area. Painted a sunny yellow, it was in high, bright contrast to the neighbors' varying shades of fashionable gray.

Herald opened the van door and stepped out. Memories of their early days there began running through his mind. They had purchased the house when their first child, Katherine, was a year old. Having a home had seemed the most important thing in the world—more so since Thea was pregnant at that time. Herald remembered painting the children's bedroom and decorating the walls with pictures of various cartoon characters. The ceiling was stenciled with maps of the larger constellations.

Recalling those stolen nights when he and Thea would sneak away from the compulsory responsibilities of parenthood made him smile. After the kids had been tucked in and asleep, he would draw a hot bubble bath and retrieve from hiding a chilled bottle of champagne tucked away in the back of the refrigerator and two frosted champagne glasses stashed in the freezer. Snuggling up behind Thea and nuzzling her neck, he would softly inquire, "Want to play?" At the always positive response, Herald would lead her to the bathroom and slowly undress her. Even after the birth of her first child, Thea still had a body to be admired, which Herald never ceased to do. Her ample breasts, thin waistline, and firm rear end were up to swimsuit-model standards, including a tight trim of her private hair.

Herald had always kept the bathwater just a little too hot. The heat would melt away their daytime worries as they eased into the bubbly water, willing their reddened skin to become accustomed to the temperature.

Facing each other, they would sip champagne and talk; their entwined legs, due to the confined space of the tub, never failed to stir physical interest. Recalling further evenings such as these, Herald zeroed in on one in particular:

He envisioned himself taking a sip of champagne and saying to her, "I feel like our daily stresses are suffocating our love life, as if it's being surreptitiously wrapped in clear plastic food wrap."

Sitting up, her breasts rising out of the cover of the bubbles, she took a sip of champagne. "Plastic food wrap?"

He nodded and continued. "You don't realize how the stress of our lives takes the form of plastic wrap and how insidious it is. The first layer of wrap easily sneaks around your head and body. You don't notice it, because you can see through it. But over time, life's stresses generate more layers of wrapping, and they cloud your sexual interest."

"Well!" Thea laughed, "I've heard many attempts to explain how the wear and tear of a long marriage, children, and dual careers diminish a couple's sex life, but as far as I know, plastic food wrap is not one of them."

"Then how else do you explain the gradual loss of our sensuality as we get more and more wrapped up in our lives? ... no pun intended." Leaning closer, he added, "There's good news though: this type of plastic wrap dissolves in a secret combination of bubble bath and champagne."

"Very punny. Very, very punny. We'll just have to see how effective your chemical concoction is at dissolving our food wrap."

Rising from the tub, the bubbles clinging to her breasts and concealing her private parts, she grabbed Herald's outstretched hand to steady her as she stepped out of the tub and onto the bath mat. Standing there dripping, Thea tugged Herald's hand, assisting him up and out.

Standing near her bubbly body, he grabbed a bath towel and took his time patting her dry, paying special attention to the areas that would stimulate her sexually. Thea then dried Herald, taking the same special attention. After finishing, she dropped the towel and grabbed his manhood, remarking, "Well, the plastic-dissolving agent seems to be stimulating at least one part of your anatomy. Let's see how the wrapper dissolver affects our equipment in bed. If there are any problems, I may have to report you to the EPA for creating hazardous waste."

Herald chanted as he accompanied Thea to the bedroom, "That's 'Mr. Hazardous Waste' to you! Wrap-a-wrap-a-wrap ... They call me 'The Happy Unwrapper.'"

Yes, the bathroom and bedroom doors were still ajar, but if they were lucky and quiet, as was most often the case, the night would be theirs. Herald and Thea were unable to rekindle the Fourth of July fireworks of the first days of their relationship, but even after two children, it was still a hell of a good party. Without fail, Herald's familiarity with Thea's tantalizing body allowed him to light her fire and bring her to a sizzle. Thea always wondered if Herald's encounter with Bright had anything to do with his ability to satisfy her. But Bright was a long time ago, before their relationship and far, far away.

Snapping back to the present, Herald approached the house's Dutch door, the top half of which was already open. Pushing the bottom half open and stepping in, he greeted his family with his familiar, Spanglish greeting. "Hola, tribe!" As he put down his briefcase, two California-blond munchkins, ages five and eight, cleared their bedroom door in a youthful frenzy. They ran to greet him, each bearing one of their usual toys. Today, Katherine and Elizabeth were carrrying their respective life-size dolls, each with a birth certificate dangling off one toe. He grabbed a girl in each arm and lifted them to his shoulder height, amid their delighted screams of, "Daddy, don't!"

Giving them each a kiss and setting them back down, where they turned their attention back to their dolls, he went to the kitchen and poured himself a glass of wine in an oversized goblet, stepped into the living room, and sank into the sofa.

Thea, entering from the bedroom and noticing the note dangling from his shirt sleeve, called over to him. "Hello, dear. I see Deborah didn't fail me in reminding you of our social commitment this evening. Be careful of too much wine. Many of our clients will be at the function tonight."

"Yes, dear," he nodded, toying with her. "However, resorting to guerrilla tactics such as stapling notes to my shirt is a bit much. Deborah threatened me with correction fluid if I failed to exit on time."

"Well, we girls have to stick together, you know. After all, except for the staple marks on your shirt sleeve, which will come out in the laundry, there appears to be little damage."

Herald smiled and took a long sip of wine. "When we were dating, I never suspected this dark side of your personality. You need to be reminded: I am a sensitive male, easily startled."

A glint in her eyes, Thea responded. "'Easily startled' is not a term I would ever use for you. But getting back to tonight, this fundraiser is a good chance to have some fun—which, I might add, is something we hardly have time for anymore—and we get to network for business." She flicked her hair—the signal something was bothering her. "And how goes the motion to get us out of hell?"

Herald paused; he first looked at the floor and then at Thea. "Not bad. However, the majority of legal decisions are against us. Just thinking about it makes me ill … But I'm looking forward to the fundraiser, and why not? I need something to break up the stress of my routine. On another note, in that wanton black, silk, spaghetti-strap, tight slip of a dress, you look wild enough to taunt the natives!"

"Thank you for noticing," she said, blushing just a bit. Then whispering in a low tone, to keep the kids from overhearing, she added, "Sometimes being the managing law partner, wife, and mother exhausts me."

A knock at the front door grabbed her attention. Turning to it, she saw the babysitter from up the street standing at the Dutch door, waved her in, pointed to the girls' bedroom, and signaled to take them back to the kitchen. "Dinner's on the table. We should be back early."

The sitter, used to the drill, took control of the bouncing children and started herding them to the table.

Herald, still feeling playful, drawled, "Yes, Mistress. I be moving, Mistress," and rose from the sofa, leaving Thea to handle last-minute instructions about bedtime.

Taking another sip of wine, Herald walked to the bedroom to dress for the occasion. He placed his large glass of wine on the nightstand, went to the closet, and pulled out a suit hanger to hang up his jacket. He finished undressing, hung the pants beneath the jacket, and placed the suit in its assigned section of the closet. Nearby, in a heavy plastic storage bag, was his tuxedo.

Removing the coat from the hanger, he draped it on the bed. The jacket fell open, exposing his embroidered nametag on the interior pocket. Plopping down to sit on the bed, he took a deep breath and stared at the jacket with eyes frozen wide. His recurring stress, banging for release from his Vietnam mental jail, intensified. Seeking shelter from the threat, his mind took him on a flying-carpet ride back to Vietnam.

YEAR 1969

AFTER BEING THERE for six months, he was allowed one week of R&R in one of several designated areas. Australia, Taiwan, Hawaii, and Bangkok were just a few of the choices. His only wish was to be away from Vietnam during Christmas and New Year's Eve of 1969. The destination matching his wish was Taiwan.

Herald's memories sprung again to his first meeting Grate while on the helicopter ride from Cu Chi to the Tan Son Nhut Air Base, where they both had several hours to kill until their next flights: Grate's to Australia, Herald's to Taiwan.

The lads were in awe of this aspect of Vietnam; in various places, there actually was some semblance of normality! As they walked off the flight line, they passed through a real airport terminal, small but neat. At the counter, a clerk checked their names to process the orders necessary to go on R&R and directed them to the weapons-storage facility, where they were to check in their weapons prior to departure. Heavily armed tourists were frowned upon in foreign countries.

"You have to love the United States Army," Herald joshed. "They may be short on the luxuries in the bush, but the lavish support when you leave is to be admired."

"I must say I agree," Grate drawled. "As a country boy, I could appreciate this opportunity more if I had just a few of the resources I see around here to use out in the … field."

"Well, we're not in the field now, so let's enjoy our brief time 'in the rear with the gear.'"

After receiving their orders, they headed to the terminal exit. The first thing both noticed was that the sidewalk was made of asphalt, not dirt. The road leading from the terminal also was asphalt.

"My God!" Herald exclaimed. "We're not kicking up any red dust!"

Next to the terminal was the weapons depot. The tight, clean-scrubbed appearance of the building stunned the boys. Leading to the front door on each side of the asphalt sidewalk was a lawn ten feet square, mowed in an immaculate fashion. The walkway was lined with the standard, odd-shaped rocks painted white used back home to enhance military-base landscaping.

A polished plywood counter was the first thing they noticed upon entering the building. On the wall behind it was a locked cabinet storing weapons organized in neat rows. Herald and Grate had not seen a building, let alone a clean, organized one, for six months.

Walking further in, they spotted an enlisted man in tailored fatigues sitting in a swivel chair with his legs outstretched, ankles crossed, and heels on top of a large metal desk, chatting on the phone. The man turned and waved his hand, motioning them to sit on the couch behind them.

Overwhelmed by the comparative luxury of it all, Herald turned and sat, rubbing a hand on the armrest. "Wow! A real couch!"

Grate, not so pleased, and pulling rank, went up to the counter, placed his weapon on it, and, in his slow—but now loud—drawl, bellowed, "Private

Wo-o-orm, I ... presume? Drop the phone, get off your rear-echelon ass, and salute the officers in front of you ... *now!*"

The private dropped the phone onto its hook and swung around in his chair, his eyes widening as he surveyed Grate standing there with no rank, filthy, his hand on the M16 with a bullet hole in the stock—resting on *his* shiny counter. The M16 recoil spring dangled from the side of the stock where the bullet had gouged a large hole.

The private stood and saluted. "What may I do for you gentlemen from the wet country?"

Grate, in his almost-Georgia pace of conversation but now less loud, continued. "It is not what we ... want, but what is required when leaving the country on ... R&R. Check in our ... weapons. You are the weapons clerk ... no?"

"Weapons clerk, yes," the private replied, now smiling and nodding.

"See, Herald, stay in this country long enough and you resort to speaking Pig English and ... nodding."

The embarrassed private reached across to the wall on his left, on which hung ten clipboards in neat arrangement. He picked one off with his left hand and, with his right, selected a pen from a cup on his desk and moved to the counter. Grate couldn't help but notice the neatness with which everything was placed; it gave him a further clue into the mind of this clerk.

Without looking at Grate, the private asked, "What corps are you from, sir?"

Grate turned and looked over to Herald. "What corps are we ... from?"

Herald rubbed his chin and looked at the ceiling. "I only know our battalion and company. We are west from Cu Chi, or east, from your point of view on this side of the world, near the Parrot's Beak in Cambodia. I'm so far down the ladder and out in paddy paradise, the question of what corps is just not relevant."

Grate turned back to face the clerk. "Well, you heard it, no corps ... info. Next ... question?"

"Well, you officers fill out the forms … there's one for each of you on the clipboard … and I'll attempt to locate your corps." He put the clipboard and pen on the counter and slid them toward Grate. Turning, he went to the map of Vietnam on the back wall. As he reviewed it, he asked, "Are there hills and jungle, or is it wet?"

Looking over to Grate, Herald responded, "More wet than jungle and no hills except for one. The entire area is under cultivation, with interconnected rice fields. The fields are all surrounded by bamboo and vegetation hedges." Grate nodded approval of the description.

"You did say west of Cu Chi, yes?"

"Yes," Grate sighed, as he clarified the location for the clerk.

Approaching the counter, Herald pumped his Browning shotgun to clear any ammo and laid the weapon on it. The rear stock had been sawed off, leaving only a pistol grip. He and Grate took turns filling out the required information and placed the clipboard and pen back on the counter.

Turning away from the map, the clerk announced, "Got it! You guys are in III Corps."

Herald handed the shotgun ammunition to the clerk, who placed it in a bin beneath the counter. The clerk then picked up the shotgun by the pistol-grip handle, admiring the unique modification. He pointed it around the room, noting the ease with which the deadly weapon could be directed in a small space, like the space afforded while sitting in a vehicle. He turned and placed it down on the desk. Grabbing a rag, he wiped his hands clean of the clay dust he'd gotten from the Browning; then he lifted it from the desk and wiped away the dust it had shed.

"Do you feel better, knowing what corps you are in?" the clerk asked Grate.

Grate looked at the fluorescent light on the ceiling, whistled, and sighed. "No."

"Me, neither," added Herald.

Grate handed his damaged M16 to the clerk.

With the weapon in his hands, the fastidious clerk examined the bullet hole. Then the recoil spring caught his attention. It was bobbing up and down from the motion of the transfer from Grate.

"This weapon's shot," he remarked, placing it on the desk, noting the serial number and dropping it into a disposal bin. Then, grabbing a clipboard with the weapons checklist on it, he turned to face Grate. "It appears you have destroyed government property. I will have to make a report, and you will be required to pay for the weapon."

Grate reached over the counter and, with his large hand, grabbed the clerk's throat, lifting him to his tiptoes. "To you," he hissed, "my weapon is but a tool for a simple country ... lad. To me, my weapon has taken on a godlike ... aura. The aura was imparted when it took a Charles bullet for ... me. A little respect is in order if you wish to remain in a healthy ... condition."

Leaning over, Herald cupped his hand over Grate's ear and whispered, "If you are in the stockade for abusing this moron, you will miss your freedom bird! Besides, your favorite weapon in the whole wide world would be easy to repair in the field, even if the stock and recoil spring were damaged. You could resurrect this baby and, if there were no other choices, exchange it back in the field for a new one and be free to accord your sacred M16 a proper funeral."

Grate unlocked his grip from the clerk's throat, and the hapless clerk went crashing to the floor. "Treat my weapon like it was your mother, if you want to keep both your ... ears. I expect my weapon to be here when I return, or you will experience line ... justice."

Herald took Grate by the arm and started to lead him away. "Easy, boy, easy. It is time for us to move on in a more genteel fashion. Threatening a petty bureaucrat is a leading indicator that this entire experience has really overloaded your circuits."

"Yes, you are right, my friend. Time for a long, long, hot, hot ... shower."

Herald looked up, cocked his face to the left, and, joking, simpered, "Thought you would never ask, you brute!"

The next stop was the officers' transient barracks and that long, hot shower. The boys luxuriated in the steaming spray for at least an hour, their skin wrinkling from the excessive moisture. In the surging water, they soaped up and rinsed off over and over again, repeating and repeating, soaping and rinsing, to clear off the dirt and stench of the field. A normal shower in the field was taken under a half-filled, five-gallon water can with a perforated bottom hung on a rack of wood two-by-fours. Showers were permitted just once a week—not much for power cleaning in a world of dust.

Living underground in a bunker in Vietnam—walls of clay and two or more levels of sandbags as a roof—resembles living in a poorly built sod house of the American Midwest in the 1800s. A fine dust coats the inside of the nose and mouth and settles in everything, accumulating everywhere. As an added bonus during the rainy season, it becomes pure goo.

After showering, Herald and Grate were issued new uniforms. The two men each were about five-feet-nine and stocky, but the generic medium-size uniforms supplied were for taller men. Herald and Grate looked clown-like in their oversized fatigues. Ignoring that detail, they pinned on their rank and strutted in their clean clothes.

Herald looked in the mirror and then turned to Grate. "I now appreciate how much better one looks in tailored fatigues, like the ones I had in Germany. When I get back to the good ol' USA, I promise to always tailor my clothes. Still, I feel *almost* human in these rags."

"You may be many things, Herald," Grate sneered, "but human is the last noun anyone would use for ... you. There was a species of ancient man that died ... out. What were they called ... Neanderthal?"

"Maybe so, but at least people note my more humanoid qualities, an observation most fail to see in your life form, which leans more toward the weasel species."

"Enough of this banter! To the Officers' Club, bub, for what I hope is a better excuse for the concept of ... food." Checking out his new uniform in the mirror, he boasted, "Pretty snazzy ... eh?"

"If you were not a man, I would date you in a second. You are truly a fine example of a well-dressed warrior. To the pub, bub, where we will consume spirits and sustenance."

The boys wandered out of the barracks and onto the well-maintained streets surrounded by mowed lawns and painted rocks—the exact opposite of anything they'd experienced daily in their drab, earthen, sandbag-and-barbed-wire world.

A strange sensation swept over Herald; everything seemed dreamlike; he was there, but he had the sense that something was just not right.

I don't get it. How could this part of Vietnam be so distant from the war?

"Grate, my man, it appears we have entered military heaven, with no war and where the three maxims apply: if it moves, salute it; if it's movable, pick it up; and if it's immovable, paint it. If I'm overwhelmed by a big Army base as an incomprehensible experience, I'm not sure I'll ever be ready to deal with going home."

"Well," Grate drawled, "*I* intend to give going home one *hell* of a ... try."

They walked past the Olympic-size swimming pool and the bowling alley, and, after obtaining directions, arrived at the main officers' mess hall. The entrance was up six levels of immaculate white stairs that led to a porch of what appeared to be an antebellum mansion, complete with white pillars. Enormous front double doors befitting a Southern plantation made an elegant entry to a large dining room and, behind it, an elaborate bar and lounge.

As they approached the bar, it became apparent they were very underdressed. Everyone else was wearing civilian clothes or tailored, starched fatigues, and sporting fresh haircuts—and looking far more civilized than either Herald or Grate.

Even the bartender was an American. He gave them a long look and, in an insulting tone, as though speaking to some lower life forms, asked, "You boys just off the boat?" Then he turned and laughed over his shoulder.

In his level, monotone voice, Grate answered, "Why, yes; whatever gave you that ... idea?"

Even though he'd known Grate only two hours, Herald smelled trouble. His senses had been honed to the nth degree in the field to sense dangerous emotions in well-armed people. Herald perceived Grate's recent assault on the weapons clerk as indicative of imminent trouble—something Herald wanted to avoid at all costs. After all, the entire point of going on a one-week R&R was *to leave.*

"Grate, my newly acquired friend, let us partake of the amenities in a *peaceful fashion* and look later for a more hospitable club."

"*Hnh!* The enlisted son of a bitch is looking at us as if we are … weird! *Us!* We are the only people here with any idea of what crap this war really … is."

"Well, from my view, we are in the distinct minority here and only passing through. So let us just do that and, later, find a more enjoyable club, with a band. I am really looking forward to a real meal—one without violence."

Spitting on the floor, Grate began to hiss again. "Are you just going to let the REMF talk to us that … way?"

"Yes, the 'Rear Echelon Mother Fucker' gets his say today, as we have other fish to fry in foreign lands, and this snobbish, delusional bartender is not going to derail my desire for a steak dinner on a white tablecloth, with a white napkin and red wine."

Grumpier still, Grate asked, "Is he keeping both … ears?"

"Yes, both ears and all other body parts intact, as well. We are not going to quibble over partial retaliation, are we?"

"OK, but just this … once. *Next* time, *some* body part must be … removed. That is country justice at … work."

Patting Grate on the back, Herald added, "Let us hope the only 'next time' you're insulted will be when you are back in the world and such a callous remark will not constitute even a minor infraction for a country boy to take action. Being in the shit for six months can alter your attitude, subsequently encouraging bad behavior."

"Bet your … bippy!" Grate shot back, laughing. "Let us adjourn this unfriendly bar for the dining … room. I will enjoy using a fork and knife for something other than desperate tools of last resort if I'm out of …

ammunition." Grate spun on his heel, and both men headed for the dining room.

The meal was grand. Accustomed to eating from their stainless-steel mess kits, dining with white china plates by itself was gourmet even before the food was served. In high spirits, they started with a bottle of white wine, to quench their thirst and marvel at their ability to have *fresh* green salads. Next they enjoyed two bottles of red, paired with their done-to-perfection medium-rare steaks, string beans, and baked potatoes. The more Herald ate and drank, the more he felt he'd become a character in an *Alice in Wonderland* sequel. Raising his wine glass and letting his hyperactive muse run wild, he sang the tea party's *Unbirthday* song as a toast to his dinner partner: "A very merry unbirthday to you, and a very merry unbirthday to me."

"Sing that one more time," Grate cautioned Herald, pointing the end of his steak knife at him, "and you'll never make it back ... home!"

The irony in Grate's warning was the realization that this war experience would be a permanent operating part of their psyches; for good or bad, it was a new concept. Everyone had heard stories about the guys who *went* home but could never really *go* home.

After demolishing their dinner, though they tried to find time to appreciate it, the boys went outside. Upon inquiring of an enlisted man as to where they could fine a good club with a band, they were directed to an outside part of the base. Approaching the club, they heard music rolling through the muggy, sweltering night air; the band's garbled music crescendoing as they neared. The club's garish neon sign pulled them in like a lighthouse beacon in the night.

"Can you believe ... it?" the amazed Grate observed, speaking in a cadence worthy of a New Orleans gentleman, "they actually have lights at ... night!"

Not fully at ease, Herald checked it all out. "Lights will never make me feel any easier about this place. I still feel under the gun."

"Herald, the trouble with you is, you need to learn to let ... go. Take me, for example, or, better yet, let's take someone who could let ... go, or ... oh, the hell with it—let's just go in and experience a real nightclub in the land of ... 'Nam."

A heavy-framed military policeman at the door noticed their new, untailored uniforms—a clear indication of their recent reclamation from the field—and advised the two to be on good behavior. Herald and Grate, assuring the officer everything would be just fine, moved through the crowd and found a booth.

Spotting a waitress, they waved her over. The waitress, a French-Vietnamese, and quite pretty, spoke in tortured English, the way Asians pronounce American words. "What you want, GI ... Numbah One Viet beer, BA-MA-BA, 33, you call 'Tiger Piss'? American beer only 3.2. Or maybe hard stuff?"

Herald turned to Grate. "*Viet beer?*" Grate shrugged and nodded approval. Herald looked back at the waitress. "Viet beer? What is Viet beer? They make beer in the middle of a war? I had real beer during my tour in Germany, but I did not expect a local beer here."

"Yes," Grate sneered while raising two fingers of his hand to the waitress, "it appears the U.S. presence has spawned many enterprises, even in this war-torn wasteland of ... poverty."

While waiting for the beers, they observed the band was a show unto itself. The instruments had seen better days. So had the musicians, improvising American tunes the best they could. The band consisted of four men, all Vietnamese, who together could not have weighed more than 400 pounds. How these diminutive people could be such good fighters was a mystery. Of course, when the first Cape buffalo in Africa was approached by a man with a rifle, the buffalo was unconcerned as well, until the first bullet hit. It does not take size to pull a trigger.

The one haunting memory of the night, as these ostensible musicians attempted to play popular songs, was the singers' pronunciation, or more to the point, *mispronunciation* of the words. The lyrics were so distorted by warped words; the distortion symbolized what was wrong in this country. The misuse of English signaled that the United States and South Vietnam were not on the same wavelength, so how could they fight a war together?

After about an hour's worth of loud, very bad music, both Herald and Grate agreed they'd had enough of what sounded like cats fighting. Rising from their chairs, they left money for the check and decided to return to the Bachelor Officers' Quarters for a romp on another treasured aspect of civilian life—*clean sheets*.

Full of good cheer, they left the bar and, in near unison, yelled, "Merry Christmas and a Happy New Year—we're OUT of this country!"

As they hurried away through the steaming, sodden air, the music and distorted words sung by the band echoed the theme song for the war in Vietnam and into their ears:

> Ve gotta get out of thes pace,
>   if it's the last thing ve ever do!
> Ve gotta get out of thes pace,
>   A bettar life for me and you.

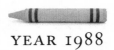

YEAR 1988

THE TAP—TAPPING of Thea's high heels on the hardwood floor jerked Herald back to the present. The clock showed he had been cruising down memory lane for five minutes. He should have been dressed by now. The simple stress of getting caught daydreaming, and not being ready on time, triggered his chest muscles to tighten with an ever-stronger urgency.

CHAPTER 9
MARCH OF DIMES FUNDRAISER

HERALD TIMED STANDING UP and picking up his bow tie from the bed with Thea's arrival—anything to conceal his romp back into history. He paused to admire his spouse of fifteen years. She was stunning, even after two kids, in her short black dress fitting her body in a revealing fashion. He twirled the tie in his left hand and gave her his little-boy-lost smile. One of the first things Thea agreed to do for him after they were first married was to knot his bow tie.

Thea picked the tie from his open hand; then, reaching her arms up and running the tie around his neck collar, she gave it a few quick, deft strokes and tied the elusive knot. Leaning back, cocking her head, and winking at him, she inspected the tie, gave it a little twist, and nodded her approval. All done, she reached behind him and gave him a pat on the rump.

"At your age," she teased as she turned to walk out, "you really need to learn how to do this for yourself. We must leave soon if we intend to have dinner." The receding tap-tap-tap of her high heels on the hardwood floor echoed in the empty-sounding bedroom.

Viewing himself in the closet-door mirror to inspect the tie job, he called out to her in the next room. "Nice work, but don't quit your day job. Ready in two."

Turning to the bed, he reached to pick up his tuxedo coat. As he grasped it, the bright-red inside label fell into view. It read, "Sam Shen's Tailor & Co. formerly in Shai China, Hong Kong, and Taiwan." Above the manufacturer's label was the familiar black silk label, with "Herald R. Lloyd" embroidered on it in red thread.

His forehead flushed as he was hit by a strong wave of memories: vivid visions of another woman and how he came to purchase this tuxedo on his Vietnam R&R in Taiwan. Herald's rent-a-woman for a week, Bright, had taken him to the tailor, where it was handmade to his exact measurements as a Christmas gift to himself.

Every time he saw this red label, it served to memorialize the absurdity of attempting to relax on a one-week vacation from the war zone, knowing he had to go back.

In Vietnam, he'd longed to return to the simple, safe, civilian college life. Away from Vietnam, any life looked good. He laughed at himself for having had this tuxedo made. What brashness to presume he would survive to wear it.

Sitting down on the bed again, he looked out the window and was swept back to the day before Christmas, walking off the plane in Taipei, Taiwan, the last refuge of the Chinese Nationalists when they lost the civil war to the Chinese Communists in the 1950s.

YEAR 1969

IT HAD BEEN a three-hour flight, no booze, no movie. The plane taxied to the terminal and jarred to a stop. The cabin door opened, and the portable steps were rolled up to the aircraft and locked in place. An eerie quietude permeated the interior of the plane as everyone rose from their seats and filed out. Stopping in the doorway of the Boeing 707 jetliner, Herald looked around, adjusting to the light while taking in the sights, sounds, and aromas of this new world.

The first thing to catch his eye was the six-foot-high, bright-red-lettered sign, "Chiang Kai-shek International Airport," beaming over the terminal. Hanging heavy in the damp heat, but nowhere as oppressive as Vietnam, the smells in the airport air were of jet fuel and Chinese-restaurant cooking oil. To Herald, those first breaths of air outside Vietnam smelled intoxicating, jet fuel or not.

Herald descended the stairs and walked the tarmac toward the terminal. Stopping after a few steps, he looked at the airport terminal sign again and tapped one foot on the ground, just to make sure he was not dreaming; the concept of being alive felt surreal. He continued to the terminal and opened the door, only to see a mountain of 100 or so drab-olive-green duffel bags, belonging to other soldiers from his plane on R&R, piled yards high.

Ah yes, only the best baggage handlers for the U.S. Army.

A Marine in the crowd from the plane shouted, "OohRah!" and scrambled to the top of the heap, picking up one bag and yelling the name stenciled in white paint on the side. One of the first items of business for a military man is to stencil his name, using white or black paint, on his duffel bag. As each soldier answered to his name, his bag was thrown down to him. Some bags were caught; others hit the floor with a dull thud.

Grabbing his own duffel bag, Herald walked to the door to the outside. The noises penetrating through the door hinted at a far-different world from the one he'd just left. Hesitating, he broke into a light sweat at the prospect of dealing with the drastic changes.

Well, I can't just stand here all day. Let's just do it!

The instant he stepped through the portal, he became overwhelmed by all the peculiar clamoring and exotic smells of civilization in Taiwan. In front of the terminal awaiting all the GIs with money and no plan were eager, frantic groups of hustlers hawking—in no particular order—hotels, women, wine, song, and dance. The backdrop of this marketing madness was a cacophonous blur of densely packed, two- and three-story cement buildings, streets crowded with moving vehicles of every type, traffic horns blaring, and the conflicting odors of Chinese cooking and vehicle and factory exhausts.

Falling into a protective trance, he asked himself, *Can this be real? If it is, I might as well play the role. What do I have to lose? In six days, I'll be back in Vietnam. Who knows if I'll make it out of there again?*

Before Herald could take one step out to hail a cab, he felt a strong hand grab his arm. He spun around and grabbed the assailant's arm to rip his hand off, when he perceived the man's broad smile. A local in his fifties, with pockmark scars extending across his face and wide blunt nose, his expansive smile revealed the deep blackness of rotting teeth.

After recovering from being startled by both physical and visual assaults, Herald discerned the cheap Hawaiian-style shirt and blue jeans the man was wearing.

"I Sunny, GI!" he hollered. "Here help have good time. Know good hotel and plenty women." His breath smelled of something Herald would *never* put in his own mouth, if indeed Sunny's foul breath was caused by food.

Looking around at the other GIs who were engaged in similar discussions, Herald shook his head in disbelief.

Hell, why not let Sunny remind me how to have a good time?

It might not have been his real name; but now, in this surreal foreign land, Herald didn't care what the man's real name was.

Sunny waved him onto a small, ancient school bus with about ten other GIs. The old bus starter emitted a painful screech as the engine came alive with a cough of diesel smoke and clacking of old, loose engine valves. The driver pushed in the clutch and, with a hellacious metal-grinding noise, forced the transmission into first gear. Herald tensed and shuddered as the clutch engaged. With a burst of black diesel exhaust, the group was off to the Imperial Hotel in downtown Taipei.

Back in the 1960s, Taipei was only starting to become an economic giant. The Imperial Hotel, likely built by the British in the 1930s, had seen better days, but it was clean. Most important to Herald, it was not in Vietnam. The lobby was about fifty by fifty yards square, with a high, stamped-tin ceiling, stained yellow by mildew, cigarette smoke, and age. Dark wood paneling on the walls was covered in a light film of something sticky that obscured the grain and cried out to be washed off. On the right was a large bar; on the left was a small convenience store offering sundries, American toothpaste, and newspapers.

Sunny had the program down pat. First stop was to check in. The clerk spoke decent English and had a room on the tenth floor overlooking something Herald could not understand but was reputed to be very good. As Herald signed the register, Sunny was right at his side, tapping like an impatient woodpecker on his arm, as if hastening to close the deal. His repulsive smile and touch gave Herald the creeps.

Sunny pointed to the bar on the opposite side of the lobby. Herald, giving Sunny a half-baked smile, moved his arm to stop the annoying tapping and returned his gaze to the clerk. The clerk closed the register log, grinned, and gave Herald the biggest hotel key he had ever seen, with a long, wide, brass handle. It must have weighed half a pound. Fantasizing it was the key to a foreboding dungeon in Dracula's castle made him chuckle. The size and weight prohibited any attempt to steal it. Herald put the key in his front pocket, making a conspicuous bulge.

Sunny's group of GIs was huddling around one table in quiet conversation. Joining them, Herald chose to sit in a chair at the back—a safe distance from Sunny's dragon breath. He looked around the table at his fellow refugees and nodded. They nodded back, but before any conversation could be initiated, Sunny began shouting what seemed to be a command, in Chinese.

Fifteen women came filing out from behind a paper divider and stood in a line. All were very young, pretty, slight, and very Asian.

Turning to the men, Sunny began his spiel. "Pick girl now, any girl you want. Pick two or even three! Special deal on more than two, today only! All are inspected by government every six months."

Herald's mind began to cave in on itself. The Western concept of dating, attraction, and the ritual of meeting someone new to woo into a sexual experience were all thrown out the window.

OK, when in the Orient, do as the Orientals do. I'll take number two. Maybe the government should be inspecting Sunny every six months, instead of the girls.

His choice was a petite, lovely young thing named Bright, five-foot-four in four-inch-high heels, and weighing, at most, 100 pounds dripping wet. With her glitter-filled acrylic shoes sparkling in any light, a short, sleeveless, embroidered, red silk dress closing high at her neck and clinging to every curve of her body, and a skip to her walk, causing her body to bounce in an energetic, sensual manner, she was a beauty to behold—and enjoy.

Herald never thought to ask if "Bright" was a "nom de trick" or the young woman's real name. But who needed real names? This was just another bizarre dream, and he had only six days to live it.

She looked him over and gave a knowing smile of experience with American GIs. Herald looked the perfect example of shell shock, with bewilderment dominating the conflicting emotions on his face.

Bright wasted no time in making this a fun date; otherwise, this GI might find *another* fun date. Her eyes signaling self-assurance, she walked over to Herald, grabbed his arm, pulled him from the chair, and, arm in arm, headed him to the bar, her little skip intoxicating him as they walked.

At the bar, she turned to face him and, with a practiced air, hopped up on the tall bar stool and crossed her legs; the slit on the right side of her dress opened, exposing the smooth, honey-olive skin of her thigh and the muscular curve of her legs.

Men's magazines aside, this was more female flesh than Herald had seen in months—and she was *the real deal.* He was entranced by the way she'd lifted one knee a little higher when hopping up and sliding onto the stool, allowing her tight dress to adjust to a seated position and not hike up. Bright's simple act of sitting showed her grace and hinted at her power: the warm secret between her thighs.

Caught staring at her legs, Herald felt a slight flush of embarrassment coming over himself. Diverting his glance upward, he became transfixed on her long, black, shimmering hair that smelled of jasmine. Her brown eyes sparkled with verve, yet hinted at a sadness in having to work in this oldest of professions.

Herald became confused. His feelings seemed disconnected and far off, as if behind some protective shield one develops in a combat zone—an acrylic barrier in his mind, allowing him to see everything but preventing him from feeling what he was experiencing. He bit his right index finger, to make sure this was not a dream, and reflected on his difficulty to feel anything but numbness:

Maybe this protective shield is the price you pay to keep your sanity when people are trying to kill you and you're hoping to return the favor.

Bright, seeing Herald bite his finger, waved her hand to the bartender, who was wearing a comic, oversized, worn hotel uniform, in the style of a British red silk foxhunting jacket. "Bahtendah, over here, have Numbah One GI, need help." Her English was broken, with a corrupted accent that seemed to pervade the speech of everyone in Asia.

Turning to Herald, in a low, sexy tone, Bright whispered, "First time with party girl?" She eyed his hotel room key and his bulging pants; then she fixed her eyes on his. "Look like you are happy to see me. We have good time … make love long, long time. You forget war. Me have boyfriend in Vietnam. Marine. He come back after war; he tell me make me his wife. I have picture."

Prostitute, boyfriend, wife, jasmine … It was all too much. Leaning over the bar with both hands, Herald ordered. "Whiskey, rocks! What brands you stock?"

The bartender, seated on a small stool with one foot on the bar sink, turned to Herald and, with the expected twang in his English, replied, "Old Crow, Old Grand-Dad, Jack Daniel's, Heaven Hill."

"Heaven Hill in Taiwan?"

"GIs come here many years for R&R. Many love bourbon, so we stock."

Herald shook his head in disbelief; his favorite brand of whiskey available in the wilds of the Orient. This trip was looking up. "Heaven Hill over ice, please—make it a double, and a bottle for my room, OK?"

Laughing, the bartender answered, "Better than OK. Why we stock, GI. You may take now. Pay on hotel bill or cash."

Herald reached into his back pocket and pulled out the resealable plastic bag that held his wallet. Removing the wallet, he crumpled the bag, left it on the bar, and whispered, "Won't need protection from the moisture on R&R."

As he opened the wallet and peered inside, the thought came over him: this little plastic wallet and the dog tags hanging from his neck comprised his entire identity, his legacy. The thin, two-sided wallet held his ID card on one side and money on the other. He looked up at the bartender: "Cash now. How much? You take American?" Herald fingered his dangling dog tags, looked again at the wallet, and shook his head. *No, not much of an empire.*

"We take anything; twenty dollar for bottle, five for drink. American good."

Herald peeled off two $20 bills and placed them on the bar. "You just may have brought me back from the walking dead. Thank you. Keep the change."

Herald turned his head and checked out the bar and the tables. All clean, but the signs of aging were everywhere: tears in the vinyl of the bar stools; stains and worn spots in the carpeting; nicks in the teakwood bar and tables telling of many years of service.

After Herald's drink was served, Bright chimed in. "You very lucky to have Bright. Other girls not care for GI as much as I do. You finish drink; we take bottle and go upstairs."

Herald was spellbound by her; the bourbon was starting to have an impact. The world seemed warmer and his emotional detachment less threatening. This first-time venture into paying for sex was generating a hunger. Raising his glass in the air and savoring the last drop, he let one ice cube escape into his mouth for his tongue to play with. One thing for sure, he was going to do everything possible to forget about going back.

Bright slid to the front of her stool and, before he could raise his arms to help her down, laughed and jumped off. He caught her, and her long, soft hair brushed over his face. Just the feel of someone soft and fun started an electric fire in his mind, and sexual energy shot through his body.

Bright grabbed the bottle off the bar and, giving him an inviting hug, whispered, "Time for us to go upstairs." Now, maybe he could rediscover some of the emotions he'd left stateside, and maybe, just maybe, this was the person to help him do it.

Herald and Bright rushed back to the registration desk. He picked up his duffel bag, pulled the strap over his right shoulder, and ushered her to the elevator. Stepping inside, their combined weight caused the car to slide a good three inches toward the rear wall of the elevator shaft. The doors jarred closed and the car rose, bouncing from one shaft wall to the other, all the way up ten floors.

Shit, man, this thing is scary.

He grasped the car handrail and, sighting the thin metal floor, imagined the fatal damages from a ten-floor drop.

Oh, well ... Let's see ... The epitaph on my tombstone will read "Died with whore in shady Oriental hotel elevator accident." Mom would be so proud.

The elevator clanged to a stop, snapping the cables and jiggling the car. Bright stumbled, and her shoulder brushed against Herald. He used his arm to steady her.

"Hotel need new elevator; GI not need more excitement on baahcation."

The doors hesitated and, with a double clunk, rumbled open. The pair stepped out of the elevator, and it swung to the back wall with a resounding *crrrunch*. Arm in arm, they walked down the long, dimly lit hallway to his room. Removing the oversized key from his pocket, he hefted it and marveled again at the size.

This thing is as good as any small weapon. Who knows? Might come in handy.

Unlocking the door and pushing it open, he gave a wink to Bright.

Oh, man, home for one week. Yeah!

Bright winked back at him and skipped inside. Herald followed right along, swinging the door shut and locking it.

Once inside, Bright wrapped her arms around his neck and kissed him with tenderness, at the same time easing the duffel bag off his shoulder and letting it fall to the floor with a soft thud. Without looking—and with the expertise of one who knew every inch of the room and the exact location of its furniture—she placed the bottle of bourbon on the small table next to the door. Not one to waste time, she unbuttoned and unzipped his pants and let them slide to the floor.

This was new territory for Herald. *I've never been with a prostitute before. Everything in my current life, from the war zone to this, is new; time to let go and go with the flow—what the hell.*

Kissing her with lightness, he moved his lips around hers, searching. After several minutes, he guided his tongue with gentleness, parting her lips and entering her mouth, his tongue touching hers with keen delicacy. She returned his touch. Her jasmine perfume caused his mind to spin, as did the feel of her body—the most sensual he could remember.

He ran his hands slowly up and down her back, kneading her muscles through the thin silk dress. A hunger for soft companionship was rising up in him like a volcano. Respectful and shy, he took his time to maneuver his right hand to the zipper at the back of her collar; his fingers toyed with the zipper pull tab for a minute, as if to request her permission.

After a moment, he eased the zipper down until it stopped at the small of her back. Then, slipping his right hand inside her dress, he explored her nakedness and soft skin. His left hand reached around and nudged the top of the dress off her right and left shoulders, allowing it to fall to her waist and expose her small, firm breasts. He returned his left hand to her back.

His right hand traveled from the small of her back over her left shoulder, fondling her neck, caressing her chest, and crossing over to her right breast. He cupped it while continuing to kiss her. His hand massaged her breast; his index finger stroked her nipple, making it rise in response.

Every so often, he wet the tip of his finger with his tongue, to lubricate and smooth his touch on her nipple. He took his time in foreplay, grateful for experiencing this freedom from a timetable.

Lifting his head from their kisses, he stopped moving his hand. His mind snapped into clarity with the realization he was seeking approval from a prostitute. Sensing the interruption, she moved her right hand to the back of his head and pulled his face down to kiss again. Placing her left hand on his right, she moved it back over her breast. His mind drifted back to what-the-hell mode, and physical hunger regained control.

Moving his left hand from her back, around her waist to her small, flat belly, he rubbed it with the back of his hand. She gave a little moan through her kiss.

Her moans are intoxicating. I'm turning her on—she's into me. Could this be for real?

His left hand traveled from her stomach down to the side slit in her dress. With a flip of his thumb he lifted the dress flap open. Feeling no panties, he slipped his hand between her thighs, waiting for permission. She slid her right hand through the scant hairs on the back of his forearm and, reaching his eager hand, pressed it hard to her soft secret.

Herald slipped his hand further and cupped her sweet damp spot. His breathing deepening and a light sweat beading his forehead, he paused. Then he uncupped his hand and moved both hands to where her dress hung at her hips. Grabbing both sides of the tight wisp of fabric, he maneuvered it past her buttocks. It wafted to the floor with a soft swish.

With her dress off, Bright backed away from him, affording him a full view of her naked body; then she placed her left hand on the side wall to steady herself near an unshaded window.

She arched her back, looking over her right shoulder, bent her knee, and in a practiced manner, raised her right foot behind her. As the back strap of the shoe came into reach, just below her buttocks, she used her right hand to slip it off and, with an air of grace, flipped the shoe off her foot. She then performed the same maneuver on her left shoe.

Watching the arch of her body in the window-diffracted light and the changes of muscle tone in her legs and torso as she moved to her choreographed shoe removal, he thought of snapshots of exquisite marble statues in the Louvre. The simple act of Bright removing her shoes was one of the most provocative displays by a woman Herald had ever witnessed. He shivered with excitement, reminiscent of feelings he thought were long gone.

With an enticing look at him over her shoulder, she skipped to the bed, paused, then crawled cat-like to the pillow, being sure to show her shaved sweet secret. At the pillow, she turned over on her back, raised her pelvis to bend her knees, and folded her calves underneath herself to push up to a seated position on curled legs; then she raised her index finger in an undulating motion, beckoning him to join her.

Herald felt his entire body flush with excitement. Removing his shirt and boxer shorts, and kicking his pants off his ankles, he walked to the bed and crawled up to her face, all the while keeping his eyes on her every body part as he passed by.

He was on his left side, she on her back, which she'd arched in an offer for him to touch her as much as he wanted. Good at following instructions, and using his fingers in the manner of a little animal walking upright, he crept down her stomach to the top of her leg and shifted to her most intimate area. He alternated cupping her pubic bone and stroking his fingers over her shaved skin. Entranced he thought, *Man, I am developing a fine fetish for the feline skin.*

After what seemed an hour of his caressing, Bright started emitting low moans, at the same time moving her hips in a circular pattern. She was either giving an award-winning performance or enjoying the experience for real. Was enjoying sex an extra perk of the trade?

Her breathing becoming heavier; she broke out in a sweat. The intoxicating smell of her sex filled the room. Damp with perspiration, she pushed him onto his back. Sliding her body on top of his, she straddled him, placing her knees on both sides of his thighs. She lifted herself, arched her pelvis, and, with the velvet feeling of damp flesh on flesh, slid up, pelvis to pelvis.

Herald, marveling at the feel of the smoothness of her skin, was stunned at his capability to feel any sensual sensation after his stint in a war zone.

Stiffening her thigh muscles, Bright took firm hold of his manhood in her right hand, placing her left hand on the bed to support her weight. With one snake-like undulation, signaled only by a shallow lift of her right knee, she slid about half of him into her. Pausing, she moved her pelvis in a serpentine manner to ease accepting his size, and absorbed him. If for no other reason than the grace of the movement, Herald forgot what planet he was on. The overwhelming sensual joy swept Vietnam from his psyche and let him know he could still be human. This was the place to forget the war.

When he regained his sanity, it was with a snap of consciousness. He realized he'd experienced this same snap when he'd let down his guard while on duty. It was during momentary lapses like that, while sleeping on ambush patrol back in Vietnam, Charles would seize such vulnerability and slit a throat. Now, Herald could only remember Bright creating the blazing white light of his orgasm, which cleansed his mind of all reference to Vietnam. Tears flowed down his cheeks.

Looking up and smiling at him, she said, "You really in for it now. Sex always got Bright in trouble in my village. Why Bright came to city where sex pays well. I love sex. When get a good man, Bright love to be touched. You touch like think Bright Numbah One. You nice to Bright, Numbah One GI. You be careful, Bright motor running now. Touching full-time job, GI. You ready?"

Herald decided the only thing that made any sense was to keep Bright for his entire week on R&R in Taiwan. Sitting up in bed, he turned, put his feet on the floor, sighed, and thought the stability of a paid relationship, if only for the week, seemed appropriate. Shaking his head, he laughed and continued thinking, *This entire rapport I feel with Bright most likely is Bright just doing a good job.* In a sheepish manner, he asked, "What would you charge for the entire week? Whatever you have, it seems to work for me."

"You touch me, Numbah One GI. Spend week with you, give special discount. You first GI of day."

Herald smiled, "I'm sure. First, a few rules: You must understand my life has been very exciting. I have no interest in leaving the hotel, ever. I have everything right here: bourbon, the hotel restaurant, store, and you. The outside world is too much."

YEAR 1988

HERALD, BACK IN CALIFORNIA, heard himself mutter the last words of his daydream, " … OK with you?"

"OK with what? Or should I ask, 'With whom'?" Thea asked, as she appeared in the doorway, flicking her hair and lowering her eyes to the bulge in Herald's pants.

Searching his face for a clue, a wisp of her blond hair slipped from the grip of her hairdo and fell over her right eye. She raised her right shoulder, and in one smooth movement of her left hand, returned the errant thin black spaghetti strap to her shoulder and continued up to her head to reset her lock of hair.

Tapping her foot on the floor three times and looking at Herald, she pronounced, "Back in the war twice in one evening, dear? Let me guess, that tuxedo swept you back to your whore in Taiwan. You may think it's nothing, but your prostitute flashbacks are disturbing. If I had spent a week with a male gigolo eighteen years ago and kept daydreaming about it for eighteen years, believe me, you would be upset."

"Look," Herald responded, his forehead muscles knotting in three tight lateral bands, "this post-Vietnam crap is like a monkey on my back. Memories of 'Nam spring from my subconscious on their own timetable, but I can handle it."

Thea flipped her hair back and frowned. "I appreciate the lingering impact of the experience of Vietnam, if for no other reason than living with you. However, you are back, married, with children and a law career. There is no shame in admitting you need help from the Veterans' Services.

As your wife, I'm entitled to be jealous of your recurring memory of your romp with a prostitute, the same way you would be entitled to be concerned about any recurring memory I might have of any of my former boyfriends. Do you even realize that the only stories you share with me about Vietnam are about your whore in Taiwan?"

Pausing to catch her breath and regain composure, she continued. "We have to leave in five minutes if we're to enjoy the dinner we paid for. What about it?"

Herald feigned a smiled. "Enough said; point well made. However, what happened to our sex life? Perhaps my flashbacks relate to sexual frustration. On another note, have you ever been with a male prostitute?"

Thea, both stunned and amused by the question, faced him down. "The deal between us was for me to supervise the schooling of two children and manage the law firm half time, which leaves little time for any type of sex life. If I had really understood the sacrifices children impose on a relationship, I would have respected my parents more."

Grinning, she concluded, "Now, is the male-prostitute question posed to me as your law partner, your wife, or the mother of your children? And before you answer, I'll tell you: it's for me to know, and you to find out! At least I keep these things to myself."

Checking on the babysitter to be sure the girls had not bound and gagged her yet, they said goodbye and promised to be back early. Driving to the dinner involved the usual chatter about the day and the kids. When they pulled up to the Hyatt Hotel, it was clear their '69 VW van, even newly painted, flunked in the status department.

Herald watched the parking attendant from the driver's seat open the passenger door and stare at Thea's long, firm legs and ample breasts pushing at the seams of her silk dress. The young man, wearing an incredulous expression with eyes bulging, likely thought it strange a babe of this caliber would ride in a car this stupid.

Herald gave the keys to the attendant and asked if he knew how to use the starter button.

Distracted, the clueless attendant, still admiring Thea's legs and breasts on the sly, asked, "The what?"

Herald talked him through a history lesson on how the Ford Model T relied on hand cranks until 1919, and before Chrysler's 1949 innovation of the key-operated, combination ignition-starter switch, the starter was often operated by the driver pressing a button mounted on the floor or dashboard to start the engine. Thea sat rolling her eyes.

Tutoring done, Herald walked around the van to Thea and offered her his hand. Grasping it, she turned toward him, hopped out of the van's high seat, almost turning her ankle when she landed. Recovering, she placed one hand on the van, raised her right leg, and adjusted the fallen shoe strap.

While adjusting the strap, she flipped her hair back and looked at Herald. "Not to be repetitive, but how goes the motion to get our posteriors out of the fire?"

He sighed. "Well, my research pretty much concludes that we are cooked. I found one case that allows for relief, but that was a mistake made by a court clerk who failed to put both plaintiffs' names on a judgment. There's nothing with an attorney making the same mistake."

Thea, irritated, wrinkled her brow. "Well, you better get a grip on the concept that I am not starting over unless you *dramatically* change your lifestyle. Have you informed the client yet?"

Shying from her gaze, he said, "No, not until I have finished my research. For Christ's sake, the client is Norman Thall, and you know how much he despises the legal system—and particularly attorneys." Herald felt stomach acid rise in his throat as he continued. "The motion must be noticed for twenty-five days. If I lose, I could bring a Motion for Reconsideration and an appeal. Plus our client would have to file a complaint against us and start a lawsuit from the beginning, which would take more than a year."

"Whether you win the motion to relieve yourself from default or not," she said as she started walking away from him, "I'm considering starting over by myself in Vermont, where my parents and sister live. Until you get help, there is nothing to prevent more malpractice. I do not intend to stand by while your problems threaten our family's future. There is nothing to prevent the same mistake from happening again. You may remain in California, but if everything goes down the tube, I will need time to sort things out by myself."

Herald stood rooted beside the van as Thea continued walking.

She looked over her shoulder and continued. "Come on, we must attend this function and at least *look* like we are still married. Be careful of how much you drink tonight."

The churning of Herald's stomach increased, acid rising and searing his throat as he faced the concept of losing not only his law firm but his family as well.

The large, fancy fundraiser dinner party, with 500 guests, was well under-way and buzzing with energy. The meal was chicken, cooked slightly dry, as is typical of event dinners, but the conversation was lively. The band played his favorite, "We Gotta Get Out of This Place." The words took him right back to the war again. The beat of the music started to meet the beat of the thumping on the steel doors of his psyche's tomb. Pushing the memories back, he focused on the here and now, living in the present by at least looking like he was having a good time.

CHAPTER 10
MORNING JUST YESTERDAY

AFTER A TENSE DRIVE HOME on bad terms with one another, they walked into the house and composed themselves enough to thank the babysitter, pay her, and wish her a good night. Herald bid Thea goodnight as she brushed past him to go into the bedroom, and he entered the kitchen to pour himself a whiskey and ginger ale.

He was too wired from the pressure of everything. Clenching his drink, he plopped down on the couch.

A light sweat moistened his face, and the muscles in his right shoulder were twitching as he reviewed his precarious situation. The notion that Pearlman's curse had caused his malpractice kept creeping into his mind. After guzzling several drinks, he dropped his head back against the couch and fell asleep. As the dreams came, the rhythmic pounding of his war experiences on his mental dungeon doors took him back to another time when everything was on the line.

YEAR 1969

IN THE DUSTY COOLNESS of his bunker, Herald had just finished his Vietnam breakfast of freeze-dried eggs with hot sauce and some mystery meat, which should have tasted like sausage.

Time to do the dishes.

Folding metal mess kit in hand, maintaining a bent stance, he started up the sandbag stairs to the blazing sunlight shade line cutting across the second sandbag step. At the sun line, he paused to inspect the calendar nailed on the wooden header to his right. Last night's occupant had been keeping tabs on the dates; it was November 18, 1969, a while before he had gone on R&R. Memories have their own timetable, regardless of their original sequence of events.

The heat and humidity were seeping past the shade line cast by the bunker's roof. Herald almost had to push through the sun shadow line as if it were an invisible shield. It was 8:00 a.m. and already apparent that the mercury gauge was going to blow.

Stepping through the invisible wall, Herald was walloped by the escalating heat.

No, I don't think so! Back to the bunker. And the dishes can wait. Time to write home.

Returning to the coolness of his "home away from home," he plopped down on his favorite sandbag pillow. The momentum of sitting caused his butt to slip off the bag and his left shoulder to rub on the cool clay wall. As his shoulder hit, a small sliver of clay chipped off and fell to the dusty floor. Picking up the piece of clay and crumbling it between his fingers, he thought, *Good enough to die in?*

Placing his mess kit on the floor, he reached into his backpack and pulled out the resealable plastic bag holding his writing pad and letters from Pamela. Opening the bag, he removed his airmail pad. The exotic smell of Chanel No. 5 from Pamela's letters made him hunger for home.

He tore off one sheet of paper from the pad, took a pen from his breast pocket, and, pen on chin, began scanning his thoughts for a topic to write home about, a witty topic not involving bloodshed.

"November 18, 1969. Dear Pamela, Everything is fine here. So far, I have not been in any major action. Just lucky, I guess. I think about you every day and cannot wait to be with you again. Thanks ever so much for your timely letters. It makes this experience tolerable. Just knowing someone remembers means everything."

Thinking of home brought back memories of war movies that had, in part, inspired his GI Joe folly. The GIs in those movies believed in childish superstitions. In a previous letter to Tom, his friend still in college, he'd written about the female volunteers who flew around the firebases in Red Cross helicopters. They were called "Donut Dollies," nicknamed for serving coffee and donuts to the soldiers.

One of these girls had struck up a conversation with the "blooper" man in AckMan's squad, jargon for the soldier who carried an M-79 40 mm grenade launcher—deadly to anyone within two meters from where it would detonate. The next day, after his conversation with "Donut Girl," the blooper man triggered a booby trap and lost a foot.

No matter how nice this poor girl was, no matter how many times she came out to the firebase after that, no one—*no one*—would talk to her or even try one of her donuts. As far as the platoon was concerned, Donut Girl was a jinx; anyone who talked to her or ate one of her donuts would have a hex on him.

Now there's a great topic for my letter to Pamela. Nothing like silly superstitions between soldiers for a silly subject.

Before setting pen back to paper, a rise of short-tempered voices, coupled with heat stealing into the quiet, cool depths of his bunker, caught his attention. Herald sensed the entire platoon was already in a foul mood.

"Ack—Dog, just try and bark your way out of—*ack*—this one!"

Try and bark your way out of… what? What the hell is AckMan talking about? Do I even want to know what that means? It's going to be a long day if we're going to be barking our way out of things this early.

The heat, dirt, and overcrowding in the other assigned bunkers for his platoon were just a few of the many splinters under everyone's fingernails. Overcrowding was a minor annoyance, resulting in the bunkers' coolness fading earlier in the morning. It was also voluntary—the direct result of no one except Dog willing to share a bunker with LeMaire.

LeMaire's arm-hair-burning, mosquito-abatement program was legendary. The smell caused even the most hardened soldier to prefer the mosquitoes. But Dog didn't mind; he reveled in having the extra space.

Herald laughed, recalling a conversation he'd had with Dog about sharing a bunker with LeMaire. He'd been sitting on his bunker roof as Dog, with his lips pushed together, had come walking by, bobbing his head in synch with his bark-singing, "Ree rotta ret rout rof ris race." Herald had recognized the tune, "We Gotta Get Out of This Place." As Dog passed, Herald had gotten his attention and inquired, "Dog, I hate to interrupt your singing, but how are you able to sleep with LeMaire burning his arm hair? Isn't the smell unbearable?" "Rarh," Dog had barked, cocking his head to explain by raising a hand to his nose and digging around with his index finger, where the jagged edge of his dirty, roughly chewed fingernail caught what appeared to be a long, stringy object. Prying the object loose, he used his thumb and index finger to get a firm grip on it, to finish drawing it out of his nose. Herald had put his hands over his eyes and lowered his head in an effort to calm the electric horror storming over his brain. This was Vietnam—but even in war there are limits, limits on witnessing another human being extracting nose stuff. Small limits, but limits nevertheless that let humans rise above the animals. Herald dropped his guard; his innate curiosity had gotten the better of him. *"Good God, Dog, that is so very, very gross! I'm sorry I ever asked! Stop! Please, stop! Oh God! No-o-o-o!"* Herald had almost lost it at seeing the revolting sight. Dog had extracted a very long, very large, very clotted something from his nose, and Herald had been riveted by the sight—riveted in the way physical deformity commands attention; he could not take his eyes off what must have been an unbelievable nasal *Guinness Book of World Records* record. Dog then nodded, smiled, and barked, "Ur Rat," and finished pulling the three-inch-long, dried mucus-and-who-knows-what-all-else-covered length of cotton from his left nasal passage, dangling it from his thumb and index finger and barking, "RUGGH." Still mesmerized by it, Herald had recognized it for what it was. Stuffed in Dog's nose, it would have blocked any smell of LeMaire's burning arm hair—or any other random LeMaire odors, for that matter.

Herald laughed and was about to write Pamela about it, when his mind strayed back to the platoon's foul mood.

The real mood breaker for the platoon was AckMan's constant *acking* all night. It was not the sound. Although obnoxious enough, the noise was buried in the snoring of all the others. *Acking*, in and of itself, was perceived as a dark premonition.

Herald grinned at the thought of composing something funny to tell Pamela about superstitions and the platoon's sleeping habits. In the middle of musing on the ridiculousness of it all, heavy footsteps outside his bunker caused him to look to his weapon.

Platoon Sergeant Pearlman, all of twenty-something years of age, jumped down the three stairs into Herald's bunker and stood in a perfect crouch to avoid one of the steel roof beams. Rocking his M16 in his right hand—and seeming distressed—Pearlman looked at Herald with perspiration beading on his forehead, the sweat accumulating into rivulets. Herald gazed at his preoccupied visitor, waiting for him to explain this sudden intrusion.

Sweat streamed down Pearlman's forehead to his frontal bone ridge, just above the eye sockets; it gathered in his thick eyebrows, saturating them; it continued its journey to his high cheekbones and down his cheeks, dripping off his chin onto the clay floor and raising tiny explosions of dry dust. As the streams of perspiration kept flowing, Pearlman's forehead and jaw muscles began twitching in alternating tight striations.

Gathering his thoughts for a few minutes, he began to share his concern with Herald, patiently waiting.

"I had a very, very, *very* strange dream last night. It started with me standing in a long line of badly wounded soldiers in torn uniforms. Two soldiers were in front of me. One was an American, the next perhaps a Russian, both of whom were poised on the lip of a steep drop-off. I looked behind me, and the line of soldiers stretched beyond my sight. They were wearing uniforms from the many countries at war during the 1960s. Every nationality was represented, including Zulus, with their elaborate head-dresses. All of the soldiers were strung out in single file on what seemed to be a dirt road running along a gigantic valley wall. It was a dream, so who cares where you wake up, so long as it's not in 'Nam ... and on it went.

"Looking around, I realized that what I thought was a road was one of many rock ledges lining the side of the canyon wall, looming over a big hole, like a huge, open-pit, iron-ore mine, miles wide. When I glanced down to the bottom, it was lost in swirling mist. Looking up, the pit vanished in drifting fog vapors. I bit my finger just to be sure it was not a dream, but on it went.

"My eyes traveled back to the bottom mist and followed up the multi-tude of ledges stacked on the gorge wall, until the levels were lost in clouds.

"I was surprised by a strong, dry, stale odor. The smell was what I would imagine to be the scent of a Roman burial catacomb. I'd read about the catacombs under Rome on my two-week tour of Europe in high school but never went down to experience them. There was no air movement, although the cloud wisps were slowly revolving.

"Peering over the shoulders of the two soldiers in front of me and down to the lower ledge, the entire ledge was completely filled with forms resembling burial caskets stacked side by side in groups, fading into the horizon. A figure in a ragged, hooded black cloak stood at the front of the line, right out of an old 1930s horror film. When the first soldier reached the edge of the ledge, the dark-caped figure pointed to the next empty burial chamber, far below.

"Keeping his finger pointed to the space, he faced the soldier, inquiring in a gravelly, low voice, 'Ready, or not?' The soldier, who seemed to be from some African war, understood the dark figure's universal language. With fear in his eyes, he looked left and right in disbelief, and repeated, 'Ready?' Poof, his body was gone and his unmarked tomb instantly filled with his remains. Part of my mind gave directions to my body to turn, run, fall to the ground, anything to wake up, but on it went.

"The hooded figure pointed to the adjacent grave, signaling to the soldier in front of me, who stepped up to the edge of the precipice. The words were repeated from the caped head, 'Ready, or not?' This soldier, clearly an American, exclaimed, 'Not even a number to mark my grave? Even the Germans in World War II tattooed numbers on their ... ' Poof, he was gone, his vault below filled in. My leg muscles involuntarily stepped me forward. Looking at the next empty burial place down below, all I felt about my forthcoming demise was regret.

"The dark figure pointed at my crypt and turned toward me. Before he could speak, I shot up awake. My teeth were clenched. My eyes bugged out, and a profound, heavy sweat exploded all over my body, soaking my shirt and pants. I huddled in my poncho and didn't go back to sleep."

Pearlman interpreted his dream. "I have a bad feeling about *today*. I've had this feeling before, but never like this. It's as if my number is up. Something cold has reached in, grabbed my heart, and paralyzed my mind." Raising his hands, he continued, "Look at my hands. Have you *ever* seen my hands shake like this?"

Still sitting on his sandbag pillow, Herald looked into Pearlman's face. Even in the diffused light of the bunker, it was clear: fear was in his eyes. Herald was stunned.

Pearlman taught me how to be a line officer, for Christ's sake.

He waited until he was sure Pearlman was finished; then he howled, "Far out! That's the most detailed dream I have ever heard. Where in the hell did you come up with it? Is it some Harvard Freudian psycho creation? All I can say is, you must have heard others in the platoon having weird dreams like this. And, when you did—did the soldier who had the dream survive?"

"Yes, everyone has so far. But this one was really bad. Like I have been on line so long that my luck has run out." Pearlman held up his trembling right hand. "Look," he repeated, "my right hand is still shaking. Before, when my hands started vibrating, I would bite my index finger, and the trembling would stop, but not today."

"Biting your finger—is that permitted at Harvard?" Herald asked, trying to amuse.

Pearlman, relaxing a bit, partly distracted by the finger-biting crack, responded, "Yeah. When I feel really stressed, and things start building up and negative energy crowds me to the point where even my supposed Harvard-trained mind starts to stall, I bite my finger, 'Harvard-hard.' It's a very simple and easy way to mentally regroup."

Herald nodded and bit his own finger very hard, leaving a bite mark that bled a bit. He looked to Pearlman, who was nodding in approval, and then put his finger back into his mouth, to stanch the minor flow of blood.

"Hey, do you know why blood tastes metallic?"

"Something about the element iron, which bonds with oxygen," Pearlman tried to recall. "I was an English major, not chemistry."

Removing his finger from his lips, Herald cajoled Pearlman. "Today is our day off after ambush. Go get some chow to nourish yourself and some sleep. We'll leave you alone for the day. I think this shit may be getting to you."

A second vibration of pounding steps into the bunker caught their attention. Both turned and faced the door while Herald reached for his weapon and Pearlman swung the muzzle of his weapon toward the steps.

The runner for the CC came charging up to Herald's bunker and jumped down the stairs. His shoulder hit Pearlman's arm, knocking him to the back wall. Breathless, he gasped, "Sorry, Sarge," took a deep breath and continued. "Get it all ready. An LOH spotted boo-coo Charles running into a small, square, bamboo-and-palm-tree forest and disappearing. It must've been part of the large raiding party that attacked one of our firebases last night. Charles made the mistake of waiting 'til dawn to 'didi' back to Cambodia. It's our turn to kick his butt. Air cav is on the way to eagle-flight two companies in, to block Charles from sneaking back to Cambodia."

Herald frowned at Pearlman, who frowned back. Looking at the messenger, Herald inquired, "'Boo-coo Charles'? 'Boo-coo' means 'a lot.' That does not really tell me how *large* a group we're talking about. Any better idea how many?"

"No," the runner responded, wiping the sweat off his face, "the chopper pilot was too excited, when he called in the sighting, to count."

Herald shook his head. "We'll be ready in fifteen."

The runner started bolting back up the stairs, his shoulder knocking Pearlman to one side again. Pearlman grabbed the runner by the arm and stopped him in mid-stride. Again the runner looked up, said "Sorry, Sarge," and ran out.

Herald looked to Pearlman for confirmation or objection. "Charles is famous for setting an ambush that starts out looking like he made a mistake and is vulnerable for the pickings. He hopes the illusion of vulnerability will entice the U.S. forces to jump in unprepared and land them a large body count." Pearlman did not respond.

Why would *Charles be caught in the open so easily at dawn?* Hearld's face flushed. *It's gotta be* us *who'll be ambushed. But, as they say, 'Ours is not to reason why ....'"*

He ordered Pearlman to have the other squad leaders report to his bunker. Pearlman nodded and headed out to alert the platoon.

Minutes later, the squad leaders and point man Dog assembled, crowding Herald's bunker and kneeling in the dusty clay. Diffused light filtered through the bunker's firing ports, highlighting sweat beading on every face as they looked at Herald, who moved to the far corner of the bunker. The word was out: it was a firefight with Charles.

Herald searched the faces of Dog, AckMan, Ferlinghetti, and Jones. All had earned their squad-leadership positions through attrition. They, the ones with all the Vietnam experience, had *the* big doubt in their eyes. They were skeptical of putting their lives on the line going under fire, when the person giving those orders had never been in a full firefight. At least Pearlman had, and would be there if Herald panicked.

Herald was the amateur. Wiping his face with his neck towel, the almost-newbie lieutenant yelled, "Get your gear together for a definite fight and possible ambush—only one meal and two canteens of water. Everyone is to carry double ammo, eight grenades, and two claymore mines—more if you are able. The brass thinks Charles has made a mistake and allowed himself to get caught in daylight before he could slip back to Cambodia. This is a classic ambush tactic for Sir Charles.

"I want at least one person in each squad to carry an extra bandoleer of machine-gun ammo; LeMaire may need it. Leave the ammo in the carton. Machine-gun ammo draped over your shoulders may look cool, but all it does is form a giant brass X on your chest as a target. More important, dirt and dust will contaminate the cartridges and linkage. Dirt on the shells and linkage causes jamming in the machine gun. Any questions?"

Jones, scribbling in his notebook responded, "OK, Kemosabe."

"*Rompo un culo!*" Ferlinghetti spat out, indicating he was going to break some ass.

AckMan just coughed a low "*ack.*"

They turned and attempted to leap up the stairs of the bunker, nearly colliding with Pearlman, who pushed them all back for an instant. Dog bared his teeth and barked a short "Rah-ROU!"

As Pearlman pushed them back, he spoke in a low, even tone. "Your asses are mine after the LT, so show a little respect. Now riki tik and get ready."

All four hesitated for a moment, formed a line, and passed by Pearlman, leaping from the first to the third sandbag step, pivoting, and fanning out left and right to their different bunkers. They knew the drill.

Herald started toward the stairs on his way to the CC to get the comics for the day's area of operations. Pearlman shook his head, brushed his long, black hair back with his left hand, and sank to the bunker floor on his knees in front of Herald. "Don't think I can do it today; I feel ill. A cold dark hand has grabbed me, LT. If I go out today, I die."

Herald looked at the dusty floor of the bunker and whispered, "We discussed this earlier. Everyone who has experienced this feeling has come back. This is just a normal reaction to stress."

"I know you're correct; others have said the same thing. But look how many men in other units *have* been right and have *not* come back. I've been here for eight months and had the feeling before; but not like this. If I go today, I will not be coming back."

"OK, Pearlman, I am *not* going to force anything on anyone who feels the way you do, especially with your experience and the brains to qualify for a Harvard education. It may cause you to hesitate and cost lives. I just hope you do the same for me, if and when I lose my nerve. What will I tell the platoon?"

"Let me tell them. They'll understand."

The squad leaders could be heard ordering their squads to gather their gear for a definitive Charles dance. The platoon members moved like silent ghosts, except for a loud *acking* from one bunker and a louder *"Mon Dieu! Merde!"* from another.

Pearlman called the squad leaders together, after they had gathered outside Herald's bunker. "Guys, I just cannot go today. If I do, I feel it will be my death, and, worse, I will not be able to do the job you expect of me."

"No way—*ACK*—Jose! You promised me we would always be—*ack*—together. We have eight months—*ack*—and two firefights. You promised and now—*ack*—you want to send us out alone with a—*ACK*—newbie LT? Just ain't—*ack*—right, man. You promised!"

Jones chimed in, "I've been here for only five months, but remember, four months ago, after the sniper fired on us? The next day, I had the same feeling of dread as you do now. You talked some sense into me. We went out and came back. OK, today we are going to a real fight. The LT and all of us need your experience in the shit."

Ferlinghetti threw his poetry book on the ground. *"Dio bastardo!* You not-a go, I not-a go. Doze-a ass'oles ... dey can-a court-a-martial-a my pasta ass! W'at-a dey gon'-a to do, e', send-a me *alla prigione*? … to prison? I still-a be alive! *Ma, che cazzo, minchia!*"

Pearlman, looking to the ground, gave himself a fast head massage, using all his fingertips, sighed, and looked up. "Guys, the LT is doing a good job, right? He has earned the right to take over."

Jones jumped in. "Yeah, he's done a good job, but not in a full firefight yet."

Herald, who was back from talking to the CC and obtaining the comics for the AO, was down in his bunker, packing. Hearing the discussion outside, he hollered up, "Thanks, guys, for the overwhelming vote of confidence!"

AckMan, looking down the steps of Herald's bunker, called out, "No offense, sir; but—*ack*—until you've been shot at, nobody knows what—*ack*—you will do. We're more than—*ack*—happy to let you be the LT. We just want the sergeant there—*ack*—the first time, in case you lose it."

Pearlman bowed his head and brushed his hair back over his head. He paused for a minute, sensing a revolution arising in his own platoon in favor of his leadership over Lt. Lloyd's. He realized Lt. Lloyd had performed well enough to deserve the respect of his men.

To force fear from his mind, Pearlman placed his index finger in his mouth and bit, hard—getting into Harvard-hard. Facing the sky, and with the taste of his blood in his mouth and tears in his eyes, he replied, "Yes, you all are right. We *have* been brothers for way too long. Even with my fear, I cannot abandon my family. I'll go."

More confident, and smiling to the squad leaders who had begged him to go, he said, "If a bullet finds me, I'll be waiting for all your asses in hell when you get there. God help you if you fuck up today." Smiling again, he raised his right hand to eye level. It was no longer trembling.

True to the CC's word, the dreaded *whop-whop* of Huey helicopters could be heard in the distance approaching the firebase with speed. Herald came out of his bunker, equipment in his sweaty hands, and moved in full stride over to where Pearlman was shouting over the oncoming noise of the Hueys to his troops. "Split up into four groups of six."

As they formed, he turned and spoke in a low voice for only Herald to hear. "I hate a hot landing zone and being transported in a copter that's nothing more than whirling metal and jet fuel attached to a jet engine. One round in the fuel tanks from a 51-cal heavy machine gun, and it's gonna be Deep-Fat-Fried GIs."

"Stop with your stupid shit, Pearlman. The hair on my neck and arms is already up! My intestines started rumbling just from the stress of our little conversation about your bad feeling. Please do not add any icing to the cake by raising paranoid nuances you developed about helicopters and hot LZs. We need to ride in different birds to protect command. Why don't you ride with AckMan's squad? He's one short, and this places you last in the line of helicopters. I'll go with Dog, Hollywood, and LeMaire in the first chopper. If the shit hits the fan, we will have one machine gun on the ground for cover fire and yours truly to call in the artillery."

With muscles knotting up on his neck and sweat beading on his face, Pearlman asked, "If I catch 'the big one' today, would you do me a favor? I'd appreciate it if you would contact my parents and let them know how much I valued their support and that I'm sorry I left Harvard."

"Man, you know more about a firefight than I do. This is my first one. If anyone is going to get it, it'll most likely be me. And don't forget: I'll have the radio—always the first target for Charles—so not to worry."

Pearlman's jaw muscles tightened at the word "worry." Starting to get testy, he said, "Listen, you're new around here. When a soldier has an intuitive feeling about his death and requests a favor, it's rude to return platitudes. Yes, I may be in error, but that's not the point. This may be my last request on this planet, and I expect a serious answer. Will you call my parents or not?"

"Pearlman, I'm sorry for attempting to make light of your request. I have yet to learn all the rules governing combat manners. Yes, I promise, the first telephone call I make after discharge will be to your parents. And you must promise me the same, OK?"

"OK," Pearlman nodded, "sure."

Then, with an air of solemnity and understood rite, as if preordained, Pearlman passed a folded mini-piece of paper taken from the small spiral notebook kept in his breast pocket with his parents' contact information already prepared for Herald, who then unbuttoned his right breast pocket and pulled his notebook from its resealable plastic bag. With one swipe, he tore out a piece of paper, enclosed Pearlman's folded note in his notebook, and put it back in the plastic bag and the bag back into his pocket.

The ballpoint-pen clip clicked when Herald jerked it free of his pocket. Pushing the rear button, he extended the ink tip and rested the butt of his M16 on his web belt attached to his waist. Placing the paper on the butt, he wrote his parents' names and telephone number on it and handed it to Pearlman, who reopened his resealable bag, removed the notebook, and placed Herald's folded paper against the spiral coils of wire holding the notebook together; then he replaced the little book back into the resealable bag and into his pocket. The ceremony was simple and brief, but the pact was sealed. Herald smiled at the irony of various plastic resealable bags holding everything from writing materials to human remains in ominous body bags.

Just as Pearlman buttoned his breast pocket, turbine jet engine screams filled the air as the flight of about a dozen slicks—helicopters used for transport—came in, flaring to lose momentum and resting their skids on the space between the wire and dirt berm of the firebase. They squatted like huge, brown, menacing vultures with their engines at an idle, rotor blades giving off a soft *whop-whop*, waiting.

"Showtime!" Herald yelled, shooting glances left and right at his men, sending them scrambling over the berm to their assigned birds and jumping in. Herald then ran to the first bird, stepped on the skid of the helicopter, and made a quick observation before placing his other foot on the floor inside, noting there was scant space in the helicopter bay with the door gunners in place. The door gunners had M60 machine guns to cover the helicopter's landing, if Charles opened fire on it.

The small bay seemed even smaller as he settled inside. With not much room for cover in such close proximity, one well-placed round was going to hit somebody somewhere. Taking his helmet off and placing it under his butt, he moved his shoulders against the back wall of the helicopter bay, letting the vibrations of the engine act as a lubricant to slide his body down the wall until seated on his helmet.

Herald, like Pearlman, had taken great precautions in leading his platoon to ensure everyone maintained a safe distance from each other when on patrol. Charles's rocket-propelled grenades or booby traps had a kill zone of about nine feet, so Herald would keep reminding everyone to stay at least ten feet apart when beyond the wire. Having spent hours being drilled to stay away from each other now created uneasiness in the platoon members crowded in the helicopters. Here, six soldiers were within one grenade blast, the realization of that giving everyone the creeps, even more so when they recalled Herald always ranting about "Thanksgiving two-fer turkeys with body-part stuffing!"—the "two-fer" being one bullet hitting two soldiers.

The increasing pitch of the turbine jet engines was followed by the deepening *whop-whop* of the rotors as they prepared to lift off, Pearlman waving from his chopper to Herald.

Herald, waving back with a weak smile, looked over his shoulder just in time to catch LeMaire spit chewing tobacco onto the foot of their door gunner.

Charming, just charming, always making himself wanted. Not going for the LeMaire Congeniality Award this year.

Exhaust from the turbine engine filled the cabin as they lifted off, and Herald wondered if he would *ever* be able to remove the smell of jet fuel from his body. With helicopter transportation as the prime mover, the life of a grunt in Vietnam was immersed in JP-4 fuel.

He laughed out loud, as he started imagining his autopsy—something he hoped would come much later in life. Visualizing his spirit floating above his dead body in the morgue stretched out on the stainless steel examining table, the pathologist powers on the electric body saw, its high-pitched whine filling the room; in one smooth movement its metal teeth open the body's chest like a sharp knife slicing melon; the pathologist, after lifting the saw from its gruesome task, catching the dripping blood with a side cloth and handing the saw to his assistant, grabbing the rib spreader, inserting it into the body's cavity, and cranking it; the chest gaping open; the pathologist recoiling at the smell of jet fuel seeping from within; his spirit listening to the doctor dictating into the morgue microphone for his records: "Number four: subject supersaturated with jet fuel; probably Vietnam Vet, late 1960s, early 1970s."

What a lovely day for a ride, Herald thought, as his mind returned to the task at hand. The slicks and two gunships circled the base to gain altitude and then headed toward Cambodia. The Vietnam countryside displayed the most vibrant color green Herald had ever seen. It was more vibrant than the dark green that he loved in his native New England in the spring.

As the helicopter force roared over the river toward Cambodia, the wind played with the short hairs on the back of his head.

He knew the most dangerous aspect of a helicopter assault was yet to come: the landing, the moment when the flying bomb hovers close to the ground to lose momentum for landing.

Big as a goddamn barn door made of dynamite with jet fuel frosting.

At least we won't be using the river boats. He wouldn't miss the mud bath, ducking snakes and leeches before being shot. There were at least some benefits to an airborne assault.

The sharp, loud cry of the helicopter turbines, plus the pressure of the rotors pushing the air down to keep the craft airborne, rendered any voice communication useless. Even the simplest audible command had to be yelled directly into another's face, if not on the microphone intercom system. By this time, jet fuel had permeated every part of their bodies, making everyone feel flammable.

As the force turned north, Herald could see the helicopter support artillery rounds bursting in three different landing zones, in an effort to clear the zones and prevent ambushes. However, Charles was deep in the ground, and the shelling usually had little effect, except to warn them that the Americans were coming to those three landing zones.

Worse, the shelling had to stop a good four to five minutes before the chopper force could form up to land. This gave Charles just the right amount of time to set up their heavy 51-cal machine gun or prepare RPGs—rocket-propelled grenades, Soviet antitank weapons that worked wonders as their personal artillery. A good hit by either would turn a helicopter into the foreboding, large, deep-fat fryer.

Guess I'll think twice about eating fried chicken again.

The force veered toward the target landing zone, a dry, abandoned rice paddy. The choppers descended roller-coaster style, giving Herald the sensation of leaving his stomach in the air. Knee-high grasses covering the rice fields appeared to rush up at them. The choppers pulled back to flare and lose enough air speed to touch the ground for less than ten seconds, before speeding away.

At the last minute, door gunners on the flanks of the formation opened up with their machine guns, probing for an ambush before dropping the grunts off for a run. The gunners' bursts were louder than the engine; together, the sounds amplified, sending a chill down the soldiers' spines and leaving their throats parched.

Each copter dropped its six- to eight-man load and made for the high country. As soon as the men hit the ground, they fanned out, dropping to prone positions and waiting. Now the silence was deafening. To go from maximum sound barrage at very high decibel levels to silence was unnerving. A huge volume of noise creates pressure on listeners' eardrums. When the source stops, the eardrums still feel and hear the phantom noise.

As was his habit when Herald stopped outside the wire to survey any situation, he always dropped to one knee to make himself a smaller target. Stomach acid began burning his throat.

So you wanted to be a gunfighter, eh?

He ordered the platoon to form a "V" formation and move northward.

After the group was positioned, he looked at the prone Hollywood lying on his radio, face in the sun.

"Stop tanning and get your ass over here!"

Hollywood hauled himself up and meandered over. Herald grabbed the hook and grated, "Piper One to Bandleader—what is the program? Over."

"Bandleader to Piper One—head north, and the LOH who spotted the target will guide us in. Alpha Company is to our right and is landing now. Do not fire to your right unless ordered by me. Out."

Herald stood up and yelled, "Dog, point; AckMan, Ferlinghetti, left leg; Pearlman, Jones, right leg; Hollywood, take off those stupid, goddamn sunglasses!"

The heat of the sun and fear of the unknown erupted in his face and body like a large, steel blast furnace. Though the day was young, the towel thick with grime around his neck was already soaked with sweat. Walking into a gunfight was a surreal experience. He felt like the living dead in a zombie movie.

Dog, taking point, barked, "Rarh-re-ROOH," and led them north at an even pace. After one kilometer, the platoon approached an overgrown bamboo-and-palm-tree grove in the shape of a square. The square was rimmed by an old, large rice-paddy berm. It offered Charles a perfect defensive position.

The LOH flew overhead, and the pilot pointed to the bamboo grove. Herald waved at the helicopter and shouted to the men, "I want everyone to form a firing line and move up together."

Moving forward together, the platoon came up on line. When they got about 300 yards from the grove, Charles lit them up. No need to say anything the grunts did not already know by instinct; dropping, they married their bodies to the ground.

The LOH pilot swept over again, pointing to the grove and leaving a high-pitched whine and the acrid smell of burning jet fuel.

"No shit, Sherlock," Herald grumbled, as he turned over with his rear firmly on the ground and waved back.

His memory flashed on his guerrilla-warfare manual. A favorite trap of Charles was to fire a small burst of AK-47, causing the target to jump into what they believed was a safe place. Spooking one's opponent into the closest perceived safe place, like a drainage ditch, was a trap. The ditch would be filled with explosives. The perceived safe haven of the ditch would ignite into a killing zone.

"Everyone move slowly to your front against the paddy wall, but watch your ass and be alert for booby traps. LeMaire, move to your far left, and set up your machine gun to prevent flanking. Dog, go with him to feed ammo and spot targets. No barking!"

"Roh-RAH."

The radio crackled. "Bandleader to Piper One. Over."

Herald crawled over to Hollywood, who, for the first time he could remember, was not tanning on his back but lying on his stomach. Herald took the handset and responded from prone position, "Piper One. Over."

"Piper One, move your platoon along the rice-paddy berm, which runs north and parallel to the grove. Over."

"Roger, already there. Out." Herald had to laugh. Without a word, his platoon had seen the only cover in this open field and had already formed along the berm for their own reasons. But they had done so with great caution, just in case there were booby traps.

"I want everyone to fire five or six quick rounds, like we are assaulting, and let's see what we're up against. But remain prone. Wait until I fire first."

Herald raised his M16 and set it on the rice-paddy berm, snapped off the safety, and opened up with eight rounds, firing deliberately on semi-automatic and spacing over the entire grove. The rest of his platoon opened up, along with the two other platoons from Herald's company, on the far right. The sounds of rifles, machine-gun fire, and the low *duuup* sound of 40 mm grenade launchers with their trailing explosions filled the air.

As soon as the barrage started, a flurry of dark-moving figures inside the bamboo forest materialized from where they had been hiding underground. The black dots fanned out and manned their own berm, the one surrounding the bamboo grove. They immediately lit up the platoon with bursts of fire. The paddy wall and bamboo hedge around all four sides of the grove made it a natural fortified defense.

Smoke from Herald's platoon's rifle fire started to form a low, gray cloud over his position.

At the first *snap-snap* of AK-47 bullets over his head and dirt kicking up in front of him, Herald moved his weapon to the left, off his shoulder. He dropped his head so suddenly, it bounced in the hard, dry clay, causing a puff of dust. A red, electric flash of fear surged through his mind and body; all he could do to hold it together was to stay below the berm and tremble. His heart pounding at a rate he'd never before experienced, he felt paralyzed. Sweat rolled off his face, down his nose to the ground. He started to chant Pearlman's "Eye of the storm" over and over.

Time seemed to stop until broken by Pearlman, saying, "Hey, we have these little people; this could actually be a turkey shoot. But, LT, you're not going to do much *commanding* with your nose two inches in the dirt. More importantly, you need at least *some* elevation to cast a shadow of your own. If you have any intention of getting out of your father's shadow, you have to have one, right?"

Composing himself, Herald lifted his head, dirt caked on his sweating face, to Pearlman, lying less than two feet away. "I may be a little slow getting the hang of this, my father's shadow aside. It takes time to get used to the fact that just one of those little snaps could seriously terminate my life form."

Herald looked over the berm, lifted his rifle, fired six more rounds, and then ducked down, came up again, fired off four more rounds, and ducked down.

"Wow, Pearlman, this firefight stuff is sort of fun … even a little boring."

Herald punched the magazine eject button, and the empty magazine popped out. Pulling a full magazine from his ammo pouch on the right side of his belt, he tapped it on his steel helmet to seat all the rounds and slid it in his rifle, waiting for the *tink* of the locking mechanism.

"Boring? Well, LT, I don't know about boring, but it's fun just to trade shots with nobody getting hurt."

After thirty minutes or so of trading fire with Charles, the platoon became shielded from the sun's direct rays by a gunpowder cloud of expended cordite. It was taking form and lingering in the air like a low, dense fog, about twenty feet up. Its acrid odor assaulted Herald's sense of smell.

He and Pearlman alternated looking over the berm to fire, keeping their bodies in the same prone position. After another half hour, Pearlman peeked over the berm at not even a full-face height. There was a dreaded *snap*, only this *snap* was very close and not the usual crisp, sharp sound. This *snaapp* had a wetness to it. Herald heard the dull thud of a head hitting the clay berm and a yelp from the trooper Boyd, the newbie to the right of Pearlman. "I'm hit! Medic!" The medic started to crawl over to him.

The enemy position took on an odd pinkish hue. There was a sickening sweet smell in the air, and a metallic flavor in Herald's mouth.

"Wow, that was close, wasn't it, Pearlman?" Herald asked, jostling his comrade with his elbow. Pearlman, whose head was resting down on the berm, was silent; the fear he'd fought off earlier now fully consumed Herald. "Pearlman, Pearlman, you OK?"

He lifted Pearlman's shoulder. Pearlman's body jerked and flopped over. His helmet was at a high angle, exposing a small black hole just above his left eyebrow. Gray, bubbling goop was splattered around the opening. Herald recognized the gray matter as superheated brain tissue, forced out by the pressure of the bullet. Black blood was oozing from Pearlman's nose and ears.

"Holy shit! Oh God! *No!*"

Herald dove again to the ground, his subconscious conjuring up the huge form of a Tyrannosaurus Rex, wearing the black pajamas of the Viet Cong. The beast had the face of a Viet Cong soldier with huge dinosaur teeth. The apparition grabbed him by the throat. He could almost feel the massive teeth severing his spinal cord as the beast shook him. Herald's brain locked up in a red-hot electric storm of panic, freezing his flattened body to the ground and blocking out any noise.

Just for a moment, after his head hit the ground and sent a swirl of dust in the air, his mind played with the prospect of merging his blood with the smell and taste of red clay. It was the same question he had asked himself in his bunker, when he rubbed the clay chip between his fingers: *Good enough to die in?*

The thought of escaping his fear by raising his head and taking a quick bullet from the sniper flooded his mind. Nobody would ever know he had panicked if he became one of the Honored Dead. Herald doubted he had the courage to quiet his paralyzing fear enough to regain control of the situation. Death was preferable to cowardice.

The gap between the cartoon violence of the pictures in the *GI Joe Coloring Book* and the reality of war had been closed. Grabbing a handful of dirt, he prayed, *Dear God, please, please help me. And, if I ever live through this, the coloring book is deep-fat fried!*

There was no answer from God, or anyone or anything else. Time stopped for what seemed like hours. In desperation Herald made a wish on the coloring book to save him.

Blasts of rifle fire began registering in his ears, forcing him to regain his senses. He began chanting in a low tone, over and over, "Remember what Pearlman said. Make this firefight your hurricane. Put yourself in the eye. With the storm around you, ride the eye … ride the eye."

The conflict in his mind was a pitched battle between duty to his men and fear for his life. Herald could see the telegram from the War Department: "We regret to inform you your son's cowardice in the face of the enemy caused his own death and the death of those under his command."

Fighting the forces of Herald's mental hurricane, this insult rose up like a piece of ship's wreckage to cling to, in his raging sea of fear. Lashing the debris and concentrating on the calmness of the eye of a hurricane, he began to reclaim control of his mind. Raising his index finger to his mouth, he bit it hard, Harvard-hard. The taste of his blood triggered a reaction. Synapse by synapse, lobe by lobe, he started recovering his brain and the ability to put simple thoughts together. He reached out and grasped a critical concept: *his men were more important than he was.*

This insight into his insignificance gave him a burst of strength and freedom. Being free from fear of personal harm left him open to protect those given to his care, and it offered a bonus: to be objective enough to know what he had to do to direct his men for them to survive. Protecting his men had the mutual benefit of protecting his ass.

A force beyond himself touched him on the shoulder, whispering in his ear, "Pearlman is dead. You have a job to do."

The dark cloud of fear receded. The sky was now blue, the sun shining hot and beautiful. He could do this!

A warm sense of euphoria filled his mind. Herald had moved beyond his fear. His men were now more important to him than any physical risk he would encounter. His life had changed forever. The feeling made him giddy, free; an almost hysterical smile came to his face.

Still scared, but now with calmness, purpose, and a huge influx of energy flooding his brain, he knew he could accomplish his job. Meeting the ultimate demon, he moved, even if at a slow pace, beyond it.

The process seemed to take hours, but after several minutes, one of the other troopers asked, "What are we going to do now, LT?"

The cliché in Officer Candidate School is: in a desperate situation, one of your men looks to you and asks, "What do we do now, Lieutenant?" Pearlman's words flashed in his mind as big as the huge, stock market ticker tape electronic sign in Times Square: "You ain't going to do much commanding or cast a shadow with your nose in the dirt."

Well, what do we do now?—the "we" referring to the different parts of his brain arguing with each other.

It didn't take long for his brain to reach a consensus: lying there immobilized by fear was only going to get him killed—or worse—all of them killed. His first rational thought was, *There is a sniper; only a sniper could have made the shot.*

Herald spit; his mouth was filled with the acrid taste of cordite mixed with the sweet, sickening metallic taste and odor of Pearlman's blood. The bullet had exploded a pink mist of blood into the air and all over Herald. Tasting Pearlman's blood caused him to grab his stomach as digestive acid shot up his throat, filling his mouth, seeping into his nose, and stinging his nasal passages. He spit again to get the wretched mixture out, but residual remained, and it would be a taste that would never leave him.

Rolling on his back, Herald roared, "Hey, assholes, there is a sniper out there, and he nailed Pearlman in the face. We'll talk about it later. Every time you fire, I want you to change your position by a few feet, left or right. Never fire from the same position twice, unless you're ready for an AK-47 facial."

Rolling back to his stomach, he shouted, "Alternate every other soldier firing on those gooks to keep up the pressure, and spare the ammunition, only one or two shots at a time. We will not be in a position to block Charles if we are out of ammo."

AckMan screamed, "Where—*ACK*—did they get—*ack*—Pearlman?"

Just as AckMan posed the question, one of the wonders of the human body occurred: Pearlman's body suddenly and violently contracted. A death rattle moaned from his throat. This gesture was the most primitive part of his brain still firing the nerves for breathing and heartbeat. Instinct was still trying to hold on; Pearlman was already brain dead, but his young, healthy body would not give it up.

"Yeah, creepy isn't it? There is no way to take one in the forehead. Pearlman's a goner. We're just being treated to *real* death: lonely, dirty and pathetic. This is the stuff they leave out of the movies. Sorry, AckMan, but as senior squad leader in the platoon, I want to congratulate you on your promotion to platoon sergeant."

The random, mysterious silence, which occasionally descends upon the battlefield, was broken by a loud *"ACK!"*

CHAPTER 11
AFTERNOON JUST YESTERDAY

HERALD, EXUBERANT ABOUT MASTERING his fear, crawled over to Hollywood and took the radio hook in his left hand. "Piper One to Bandleader. Over."

"Bandleader to Piper One. Over."

"Bandleader, this would be a great time to show Sir Charles what 'calling in the world' as a fire-support restaurant really means. For an appetizer, how about a selection of artillery? I have one trooper casualty and my platoon sergeant KIA. By just sitting here, we, not Sir Charles, are the ducks in the shooting gallery. Charles is in a naturally fortified position, and we are in the open and exposed. This is not the type of operation it was quacked up to be. Over." Herald put the hook down and laughed at his pun. The joy of mastering his fear made him giddy beyond words.

"Piper One, Bandleader, arty is already on the way. Just hold your position and, if you find humor in our situation, no jokes on the radio. Out."

A 105 mm howitzer can throw a thirty-three-pound shell nearly seven miles at 1,548 feet per second and has the same effect as tying together two, large, sixteen-pound steel bowling balls, hollowed out and filled with explosives. When it hits, it hurts.

Coming from over the river to the front of the platoon, the first 105 mm shells blasted the grove. Audible for about two seconds prior to impact, the shells had a high-pitched whistle. The ground barely shuddered as small clods of dirt flew into the air. A few bamboo trees were shredded, but the vegetation survived the shelling; Herald was surprised by that.

The twenty-minute barrage of at least fifty shells covered the grove in a methodical manner; propelling hot, jagged bits of metal through the air at near-supersonic speed, and plowing into the ground seventy-five yards or so in front of the berm shielding the platoon.

Herald imagined Charles's tunnel complex under the bamboo grove. He had learned from his Wolfhound training camp that some of these Viet Cong tunnel systems went sixty to one hundred feet deep, with up to four or more levels. Depending on how the VC responded to the attacks, coming out of the tunnels or not, would identify how deep the tunnels were estimated to be and dictate what kind of arsenals were needed for the job.

The 105 mm shells were invading the top level of tunnels. He sympathized with Charles, questioning his safe haven in these deep shafts, which would become their graves when the unreinforced dirt walls and ceilings crumbled from the blasts.

About five minutes after the barrage stopped, Herald shouted, "OK, let's play it again, Sam, to see how deep this tunnel complex is."

The platoon opened up. Large numbers of little people dressed in black scurried out of their bunkers and opened fire, sending the telltale *snap-snap-snap* of their bullets over the soldiers' heads. It appeared 105 mm was not big enough to penetrate Charles's bunkers below the first level or to dampen his enthusiasm. A brownish cloud of low-lying smoke from the explosions of the artillery shells snaked its way between gaps in the bamboo and spread over and around the grove in the hot sun.

"Piper One to Bandleader—it appears there was no effect on lower tunnels, as Charles is still coming out in force; perhaps something bigger? Over."

"Piper One, we have 155 mm on the menu, and they are on the way. Bandleader, out."

A 155 mm howitzer, capable of throwing a ninety-five-pound shell more than nine miles at 2,244 feet per second, has the same effect as throwing six sixteen-pound steel bowling balls, hollowed out and filled with explosives and wrapped together. The shells have their own distinct whistle, and one can feel the intense energy being transmitted through the air as the shells slam to earth.

Artillery like the 105 mm and 155 mm are designed to shoot off-center of a target by minor increments. Though the guns have the same target setting, the effect is to have each impact spaced apart rather than having all the guns calibrated to hit the target at the exact same spot. Surrounding the target achieves a wider shrapnel zone.

As each of the larger shells exploded, the ground beneath the platoon convulsed. Again, for twenty minutes and with mathematical precision, fifty of these far more powerful and accurate shells rained down on the bamboo grove, blasting enormous clusters of dirt, debris and entire trees into the air. The larger shrapnel shot farther from the detonations, whizzing into the dirt just thirty-five to fifty yards in front of the platoon's protective berm. Empathizing, Herald could imagine the fear and screaming of Charles as the first and second levels of passages collapsed.

No way for a soldier to die.

When the barrage ended, Herald roared, "Let me hear you guys bark! No offense, Dog."

The platoon opened up, but again Charles seemed to be unaffected; he did not back off. What seemed an endless supply of Charlies emerged from their bunkers at each round of small-arms fire, taking cover behind the bamboo berm and returning fire, snap-snap-snap, a cat-and-mouse game lasting four hours. The day was still young, and the unrelenting sun began raising blisters on unprotected light skin.

A low, darker cloud of smoke, from the 155 mm artillery shell blasts, streamed out, enveloping the smaller brownish 105 mm smoke trails. It hugged the ground.

What in God's name is that smell? Herald wondered, as the tentacles of smoke coiled their way to his nostrils, 300 yards away. They had the same sickening sweetness he'd just experienced with Pearlman's blood and cordite, plus an acidic overlay of black-powder residue, the same smell he remembered as a kid when he'd set off fireworks on the Fourth of July. The same black powder used in those fireworks was identical to that used in the artillery shells. *It had mixed with Charles's blood.*

The explosions had consumed enormous amounts of human flesh and atomized the blood of the victims, as though a creature from outer space had consumed its kill in some ungodly fashion, leaving only a disgusting blood-and-gunpowder smell as evidence of its feeding.

Herald grabbed the hook and keyed the mic, remaining low to the ground, mindful of at least one sniper in the bamboo grove. "Piper One to Bandleader—do we have any eight-inchers in range Charles can suck on? Over."

"Bandleader to Piper One—watch the language. Yes, it is taking a little time as only the big brass may approve this level of artillery. Out."

Eight-inch artillery was one of the largest cannons the U.S. used in Vietnam. It could fire a 200-pound shell more than ten miles at 1,952 feet per second, having the effect of strapping together twelve-and-one-half of the sixteen-pound, hollowed-out, steel bowling balls filled with explosives. The shell was mammoth and, more important, capable of going deep in the ground before exploding.

A giant explosion shook the ground. Another shell hit, and a large palm tree completely vanished. With each burst, large portions of trees and gigantic masses of dirt went flying into the air. The earth shook, each blast sending shrapnel whizzing into the dirt surrounding the platoon.

"Keep your head under the cover of the berm or enjoy a shrap lunch," Herald bellowed over the assault. "You can check out the show later!"

The larger shells broke through the ground with delayed fuses. He knew from his training they would penetrate deep, with each shell upon detonation transmitting a shock wave, collapsing the roofs of the lower level of tunnels. Again, Herald imagined Charles's horror of suffocating deep in the moist clay of the narrow, crowded tunnels as the ceilings collapsed.

Herald feared being buried alive. Getting shot or dismembered by a booby-trap blast seemed a better way to go.

At least you could see the sun and have air in those last moments.

Eight-inch cannons have a bizarre aspect: the length of the barrel is perfectly matched to the shell. The cannon's trajectory can be aimed to hit the same exact point every time—the opposite of what the Army normally chooses.

But for this little show, the eight-incher was just what the doctor ordered. After one hour with more than thirty deafening blasts, Herald shouted, "Open fire." The *crack* of M16s, M60 machine-gun fire, and the *duupp* of 40 mm grenades concluded the earsplitting show of strength. Charles surfaced from his bunkers, but much more slowly and in fewer numbers.

What the hell kind of bunkers do these guys have?

The bamboo grove looked like a chewed dog toy. Elephant trunks of blackish smoke, oozing the smell of black powder and blood, filled the air 200 meters beyond Herald's position. He had to hold his stomach to stop from retching; the acid bile burned his throat, leaving a vomitus taste in his mouth.

Herald swallowed his bile, grabbed the hook, and keyed the radio mic. "Bandleader, this is Piper One. Bring in the flyboys, and let's do a little USA 250- to 500-pound-bomb babies show. This must be a huge underground complex, a reverse Empire State Building of Charles's tunnels. Over."

"Already on it, Piper One. They should be over you shortly. Matter of fact, pop yellow smoke now. Be sure it is yellow, or it will be your ass. Over."

"Roger, yellow smoke now. Out." Grabbing a smoke grenade, Herald pulled the pin and threw it as far as he could in front of his position.

The first Phantom jet came in close over them to give the big looky-loo. As the jet came around again, Herald rolled over on his back and looked up. Bombs were being dropped 200 yards behind him and floating over his head, like harmless large pelicans. Just as it seemed the bombs would overshoot the bamboo grove, air brakes, which looked like paddles on a windmill, opened at the rear, and the bombs dropped straight down on the now-shredded bamboo grove. The first two bombs hit, their explosions causing the ground to shudder.

More clay in my mouth, Herald wisecracked, as his head rebounded. "Who's hungry now?"

After what seemed an inordinate amount of time, a hail of shrapnel from the bombs slammed into the front and even the back of the platoon's berm. The *whizzz* of spinning shrapnel could be heard as the sharp metal pieces plowed into the earth.

"Keep your face in the dirt," Herald ordered as he snuggled up tight to the berm. "This friendly fire will take off your nose!"

He knew the havoc these bombs would wreak. Now they would be collapsing and compacting the entire Viet Cong tunnel system. This hiding place had become a prefabricated graveyard.

After two passes by the jets, with four bombs exploding, Herald seized on an idea. If his platoon opened up with small-arms fire just as the bombs were released from the jet, Charles's response would be to leave his bunker to return "Mr. Snap-snap." This would coincide with the arrival of "Mr. Bomba": *a surprise party for Charles.*

Hey, what was that song? 'La La Bamba'? Or, 'Bye-Bye, La Bamba'? A theme song! What a great idea to take the fear out of every soldier in this platoon!

He yelled to his men, "OK, guys, we are going to have *some fun today!*"

"LT, there ain't no way—*ack*—to have fun with Mr. Charles in our—*ack*—face. Have you lost it?"

"Look, guys, every time we open up with small-arms fire, Charles's response is to get out of the bunkers to repel a ground assault. I'll be on my back. Just as the jet-jockeys line up to release their bombs, I will signal, and you guys open up. Our firing will give Charles enough time to get out in the open, just as the bomb arrives to give him a taste of 'La Bomba.' But remember, Mr. Bomba has a real bad, shrap-breath problem. When you see the explosion, stop firing, and drop down behind the berm."

"Well, LT," AckMan started protesting, "we—*ack*—*have* been pounding Charles with all our big guns—*ACK*—and he is *still* operational. So even if your idea is *really stupid*—*ACK*—as long as we are not standing up and charging Charles's machine guns, I, AckMan, will go for the—*ack*—weird."

"Does anyone remember the song 'La Bamba'?" Herald asked around.

"*What?*" Jones demanded. "LT, in between focusing on Charles and friendly fire, we're just a bit distracted ... and I don't think I need to remind you that Pearlman is lying dead next to you, which really brings home that this is not a drill. Remembering popular songs at this time is *not* on the radar; as a matter of fact, my song-memory lane is closed. Could you remind me ... and sing a few bars?"

That was the longest speech Herald had ever heard from Jones. Being stone silent, chewing his dirty fingernails, and writing in his notebook for his novel were his ways of dealing with the madness of Vietnam, but today's excitement had loosened his tongue.

"*Ammaestrare, maestro,*" Ferlinghetti piped up, "You teach-a, no?"

Herald laughed and attempted the tune for them. "OK, with my modification, it goes something like, 'La La Bamba, Bye Bye Bamba, it's sad to see Charles go.'"

"*Aye! Si, si, yo sè!* I know eet!" hollered over a Mexican trooper from San Jose. "Is a Spanish song. Goes like dees: '*Para Bailar La Bamba! Para Bailar La Bamba!*'"

Herald grinned as the trooper belted it out, making it come alive for everyone. "OK, everyone, listen up," he yelled. "I'm going to change the song and sing the first bar as 'Bye, La BOMB-ba!' When you hear it, I want you to sing back with 'Sad to see you go' and open fire for the second bar ... *and keep your damn heads down!* Got it? Or it's suck shrap."

A disbelieving chorus of voices came back with, "O-O-O-O-K, LT."

As though right on cue, a jet flew over, lining up for a pass. A second before it released its bombs, Herald sang as loudly as he could, "Bye, La BOMB-ba!"

Without skipping a beat, the platoon raised their weapons, sang back, "Sad to see you go," and opened fire. Charles, also on cue, came scurrying out, like scores of ants from a nest. The dark figures were lost in the glare of the explosions. "Sorry, Charlie," Herald whispered.

Herald felt neither remorse, horror, nor jubilation about slaughtering the little men in black pajamas. It was a dreamlike event. When he closed his eyes, he could feel the terror within the entire tunnel complex, deep below, as the carved clay sanctuary collapsed, burying all. It was a wonder the last of Charles continued clawing his way through the tunnel debris to the surface, to fire on them, even in the face of 250- to 500-pound bombs. The most basic point of honor in being a soldier is dying per the warrior's dream—death with a good sword on a sunny day.

Having grown up in the United States in the 1950s and '60s, Herald had no concept of respect for insect life forms. If they invaded your home or garden, they were fair game for wholesale chemical destruction.

To get rid of ants on the patio, when he'd worked one summer on his stepfather's dairy farm, Herald would pour gasoline on anthills. The ants would come streaming out to avoid the toxic liquid. After they'd exit, Herald would light the gasoline with a match, set them on fire, and back up to avoid the intense flame and heat. The ants milling around the mound entrance would curl up and burn, but other ants continued to file out, long after Herald thought they would have sensed the danger and stopped. Now Charles, like the ants, continued to file out and curl up in the fire.

"Not bad," Herald yelled, "but let's do a Charles psych-op treatment and sing it so Charles can hear it. 'Mr. Fast Mover' jet fighter is lining up. Here we go!" Raising his voice to its loudest pitch, he roared, "Bye, La BOMB-ba!"

With a much louder response, the platoon picked up its cue. *"Sad to see you go!"* The words reverberated off the bamboo grove with the echo of ground fire. As if driven by their military programming, Charles continued to file out into the blinding light of the titanic explosions.

With each blast, the soldiers dove to the ground as large amounts of shrap showered upon them. Herald was still crawling two inches below berm level to avoid another Pearlman episode. Moving behind the platoon, he commanded over and over, "After you see the explosion, get back down fast."

Everyone got the drill; 'La BOMB-ba' went on for two more 'Mr. Fast Mover' passes.

"LT," AckMan yelled, "you better get your—*ack*—ass closer to the paddy berm, or you may become a—*ack*—victim of your own theme song!"

No sooner had AckMan said that when Herald's body went bouncing off the clay from another 'La BOMB-ba' blast. Herald heard a very close, vicious *whizzz* and felt a hot pressure on the left cheek of his buttock. It was followed immediately by a warm wetness in the crotch of his pants.

Oh, great! Just what the doctor ordered! I can already hear myself telling everyone back in the states the awe-inspiring story of how I qualified for a Purple Heart by singing 'La Bamba' and taking a piece of American shrap on my ass. Charming ... just too charming for words!

Scrambling close to the berm and lying parallel to it for the least exposure, he grabbed his field bandage, pulled off the wrapping, and unbuttoned his pants. While still keeping at least two inches below berm level, he slipped the dressing under his pants, down to his lower left cheek.

Christ, I can't even see how serious this is! Oh well, at least I can imagine the letter from the War Department: "We regret to inform you your son died bleeding from his ass."

This day was just itching to terminate his life in the most embarrassing manner possible.

He was almost finished with bandaging his wound when AckMan looked back and said, "LT—*ack*—now is not the time to be playing with your butt.—*Ack*—shit, I mean really, man, there is a time and place for everything. Get—*ack*—a room!"

"AckMan," Herald snarled, "you never saw a thing ... or you will have a serious accident with a large blunt instrument that has your name on it!"

Jones, looking over his shoulder, couldn't help but toss in his own smart crack. "Kemosabe have strange masturbation habits. Next time LT 'calls in the world' for fire support, I bet his ass he'll be a little farther away!" Laughing loudly and lowering his head to the ground, he dug out his notebook and, keeping himself very horizontal—but still quaking with laughter—began to scribble.

Ferlinghetti, laughing at Jones's joke, jumped in with a tease. "*Ma, lascia lo stare!* 'ey, I 'ave una poema."

Dog smirked at Herald bandaging his posterior and barked over his laughter, "ROUH-rah-HA-HA."

Herald paused from his buttock bandaging and blasted, "No poems now, Ferlinghetti. And, Jones, if you write this in your book, I will hunt you down, no matter where you live."

The sickening stench of blood and black powder hung heavy in the air and smelled and tasted greasy. The revolting cloud now covered the platoon's entire position, its shroud streaming far to the rear and clinging to their faces and clothes. The vile taste of vomit overwhelmed their mouths; in prone position, they placed their towels over their noses and mouths, seeking relief that did not come, and held their stomachs to keep from retching. It is one thing to face an enemy and fight; it is quite another to witness an enemy being atomized and suffocated in his tunnels and inhaling the results.

No fighter wants to end up in his own blood cloud knowing the only major effect he has had on his enemy is to render him slightly ill.

At this stage, everyone had some sympathy for Sir Charles, trapped below ground, dirt pressed against his body and face, suffering a dark, lonely, and suffocating death in a place he called home.

Done with dressing his wound, Herald turned over. In the time it had taken him to bandage himself, the air support had headed home. Now an ominous quiet settled over the grove, which was darkening as evening began to fall.

Herald commanded his men to open fire. Mr. Charles did not return the usual AK-47 *snap-snap*. He ordered a second round. Still no response. Grabbing the hook and keying the mic, he shouted, "Piper One to Bandleader, it appears Charles has been temporarily neutralized. However, we are spread out, low on ammo and, most important, facing in one direction. We cannot defend a Charles attack from Cambodia at our rear, coupled with an assault from what is left of Charles in the grove. Over."

While awaiting a response, Herald rubbed his nose with his sleeve and put his head on the ground.

I may forget many things about today, but the death smell of greasy black powder residue and blood will not be one of them. I promise I will never burn another anthill.

CHAPTER 12
YOU GOTTA BE KIDDING ME!

"Piper One, this is Bandleader. Over."

"Piper One. Over," Herald responded.

"Piper One, it is very close to nightfall, so we are going to move en masse for the helicopter pickup with Alpha Company starting in five minutes. Over."

"Roger, will wait for your first movement. We will move a bit slower due to casualties, but remain in position to provide cover fire if necessary. Out."

HERALD TURNED ON HIS BACK and began shouting orders. "OK, guys, it's getting dark. Charles, if anything is left of him but body parts in the grove, or his buddies in Cambodia less than a klick away get ambitious, they may decide to go hunting GIs. Unless we want to be the meat in a Charles sandwich, it's time for us to go. There is a helicopter pickup with Alpha Company in progress. We have to collect ourselves and move to the right, all at the same time.

"AckMan, since you are now platoon sergeant, pick two from your squad to wrap Pearlman in his poncho and bring him with us. Have the remainder of your squad grab Boyd. You'll have to pick your replacement

215

squad leader later. Watch the bleeding on Boyd's leg; it's where Pearlman's bullet ended up—a goddamn two-fer. Dog, lead off point. LeMaire, hang in the back, and protect our rear."

Dog barred his teeth and growled, "Rarh-re-ROOH," as he moved to the head of the platoon, and Herald continued booming out orders.

"Ferlinghetti, take over AckMan's squad for the time being and have two of your men help carry the weapons of those who are busy with Pearlman and Boyd. Have the men carrying those weapons hang close to the guys handling the casualties. If things get hot, they will need their weapons fast. We are heading out in five minutes!

"Keep your weapons trained on the grove, and do not move for at least one minute after the company commander starts to move to the landing zone for pickup. We want to see if the CC draws 'Mr. Snap-snap' from Charles. We may have to stop and provide cover fire for the rest of the company. And for Christ's sake, keep your weapon on safety. We've lost enough people today! That's it. Do it!"

So you wanted to be a gunfighter, eh? Happy now?

"Got it," was the collective grumble from the platoon.

AckMan picked two men from his squad to deal with Pearlman. They crawled over to him, took out the poncho from his backpack, and spread it out next to his body. This usually easy task was difficult because they had to hug the ground as they crawled around their dead friend, to avoid becoming another easy target for a sniper. Nobody wanted to gamble; there was no way to be certain all the Charlies were vaporized and floating in the smoky cloud above them.

After the poncho was spread, the men crawled to his right side and rolled him into it. Both fought nausea upon seeing the black bullet hole, the bubbly gray brain tissue protruding from his forehead, and dark blood still seeping from the back of his helmet.

One soldier had his hands under Pearlman's armpits, and the other was holding his ankles when Pearlman's body convulsed, looking for another gasp of air. Both jumped back a foot off the ground from their kneeling positions, mindless they were now visible targets.

"LT, HE'S STILL ALIVE!" yelled one, in the voice of a person horrified by the final spasms of life from a clinically dead person.

Seeing their alarm, Herald shouted, "Look, Pearlman is very dead. Any last movements are involuntary reactions of his body not realizing his brain is already dead. If you look at the inside of the back of his helmet, you will see it's over. We, the living, need to move out—unless you feel like spending the night. We are *not* leaving our dead, so let's just get on with it."

"OK, LT," one of the soldiers with the body detail replied, "but this entire thing gives me the creeps. Bad luck to touch the dead."

As the CC, with his Charlie Company command team, and the Alpha Company moved to the landing zone, Herald waited, his attention riveted on the smoking bamboo grove. There was nothing but total silence.

Looking over the grove, Herald yelled, "Let's move at a half-crouch, carefully, with your weapons on safety. Be ready if we take any fire. If any of you leave your weapon off safety and kill me, my ghost will haunt your ass forever. Check them all *now*."

Half-crouched, the platoon started moving. The men transporting Pearlman struggled to carry his limp dead body, with the extra exertion of doing so from a crouched position. Within the first fifteen yards, Pearlman slipped from their grasp.

The lead soldier on the Pearlman-body detail stopped and whispered, "I'm truly sorry, Sarge. I mean no disrespect. I just can't seem to get a grip on you, old buddy."

"Me, too," the other nodded and agreed. "For someone who is going home, you are very hard to hold onto. Forgive me, man."

Pearlman's body was dropped at least four more times. Each time, a short prayer was said by those who deeply cared for him and were bringing him home for the last time. They were giving him the same simple respect they wanted for themselves if their places were traded.

The movement went smoothly, with both Alpha and Charlie Companies spread out parallel to the grove in six-man sticks, each to be picked up by the twelve helicopters. Being positioned in front of the grove made Herald anxious, feeling vulnerable to another attack from Charlie.

We're like two lines of ducks in a row in front of Charles's circus shooting gallery.

"Piper One, this is Bandleader. Over."

"Bandleader, this is Piper One. Over."

"Piper One, a VC is waving to surrender. Battalion has ordered we take him alive as a prisoner. Looks like we'll have another chieu hoi working for us. My radioman, first platoon leader Lt. Chump, and third platoon sergeant, acting as third platoon leader, with our chieu hoi will go get him. Meanwhile, you stay where you are. Over."

Herald grabbed the hook and keyed the mic, fearful of the potential consequences from the CC's lack of judgment. "Bandleader, you are taking the top level of your entire command structure to an armed soldier with unknown intentions. If this is a trap, it will destroy your command structure and get you killed. Over."

"Piper One, you just worry about staying where you are and keeping control when the copters arrive. Charles is beaten. What else can he do after that pounding? You have your orders. Out."

Herald watched the band of five move with caution in single file toward the potential prisoner. When they were fifteen yards from him, he jumped out of sight for a second and popped up with his AK-47. Leveling his weapon, he emptied the entire thirty-round magazine at the group in measured killing bursts of four to five rounds to keep his weapon on target over the weapon's recoil. *BRAAP! BRAAP! BRAAP! BRAAP! BRAAP! BRAAP!*

The chieu hoi, first in line, took three in the chest and flipped a backward somersault from the impact. The third platoon sergeant took one in the thigh, spun around from the impact and also went down. The burst missed Lt. Chump, who fired back wildly in the air as he dived for safety.

The CC took a hit in his upper thigh, was knocked backward, and went down. His radioman, unhurt, dived for the dirt.

When the VC jumped down into his bunker, most likely to reload, the platoon sergeant threw a grenade, and the party was over for the moment, as bits of Charles and smoke flew twenty feet into the air.

Watching the grenade blast from 200 yards away, Herald called on the radio, "Bandleader, this is Piper One. Over. Bandleader, this is Piper One. Over." Only lonely static filled his radio speaker.

Herald looked to AckMan and Ferlinghetti. "You guys stay here and mind the platoon."

"Dog, Jones," shouting orders, "get with your squad, and come with the medic and me. I have to go to the CC, if for no other reason than to find out if I am the new company commander. LeMaire, set up your machine gun toward the grove. AckMan, line your squad on the left side of this paddy square. Ferlinghetti, set up your squad to the right of it, with LeMaire's machine gun as the center point on the berm corner. Hollywood, you stay here. AckMan, if I do not return, it is your party as acting platoon leader, and Ferlinghetti, platoon sergeant. Both of you have your squad-leader replacements in mind, if I do not make it back."

AckMan and Ferlinghetti nodded and turned to their squads, ordering them to form up on LeMaire.

Herald motioned to Dog, who went first, with a short "Rarh-re-ROOH," as they started crawling to the CC's last location. Jones's squad, with the medic, followed.

Inching on their hands and knees, it felt like it took forty-eight hours to crawl the 200 yards to the CC. Every twenty to thirty yards, they had to stop to regain their wind and wipe the sweat from their faces.

Herald never imagined the determination and self-discipline it would take to crawl in the intense heat and humidity, with more than 100 pounds of equipment strapped on him, to unknown danger. The physical strain, combined with the gnawing fear of approaching the very spot where Charles could fire on him at point-blank range, was a horrifying nightmare. With every movement forward, he kept one eye on the berm and his weapon ready. It was a slow, exhausting, excruciating experience.

A real Vietnam cocktail? Let's see ... Two shots sweat, heat to 100 degrees, add one shot intense fear, stir, pour into empty C-ration can, top with a pinch of the essence of black gunpowder mixed with blood, serve straight up.

Parting the tall grass, at last Herald found the CC and his radioman, with Dog nearby. Dog looked at the CC grabbing his bloody groin, gave a toothy grimace, "Grrh," and looked back at Herald, nodding to indicate, "You take care of this officer mess." He moved past Chump to the wounded third-platoon sergeant.

Herald looked over his shoulder to Jones and his squad. "Move past the dead chieu hoi and set up a base of fire." Jones nodded and, with his squad, crawled by the chieu hoi and spread out.

Herald turned to the CC, who was sobbing, bobbing back and forth on his left side, and grabbing at his groin. "Captain, Captain, we need to get back to the company. What the hell are you doing grabbing your crotch?"

"Hell, Lloyd, I took one in the balls. The bastard shot me in the balls. *The balls!* I never thought they would go for my balls!"

"Captain, I am sure Charles was just firing a burst into the crowd. There were five of you. Nothing personal. He just wanted some payback for us shelling him, bombing him, and killing his buddies all day."

"The hell with you, Lieutenant. You wouldn't be so cool if he was firing at *your* balls! What do you know? Jack shit! Help me find out if everything is there. I need an inventory, man."

"Captain, it has been a very long crawl to find your butt. I've found you, Charlie is not firing at us, and the best person to take inventory of your manhood is you. I will be back, but I am not a medic, and I am not touching your genitals, shot or not. Remember, you *do* have a company to think about."

"Congrats, Lt. Lloyd, you are now in command. Be sure to write! The only thing important to me now is my balls. There's just so much blood, so much blood. Where are they? Are they hurt but still working? Am I to be denied children?"

Realizing the war was over for the CC and his balls, Herald moved to the CC's radioman and asked, "Are you in contact with the battalion?"

"Yes, but the captain just keeps looking for his balls, and the battalion commander is yelling at me. What can I do?"

"Give me the radio. What's the battalion call sign?"

"Road Warrior," the radioman replied.

"Road Warrior?" Herald sighed, shaking his head in disbelief.

" … uh … yeah, Road Warrior."

Laughing, Herald triggered the hook's mic. "Road Warrior, this is Piper One with Bandleader. Bandleader is down and not functioning. Repeat. Not functioning. Over."

"Piper One, this is Road Warrior. You are now in command. The first group of choppers is inbound in five minutes. Move the casualties back to your platoon's position. Hold Charlie Company in place for the next run. Repeat, hold your force in place for the next run. This pickup is for Alpha. Do you copy? Over."

"I copy, Road Warrior. However, the area is not secure. Repeat. Not secure for choppers. Over."

"You have your orders. Out."

Just as the radio communication finished, Herald heard the *whop-whop* of the helicopters in the distance. It had been a long day, and for the second time, a person in command had said, "You have your orders." He felt a chill come over the back of his neck and run all the way down to his family jewels, which began tightening up against his thighs. What could happen if this order was wrong, too?

Oh, my God. My company—oh, God—my company is spread out and disorganized. Charlie Company has lost its command structure! Fear is infecting everyone! How am I supposed to explain in the midst of all this chaos to them that there are only about a dozen helicopters coming to evacuate both Alpha and Charlie Companies, and not to run for the first evacuation with Alpha? It'll take a minimum of two runs, one for each company, to evacuate all the men. With a minimum two-hour turnaround, it'll be dark; the choppers won't have sufficient light to pick the rest of us up. We'll be spending the goddamn night here! Good luck, Chuck!

Herald instructed the radioman to contact the other platoons' radiomen and order them to hold; then he moved to the third platoon-leader sergeant, also hit in the thigh. It was clear to him this man was doing much better with the medic at his side.

The medic was acutely aware of the extreme danger of their position, being so close to the bamboo grove without enough men to secure the berm. He kept looking every few seconds to the grove while fumbling with a bandage on the groaning sergeant's bullet wound.

Chump, first platoon leader, crouch-sitting, was looking at the berm and rocking back and forth, muttering, "Got that fool. Yeah, I got that fool."

The wounded platoon sergeant groaned and blasted back, "You got nothing, fool. *I* tossed the grenade. All you did was a great imitation of a rabbit-in-the-headlights look."

"Chump," Herald snarled as he crawled over, "the captain turned command over to *me*. Get back to your platoon. The first run of choppers is for Alpha Company. You are to take the CC and his radio to the pickup point for medical helicopter dust-off and then return to your platoon and wait further orders. We are to hold for the next run. Do you understand?"

"Choppers on the way, great. I will get back there on the double. Yes, the first run is for Alpha, and I will hold."

Herald moved to the body of the chieu hoi tracker and rolled him over. He confirmed the chieu hoi had taken the full boat. Three in the center, heart-chest area was a death warrant.

There were only two places that spelled immediate death, the head and the heart. When wounded soldiers came back to a field hospital, attention was given to those who did not have a wound in the head or heart. No need to waste time on hopeless cases. Their chieu hoi had rolled the AK-47 dice and came up with snake eyes.

Herald went back to the company radioman. "Do you have other platoons in communication?"

"I've got them, but there's a lot of confusion and just plain fear out there."

Herald looked around, yelling, "OK, guys, we're outta here before Charles gets any other fancy ideas! Get it together, and let's run for it!" He breathed heavily and rapidly, over and over, to store up as much oxygen as possible to build up his stamina.

"Rarh-re-ROOH," came Dog's bark. Jones nodded, and they were off, dragging the wounded platoon sergeant, with Jones taking the left arm and Herald the right. The sergeant kept moaning from the pain as his leg bounced on the uneven ground. Jones's squad carried all the weapons of those who were wounded and killed, and they trailed Herald to provide cover.

As Herald ran at a crouch, dragging the wounded sergeant, an old Christmas carol came to mind. He started singing in a hushed voice, using his own poetic license, "Dashing through the grass, on my one-horse open ass, o'er the fields I go, laughing all the way, ho, ho, ho." Jones smiled, nodded, and made a mental note to write the song down for posterity.

Chump, the CC and what was left of his balls, and the CC's radioman moved off in the direction of the liftoff point to catch a chopper out with Alpha Company. This would remove the CC from the battlefield, but Herald had other, more pressing concerns. The CC had passed the command baton, leaving Herald to fend for the company.

This must be my lucky day.

Just as Herald arrived back at his platoon, the first lot of Huey helicopters arrived and, as though on an expected cue, two dark specks came alive in the shredded bamboo grove. It was Charles, setting up a 51-caliber heavy machine gun on a tripod on the same berm in the grove where the supposed would-be VC prisoner had ambushed the CC and group, killing the chieu hoi.

Herald could hear the metallic clunk of the large steel bolt being pulled back to engage the six-inch-long shells that hurled high-velocity bullets, over one inch in length and one-half inch wide. Just one of them could sever body parts or turn a helicopter into a fireball.

The methodical *BOOM! BOOM! BOOM! BOOM! BOOM!* of Charles's machine gun gave off brick-sized green tracers showing the trajectory of their fire on targets far out in the landing field, mowing it in a calculated stream from left to right and creating a green umbrella. Charles wanted the big score and, after this day, who could blame him? His machine-gun fire was the last straw for American discipline.

Everyone from both companies ran at a crouch to the helicopters and piled on.

Herald paused and dropped to one knee, panting to recover his breath. He looked toward the choppers and was amazed to see one-and-a-half companies with more than 100 men jump on the twelve copters. A full load for this number of helicopters would be one company, numbering about seventy-two.

So much for command and control, he thought, as again he shook his head in disbelief.

People sandwiched each other, standing on the landing skids and throwing their weapons and gear off to lighten the load. The copters were so overloaded each pilot should have been decorated for bravery if they could get them off the ground. It was a fantastic feat, lifting those machines into the air, cocking them forward at an angle, moving ahead as if in a slow-motion movie to gain momentum, and then gaining getaway speed and altitude, as green tracers chased them from the field.

It could have been a recipe for disaster. The overloaded helicopters were easy targets as they lifted off the ground—just like shooting fish in a barrel. But luck was on their side. The VC machine gunners, overwhelmed by the huge number of moving soldiers and helicopters, failed to focus their fire. The horrifying scene resembled the strategy of schooling fish to swim in a fast, high-density cluster, creating a sensory overload for the predator's visual channel on the mass moving target.

While Herald was gasping at the "panic circus" going on in ring number one, overhead he heard the different "swish-swish" of a Cobra attack helicopter's blades. The sound signaled a new show about to take place in ring number two.

A Cobra gunship, nicknamed "Snake," was a special helicopter, the sole purpose of which was mobile firepower. It had rockets, a Gatling machine gun firing at 6,000 rounds per minute and—the icing on the cake—an automatic 40 mm grenade launcher. All this was mounted on a frame that, unlike the Huey at about six feet wide, was only three feet wide. This added up to a very small, hard, fast-moving target for Charles, with lots and lots of teeth.

Charles was still busy belching out his heavy machine-gun *BOOM! BOOM! BOOM! BOOM! BOOM!* when the Snake pilot saw Charles's single stream of green-light machine-gun tracers arching up toward the gunship. Opening up with the Snake's Gatling machine gun's six barrels spinning—*VERUUUUUP! VERUUUUUP! VERUUUUUP!*—his return fire emanated red tracers, to show his line of fire, blanketing the target. Four 2.75-inch rockets *whooshed* down, and the *BLAM, BLAM, BLAM* of their explosions obscured Charles and his machine gun from view. The dueling tracers and rocket trails created a crisscrossing pattern of neon death. It was a beautiful dance of destruction, which only Picasso could have captured in one of his grotesque surreal paintings of the Spanish Civil War.

Except for a few curls of smoke where the machine gunner stood, it was over in less than ten seconds. The gunship banked to the left, leaving only a soft swishing in the air, and continued to circle, hunting. Many hours later, the grove of burnt sticks still had numerous thin, dark smoke trails spiraling languidly into the darkening sky.

Still squatting, Jones took a moment to jot a note in his finger-blood-stained notebook. He looked at the grove and, in awe, sighed to Herald, "LT, just a few more minutes recovering the CC and his crew, Charles would have cut us into little pieces, like fish in a sushi barrel."

Smiling at Jones, Herald agreed, "Gives one a good reason to believe in God, doesn't it? Let's hope our luck account has not been totally overdrawn. This ain't over yet!"

CHAPTER 13
IT CAN ALWAYS GET WORSE

THE OVERLOADED HELICOPTERS DEPARTED, turbine engines screaming under the weight of too many desperate men. Both Alpha and Charlie Companies were packed inside and out; those outside clutched each other as they stood on the landing skids.

Only the wounded and those who had been unable to pack themselves into the choppers remained, scattered between Herald's platoon and the grove of dark, headless tree trunks, from which smoke still swirled into the receding light.

Noise pressure from the twelve helicopters' jet turbines slammed against Herald's eardrums, generating a painful sensation. Even eighteen years later, when he recalled this event, the whine of the turbine engines reverberated.

Herald directed his platoon to spread out in an angle facing the bamboo grove. Scanning the area between where they stood and the jagged, smoking stubble, they spotted about forty abandoned men from Alpha and Charlie companies in clusters milling around.

Herald detected faint sounds of weeping; others were sitting with their heads in their hands or looking with a blank stare into the night sky in the direction the helicopters had departed.

At dusk a humid, tropical mist formed in the grove and oozed out between the spaces in the line of charred stumps. The fog amplified the smell of black powder and blood spilling deep into the abandoned rice-paddy field.

The mist reached Herald; the nauseating smell repulsed him.

So-o-o, you wanted to be a gunfighter, eh?

It was time to move into high gear. The helicopters were not coming back that night, and it was already too late to take defensive measures.

"Over here," Herald shouted, "and make it on the double!" The abandoned men wandered without direction, but after a few minutes, they moved to him and formed a group.

"OK, everybody, down on one knee," Herald said in a quiet, even tone. "We're all alone. Charles's buddies are just one klick away over the border. They may join what is left of his survivors in the grove and seek revenge on some GI ass, so riki tik, identify yourself by name, rank, and weapon."

One by one, each man introduced himself. It was a mess. Men outnumbered weapons, so Herald assigned two men to a weapon and ordered the platoonless soldiers to be split evenly among his squad leaders. Spacing his squads to all four sides, he created a rice paddy redoubt, a stronghold of about forty square yards.

The last unassigned man, sitting off to the left side of the group, was clutching an unloaded Russian RPG rocket launcher. He had a baby face, in stark contrast to his six-foot-plus height and muscular build. Herald looked twice at him and, sure enough, detected a bloody, dotted cleat impression on his chubby left cheek from the heel of an American combat boot.

"What's your name, and do you realize you have a boot mark on your left cheek?"

The boy giant looked up with tear-streaked cheeks. "Timmy O'Hara, sir. I'm called Little Timmy at home, and the boot mark is from my squad leader." He looked down again at the ground.

Herald bent over and surveyed the individual cleat marks on Timmy's cheek, some with coagulated blood in the deepest marks. "Are you in pain from those cleat marks?"

"My squad leader said he would take care of me, but then he kicked me off the helicopter." Timmy stopped staring at the ground and looked up with an empty gaze, tears welling in his eyes.

Herald, glancing at the launcher Timmy was holding, felt a betrayal and stared deep into his bloodshot, anxious eyes, questioning in a soft voice, "Where is your weapon, Timmy, and why do you have an unloaded Russian rocket launcher?"

Timmy hefted the launcher. "I dropped my rifle to jump on board the Huey. The chopper barely moved when we tried to take off. When it could not lift, it was clear we were overloaded. My squad leader yelled at me to jump, and when I didn't move fast enough, he kicked me off. After I fell, I couldn't find my rifle in the tall grass. I saw the rocket launcher and knew I'd better have some weapon, no matter what."

"How old are you, Timmy?"

"Eighteen, sir. I signed up after graduation." His bloodshot gaze returned to the ground. "This is my first night outside the wire."

A multitude of emotions was overwhelming Herald. Calling up his officer training, he replied in a calming voice, "Well, Timmy, hold onto the launcher until a weapon opens up. If we are attacked tonight, there will be weapons to go around—not to worry."

Poor kid. Hey, what am I thinking? It's my first firefight, and I'm just twenty-two. Who do I think I am, Victor Mature?

Timmy's body began quivering, starting at his left shoulder, moving to his right arm and down to his hand. Dread had him by the throat.

Smelling Timmy's fear, Herald piped up, "When I first got to 'Nam and went out on my first night ambush, my Platoon Sergeant Pearlman, God bless him, said to me, 'When we go out in the bush tonight, I do not want you to laugh.' My response was, 'There is no chance that I, a total newbie, will laugh about anything.' Then Pearlman explained, 'Frogs in 'Nam make a croaking sound particular to this country that sounds like the word '*re-up*.' Not to be outdone, the lizards nesting next to the frogs have their own song that sounds like the word '*fuk-youuu.*' So it may sound silly, but the frogs croak *'re-up,'* and the lizards answer '*fuk-youuu!*'"

Warming up, Herald continued. "The Army continuously pushes everyone to re-enlist; even guys in 'Nam. Their marketing phrase is to 're-up.' So it's just a little humorous; the lizards' response to the frogs singing *'re-up'* is '*fuk-youuu.*' So, I say to you, no laughing when the show starts later, OK?"

Timmy looked up. "I promise not to laugh, sir, but what a stupid story."

"You're right. Now get over to that rice-paddy berm. Your squad leader is Jones, got it?" Timmy crawled over to Jones, who placed him in his squad.

Herald reviewed the placement of his squads. AckMan, now platoon sergeant, was in the center rear with Hollywood; Ferlinghetti had the right side of the square and Jones the left. There was a man every three feet around the now-fortified redoubt. LeMaire had his machine gun facing the grove; it seemed the most probable area of enemy approach. Dog was at LeMaire's right side, as a spotter and ammo feeder.

The situation was bleak. No food or water except for what his platoon had left, after a full day of "fun in the sun." Dog bared his teeth and emitted a barely audible "GRRrrrr" as the last streaks of sunlight faded.

Great, just great. They never played this option out in Officer 'Cantaloupe School' at Fort Benning. No time to be scared. Let's get to the radio.

As he turned to Hollywood, the platoon sergeant from third platoon, whom he and AckMan had dragged from the fake-surrender ambush, yelped from the pain of the bullet hole in his thigh.

Herald moved to the sergeant and knelt down, whispering, "Sarge, we are out here alone and don't have enough weapons for everyone. Worse, we're here for the night, all eight hours of it, and when you make noise, it's a road sign for Charles. He may have a major case of ass over the day's events. Letting him know our exact position by your groaning is not just a bad idea but perhaps a fatal one. I know this suggestion is reminiscent of those John Wayne western movies, but it's time to cowboy up. Chomp down on something; chew if you need to, but no noise. If you can't control the pain, enjoy a little more of the medic's morphine, or it's gag time. Got it?"

Lying next to the sergeant was Boyd, the newbie concerned about LeMaire's tonguing his machine gun. Boyd had taken the spent bullet that killed Pearlman. Looking over to him, Herald inquired, "How goes it, Boyd?"

Propping himself up onto his right elbow and using his left hand to steady himself, he looked up with bloodshot eyes. "Not bad, LT, after I got over the shock and went into the land of the morph. Examining my leg, I realized the bullet is just below the skin." Reaching down with his steady left hand to just below the calf of his right leg, he lifted his pant leg and moved a solid object in the shape of a bullet head. "See, I can move the bullet under my skin. Pretty cool, eh? What a great good-luck charm for me to take back home. I'm OK. Don't worry about me, I'll be ready."

Herald smiled weakly, watching Boyd manipulate Pearlman's instrument of death under his skin. The bullet's movement caused Herald's stomach acid to creep up into his throat. Averting his gaze, he said, "Well, Boyd, ready or not, if and when we get out of here, you can return to base and have a doctor remove it properly. You go back on the first chopper."

The old proverb, "One man's meat is another man's poison," came to Herald's mind, and he just shook his head. The irony that the same bullet that killed Pearlman could be another's good-luck charm blasted Herald's emotions the way Charles's machine-gun fire had torn into the landing zone earlier in the day.

It would be nice if Boyd did not play with the goddamn thing like a Christmas toy.

Herald felt it was time to contact battalion. Stage one of "Get organized and get your defenses in order" was completed. On to stage two: communications.

"Road Warrior, this is Piper One. Over."

"Piper One, Road Warrior. What is your status? Over."

"Well, we are organized for a fight if it comes. Low on just about everything, so any argument with Charles will be brief. The light is almost gone, and there is low cloud cover. It will be a pitch-black night. If you could pop a flare over the bamboo grove we hit all day, I could plot some fire support. Over."

"You got it in two minutes; flares will be fired from Firebase Jackson. What is your strength? Over."

"We have forty men, plus twenty from my platoon, with one KIA, two wounded, and one officer: me. It would make everyone feel better about our chances if we could light up the field to break up the gathering darkness and see if Charles is starting to maneuver on our position. Over."

Just as Herald unkeyed the mic, there was a loud *pop*, and the five-acre square surrounding the men took on a bright reddish hue. With the light, everyone either dropped to the ground or stayed on one knee. The entire group scanned the area around them with vigilance. There was not a movement or sound, except the rustling of tall grass from a slight breeze, and the hum of insects.

The near-complete stillness meant little. The high, overgrown grass was more than enough to conceal Charles. He was a master of camouflage, and grass was more than he needed. The light from the flare, dangling from its little parachute to slow its descent, was comforting, even though the distant view was of smoking, beheaded black bamboo and palm tree trunk stubs.

Herald whispered just loud enough for the group to hear. "This may sound stupid, but keep a close eye out. Better yet, without starlight or moonlight and with this low cloud cover, keep a close ear out when the flare is gone. If there is an attack, we may have to move to the river—fast. I know on many night ambushes, one man sleeps and one watches, but not tonight. We need every eye, and, most important, every ear in every direction. When the flare ignites, look for any movement in the grass. If there's too much movement, we may have to run for it. There is not enough ammunition to stand and fight. We cannot allow Charles to cut us off from the river at night; that is our only exit by patrol boat back to base camp. If he cuts us off, it will be our Custer's Last Stand. And I'm not in the mood to be mutilated tonight.

"Further, the river boats provide our only source of cover fire if Charles forces us to make an escape before the choppers get back in the morning, but, first, we have to get to the river, and, second, we have to give the patrol boats time to find us. AckMan, Jones, Ferlinghetti, I want you to keep moving around to keep everyone awake."

Another flare ignited, and all eyes left him to scan the assigned area in front of them.

Herald picked up the radio hook, keyed the mic, and whispered, "Piper One to Road Warrior. Over."

"Piper One, this is Road Warrior. Over."

"Mark the last flare-firing coordinates as the midpoint for a covering fire grid, and we are down for the night. Over."

"Good night, and see you in the morning. Choppers back at dawn, and all the Charlie Company men who left in such a hurry are to be returned to you for final mop-up tomorrow. Expect a flare every ten to twenty minutes. Good luck, Piper One, and watch your posterior. Out."

Just as he clicked off the radio transmission, one of the boys from Alpha Company sneered in a hushed growl, "We were to be lifted out first! I was the radio operator for the Alpha CC. I had to lose my radio to find a spot on the landing skid, and two of my own buddies kicked me off. Charlie Company cowards skipped, and we are left here to die. Charlie Company ran, and now we're in the shit!"

Herald moved at a low stance over to the grumbling soldier and looked him directly in the eye as the flare's light was fading. "You may be right or wrong, but look around. There are sixty of us, more or less, to deal with a very pissed off Mr. Charles. We'll work out the blame game in the morning, if we're still alive. We all need to be on the same program tonight. Look, I am the only officer left. I'm from Charlie Company and have the only radio to call support. Did I run? No. I'm here with my entire platoon, looking you in the eye. Now, if you want, take a vote, and all you Alpha men who want to leave and set up another perimeter, go; otherwise, shut up!"

Silence was the response. Everyone understood it was time to pull together, or it was "Snuff-o-rama."

As Herald walked back to the radio, AckMan noted, "—*Ack*—LT, you have blood on your ass." He chuckled as he noticed that Herald's bandage, previously inside his pants, had slipped from his butt cheek and was hanging on his boot. "What's with the bandage around your ankle? Trying to get in touch with your feminine side? What is this, your—*ack*—time of the month?"

Herald felt his posterior and assured himself that the wound was only minor and had stopped bleeding on its own.

"AckMan, please keep my diaper a secret between just us, OK?"

AckMan was still snickering. "Have you been hiding something from us, LT?"

Giving a mighty sigh, Herald sat down next to the radio in the soft light of the descending flare. "I just hope all the excitement is over and we get out of this mess."

Time slowed to a snail's pace, every minute refusing to pass. It was as if a fiendish, grinning Charles were sitting next to the pendulum of the great-grandfather clock of time. As the clock's pendulum would reach the apex of its swing, Charles would snatch it, just for a moment, to hold time under his control for an instant, at his whim; then, with a hiss, he would release the pendulum back on its inevitable course.

Each rustle in the grass raised the hair on everyone's neck all night. With the flares, which came every ten to twenty minutes, every blade of grass, crevice, and knoll of the battleground was eyeballed for any hint of movement by Charles.

The flares themselves created shifting shadows in the tall grass. As the flares dropped, the angle of their light on stationary objects, such as tall grass stems and twigs, cast what appeared to be moving shadows. It made for a long, long, difficult night.

The low cloud cover and smoke from the bamboo grove merged; the soldiers could not see their hands in front of their faces. Visibility of any kind was possible only in the flare's harsh glow. Except for the hum of the insects, the only other sounds were the muted moans of the wounded sergeant and Dog's low *GRRrrrrs*, mixed with small, muffled *acks* from AckMan on the far side of the square. Boyd could also be heard whispering to different people when a flare cut the blackness, "Hey, want to see my bullet move under my skin?"

After about an hour, just as another flare popped and its reddish hue lit the landscape, Herald rose to a crouch. Moving in a zigzag pattern to avoid snipers, he crept over to Pearlman's body, knelt, and slowly opened the left flap of the fallen soldier's poncho. It gave off a solemn, rubbery sound. Pearlman appeared to be resting on his back. Pausing, Herald then lifted the right flap of the poncho, which was covering half of Pearlman's face. The smell of early decomposition filled the air as Herald raised and placed the right side of the poncho on the ground.

Something was out of place—wrong—but the aura of the last flare was dying out, and Herald lost Pearlman's image in the flat darkness. He sat in the emptiness of the night, with the smell of decay and the hum of mosquitoes, waiting for another flare.

Perfect. Just perfect.

After ten minutes, another flare popped high in the sky, and Pearlman's body was illuminated again in a ghostly red hue. Tears squeezed from Herald's eyes as he viewed Pearlman's figure, lying chest down, his open, dead gray eyes looking back at him. Something was very wrong.

And then Herald recognized what it was: Pearlman's head was on *backward*.

"Oh my God!" Herald gasped, his stomach convulsing at the sight of his friend's grotesque condition. Transfixed by the sight, he couldn't stop staring.

The bullet's pressure entering Pearlman's brain had pushed dark arterial blood out of his eyes, ears, mouth, and each nostril. The blood had mixed with dirt, making his face look like some macabre zombie mask.

Herald coughed and threw up into his right hand; the vomit flowed in brown rivulets between his fingers. He coughed up again, spit, and looked closer. Pearlman's face was turned 180 degrees and now positioned not over his chest but between his shoulder blades. His arms were also splayed in unnatural positions. Pearlman looked like some vandalized, cheap, department-store mannequin left in an alley on Halloween.

Herald figured the hasty movement of the corpse-carrying detail, with its numerous drops of Pearlman's body, had broken his neck and turned his head so it was twisted and facing backward. The flare's red gleam died, leaving Herald to his grief with the humming of thirsty mosquitoes to keep him company in the jet blackness.

Pop! Another flare lit up the area, this time casting a yellowish glare as it dangled from its little white parachute. Herald, in a rush to finish in the flare's short life, wiped his vomit-soiled hand on his pants, turned Pearlman's body over, and twisted his head back to normal. As he moved Pearlman's skull, the neck bones emitted an eerie crackle. After maneuvering Pearlman's rigor mortis-stiffening arms to lay crossed over his chest, he straightened and buttoned Pearlman's uniform and swept his long black hair back using his left hand, as was Pearlman's habit. Pearlman now lay in a manner befitting a revered ancient Viking chief. Herald kept straightening the profile of Pearlman's head, but it kept drifting to the right or left—the neck had no intact vertebrae to hold the head in place. Herald gave up.

He moved his right hand to the canteen at his waist. Feeling it, he snapped off the restraining cover with his right thumb, rotating the cap as he lifted the half-full flask.

The grieving soldier poured water over a corner of his towel and, with respect, tried to remove the coagulated blood, mixed with dirt, off Pearlman's face. Without support, Pearlman's head kept moving away from his touch.

Herald had to hold Pearlman's chin in the palm of his hand to finish cleaning his face. It was as if Pearlman were a little boy shying away from his mother's washing him. As Herald cleaned his friend's cheeks, he talked to him. "I should have let you stay at the firebase. Sorry, man, but I really needed you today."

The yellowish flare's luminosity was fading as Herald finished cleaning up Pearlman, making him ready for his platoon family to say goodbye.

Returning to his position just behind Dog and LeMaire, he announced in an elevated whisper, "Anyone who wants to say goodbye to Pearlman, do it now, one at a time."

As the last glimmers of another flare expired, Dog rolled on his side and rose to a crouch. He zigzagged to Pearlman, knelt down beside him, and sat in quietude for ten dark minutes, waiting for the next flare to see Pearlman. When it went off, Dog saw Pearlman's eyes were still open. He gave a quiet, startled "Roh-ra-Roh!" and jumped back. Recovering after a minute, he slid closer to Pearlman to have a last full look, head bowed, rubbing his hands together. As the flare died, he sat back on his heels, looked to the inky void of the sky, extended his lower jaw, pushed his lips together, and, in low, mournful tones, whimpered the melody, "Taps." "Rooh-de-rooooh. Rooh-de-rooooh. Rooh-de-rooh, rooh-de-rooh, rooh-de--rooooooh … "

His soulful, soft yowls raised the hair on the necks of the entire platoon and sent shivers down everyone's spines. As he intoned the solemn notes, his right hand extended with tenderness and closed Pearlman's eyelids. At the burst of the next flare, Dog rose to a crouch and zigzagged back to LeMaire.

As Dog moved, Timmy crawled over to Herald and asked, "What was that all about?"

Herald, grief stricken, turned away from Timmy, pretending to eye the flare wafting down. Unable to stop the flow of tears from his own eyes, he replied, "Dog was singing 'Taps' for Pearlman. Here in 'Nam, a platoon is like your family. You may pick your friends, as the saying goes, but you cannot pick your family. Dog lost two of his Army family in the last three months. After the loss of his best friend, he blamed himself and stopped speaking English. This is his only time to say goodbye to Pearlman.

"When you are killed here, there is no funeral or ceremony. The Army 'tags and bags' you, and you're sent back; there's no time to say goodbye. This was Dog's last chance. Like all of us, he may have a hard time when we rotate back."

"What is 'Taps,' sir?" Timmy inquired.

Herald jerked his head over, wiped a tear from his right eye with his right sleeve, and in direct eye-to-eye contact murmured, "Guess you'd better find out."

Timmy nodded and crawled back in silence to his position just as the flare died.

In the last rays of the flare, Herald noticed AckMan moving in a crouch while finishing his inspection of the entire perimeter. When AckMan was close enough to hear, Herald admitted in a low tone, "It's my fault. When Pearlman was spooked about today, I should have let him stay at the firebase. I have to wonder if I would have been able to make it without him."

AckMan paused, eyes fixed on Herald, and wrinkled his brow for a moment. He murmured, "Pearlman—*ack*—knew the risks. This is the way he would have wanted it: quick. He would have—*ack*—hated losing a limb to a booby trap and going home a cripple. If it has to be a bullet, let it not be a gut shot, where—*ack*—in agony you slowly bleed to death internally, or a sucking—*ack*—chest wound, where you drown in your own blood. A quick death with his platoon family would have been his choice.

"If you blame yourself, you'll end up like Dog. What the hell is Dog going to do when he rotates back to the—*ack*—world? Go back to school and get a PhD in canine diplomacy with his—*ack*—thesis in dog linguistics?"

Puzzled, Herald repeated, "Dog linguistics?"

"Dog language." He cocked his head and, scratching his chin, pondered, "Well, Dog could always fall back on the—*ack*—family business of tracking criminals with bloodhounds. Come to think about it, if he—*ack*—hires a manager who becomes fluent in dog to run the business, he could make it, but that is not the—*ack*—point.

"Let Pearlman go. Be happy you lived and—*ack*—learned to keep your head under fire. It could have been much—*ack*—worse.

"Pearlman is well to be out of it. None of us will be—*ack*—right when we get back. This war has infected us all. You've heard the old saying about being strung out on drugs. It's like having a monkey—*ack*—on your back. *We all carry 'Nam baboons.*"

AckMan and Herald sat in silence, waiting for the next flare. When it exploded and dangled from its chute, AckMan nodded his head and used the flare's light to guide him to Pearlman's body, where he knelt at his side. After a few minutes, AckMan returned to his post, wiping his eyes on his sleeve as the flare's halo ebbed. Everyone in the platoon visited Pearlman during the night, even LeMaire, who, as the last, with a gentle hand, covered their friend with his poncho.

When all had paid their respects, Herald was overtaken by a sudden feeling that Pearlman's cold, dead hand was on his shoulder, and a shudder surged through his body. Jerking around, he glared at the body.

Goddamn it! I remember the promise to call your parents. Stop yelling at me! Now is not the time. I'm not out of this yet, so back off! I promised, and I will keep my promise.

The mosquitoes were swarming with an extra vengeance. The normal scent of sweating humans spiced with the hormone of fear created a smell all its own, intoxicating to the little bloodsuckers.

Enduring two hours of buzzing, biting, stinging torture, and sensing the mosquitoes had crowded just about as many as could fit sucking at one time on his forehead, Herald turned his right hand outward and swiped it across his brow, squashing as many of the annoying pests as possible. Surveying the palm of his hand of the black band of corpses, he was sure it was a new personal record for mosquito kills.

Well, if this is to be it, so be it. If I live through this, I am going to find the coloring book when I get back home and guard it forever as my rabbit's foot.

Lifting the towel from his neck, he wrapped it around the lower half of his face and neck, as a shield from the mosquitoes, imagining he was an Arabian desert warrior.

The night dragged on, with only the flares to break the monotony. Herald sat on the hard clay of the rice paddy and surveyed the 360 degrees of his command. Light from the flares cast a shallow shadow beside the lonely poncho holding Pearlman. For the first time in many hours, Herald had a chance to stop and take stock.

Staring at Pearlman's body as the light of the flare died, he became aware of the nauseating smell of black powder and blood. Sniffing around, he found the source—*his shirt*. The vile odor was clinging to his clothing, even his skin. In the excitement of the day, the smell had gone unnoticed. But now he could even taste it.

Black powder from the explosives, plus blood from the wounded and dead, had combined to form a syrupy cloud floating through the air like cooking grease, the almost-solid essence similar to yellow stains that coat the walls of greasy diners. Herald now understood from old war movies what the term "smell of death in the air" meant. With this realization, his left shoulder muscles jerked involuntarily, and his heart and chest muscles all knotted. Stress has its own way of wreaking havoc on the human body.

As the night wore on, the frogs continued their *re-up* chant, followed by the lizards' answering *fuk-youuu*. Herald looked over to little Timmy and caught his eye after another flare touched off. Timmy, grinning and nodding back, ran his finger across his lips to signal they were sealed and he would not laugh.

Herald moved at a crouch over to the young GI and whispered, "I guess you'll be happy to get back to your unit tomorrow."

"Oh yes, sir," Timmy said, facing Herald with a steady gaze and a wry smile. He began to pick at the blood clots on his face where he had been kicked. The indentations of the cleat marks had swollen during the night; they now looked like large, inflamed acne bumps. As one of the larger clots came off, he looked up with a smirk. "My squad leader and I have a lot to catch up on."

Herald nodded in agreement.

As the light from the flares vanished, he crouched away from Timmy, all the while shaking his head and laughing to himself.

Oh brother! Oh great!

Returning to his spot, he thought back to college when Tom-Tom had posed the question, "Do you even *know* how to spell *gunfighter*?"

Know how? Ha! Now I can spell the hell *out of the goddamn word!*

CHAPTER 14
THE RETURN OF CHUMP

MOMENTS BEFORE SUNRISE, as the ink black night broke into shards of gray, the mechanical birds were heard in the distance, blocking out the sounds of the normal avian population. The *whop–whop* of chopper blades, growing louder by the second, signaled the return of those who had fled.

As the sound levels increased, the stranded men started grinning and looking to each other in awe and elation.

Having a mystical moment, Herald wondered if maybe there was a special reason he was still alive. The only answer: he firmly believed his survival was attributed to the talisman of the *GI Joe Coloring Book*.

In history, men have gone to war over grand ideas: the British had their Magna Carta; America had its Declaration of Independence. Considering that, Herald scratched his head. He wanted his Bill of Rights to be more profound than a child's fanciful GI Joe, but the book's magic had surely saved him.

Better safeguard the coloring book, just in case I have to invoke its power again.

Out-of-range blasts of exploding artillery from base camp broke his concentration, and he was back in the zone. The U.S. artillery had opened up on the bamboo grove to cover the approach of the helicopters.

The grove had been reduced to sticks and splinters the day before, but this did not make it any safer, just a more beguiling trap. Charles could have reinforced and placed heavy helicopter-destroying weapons in the shattered bunkers overnight, hoping the Americans would think he'd been beaten. When landing, helicopters become an easy target. Without artillery fire to keep him busy, Charles would have the opportunity to open up with a wave of destruction on the troops unloading and loading onto the choppers.

For a change, Herald and his crew got to witness the overwhelming effect of a helicopter assault. The *whop* of the blades and screaming jet turbines of the fifteen helicopters in formation were enough to awe anyone. In a matter of ear-shattering moments, the number of armed soldiers—and firepower—mushroomed in an area where, two minutes before, there had been total silence. The helicopters flared just enough to drop off the Charlie Company personnel who'd run, and copters sped away to avoid becoming targets. There was not one bullet from Charles.

The overnighters were inspired as the first wave of Charlie Company soldiers returned and marched to where Herald had popped smoke, marking the position for them to assemble. Sitting on the rice-paddy berm, Herald identified the first person to approach.

Oh brother! The one and only Leave-My-Post-Under-Fire Lt. Chump.

Thinking that an officer leaving his command under fire was the worst offense an officer could commit, Herald pondered what to do. Lt. Chump was followed by his platoon and the rest of Charlie Company.

When Chump was five feet away, Herald, still seated, moved his hand up and down, signaling to everyone to lower to one knee. All followed orders. His M16's muzzle was just two degrees off Chump's head. Chump, still in character, remained standing. Herald, shaking his head, yelled, "Christ, Chump! On one knee! The absence of incoming at this instant does not mean Charles doesn't have you in his gun sights."

Chump dropped to one knee. Herald, in his sly way, continued. "And a good morning to ya, Lt. Chump. Have a good flight? What happened to the Captain?"

"I got him to the chopper, but he bled out on the way back."

"Shame. Shouldn't have happened. So, Chump, what is your date of commission?"

"June 1968."

"Well, mine is March 1968," Herald came back, trumping Chump's ace, "and that puts me in command. Any problems with the concept … 'chump'?"

"No," Chump responded. "I understand, Lt. Lloyd."

"*Good*. Would've hoped you'd stuck around for the party last night. Well, in honor of your auspicious return and in order to ensure there is no communication gap, you personally—not your point man—will walk point today for the entire company. Any questions?"

"You don't think I bugged out, do you, Lt. Lloyd? I mean … I … I was … I was helping with the wounded CC and … you know, Lt. Lloyd, I would feel a lot more comfortable if the muzzle of your weapon was just a few degrees more to my right."

Pausing for a moment, Herald remembered stories of fragging. In Vietnam there was a practice of throwing a grenade into the bunker of a soldier he'd been arguing with. Grenades leave no trace of ownership. To embarrass Chump further would be a stupid and maybe fatal mistake. The better choice was to put him on point for all to see.

Readjusting the angle of his M16, Herald gave his attention to the men. "Everyone not in Charlie Company move to the landing zone to be evacuated out. Timmy, you pick someone to handle our wounded and dead, and sort the returning men into sticks of six. Boyd, you go with Charlie Company … and stop showing everyone how your bullet moves under your skin. It creeps me out! When all are in position, I will call back for pickup."

Addressing Timmy alone, he added, "Timmy, this could have been nasty, and your presence was greatly appreciated. Hope you enjoyed the frog-and-lizard show! Goodbye."

Picking up the hook and keying the mic, he continued. "Piper One to Road Warrior. Over."

"Piper One, this is Road Warrior. Over."

"Road Warrior, all Alpha Company personnel formed for pickup. Over."

"OK, pop red smoke for the pickup, and Charlie Company sweep the grove. Report back when completed for pickup. Out."

Herald turned to Chump, lowered his head, and met him eye-to-eye. "Lt. Chump, move your platoon first. My platoon will follow, with the third platoon in the rear."

Returning his attention to the men, he shouted, "The word of the day is *not* to save ammo. Every dead body you see, mark with a bullet. This is not a drill. We do not want to die because you were unsure Charles was dead and hesitated. If you're worried about the cost, take it out of my allowance. Now move out and disperse, at least four abreast. No two-fers today! On the other hand, if there is a clearly wounded Charles, he is worth a lot in information; so call it in, and we'll get him out. OK, move out."

As Herald ordered Chump to walk point, Dog sat up, raised his head and barked, "Rah-TA-RATH!"

Again, they were treated to a blinding, sweltering, steamy day for mop-up and body count. The battalion commander was not just furious—he was outraged and embarrassed. Enough ordnance had been fired or dropped on the bamboo grove to win WWII, yet it had been impossible to obtain a body count last night. The battalion had lost one company commander and several other men, and what should have been an orderly withdrawal of one company became an unorganized mass flight of two.

It had not looked good for his battalion when the helicopter battalion commander reported to the corps commander that the companies of the 2nd Battalion of the 27th Infantry had fled the battlefield. The panic had caused overloading, nearly resulting in the destruction of two troop-heavy helicopters, and leaving men in the field exposed for an entire night. Such disorganization leaves a bad mark on the battalion commander's record.

When they'd fled, the battalion commander had met every helicopter as it arrived back at the base and personally took the names of Charlie Company personnel who had run. He made sure the next day they all went back to face those who had spent the night. And Charlie Company was now the laughingstock of the battalion, if not the entire corps.

Herald never found out and never asked if the battalion commander had insisted Herald's company commander expose himself to capture the VC.

As Chump approached the first berm of the still-smoking bamboo grove, he threw a grenade to check the area. He also had his machine gunner open up with two long bursts, just to provoke a response. There was none—just silence, the oily smell of death, and small spirals of gray smoke heading skyward from the grenade blast. As Chump came over the berm where the 51 mm heavy machine gun had opened up, all that was left of the gun was broken shards of metal. The only body part, exposed above ground, was one bare cheek of an enemy soldier's buttocks.

"Piper Two to Piper One," Chump reported, "have located part of one body so far and moving on. Watch out for the smell. Out."

Herald's platoon soon reached the scene.

Climbing the six-feet-high berm, Herald surveyed the vicinity. The only item of note was the same exposed cheek, where just a scant ten hours previous at least two human beings and one heavy machine gun had ruled.

The second Charles of the machine-gun team had been either buried or vaporized by the destructive force of the Gatling gun and rocket blasts. Herald guessed one of the benefits of overwhelming firepower is automatic burial or complete dismemberment, leaving scraps not worthy of burial.

The grove was decimated, as though it had been part of an atomic bomb test. Bits of human flesh were scattered everywhere, and the slightest breeze sent waves of an intense, vile odor wafting over the platoon. Everyone gagged, and at least two vomited. Jones, stopping for a moment, scribbled in his book and sneered, "I will remember this smell for the rest of my life!"

Herald groaned and pulled the towel from around his neck over his nose.

On the menu today we're serving black powder and blood, with a side of decomposition ... pair with the 'Vietnam cocktail.'"

Yes, the climate in Vietnam was so tropical and loaded with bacteria, twelve hours was more than sufficient to coat an entire dead body with decomposing mush. The mush pulsed with swarms of feeding maggots. The flies never missed an opportunity to start a new generation.

Herald raised his hand and waved it forward like a wagon-train master out of the Old West, signaling to move out. Dog wrapped his face in his handkerchief, took point, bared his teeth, and gave a low "GRRrrrr." The platoon spread out into its four squads, weaving between the bomb holes and counting body fragments. Herald, with AckMan as platoon sergeant, walked straight to the other side of the grove.

AckMan turned and, looking over the black-scape, *ack*-ed so hard he threw up. The sight and sound of one person vomiting spread like an epidemic through the platoon.

Only LeMaire was untouched by the sights and smells. "*Merde*. I youngust; buucherr'd kill, whethar be beaver, deer, or moose, even road kill. This, not so *mauvais*."

"LT, what happened to the—*ack*—Captain?"

"The CO bled out on the ride back," Herald responded, shaking his head.

"That's too bad."

Herald gave a grim smile. "Well, at least he died with his balls on."

"Don't you—*ack*—mean with his *boots* on?"

"No, the Captain's last worry was his balls. Maybe he should have been more concerned about stopping the bleeding than looking for his balls ... but the follies of war ... "

AckMan laughed. "*Ack*—died with his balls on. Not the same ring of heroism as dying with his boots on, eh?"

Herald smiled, "Yeah."

Ferlinghetti, with his squad in the rear, crested the last berm. Looking in every direction for any movement of Charles but seeing nothing but death and destruction, he groaned, "*Porca miseria!*" and then changed his tune. "'e, LT, I 'ave *una poema per questo momento*." Pulling out his book of poetry, he turned to a page marked by a dried marijuana leaf and read.

One of those paintings that would not die'
   its warring image
                 once conceived
     would not leave
             the leaded ground
no matter how many times
               he hounded it
                    into oblivion
Painting over it did no good
     It kept on coming through
              the wood and canvas
and as it came it cried at him
          a terrible bedtime song
     wherein each bed a grave
           mined with unearthly alarmclocks
        hollered horribly
           for lovers and sleepers

(A Coney Island of the Mind: Poems, page 27)

"W'at-a you t'ink-a, LT?"

Herald grinned wryly at Ferlinghetti and wiped the sweat off his face. Gazing back over the death and destruction of the once vibrant green bamboo and palm grove, he sighed. "This grove is a warring image that will never leave my mind's canvas, no matter how many times I try to paint over it. Good poem, but back on task. Get on your weapon, and get to your squad."

As the company cleared the grove on the other side, Herald called back to the battalion, "Piper One to Road Warrior. Over."

"Piper One, this is Road Warrior. Over."

"Well, we finished the sweep, and there is nothing left alive or even in one piece. I estimate from all the bits of flesh and uniform scraps, they are North Vietnamese Army, twenty to thirty were killed, with an unknown number underground. What is next on the hit parade? Over."

"Pickup in fifteen minutes. You know the drill, Piper One. Out."

Putting down the hook, Herald considered the oddest aspect of the sweep was that not one dead-body shot had been fired. There were no bodies intact enough to pose any possible threat. "OK, spread out for pickup."

The company spread out into groups of six, as the *whop-whop* from the chopper blades grew louder.

How about just a nice dull day today ... a day to appreciate being alive.

Moving to the lead helicopter, Herald paused to look back at the grove and assess the human and financial cost of the blackened ground. Saddened by the sight, he sighed and shook his head.

With his body engulfed by jet fuel exhaust, he turned in the face of the screaming turbine jet engine, stepped on the helicopter landing skid and up into the trembling helicopter bay. In a crouch, he walked to the rear panel of the helicopter, pulled off his helmet, and placed it under his butt to aid protection against explosions. Leaning his head and back against the wall and vibrating with the engine, he slid to the floor.

He felt a pinch of pain from his wound as his butt rested on his helmet, which sent his mind floating back to the University of Vermont, where he should have appreciated how good it was just to be alive.

YEAR 1988

HERALD FELT PAIN in his arm, prompting a slow climb out of his alcohol-induced sleep. It was 3:00 a.m.

He had fallen asleep on the sofa, leaving Thea alone in the bedroom.

The nightmare of his first firefight and how he came to face his fear of death or dismemberment set the stage for the next event; he had to inform his client of his malpractice. Herald knew from Vietnam that being able to face his fear was the one true gift nobody could take away from him. If he expected to get out of this mess, he had to confront the legal puzzle and think his way out of it, or at least minimize the damage.

Herald went back and forth to the kitchen for several consultations with Mr. Bourbon over the rocks. The lyric of a Fine Young Cannibals

THE RETURN OF CHUMP   249

tune came to mind and he began singing it. "What is wrong with my life that I should get drunk every night?"

One thing for sure, he did not need any counseling; he could handle this. After all, he had conquered his fear of death in combat; why should he be afraid of a few memories?

In the dark recesses of his mind, he could hear those memories pounding on the thick doors of his psychological vault. Herald went to bed for what little was left of the night. In the morning, he woke up, took a shower, and went to work. It was another MD.

CHAPTER 15
TIME TO 'FESS UP

HERALD ARRIVED AT THE OFFICE on Tuesday, MD 24. The second item on the agenda was to phone his client and tell him of the malpractice problem; the first was to stiffen his coffee with several shots of bourbon.

Walking back to the Parrot Room, coffee mug in hand, he sat in his high-backed, leather swivel chair, put the mug on his desk, buried his face in his hands, and shook his head. A light sweat began to erupt on his flushed forehead. It was time to inform the client of his mistake. The word *MALPRACTICE*, in giant, electric red letters, rolled across his brain like the Times Square electronic ticker tape.

Herald took a long swig of coffee-laced bourbon, took a deep breath, and was reaching for the phone when an electrifying pain shot into the left side of his chest. Needing reinforcement, Herald returned to the coffee room for another mugful, this time stronger on the bourbon. He returned to his chair nursing his drink, sip by sip, and calmed down.

Reaching for the phone again, Herald punched in his client's number, the finger of his right hand performing as if a ten-pound weight were attached. A pause, punctuated by electronic clicks, hung in the air for what seemed like ten minutes instead of seconds, as Ma Bell made the connection. The first ring fired through his head. On the second ring, sweat formed on the back of his earlobes. He toyed with the hope that, just maybe, no one would answer—just a short reprieve before the "Sorry, but my mistake cost you $2.4 million" conversation.

Partway through the third ring, the secretary answered, "Thall Consulting Services. May I help you?"

Now, that's the understatement of the day!

"Norman Thall, please. This is Mr. Lloyd." As he spoke those words, his long hours of legal research and what course of action he must take flashed through his mind. The minute he was kept waiting for Norman to pick up the receiver felt never-ending. At last he picked up.

"So what more do you need from me? I paid your last bill on time," Norm sneered into the phone. "You legal gangsters with your construction-defect lawsuits have killed my civil engineering profession, and that goes for general contractors, too."

The 1980s had seen tough times for the construction industry. Litigation had erupted on a mass scale over defects in single-family dwellings. A change in the law made developers and general contractors strictly liable; suing them was easy money. The litigation costs alone had precluded the insurance industry from offering insurance to geotechnical engineers for this type of coverage.

Herald massaged the pain on the left side of his chest with his right hand as he answered. "I need to inform you of a problem in one of your cases—it involves the Sunset Condo Case, where the plaintiff had taken the default of your company and of you, as an individual, with the civil engineering license. I negotiated a deal where the default was lifted for both. Do you remember?"

"Of course, I remember … and you actually did your job. We investigated, and it appears we have no liability. What's the problem now? Don't tell me you need more money?"

Knotting up, Herald exhaled to calm himself and, in a slow, even tone, to be sure Norm understood, answered, "I need to get right to the point. It appears I forgot to include your name in the stipulation for relief from default in the Sunset Condo matter. Now the plaintiffs are making an issue of it."

Silence. Then the receiver exploded with Norm's booming voice. "For God's sake, how could you have been so stupid? This will wipe me out! You'd better find a way out of this, or it's going to cost you dearly. Christ, I should have known an attorney would end up being my Achilles' heel. You'd better be insured for this!"

Herald coughed and spit stomach bile carrying a slight metallic taste of blood into the trash can to his right. Sweat beading on his face and running down onto the receiver, he replied, sounding calmer than he felt, "I lost my malpractice insurance last year, due to meritless claims. None of the claims resulted in a judgment against me, but the carrier still had to hire an attorney to defend me. Just as the insurance companies refuse to insure your business, they have refused me malpractice insurance. We insureds may have no liability in claims made against us, but insurance companies don't like the high legal cost to defend a case, and are aware of capricious juries often made up of biased homeowners. Further, owners are easily confused by conflicting expert witness testimonies and tend to rule sympathetically for the homeowner. However, I have carefully researched a motion to solve our problem, and I need your permission to go ahead."

Norm paused to gather his wits. "How appropriate that leech lawsuits have placed you at risk. But your kind started this. What are the chances you'll win the motion?"

Herald took a long drink, the bourbon coffee tingling on the way down. "Well, it's a tough road. My opinion is, we could win. There are cases in my favor and declarations from witnesses clearly acknowledging the agreement was to include you specifically. I would like the chance to beat them on my terms, especially since this is *my* ass as well as yours. We're on count-down. The motion for relief from default must be heard in twenty-six days, or the court loses jurisdiction to grant relief."

"Lloyd, I cannot afford another leech attorney! From what you're telling me, there's not enough time for another legal sleazebag to review the case and make the right motion."

There was a pause, as Norm contemplated the situation before continuing. "All right, listen … and listen good! Here are my terms. I will send over a written agreement specifying that, if you lose the motion to solve your malpractice, you will sign over your office building *and* your home, and agree to give me a percentage of your earnings for ten years. The agreement will be with my son, to avoid any of your malpractice-judgment creditors from finding those assets. Agreed?"

Herald coughed and spit again. "All right, I agree. Send over the agreement, and I'll sign it."

"And your attorney wife—she signs, too."

Herald paused, his breathing shallow with trepidation. "There might a problem, but she most likely will agree."

After the word "agree," a distinct click rattled the line as Norm slammed down his phone. Herald hung up and raced to the bathroom, the thumping of his Vietnam memories drumming louder in his head.

He closed the bathroom door and threw up all over the toilet, even before he could kneel down and open the seat. If Thea was forced to sign over all their assets, his marriage was gone, along with his children. His stomach continued to pulse for several minutes as the various consequences of this disaster battled for supremacy in his brain. Maybe he could *not* handle this.

Herald splashed his face and mouth with cool water and, contrary to his usually fastidious nature, left the rancid bathroom unattended to return to his desk.

The legal question continued to be daunting. Ninety percent of the rulings were against him. As he rubbed his forehead, the familiar sensation of rising stress acted on Herald's mind in the manner he most dreaded. He could almost hear the "stress coin's" *plink* as it was inserted into his mental slot machine of random-flashback choices. The handle was pulled, and the colorful reels began spinning. Today's roll settled on three little pictures of Lt. Chump.

The "Chump selection" focused on analyzing what appeared to be a hopeless situation, later proving to be not as bad as it had first appeared. Even before leaning back in his chair, Herald was playing out the memory in vivid technicolor.

YEAR 1969

HIS PLATOON WAS AT weapons practice at the firebase range. Weapons practice allowed everyone to have fun. Recreation is limited in a combat zone. Every two weeks, Herald took his platoon over for target practice after all-night patrol, when they had the morning off—in a manner of speaking. The three other platoons on the base took charge while Herald's second platoon had time off.

This accomplished three practical goals. The first was to make sure the day-to-day exposure of their weapons to dust and dirt did not cause a jam at the worst possible moment. The second focused on the ammunition they carried. No matter how careful they were, it would become contaminated by dust and dirt; fouled ammunition could also cause a malfunction. What better way to ensure their weapons were operating right but to fire them? Third, and most important, walking around waiting to get shot is nerve-wracking. There is no better way to shrug off a little anxiety than by firing a military weapon on full automatic. It is the type of thrill that builds confidence in abilities and weapons—just the type of diversion a soldier needs to stay sharp in the day-to-day stress and fear. The entire platoon, in groups of four, shot at the targets. Herald stepped up to the firing line with AckMan, Jones, and Ferlinghetti.

This was not a formal military firing range, just a dirt ramp where the soldiers stood to discharge their weapons. The bulldozer which had formed the berm around the firebase had also scooped out a section about 100 yards away for the backsplash. The targets were beer and C-ration cans on separate bamboo poles, a poster of the Squaw Valley ski resort on a plywood backing, and an array of coffee and other containers scattered on the bulldozed backsplash of dirt about six feet high.

Just before practice began, Dog raised his face to the sky and barked, "ROUH-rah-HA-HA," and Jones asked, "May we add two more targets?"

Looking up, Herald smiled and replied, "Sure. Why not? Go ahead."

Walking downrange, Dog and Jones removed pictures of their girlfriends from their wallets. Each picked up a stray two-by-four and forced them into the dry clay ground; then they attached the pictures to random nails on the wide part of the board. They chuckled as they returned.

Unable to see the posted images and curious over the men's chuckling, Herald asked, "What are those pictures of?"

"Our former—girlfriends," Jones replied, to which Dog added, "Rarh," sending the entire platoon into gales of laughter.

The squad leaders and Herald were the first to open fire. Some took their time picking out a target; others went full automatic. Herald emptied a magazine on full auto, punched the eject button to let it drop to the ground with a *tink!* and slapped in another clip.

He decided to find out what extremes his M16 weapon could endure. After about 100 rounds, or five magazines, his weapon felt fiery hot through the plastic barrel cover. *Odd,* he thought, slapping in another magazine. Before he could close the breach, the top round cooked off in the chamber, exploding.

Tiny shards of brass from the cartridge case riddled his shirt. Little traces of blood appeared on his face and neck, and spotted his shirt. Unbuttoning his shirt to be sure the damage was superficial, he turned and hollered, "Cease firing if you are close to 100 rounds, or you will get a brass necklace, like I just did!"

The squad leaders stopped firing, looked at him, and muttered in a collective manner, "Hard core."

Herald walked off the firing line wiping the blood off his face and chest with his towel and ordered Jones to move his four-man squad into position. After the soldiers expended their weapons, the other two squad leaders took turns moving their four men to the firing line for practice.

Rather than the wholesale barrage Herald had engaged in, the squad leaders had a program. First, one full magazine on full automatic, to help the men exercise better control of the weapon when used in this manner. An M16 was a wild beast on full auto. It took rehearsal to hold an M16 at gut level and fire five-to-six-round bursts with accuracy. After walking around in the bush on semi-auto, full auto was nirvana.

When they finished with full auto, the next exercise was to fire three full magazines on semi-auto, focusing on hitting the targets dead on. The last drill was to have the squads practice Fire and Maneuver. This permitted one squad to maintain fire on a target and keep it pinned down while popping smoke to conceal another squad's movement to a superior position, closer to the sniper. The squad, having just moved to a new position, then performed the same strategy of fire, smoke, and maneuver to allow the other squad to move closer to the sniper. The squads alternated this strategy of firing and covering one another until they neutralized the sniper.

After a fun morning at the range, the entire platoon spread out on the bunkers and cleaned their weapons, enjoying a rare moment of contentment.

Adjusting his surfer sunglasses, Hollywood grabbed the tattered, folding aluminum chair and called out, "Anyone for deep-sea fishing?"

AckMan, doing a bad English accent, countered with, "Righto!"

Jones sat on the bunker closest to the chair, removed his notebook, and started writing in it while tapping on his chin with his left index finger.

Ferlinghetti, surveying the compound for any possible intrusions and seeing none, exclaimed, "*Siamo di buon umore. Ecco: una poema!*"

Dog gave a "Ruff" and ran over to the fishing chair.

But before anyone could start, the new company commander rushed over with his map shouting, "Chump is pinned down by several snipers! Grab your gear and go get him!"

"What's his location?" Herald asked.

Gesturing on the comics, the CC pointed to the area of assault. "Over here by the old bombed-out church, where the rice fields have been overgrown by bamboo. The villagers are clearing the land, and Chump's platoon was to cover them if any Viet Cong objected. We're not sure, but we have intelligence Charles has a strong point in the area. Your radio call sign for today is Butter Two, and Chump is Butter One. I am Apple One. It appears Charles is changing tactics and is now trying a daylight attack. I sent helicopters over, and they could not spot anything. Lt. Chump is convinced he is under serious attack. Be very careful. It's just weird nobody has been killed or wounded yet. The firing has been going on for more than thirty minutes. Very odd. Could be a setup for an ambush."

Looking up from the comics at the CC, Herald cocked his head and squinted one eye. "Are you trying to butter me up by sending me out as Butter Two?" Grinning like a Cheshire cat, and not waiting for a response from the CC, he turned to his platoon. "Mount up. We're out to rescue first platoon. In case this is an ambush, I want everyone to carry a full ammo load, four frag grenades, three smoke grenades, and two claymore mines, and extra water. It could be a long day."

The platoon assembled its weapons in record time and formed up. Herald returned from the company mortar platoon working out the grids to call in fire support. The trusty band headed out in silence. Each man had only one thought on his mind: sniper.

Sniping was a one-way road for Charles. His mission was to kill or maim as many Americans as possible before they got him. Everyone was wondering whose number would be up that day, as the only way to find a sniper is to let him fire first. A sniper's objective was to create a casualty, which generated a higher cost than a fatality. A casualty required several soldiers' attention be diverted to caring for the wounded, instead of fighting. Although Charles had cover and time on his side to wait with patience until he had a clear shot, the report of his weapon telegraphed his general area.

With his location revealed, the platoon performed the Fire and Maneuver sniper drill just as they had practiced.

Today's bonus was that the snipers were already firing on Chump; their position had already been revealed.

Four hundred yards from what appeared to be Chump's locale, Herald split up the squads, having each approach on the same angle but starting 100 yards apart; then he shouted maneuver orders.

"OK, listen up! Sniper drill! Move slowly, and keep your distance from each other. Each squad to maneuver under smoke while the other squad stays in place and provides cover. Always pop smoke before moving to a new cover location. Keep it up until you're close enough to take him out, and if someone takes a hit, leave them to the medic. *No heroics, and nooo two-fers!* OK, let's move out!"

The day was a scorcher; fear makes a hot day insufferable. The real heat was inside the brain. There was no chatter among the platoon as they walked. Grim faces showed the stress. No one wanted to be the sacrificial trooper the sniper wounded or killed to give away his position.

Sweat poured off each man's brow as they moved, searching every tree, bush, six-foot mud wall, and rock, all while watching for movement in tall grass.

The crackle of the radio startled everyone. "Butter Two, where are you? We are unable to move, under heavy fire. Help! Over."

Herald picked up the mic, his perspiration dripping down and soaking the instrument. Wiping the sweat off himself and the mic with his neck towel and keying the mic, he whispered, "Butter One, we are on your west side moving in on your position at two separate angles, 100 yards apart. Pass the word to your troops, we're on the way, and they are not to fire on us. Where is the fire coming from? How about a direction? Over."

Hearing only static as the answer, he turned to his platoon. "Remember, the first rule is, Charles knows we are here, and this is a trap. Take it real slow. First platoon has not taken one casualty yet, which really spooks me, so go real, real slow. Our approach may be booby trapped as well, so pay attention.

"AckMan, you take Jones's squad. Jones, you follow AckMan's order. I will take Hollywood and Ferlinghetti's squad with LeMaire and Dog. Remember, all squad members move together. Before you move, be sure to pop smoke for cover. Move only as far as you throw smoke. With one squad providing cover for the other, it will be harder for the sniper to pick a target in the smoke of the maneuvering squad."

"Butter Two, this is Butter One. The firing is all over the place. Hurry up! Out."

"OK, men," Herald shouted, "let's get this party started!"

AckMan ordered Jones's squad to throw smoke grenades, and his squad started moving forward. Herald, with Ferlinghetti's squad, lay in the hot dust, emitting small bursts of M16 fire. The sun beat down on everyone, compounding the physical carnival of "maneuver and wait to get shot." Each man was not just hot but close to becoming molten with fear. And where were the snipers?

After two movements, one of the newbies in Jones's squad flopped down to take up position and vomited on his rifle—a reaction to the oppressive heat, stress, and physical demand of running, dropping, and crawling. AckMan started *ack*-ing in lower but audible tones by the second maneuver. By the third movement, LeMaire bellowed at Charles, *"Merde*. Come and get some, stupide gook salaud." Tension hung in the air like the 100 percent humidity. The boys were losing their sense of humor.

Herald yelled to everyone, "Easy, guys! By the numbers! This could all be Sir Charles's plan to suck you in and blow it out your ass! A bad temper is a quick way to lick on a bullet popsicle. Everyone, calm down!"

Feeling the muscles in his left arm and chest tightening, Herald began massaging his torso. LeMaire, catching sight of it, laughed. *"Mon Dieu*, LT, rubbing your grands tetons?"

Herald smirked at his comrade, "Wish only stress was gnawing at me. It would be nice if the chest pain did not feel like a heart attack."

Each member of each squad felt the apprehension of an expected head shot every time the group rose to a crouch to move. Movement toward a sniper is target time for the VC. One of Ferlinghetti's boys threw up on his buddy as he moved past him. The smell of even more vomit further enhanced what Herald referred to as "the usual delightful smells of this backwater country."

This maneuvering continued for an hour until Herald's platoon was only forty yards from Chump. The entire platoon could clearly see Chump's platoon bunched together along a decaying masonry wall.

Where the hell are the snipers? We should be taking some of the heat now that we're this close.

Herald was perplexed and assessing the situation when he noticed smoke rising from a fire behind Chump's position. It was a bamboo fire set by the locals in the process of clearing their land. He remembered from an earlier patrol how, as bamboo burns, it gives off a *snap* sound. The sudden crack had caused him to jump; it sounded just like an AK-47 round passing overhead.

Noticing one of the farmers throwing on more bamboo, Herald rose off his knee, looked to Ferlinghetti, and pointed to the left flank. Using sign language, he indicated to Jones that his group take the right flank. Then he walked over to Chump, yelling, "AckMan, cover the rear with LeMaire; Dog, with me!"

"Are you mad?" Chump hollered. "There must be ten or more snipers out there with all the firing!"

"Chump, stand up. I want to show you something."

Chump crawled over to him. Herald grabbed Chump by his fatigue-shirt collar, his feet twisting in the dry clay from the effort, and lifted him up so he had a view over the earthen wall. A farmer was piling more bamboo onto the fire.

Smirking, Herald pointed at the farmer. "Bamboo is made up of sealed segments. When it's burned, the water in each segment begins to boil. The boiling punctures the segment, making a snapping noise not unlike an AK-47 round going off over your head. The fact nobody has been hit after several hours is a clear sign there is no sniper.

"The first time I heard burning bamboo snap while on patrol, I jumped, too. Seeing the farmers clearing the land here, I realized the snap was not small-arms fire, but bamboo burning. It appears the noise was not as lethal as it seemed," Herald concluded, laughing with relief.

Looking over his shoulder for Hollywood, Herald caught him on his back tanning again. Attuned to Herald's disapproval, he jumped up and hurried over. Herald gave him a frown, picked up the radio's hook, keyed the mic, and spoke. "Butter Two to Apple One. Over."

"Apple One to Butter Two. Over."

"Butter One, snipers cleared from area, no casualties, but many dead bamboos. Over," he laughed into the mic.

"Dead bamboos? Butter Two, what are you talking about? How is Butter One? Any wounded? Over."

"Apple One, we are coming back. Butter One was bamboozled. Only wounded egos on this mission. Out."

AckMan moved next to Herald, knelt down, and yelled so Chump could hear, "No sniper or snipers?! What the—*ack*—hell—*ack*—is going on? We crawled—*ack*—four football fields in this heat for one hour, waiting to be shot, and no—*ack*—snipers! LT, *we* are going to kill this bastard for his and all our own good! If we don't stop his stupidity now, why—*ack*—he could breed, and there could be more stupid bastards giving us heart attacks."

"Rr-rr-*ruff*!" Dog approved, tossing in his two cents, "GRRrrrr!"

Chump, fear still in his eyes, stammered, "I thought for sure it was a sniper. My fear panicked the entire platoon. We just froze, waiting for the first person to be killed. My hands would not move, and my brain was locked, except to call for help. Now I feel stupid."

Grinning over Chump's admission, Herald was generous, "Fear will do that. I've read many military journals telling where fear has panicked entire units. However, had you thought through your fear, it would have seemed unjustified, as the supposed sniper had not wounded even one person. I just hope you do better when Charles really comes calling. We all have fear, Chump. We all must learn to face it, like it or not."

LeMaire freaked and ran to the top of the earthen wall. "Imbecile, tak zeese you bad'th bamboo. *Mauvais bambou, mauvais bambou!*" As he bellowed, he fired 100 rounds from the machine gun and made everyone laugh and relax, except for the farmer, who must have thought the Americans had really lost it.

What the farmer had witnessed was one group of soldiers huddled on the other side of his six-foot wall for three hours doing nothing. Later he watched another group popping smoke and running around, looking like they were attacking the first group. The soldiers finished by standing around together laughing, while one of them fired into his burning bamboo—crazy, crazy Americans!

Ferlinghetti looked all around, laughed some more, sat on the ground, and pulled out his book of poems. Wiping the sweat off his brow, he muttered, "Chump, *mannaggia la miseria,*" and read:

> Christ climbed down
> from His bare Tree
> this year
> and ran away to where
> there were no rootless Christmas trees
> hung with candycanes and breakable stars
>
> Christ climbed down
> from His bare Tree
> this year
> and ran away to where
> there were no ...

(A Coney Island of the Mind: Poems, page 69)

"Not now, Ferlinghetti!" Herald called out. "It's not even close to Christmas. We've spent too much time out here in the open. Form up and move out. Chump, take your platoon home to the left of us."

YEAR 1988

HERALD SMILED, RECOLLECTING all these years later the look on Chump's face after he saw the bamboo fire on the other side of the high wall. Things seldom are as bad as they seem, and thinking through the problem helps to put it into proper perspective. With that lesson in mind, Herald hit the law library and began the arduous task of pulling his ass out of the fire.

Many hours later, he returned to the Parrot Room and began the process of creating a motion to save his family, economic future, and legal ego. With special care to integrate the case law with his facts, he dictated the points and authorities into his handheld recorder. This is the legal format lawyers use to compare past appellate case law precedents with the facts of their own case, in order to persuade the court to adopt their point of view.

Analyzing the primary opposing cases, he used the law or facts of the cases to differentiate them from his own situation. Then he went to the sleaze bar down the street for a consultation with Mr. Bourbon. Two doubles fortified him enough to face the music at home. He climbed into his VW van and, without a single flashback, hit the road.

As usual, he entered the front door, yelling a group "Hola!" and passed through the small dining room, heading for the kitchen. Cooking was Herald's way of calming his mind after a stressful day. He surveyed the refrigerator to determine what to make for dinner. Grabbing a previously opened bottle from the wine rack, he removed the cork with his teeth and picked up two wine goblets. Holding the bottle in one hand and the goblets in the other, he moved to the dining room.

His eight-year-old daughter Katherine, the more serious one, was doing her homework, intent on moving her crayons over the picture due the next day. Bending down, Herald gave her a brief hug. She placed one arm on his shoulder, just enough to acknowledge her dad without breaking her concentration.

Leaving, he entered the living room, said hello to Thea, and tried to give her a small kiss on the cheek, but she turned away. Placing the goblets and wine on the coffee table, he continued toward the back end of the house and entered the kids' bedroom to find Elizabeth playing inside her yellow Toys-R-Us tent with her Barbie dolls. She came out for a brief hug but went back in to finish her adventure. Returning to the couch, Herald sat down next to his spouse and poured both glasses of wine. He gave one to Thea, and with a sigh, raised his right hand with the wine glass toward the ceiling, as if in a salute.

Thea flicked her hair back, looked into his eyes, and demanded, "How bad is it?"

He took a quick breath and asked, "Is this a law partner, wife, or mother question? Actually, this mistake is serious enough to concern all three personalities. We could be toast."

Thea stood up, flicked her hair again, and, ignoring the red-wine-stain consequences, threw her full wine glass into the fireplace, and faced him, hands on hips. "I have tried to get you to slow down when dealing with legal documents. But oh no, not you; you just have to get it done. Well, with the way you have been abusing alcohol, this was bound to happen. How bad? It has been more than a week since I asked you. And I do *not* want to hear your flimsy excuse about some curse over a failure to call a dead guy's parents after you were discharged."

"OK," Herald shrugged, "so *now* this is a spouse, not a legal partner, question ... and there's no 'First, the good news' about it. If I lose, we could lose the house and be forced to start all over again. Norm, always the charmer, wants us to sign over the office building and our house, and pledge a percentage of our earnings for ten years. Also, do not underestimate the Pearlman curse."

Wringing her hands and pacing the room, she cried, "O God! The children!" and covered her face with her hands to collect her thoughts. After a minute, she lowered her hands and, turning to face Herald, snarled, "What a viper Norm is! He may hate attorneys, but he sure knows how to act like one of the worst legal leeches by having us sign over everything we own. I cannot do 'start over,' not with the probability that you will make the same mistake in the future. Nothing is going to change if you continue to drink and refuse to seek counseling. If you lose this motion, the girls and I are going back to my parents in New Hampshire. You can deal with old curses on your own time.

"Changing gears: for Christ's sake, call them tonight! You've kept Pearlman's telephone number in your wallet all these years. Call them now!"

Herald's mind blazed red. With a studied coolness, he put down his wine glass, rose, and walked out the front door, careful to not let it slam shut. On the way to the van, he massaged the pain of his tightening chest muscles; then, opening the door and jumping in, he accidentally smacked his forehead on the doorframe.

Starting the engine, he headed to the rundown bar near his office. Nausea wracked his body; his head ached, both inside and out. Now he was sporting a goose-egg-sized bump on his forehead from his collision with the van's doorframe, and the mental pressure of his mistake was giving him a colossal headache. On the bright side, his head pains silenced the war memories that tortured his soul.

To escape the feeling that his brain might explode, Herald forced his thoughts to the brass vases he'd brought back from Vietnam and which now sat on the mantle above the fireplace at home. It was a positive memory from eighteen years earlier, one that would not feed his anxieties.

CHAPTER 16
THE GOOK IRONMAN CONTEST

YEAR 1969

HERALD WAS SITTING on top of an outside bunker wall next to the main gate, having breakfast. He'd been relieving the two gate guards who'd gone on break to get their own morning meal. The two bunkers on the parapet guarding the main gate were different in design from the perimeter bunkers. The main-gate bunkers protected the weakest point in the firebase, the access road; therefore, they were larger but dug into the ground only four feet deep, as opposed to the six-feet-deep perimeter bunkers. This raised the view slits almost two feet high off the berm, increasing the area of surveillance. The road, plus every square inch within twenty yards of it on both sides all the way up to the bunker footing, gave maximum visibility to repel attackers. This would prevent a sapper, a Viet Cong infiltrator armed with an explosive device, from crawling up and placing an explosive charge at the base of the bunker without being seen. The bunkers on the perimeter were part of the defensive wall and did not need the extra view required at the main gate. The rear outside wall of this bunker faced the interior firebase and was a perfect breakfast backrest.

Halfway through his meal, Herald heard the shuffle of footsteps. As the only person on main-gate duty, he was now on full alert. Adrenaline raced through his veins, his face flushed, his breathing increased, and sweat formed on his forehead and palms.

In a flash, he moved to seize his rifle and, in his rush to rise, upended his meal kit, tossing freeze-dried eggs with hot sauce and sausage all over his weapon and hands. Grabbing his rifle, heart pounding in his ears, he crouched behind the bunker wall, peered over, and, with his mouth still full of food, he shouted, "Halth er I will flire!" sending bits of egg and sausage flying onto the bunker roof.

Yep, that's why my parents taught me not to talk with my mouth full.

A solitary Vietnamese man approached the gate with a bulging rice bag the size of a large explosive charge. By his slow gait, slouched shoulders, and thin, five-feet-two-inch frame, he appeared to be old and weigh no more than 100 pounds. Naked except for a loincloth and barefoot, this was the typical garb worn by the natives when planting the rice fields. Constant exposure to the sun weathered the Vietnamese skin, making their ages impossible to estimate. This man could have been anywhere between forty and sixty years old and was most likely from the farming village two kilometers away from the base.

He stopped and pointed to the bag. "You lookee, you lookee, trade, trade."

Herald raised his crouch just enough to allow his head to pop up in a glimpse but continued to expose his left arm as a sign of deference. He motioned for the man to drop the bag, conveying the message by pointing at it, then flipping his finger down to the ground, all the while keeping his rifle on target.

The native understood this pathetic excuse for sign language and dropped the bag. He knelt to one knee, opened the bag, and pulled out what appeared to be two brass objects. Placing them on the ground, the old man looked at Herald and enunciated, "Trra-a-a-ade, trade, OK?"

Herald felt like *he* was the less-civilized participant in this conversation, being unprepared to barter. "OK, what do you want to trade?" He said the words in a plodding manner, as if by speaking more slowly, he would help the old man understand English.

Herald wanted to engage with the old man and, per previous orders, had, in fact, been required to do so. The Army had mandated that, when possible, the outlying firebases were to interact with the villagers and provide them with equipment for their own defense. It was part of the Hearts and Minds Program of the U.S. Army, to befriend the South Vietnamese.

The farmer reached for a small piece of torn paper from inside the limp bag, waved it at Herald, and placed it on the ground. Searching the roadway for a moment, he picked up a small stone, glanced back up at Herald, nodded, smiled, and placed the pebble on the paper. The tough but fragile-looking man then bowed, moved back about five meters from the brass objects and paper, and squatted in the dusty road.

With my inability to grasp the simple concept of trade, this poor man must really wonder how the U.S Army could ever save them from the Communists!

At a crouch, Herald moved around the bunker corner and took quick steps to the paper and objects. Keeping his right hand on the pistol grip of his M16 rifle, the muzzle trained on the villager, he knelt down and eyed the objects and paper; then, picking up the empty rice bag with his left hand, he checked it for weapons and, finding none, let it drop. Next he picked up the paper with writing on it and held it up in a way that he could read it while keeping an eye on the Vietnamese through the sights of his rifle.

Scrawled on the paper, in the jerky, pencil-printing style of a first-grader, were the words, "One 55-gallon drum gas, 50 engineer stakes, two roll barbed wire."

Pretty good for a native, Herald thought, eyeing the paper and alternately keeping track of the old man, still patiently squatting on the road. This trade gesture *could* be nothing more than a trap to get him away from the cover of the bunker. The farmer continued nodding, smiling, and pointing to the paper.

Still on one knee, Herald picked up one of the duplicate objects with his left hand, realizing it was a tall, sculpted vase with a full middle section, a graceful opening with scalloped edges and narrowed at the bottom just above the round base. Turning it, he felt its impressive weight. It was solid brass, not mixed metal, and not cheap. On one side of the vase was a delicate etching, stylized in graceful, sweeping, feminine lines. It was an artful, hand-engraved scene of a deer with antlers standing next to a tree on its left. On the right flew a flock of birds in the foreground above a landscape of tall grass and rolling hills in the background. Herald knew that brass was not the hardest metal to work with, but not the easiest, either.

Wow. These would be really expensive to make commercially.

Continuing that thought while spinning the vase by its neck to view the base, he checked for identification as to where it was cast and dumbstruck by what he discovered. In the middle of the bottom was a small circle of a different metal in its center. Examining it closer, he read "105 MM M14" arched along the top of the circle. This vase was a reworked American 105 mm artillery shell casing!

An artillery shell casing would be weird enough, except Herald knew all his Vietnam-era 105 mm shell casings were made of a thin, cheap, brass alloy. This was a solid brass casing, which, due to the huge expense of brass, had not been used since WWII. He was holding a piece of history from a war-torn nation dating back to WWII, when the Vietnamese ousted the Japanese, or the 1950s when the French used American WWII weapons against the Viet Cong, before the division of North and South Vietnam.

Standing, Herald walked to the Vietnamese, checked him for weapons and pointed for him to pick up the empty rice bag. As luck would have it, the engineer stakes and barbed wire were right next to the gate bunker. They were kept there for quick perimeter and gate repairs. He showed the villager those materials and then pointed to a fifty-five-gallon drum of gasoline behind the bunker. It was meant for one of the medical generators.

The crafty Vietnamese trader jumped up and down with delight at his good fortune, placing the vases at Herald's feet. Beaming with satisfaction, the gaunt little fellow grabbed the two rolls of concertina wire, fifty pounds each, still in the original protective covering, and headed down the road to his village.

Twenty minutes later, he was back for his first load of engineer stakes made of metal, eight-feet long, and stamped into a long "U" shape for strength from a flat piece of steel about six inches wide, and one-third inch thick. Stakes were used to support barbed-wire fencing. They have a point at the bottom to be driven into the ground, and have a small, punched-out, hook-shaped "V" every inch from the top to about two feet from the bottom. This allows soldiers or, in this case, Vietnamese farmers, to loop the barbed wire under the metal stamped "V" and hammer it into the face of the stake, holding the wire in place. Back in the U.S., a similar form of engineer stake is most often used to hold traffic stop signs at intersections.

With each stake weighing about five pounds, the ambitious trader hauled twenty to thirty stakes at a time back to his village, taking just two round trips to complete the second part of the deal.

Herald was amazed at his strength, and by this time, AckMan, Dog, and Ferlinghetti, back from chow, were watching the show and hollering to others to come see. Hollywood interrupted his tanning session to run over to the commotion; Jones was already there, pen in hand, writing in his notebook.

At last the old man came back for the fifty-five-gallon gas drum. As before, he had no cart to haul his merchandise. He moved to the drum and, from somewhere in his loincloth, pulled out a worn silk scarf, ten feet long. Placing it beside the thirty-five-inch-high drum, he put his shoulder to the top of the drum and, using all his body weight, tilted it slightly to one side, while simultaneously kicking the scarf under its base. Dropping the drum, he crossed both ends of the scarf over the top. Smiling and nodding, he moved around to the other side of the drum. With each hand, he picked up one end of the scarf. Raising both ends, he tied the scarf around the drum, leaving it a little loose. Turning his back on the drum, he reached behind and raised the loose portion of the scarf over his head, adjusting the knot to the middle of his forehead. He was now ready to lift the drum. How he would be able to do this, with his small frame and weight, was a mystery to the observers who had gathered to watch.

By this time, news of the old man's feats had spread throughout the firebase. The curiosity had been sparked when one GI noticed the tiny man hauling away a large number of heavy engineer stakes. He told his buddies, and twelve additional bored GIs gathered to watch the villager carry off the rest of the materials.

Simultaneous with the old man positioning his scarf, AckMan, always on the lookout for a good time, yelled, "I'm—*ack*—taking—*ack*—taking bets the old man will—*ack*—move the gas drum."

Ferlinghetti, looking all around, saw an opportunity to exploit the eager crowd gathering. "*La cosa da nulla, il gioco da ragazzi!* Ma, 'oo wan-a to bet 'e no can-a do dis?"

Two men from the growing crowd moved the old man to one side and gave the drum a shove themselves to make sure it was full.

"This mother's full as shit!" one hollered.

"Damn right, sure is!" hollered the other.

"So let's see," the first one said, as he began to calculate, "a gallon of water weighs, what, about eight pounds? And gasoline floats ... "

"So does shit!" the other interrupted, sending a wave of cackles through the crowd.

"Hey, I'm counting here. Shut yer dumb face! So, let's say a gallon of gas weighs ... uh ... six-and-a-half pounds. That makes fifty-five gallons of gas weigh ... *about 350 pounds? Impossible!*"

"The gook maybe weighs 100 pounds drippin' wet ... and he has to walk two damn kilometers to his village ... *in this heat!*"

"Yeh, that's right!" shouted another.

"OK, Ferlinghetti," called out yet another, "I'll take your bet!" In a flash, his bet was echoed by ten others.

Ferlinghetti now had two-to-one odds the old man could do it and shouted, "*Ecco il fuoriclasse!* 'e can-a do it!"

LeMaire was in charge of holding the money. Everyone knew, or knew of, LeMaire as the five-feet-ten, 260-pound, mad French-Canadian, U.S. machine gunner. He was the perfect candidate to hold the money; nobody would dare steal from the psychopath. If LeMaire decided to steal the money himself, no one was going to go after him, either. After LeMaire collected all the bets, he looked at AckMan and yelled, *"Jouer balle!"*

The group quieted and moved away from the old man to give him space and get back into position with the drum. Every time he started to lift the drum, rounds of shouting erupted, and new bets were made.

Unsure of the meaning of the commotion, he would drop the scarf from his forehead. Not knowing English, the innocent man had no way of understanding what the yelling and mayhem among the GIs was about. He could understand it had something to do with his attempts to pick up the drum, but he didn't know what the GIs intended, and he feared for his safety. Putting the scarf down, he turned with a sour expression and started to walk away for good, thinking this whole trade was a joke on him and that the GIs intended to cheat him on the deal for his artful vases. It was time to leave the gasoline and vacate the grounds before they killed him.

But each time he tried to leave, the GIs would bring him back, point to the drum, slap him on the back, and smile. Again the old man would try to move the drum, only to feel threatened by the yelling, so again he would put the scarf down and start walking away. Again the GIs retrieved him, pointed to the drum, and smiled.

The poor, confused man was escorted back to the drum for the fourth time and placed in front of it while the crazy Americans roared. He looked around at the smiling GIs and decided they wanted him to take the drum after all. He backed into it, lifted the scarf over his head, spread it evenly on his forehead, and put his buttocks against the drum to tilt it on his back. Flexing his small but capable, walk-all-day-in-the-rice-paddy-mud legs, he leaned forward and lifted the drum. It moved up in the air a couple of inches, quivered, and dropped to the ground.

Excited cheers erupted from the GIs, who now numbered sixty. Additional betting started when the old man tried to stand up with the drum again and dropped it. After the second failed attempt, two GIs went over to the old man. Each picked up one of his skinny brown arms and raised both straight into the air, waving them over his head; advertising that this was a champion in the making—and a call for more bets.

We must look totally crazy, Herald thought, *with our Las Vegas casino betting on this poor man and his gasoline.* Then he shouted, "The betting is closed. If we keep up this insanity, the object of your bets will freak out and run. I certainly would if I were this Vietnamese farmer facing a group of madmen. Everyone smile, point to the drum; continue smiling and pointing to the drum. No yelling!"

In a low chant, the group began: "Point at drum, smile; point at drum, smile; point at drum, smile."

"OK, OK," Herald called out, "Enough! Now, quiet! Let the man work his magic."

The group moved farther back from the old man, either sitting down to watch or standing, waiting in anticipation. There was total silence, except for the medical generator's humming. The old man turned around again and placed his butt against the drum. He took a slightly different angle, re-knotting the scarf. Cocking his body at the waist, the fuel drum rose with hesitation four inches from the ground. The farmer shifted his weight slightly to the left and right as he steadied the load. He took one step, paused, and then took another step. A stunned silence hung over the crowd.

He proceeded slowly, taking four or five steps before stopping and allowing the drum to rest on the ground for a minute or two. He continued in this manner, lifting, taking four or five steps, and resting for a minute or two. Before anyone could believe it, he was a distant black dot fading into the green landscape.

The GIs realized they were up against a people who had a superhuman will and strength of character. A new respect was accorded the Vietnamese that day—and Ferlinghetti was a wealthy man.

Jones, with left middle finger pressed hard against his front teeth, wrote in his notebook, "The Vietnamese people: incredible strength of will, no brains. He could have rolled the barrel instead of picking it up. These gooks do everything the hard way."

After the old man left, Herald gathered his platoon for daylight patrol. "Circus time is over. Back to work. Get your gear."

The little band formed up and headed out. As they cleared the gate, Herald yelled over his shoulder, "Got a candy run today. Down to the river, around Charles Park, back over the dry rice fields, and home—cake walk, all easy with no hot spots." ... *What a lie.*

With each step outside the wire, the effect was the same: stomachs tightened, adrenaline flooded the body, eyes narrowed, and the feeling of being fully alive dominated the psyche.

CHAPTER 17
CIRQUE DU 'NAM

YEAR 1970

ACKMAN, FERLINGHETTI, AND JONES started to chant their own version of the Wicked Witch of the West's soldiers' mantra from *The Wizard of Oz*. With each step outside the wire, they droned, over and over, "Oh-ee-o ... Y-O-O-O-um. Oh-ee-o ... Y-O-O-O-um." Within minutes, the entire platoon began joining in. The annoying droning went on until an irritated Herald stopped, turned and shouted, "Enough, already, for God's sake! This is not a walk on the beach, and you guys are bunching up. No two-fers!"

The river was about two kilometers away over clear ground. The platoon stopped at the river's edge. A crowd of Vietnamese children came out of the nearby village. They knew from past experience the GIs were suckers for children and passed out candy.

Every soldier's C-rations always had something sweet for a dessert. Candy was also available at the base for the soldiers to purchase. Hard candy was one of the few luxuries, and it did not melt in the heat. Many care packages, sent from relatives unaware of tropical conditions, contained items susceptible to heat and would arrive in a molten state.

278 CURSE OF THE COLORING BOOK

Herald never lost an opportunity to generate a nice rapport with the children. Interacting with them led to good public relations with the nearby village and was in agreement with the initiative to "win the hearts and minds of the Vietnamese." Having good manners with the children was a favorite job and gave the soldiers a break from their dismal days.

Herald posted guards at all points of the compass in twos, to warn and stall in case of an attack. This left twelve GIs to interact with the children. This guerrilla war demanded everyone be on guard at all times. If they snoozed, they did not just lose, they died.

The soldiers always carried food and candy on their patrols, to make sure they were properly fueled. However, because heat and fear tended to curb their appetites, they were glad to share half their allotment with the children. Those who wanted to give would approach the youngsters with gentleness, smiles, and hand gestures, and they would speak in pidgin English as they passed out their food and candy.

Herald went over to where a stream joined the river and called to several wary children standing shyly off to one side. Waving them over with the Vietnamese signal to come, which in the U.S. is the hand motion to say goodbye, he encouraged them, and they inched their way over. "Fish?" he asked as he pointed to the river. One of the older children knew what the word "fish" meant and nodded yes.

Taking out a hand grenade, he pulled the pin. The children screamed and started to run. These young people knew about grenades. Most likely it was one of their first words of warning, similar to American children learning, "Stove, HOT; fire, HOT!" One of the first things a Vietnamese child learns is, "Grenade, BOOM! Booby trap, BOOM!"

"No, no! OK! OK!" Herald called out, waving them back.

Stopping in their tracks, not hearing any "BOOM! BOOM!" and deciding it was safe, the children returned. Herald let the safety handle ping off the grenade and, well within the five-second delay, tossed it into the stream-river junction and waved his hands for everyone to get down, which they did without much prompting.

As they ducked, the grenade went off with a loud *WUUUMP!* A plume of water shot ten feet into the air. Herald gathered the children to the stream. Sure enough, a large number of fish, stunned, some live, some dead from the explosion, popped up to the surface. Seeing the fish rise to the surface, he laughed, remembering the stories from his relatives of dynamite fishing in Delaware. This illegal fishing was accomplished by lighting a waterproof fuse with a blasting cap inserted into a stick of dynamite and throwing it in the water, resulting in an explosion that stunned the fish.

Ferlinghetti carefully scanned the area to his left and right; then he came over to Herald and his young enthusiasts, waving his small book in the air. *"Ah! Che colpo di fortuna!* You 'ave-a good-a luck, LT! I 'ave una poema delle pesci ... a poem about-a de fish-a. OK I read'a?"

Herald, laughing at the children jumping for the fish, replied, "Why not?" Ferlinghetti smiled, opened the book, and started.

> Cast up
> > the heart flops over
> > > gasping 'Love'
>
>
> > a foolish fish which tries to draw
> > its breath from flesh of air
>
>
> And no one there to hear its death
> > among the sad bushes
> where the world rushes by
> > in a blather of asphalt and delay

(A Coney Island of the Mind: Poems, page 40)

Before responding aloud, Herald considered, *Indulging Ferlin in poetry may be good for Ferlin, but it's starting to get on my nerves!* "Off the top of my head, the poem seems to be a metaphor for the futility of falling in love.

Love, like a fish trying to breathe fresh air, is destined to die in the rush for status and wealth back in the old capitalist USA."

"LT, *che cavolo dici? Ma*, I no can-a wait-a to get-a 'ome, *pesce si o pesce no!* Hey, LT, you miss-a Pearlman?"

"Not a day goes by that I do not miss him. That bullet could just as easily have been mine. He was less than an arm's length from me. Somehow rather than feel guilty, I feel he gave me an important gift ... the perspective that life is fleeting, and to appreciate every day. Does that answer your question?"

"*Si, si*, I joost-a wan-a to get-a 'ome, too, *sai?*"

Herald's attention was drawn back to the noise of the children splashing in the water. Rambunctious, they were jumping into the creek, grabbing the stunned fish and tossing them to shore. The more enterprising ones used sticks to corral several fish together and push them to the shore, en masse. This was a special treat to take back to their parents. It was like an all-American Easter egg hunt and the best use of a grenade he could think of. The irony that the slang word for grenade was "egg" crossed his mind.

As the youngsters were gathering fish, one of the village elders came over to Herald, held out military scrip and pointed to one of their women, who in turn gave Herald a snaggle-toothed smile, indicating she was willing. Herald was about to say no, when LeMaire, Hollywood and four others came over and begged to do a little sporting with the woman.

Alarmed at the idea, Herald gasped. "No way in hell." But the desperate look of the men and concern about upsetting LeMaire gave him cause for empathy. Relenting, he negotiated the deal, informing his merrymakers, "You've got thirty to forty minutes, max, so have a ball. And I hope to God you guys have condoms." Ignoring him, the men disappeared with the woman inside her hut.

Jones walked to the main gate of the village and sat on a sandbag wall to the right of the gate. He had seen the woman who was the object of attention, reflected and shook his head no, pulled out his notebook, and began scribbling and sucking on his left thumb. Ferlinghetti walked over, eyed the village for movement of any type, and hoisted himself up on the sandbag wall beside Jones. He started to pull out his book of poems, but before he could open his mouth, Jones looked up and said, "No way, Jose! I'm busy."

Ferlinghetti frowned, jumped off the wall, and walked away reading poetry to himself and muttering, *"Ma che rompiscatole ... pain in de ass!"*

After confirming visually that the nonsporting soldiers were in proper positions to maintain security while the sportsters had their fun, Herald leaned up against a hut pole in the shade. Memories of New Year's Eve with Bright, his rent-a-woman in Taiwan, began dancing in.

YEAR 1969

THEY WERE IN HIS hotel room discussing how to ring in the New Year. She had selected a certain bar in downtown Taiwan, one of the few that had a live band that played American rock and roll and allowed prostitutes.

"I don't know," he hesitated, "I'm still concerned about leaving the hotel on a big holiday. It's a perfect time for a surprise attack. Besides, we have everything I need here: a restaurant, a bar, a bed—and you. Outside makes me nervous."

Fixing her eyes on him, she spun around in the only item of clothing she was wearing—her high heels. "What? Brave GI come to Taiwan and never see sights? You only leave hotel room three times on six-day holiday and thousand miles from Vietnam? What do when get home, live in cave? What tell friends saw in Taiwan, hotel room because fear going out? They laugh at you. If you want Bright to stay, must go out and have fun. You not be scare-cat." Pouting, she crossed her arms and plopped down on the bed. Crossing her legs, she bounced her upper foot so the glitter on her plastic shoes sparkled.

Herald relented. "OK, we go out. But if I start feeling uneasy, we're heading right back. And by the way, the word is 'scaredy-cat.'"

Jumping up, she grinned at him, and bent over in a provocative position, showing her privates, and began rummaging through her travel bag. Still beaming, she pulled out a red leather halter-top, waved it over her head and shouted, "OK!"

After she finished dressing, they went to the elevator for the ride down. Pushing the call button, he remembered his fear of this particular lift. When it arrived, the door hesitated again while opening, but the right side panel creaked open enough for them to enter. Feeling nauseous as the car bounced from side to side in its descent, Herald grasped the handrail. Riding the ten floors down was enough to make him break out in a cold sweat.

The car doors rattled open, revealing a lobby alive with the sounds of new GIs on R&R inspecting Sunny's female inventory lined up by the bar. It was the same drill as when he'd picked out Bright.

"I have best GI here!" Bright announced, flashing her eyes again as she took Herald's arm and paraded past the lineup. "He real good to me! He Numbah One!"

As they approached the front door, Herald felt his chest and shoulder muscles tighten from anxiety. He hesitated as the noise of the city filtered in. Opening the door, he became overwhelmed by the sensations of the city. After adjusting in record time to the raucous energy of the street, he looked at Bright. "I'm getting better at this, aren't I?"

"Yes, my brave GI, getting better."

She waved for a taxi. A driver spotted her and, as was the custom in Taiwan, without signaling, cut across three lanes of traffic and stopped at the curb. The drivers he'd cut off exploded in a frenzy of objecting horns and hand gestures.

Once inside the relative safety of the taxi, Herald calmed enough to start noticing aspects of the city that at first had been obscured by his unwavering focus on danger. That finely honed skill, developed in Vietnam, was of little use here; yet it had taken him nearly a week to begin reprogramming himself. He started by noticing the buildings of the city. Unimaginative cement blocks, three or four stories high, they were covered, ground to roof, with flashy neon signs hung one on top of another, additional signs filling in every exposed gap—a total hodge-podge of information, bombarding again and again.

The streets were twice as narrow as those in an American city, and every square inch was utilized. Ground-level stores or selling stalls had their wares stacked on six-foot-long tables jutting out onto the sidewalk. For-sale goods hung from the ceilings, backs, and side walls of the tiny booths. No space was left empty. Every color of the spectrum infused the surroundings, radiating from the cornucopia of colorful signs, merchandise, and people hustling through the crowded streets. Ancient yellow taxis sported various shades of light brown and rust, showing their age and abuse.

Arriving at Bright's favorite hangout, the entrance of the bar was ablaze with lights blinking around a large, red neon sign flashing the name, Rick's Café Américain, in both Chinese and English lettering. It stirred his memory of the famous movie *Casablanca*, in which Humphrey Bogart's bar bore the same name.

After sizing up the doorman, Herald grinned and teased, "Mr. Bogart, I presume?"

The doorman returned a smile. "No, my name Sam. Ten dollar."

"Could you play that again, Sam?"

"You GI very funny. First one to make movie joke. Ten dollar."

Herald handed him a ten-dollar bill and started in, but the doorman grabbed Herald's arm. "You play ten dollar again; ten dollar each."

"Touché," Herald grinned as he handed the doorman the additional ten bucks.

Stamping their hands "Paid," the couple ambled into the club—right into a haze of thick cigarette smoke that obscured everything beyond six feet. Taiwan cigarettes, far stronger than their American counterparts, are filled with a mixture of malodorous ingredients resulting in the dense smoke; moreover, the harshness of the inhaled smoke, first- or second-hand, was toxic to the lungs and irritating to the eyes.

Passing the entrance podium, Herald pocketed several brightly colored matchbooks bearing Rick's Café Américain logo, and mused, *Imitation: the sincerest form of flattery.*

There were many Americans in the bar with their own rent-a-woman, but what caught Herald's eye were the yellowish-tinted Christmas lights strung around the bar. They looked cute until closer examination. Touching one he reeled with disgust: a half inch of smoky grease and dust debris had built up on each tiny light bulb and the electrical cord. It was a wonder they emitted any light at all, and it was apparent they'd been hung many years ago for holiday parties long past, and never taken down.

Well, it saves on decorating costs.

Viewing the peeling paint on the walls and the torn bar seats, he concluded, *This makes the sleaziest bar on Bourbon Street in New Orleans look like the Ritz. What a perfect place to spend possibly my last New Year's Eve on earth. Perhaps I deserve such chaos as my last memory of this insane world.*

Bright, on the other hand, was in a particularly frisky mood. With her supple, red leather miniskirt that matched her halter-top, both so tight they fit like a second skin, she enjoyed being a female reveling in her sensuality. Her body was tingling after the nonstop days of sex with Herald, who'd been using intercourse to bury his fears. She loved the fact he had left no part of her body unattended.

Her eroticism lit Herald's spirit and made him laugh. He figured the war gave Bright the ultimate economic playground. In one year, she'd earn what a woman of her class could not make in ten years of honest labor. And, Bright provided a kind of social service for the traumatized men who needed to forget the war.

Now, here at Rick's, was an American-style New Year's Eve party for the GIs in progress. But this party was about thirty degrees off center, as produced by the enthusiastic Asians—the best example being the band. They played well enough, but English words sung with a Chinese accent did not really work. The mix of cultures made the lyrics to all the songs the band was singing appear to be a mockery of home.

Herald was pondering that while he and Bright were standing at the bar. Bright whispered to him as she raised her right leg, exposing her inner thigh, to the bar rail, "Touch me under skirt. Have surprise."

True to her word, the surprise was she had no underwear on. An electrifying sensation of passion passed between them as his fingers stroked her wetness. He loved that no one could spy his fondling under her skirt. Playing with Bright in public titillated him beyond all comprehension, fulfilling some dark fantasy of which he had been completely unaware.

He nuzzled and kissed her face and neck at the bar. She pulled him closer, to avoid anyone observing their play, and moved her hand to his zipper. With an erotic tease, she pulled the zipper down, placed her hand inside and rubbed him. After a few minutes, she parted his underwear front seam and held him in her hand. He felt as if his brain was racing into a void of white light. Removing his now very wet fingers, he rubbed them together. Her scent was everywhere, intoxicating.

Bright looked into his eyes and murmured, "We go to bathroom." She removed her hand, pulled up his zipper, and grabbed his arm with the other hand. Entering the large men's bathroom, they headed to one of the enclosed toilet stalls.

Once inside and latching the door, he placed both hands on her waist and lifted her to the top of the toilet water tank, her skirt rising and exposing her. Straddling the toilet bowl, he yanked down his zipper, took himself out, and pulled her onto him until they were fully joined. As they moved together, she cried out, "You good, GI! You so, so good! HARD, HARD, like no tomorrow!"

Why indeed? Why not hard, like there's no tomorrow? Who knows if there'll even be one?

Their passion boiled over with wild movements thumping on the walls of the stall so loud they could be heard outside the bathroom over the blaring band. At last, they hung clinging together for a time. Herald continued to reflect, *Why not go for a walk on the wild bathroom side? Maybe we've found a special relationship in the chaos of the war. After all, we've already spent five days together. Who knows? It could happen, couldn't it?*

Just then, in the next stall, he heard another GI's rent-a-woman say the exact words Bright had been using on him: "You good, GI! You so, so good! You Numbah One GI!," accompanied by the same stall-thumping sounds and exchange Bright had been baiting him with.

Unbelievable! I guess I'm not as special as I'd like to believe. This public sex in the bathroom fantasy is just part of the Standard Taiwan Prostitute Program.

Herald had been fooled again by his naiveté and emotional hunger. The sounds from the next stall confirmed he and his fellow stall-mate were with skilled women trained to earn money by nursing emotionally sick soldiers, making them feel special, at least temporarily.

His fantasy crushed, he threw his head back for a diversion and noticed the paint peeling from the mold-stained cement-block ceiling. The absurdity of this world made his head spin.

Bright could fuck my eyes out and piss on my grave.

Lifting her off him, he sat her on the toilet seat while she continued to rub his neck and kiss his face.

They returned to the bar, just in time for the clock to strike midnight. It was 1970.

Bright, continuing with her good spirit, began singing with the patrons "Auld Lang Syne," with her distinctly Chinese accent; Herald joined in, and they waved their champagne glasses at each other. For closing, the band played the soldiers' theme song of the Vietnam War, "We Gotta Get Out of This Place." Everyone who was American joined in the chorus, using the same Chinese mispronunciations as their hosts, "VE GOTTA GET OUT OF DIS PACE, IF IT'S THE LAST TING VE EVER DO!"

The Asian accent of the band was the icing on the theme-song cake rattling around in his mind and mocking him.

Here comes that cartoon feeling again.

He looked around, acknowledging the only American things in the room were the Americans themselves. Everything else was a cartoon replica of what the Taiwanese thought Americans wanted while on vacation from the war.

A small child looking for candy grabbed his hand; his thoughts went rushing back to being on patrol in Vietnam.

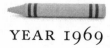

YEAR 1969

HERALD HANDED THE TINY Vietnamese girl a slightly mushy chocolate bar and looked over to AckMan. "Has it been forty minutes?"

"Ack," came the weak response, as AckMan looked at his watch and nodded.

"Form up!" Herald shouted, circling his right arm over his head. "Time to move around Charles's Park. Everyone on your toes! Next stop, 'Charles Town,' and we never know if he's in a bad mood—but he *always* knows when we're on his doorstep. Dog, point."

"RUH-Roh," Dog barked as he looked up.

As the platoon arrived outside the overgrown bamboo area, the newbie, Private Boyd, back from the base hospital, moved out of position to walk next to Herald. "Why do we avoid entering Charles's Park?"

Herald, whose eyes never stopped searching the trail and adjacent terrain except when confirming map landmarks to track his general location, continued scanning and apprised, "Charles marks his territory with booby-trap signs and visible fishing-line triggers. See that small sign on the bamboo trunk right over there, the one with the primitive drawing of the skull and crossbones and the words, 'Thu Dia'? It does not take a rocket scientist to figure out that 'Thu Dia' is not a hospitable welcome.

"Now look over there, between the bamboo trunks, in the sunlight. If you peer at an angle, you will see the clear fishing line. Each wire is attached, or could be, to a booby trap. Man, just look at the number of wires in this patch of bamboo alone! It appears like a berserk spider's web, spun from fishing line.

"If you take one step inside the bamboo tree line and trip one of those wires—Bam! Most likely you'll be missing a foot, or even more. The only way to get into his park is with heavy equipment. Specially equipped bulldozers or tanks are all that can safely trigger the booby traps. Charles knows that for us to obtain the armor to trigger his booby traps takes a major effort, so we maintain a mutual temporary armistice. If he stays quiet as we pass, we do not call in the armor. Understand?"

Boyd, flummoxed by it all, shook his head from side to side. "This place is really weird ... a safe-haven park for Charles."

"Our Company alone lost sixty people to booby traps over the last ten months. Sixty people amounts to almost an entire operating company in the field. Needless to say, everyone must be *very* aware of their movements and observe what they are stepping on.

"Picking up anything is absolutely *verboten*, to use the German slang for 'forbidden.' An example of how bad a booby trap can be came from Alpha Company, in fact, close to where we are now. In a brief moment of forgetfulness, a squad leader stepped on what appeared to be a large knot of wood, which should not have been on a paddy dike. While this is something in the States you'd think nothing of, here it was the trigger for an unexploded, 250-pound U.S. bomb that had been dropped by the U.S. Air Force on Charles; but the fuse had malfunctioned. Charles, in his genius, recovered it and replaced the malfunctioning trigger with one looking like a large knot of wood. Charles is very clever and resourceful. He'll take anything we leave and use it against us.

"To hear the witnesses tell it, the squad leader and all his gear evaporated in a blinding flash. The blast threw everyone within fifty yards to the ground. After the explosion, it took fifteen minutes for all to compose themselves enough to take inventory. It was only because the bomb was buried that the entire force of the blast focused upward, taking out just one soldier. The complete company searched the area for two days in an attempt to find enough of the squad leader to declare him dead. But there was nothing left, so a Missing In Action report had to be filed in place of a Killed In Action.

"This guy's poor family will never know for sure if their boy is dead. The witnesses were sure, but that's not how the Army looked at it. As far as they were concerned, he went AWOL and was residing and partying in Honduras. And now, Boyd, do you know the reason for the answer to the question 'What's The Word?'"

On cue Boyd delivered his lines in syncopation.

Herald nodded in approval and then changed the subject. "By the way, Boyd, how's the leg?"

"Fine, sir. Pearlman's bullet was only a nick. See? Not even a limp. And, look at this! Had a nurse save the bullet for me—so nice she drilled a hole through the end—and got me this gold chain so I could wear it!"

He opened his shirt, and with his right index finger, he lifted the necklace dangling the copper-jacketed bullet, which swayed back and forth like a king cobra ready to strike. "It's my good luck charm!" he beamed. Grasping the pendant, he rolled it between his index finger and thumb. "Looks brand new, don't it?"

Herald could only turn away, feeling nauseous as stomach acid seeped into his throat. Boyd replaced the bullet inside his shirt and walked back to his place with his squad.

Just as the platoon came abreast of Sir Charles Park, the sky filled with helicopters. The entire platoon nosedived to the ground. None of them wanted to be caught upright if Charles Park was the helicopters' target.

Herald rolled over on his back and focused on the three choppers.

"Piper One," the transmission came crackling in, "Road Warrior, new battalion commander, first inspection. Over."

Herald reached over to where Hollywood was lying on his back catching a few quick rays, and grabbed and keyed the mic. "Road Warrior, this is Piper One. Over."

"Piper One, I want you to go into the bamboo and search and destroy Charles. This hiding place is to be shut down under my command. Over."

"Road Warrior, I do not have the equipment to deal with Charles and the booby traps. Must hold here for armor support. Over."

"Piper One, you're a damn coward. If I have to come down there and show you how to do it, I will. This is a direct order. Move your men into the bamboo. Over!"

"Road Warrior, Piper One. Will not move without armor. We'd be cut to pieces for nothing. Over."

Herald took into account how a successful assault had been orchestrated on another Charles Park. First, artillery and napalm were dropped by aircraft, to soften up Charles's defenses and trigger some random booby traps. Only after the air assault did the special bulldozers equipped to trip the traps move into the park. Working in unison with the infantry, the bulldozers' job was to spring the booby traps, absorbing the explosion so no one would get hurt. The infantry's job was to provide cover; holding Charles's head down to keep him from attacking the bulldozers. Moving men into a marked, booby-trapped zone without armor was a death warrant.

"Piper One, I am coming down there to take command of your platoon. You, a complete coward, are now relieved! Out," was the final, roared message, as the command chopper and its two support choppers circled. The roar of the three turbine jet engines increased to a scream as the choppers circled lower to land around the platoon. Herald signaled his men to spread out and provide cover for the choppers.

A battalion commander travels with a minimum of seven radios for contact with four companies, Corps headquarters, the Air Force, artillery and more. From Herald's experience, just one helicopter next to Charles Park would provide an irresistible target—too much for Sir Charles to pass up. Now they had three helicopters plus more brass command than Charles could hope to kill at one time. All these juicy targets were having a picnic next to his park without proper infantry support—a movable feast for Charles. Time to duck and cover.

The command helicopter touched down, and the BC jumped from the bay.

"Lieutenant, give me your weapon. You are relieved! I will lead this group to show Charles who's the boss here. I may have just taken command of this battalion, but I've seen enough. I will not tolerate a direct disobedience of my orders. I have seen more courage in Korea in one fingernail clipping than from you in Vietnam! All of you are cowards, just cowards. It's time a *real* commander showed you how to do it!"

Herald handed over his M16. The battalion commander turned and took six steps toward the bamboo tree line. Already on one knee, knowing what was next, Herald turned and dove to the ground. Dog followed suit with a short "WRRRrr Rot!" Hollywood, lying on his back, flipped over, his sunglasses flying off his head, followed by the entire platoon diving to the ground. He covered his head as the battalion commander took his next steps in the direction of the bamboo hedge.

Herald's platoon had been drilled to always keep their distance away from one helicopter—let alone three—and to stay away from any radio. Now they were surrounded by ten radios and a good part of the battalion command structure, which included the artillery forward observer, air force liaison, three other assorted officers, each with their own radioman, ripe for the picking.

The eyes of the platoon members said it all. They were horrified by all the equipment, radios, and officers gathered in a close group. It was a nightmare coming true. A circus had dropped out of the sky with the sole intent of baiting Charles to kill them all.

"I have been relieved of command," Herald yelled to his platoon. "The battalion commander will take over from here!"

This was the icing on the cake for the platoon. LeMaire blasted, *"Mon Dieu, merde!"* He started slithering away from the helicopters in a scramble, digging his toes and angling his body so his heels pushed on the ground for leverage, sliding his left arm and hand forward to claw the dirt, pulling himself forward, while dragging the machine gun with his right, which bumped up and down on its support legs. He could stand only so much stupidity for one day.

"Holy—ack—shit!" AckMan gasped, as he and Jones moved in the same snakelike manner as LeMaire, as far from this lunacy as possible. Their squads followed suit. Only Dog and Hollywood stayed with Herald.

"*Bastardo! Che cazzo!*" hissed Ferlinghetti while crawling away with his squad. "*Andiamo dai coglioni!*"

The basic rules of survival had been drilled into all of them, day after day. What they had been disciplined *not* to do was now being flaunted on Sir Charles's doorstep.

The battalion commander's seventh step pushed against one transparent fishing line in the bamboo hedge. A faint *pop* was heard. Those knowing the meaning of that sound went into full alert. The tension hung in the air as the group hoped beyond hope that what was about to happen would not. Seconds later, *BACKRACKK!* Instantly the acrid smell of gunpowder mixed with blood filled the air, shrouding Herald. He retched up into his throat as the greasy taste of black powder and blood flooded his nasal passages.

The commander flew back three meters from the impact of the explosion, landing near Herald's feet. Rising to one knee, Herald turned around, and moving in a crouch, grabbed the commander under the armpits, lifting his chest and dragging him away from the hedge.

Initially in shock, the commander regained his senses and began groaning. Collecting himself, he did a quick, body inventory scan, and finally eyeballed his leg, "YEEAAAAAAEEE! AAAAAEEE!" he screamed at the exposed bone where his foot had once been.

All the radiomen and support staff freaked and started running for the choppers. Herald and his platoon medic acted with swift precision, tying a tourniquet and bandaging the commander's foot so he would not bleed to death. At least the medic knew his job. The two grabbed the commander under his arms, carrying him to the helicopter, and laid him down in the bay. All the support staff, radios, and excitement left in a roar of turbine engines. Silence hung heavy in the air with the smell of charbroiled flesh accented by burnt jet fuel—and the echo of the hare-brained commander's screams.

Herald knelt on one knee for several minutes, fist pressed to his head, collecting his thoughts. Never in his wildest dreams had he imagined the battalion commander would act in total disregard of his own command safety and that of his platoon.

Nobody will ever believe this!

Surveying his platoon, all in varying degrees of shock, he contemplated, *Vietnam is just too weird for anyone to understand. You spend all your time— when you first get into this godforsaken country—feverishly trying to learn how to survive. You memorize, not just mentally, but physically, too, practicing every rule of the bush. You strive to coordinate the mental and physical rules to react with the same precision as an Olympic athlete. You train diligently at the optimal level, knowing one inch may be what's needed for an additional one percent advantage that could keep you alive. Just as you start to feel at home with the fear and the rules to live by, the Vietnam version of a New Orleans Mardi Gras parade of uncontrolled and dangerous surprises comes to town. It's just too disjointed, Picasso-like, a surreal, psychotic cartoon parade, complete with Huey helicopter floats.*

Jones walked by, delivering a sarcastic laugh. "Yeah, this is why I keep a journal; nobody will believe this shit!"

For ten minutes, Herald waited for instructions from the radio, but there was only static. Assuming he was back in command, he called out to the platoon, "Listen up—looks like yours truly is back in command. Time to head out."

Sighing to himself, Herald rationalized, *I may be court-martialed when we get back. Or not. Best I face this as soon as possible, to get in my side of the story.*

Picking up his M16, which the battalion commander had dropped when the booby trap exploded, he used the end of his towel to wipe off several blood spots and small bits of skin. Stomach acid began to rise in his throat at the sight of human tissue on his weapon.

This just as easily could have been mine!

The platoon moved about a quarter of a mile from Charlie Park and sat down to rest.

"LT, give me just a minute," Jones chimed in, while rubbing his index finger on his lips and writing furiously in his notebook. "I need to finish this. It is just too much."

Ferlinghetti, shifting his eyes from left to right, came within three meters of them, *"Quest' è troppo!"* 'E, LT, I wan'-a to read una poema, OK?"

"A poem?" Herald snapped. "What the hell is wrong with you?" Pausing, he reconsidered, *Why not? This day has been weird enough.* "Go ahead. Can't wait to hear what part of any poem is appropriate."

Ferlinghetti opened his now-worn book and read the beginning of the long poem:

> And that's the way it always is and that's the way
> it always ends and the fire and the rose are one
> and always the same scene and always the same
> subject right from the beginning like in the Bible
> or The Sun Also Rises which begins Robert Cohn
> was a middleweight boxing champion of his class
> but later we lost our balls and there we go again
> there we are again there's the same old theme ...

(A Coney Island of the Mind: Poems, page 44)

Herald nodded his head, conceding, "Ferlinghetti, I have to say the fire and the rose were the same today. Time to go. Saddle up."

The platoon picked itself up, taking longer than usual, in horror of the flying command circus. They donned their dropped equipment, shifted ammo and arranged their packs into proper place. The band headed out at a safe pace, conscious of booby traps but walking as fast as they could. Each one wondered what fate would befall them when they arrived back at their firebase. With the battalion commander blown up, someone was going to take the hit, and just one measly lieutenant would not be enough for the brass.

Herald cleared the base's perimeter fence, walking straight to the CC's bunker, who, looking up as he entered, inquired, "Anything interesting on your milk run today?"

Herald looked around, waiting for the Military Police to arrive, and muttered, "No, nothing unusual. Anything up around here? I hear we have a new battalion commander?"

The CC replied, "No, other than I heard the battalion commander had an accident and was shipped to Japan. Rather odd change of command so early in his tour, but what do I know? All the brass tells me is that he had an accident."

Herald inquired, "Who is taking over?"

The CC looked down at his map and added, "A new boy from Korea. Hope he understands Vietnam is nothing like Korea."

Herald gave a weak smile and agreed. "There is no doubt in my mind, after some time in country, he will understand Vietnam is nothing at all like Korea. There is no danger of freezing to death in this hell hole."

As he left the CC's bunker and returned to his platoon area, Herald contemplated, *Could I really have gotten away with direct insubordination? Maybe they forgot who I am. Maybe the BC, now in physical and emotional pain from losing his foot, forgot to blame me for not following his order to clear Charles Park. Maybe losing his foot made BC embarrassed he caused his own mutilation by being so stupid. Maybe the whole day never happened. Maybe I'm just living in a cartoon. Maybe.*

Back at his bunker, Herald looked over to where Dog was sitting and posed the question of the day: "Did today start with a Gook Ironman Contest and finish with the BC blowing himself up?"

Dog looked over and nodded, "Ruff!"

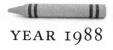

YEAR 1988

HERALD LOWERED HIS HEAD and barked, "Ruff!" at the steering wheel as he parked the VW at the law office. He jumped out carefully to avoid bashing his head on the door frame for a second time.

Shutting the van door, he walked with purpose to the bar down the street, still angry about the argument with his wife.

This section of Redwood City had become dilapidated in the 1980s. Many of the storefronts were abandoned and boarded up. On one corner was a bar called "Mustang Ranch." It had been a rundown "Mustang Auto Parts" store for thirty years before being remodeled into a bar. Herald wondered if the original owner had—tongue in cheek—named the shop after the whorehouse of the same name, near Reno.

The bar had distressed wooden flooring, dirty and cracked plaster walls with peeling paint, and Western movie posters from the 1930s, unframed and stapled to the wall. Lighting consisted of four 100-watt bulbs, bare and glaring, suspended somewhat evenly throughout the room. A Western saddle, its stirrups dangling, hung in the center of the ceiling, with one large bare bulb in the middle of the saddle, and four smaller satellite bulbs irregularly placed, giving the effect of a macabre cowboy chandelier. The bar counter was constructed of salvaged plywood previously used for building forms and still showing traces of concrete, which gave off a faint dusty taste of the building material. The hard-liquor display cabinet behind the bar was of early 1960s board-and-cement-block construction.

Crossing the threshold, the familiar, acrid smell of cigarette smoke mixed with stale beer irritated Herald's nose. He sneezed, rubbed his nose, and approached the bar stools—1930s steel tractor seats on sturdy wooden posts.

Herald surveyed the room, as was his habit from Vietnam. It was the usual array of about twenty suspects; still-dirty construction workers, bus drivers, unemployed misfits seated at the bar and tables, along with isolated pockets of prostitutes and lonely women drinking their welfare check.

He slid onto a bar stool, and acknowledged his rapport with the bartender, "So, Checkers, how goes the war?"

"Ah, Herald! Haven't seen you in a while; we've missed you."

"Yeh, been busy killing trees. I'll take a Tanqueray martini, very dry, up."

"Killing trees?"

"Yes, it's a joke for legal pleadings using up huge amounts of paper."

The Mustang Ranch's idea of a martini was three ounces of gin, poured into an unchilled, stained water glass; no olive.

Feeling the pounding of his heart and throbbing of his brain, Herald hammered the drink down. The raw gin stung his throat and slammed into his stomach like napalm.

Herald pointed to the glass as he coughed and his eyes watered. Checkers nodded and poured another.

Checkers was the offspring of an English father from London, who immigrated to San Francisco, where he met Checkers's mother, a Hawaiian. Six feet tall, lanky and affable, he was the perfect bartender. Cordial to one and all—and intuitive—he sensed something was bothering Herald.

"Man, you look like shit. At the rate you're sucking down these pocket rockets, you'll be on the floor or dead in fifteen minutes. What's going on?"

Herald looked up at Checkers, muttering, "My career is in the toilet, and the handle's pushed. All that's left is the wild circular ride down the hole. I do not deserve this. I was in the Army—did my time in 'Nam—came back— sucked up being spit on by some damn hippies and yellow-robed Hare Krishnas in the San Francisco airport—went to college and law school … Shit, man, we did not start the war! But we sure got the brown end of the stick when we got back. In college I was thought of as a drug-addicted baby killer. What the *fuck*?!"

Checkers, familiar with this type of self-abasement from his customers, understood the only way to deal with Herald's rampage was to let him babble on. "Hey, man, you haven't connected the dots between Vietnam and whatever legal problems are stalking you now. I didn't know you were over there. What'd you do?"

Herald pointed to the glass as a reward for more information. Checkers winked back, poured another, and leaned forward, placing his elbow on the bar. He knew Herald only as the attorney down the street. Checkers

298 CURSE OF THE COLORING BOOK

had always wondered, when he was in high school, why Vietnam veterans were scorned.

Nodding appreciation for the drink, Herald continued. "Was a combat, infantry lieutenant platoon leader and company commander on the Cambodian border in '69 and '70. It was my year of fear. A goddamn paratrooper and assigned—not to an airborne unit, but a leg unit. Lucky for me, my troopers were all good, straight leg or not."

"So, airborne or leg, whatever; did you see any action?"

Herald sighed and glanced to the ceiling. "Yep, but it was the day-to-day shit that got to you. Then you come home and are discharged—and society treats you as if you should be punished for misbehaving on some high school outing. Lately, my continual war flashbacks about 'Nam have been escalating, and they're really pissing me off."

Entertained, Checkers asked, "So, how was it to be a paratrooper? I've always wanted to sky dive."

"Well, being a paratrooper isn't anything like sky diving. Ever see a parachute landing fall?"

"A parachute landing *what*?"

"Here," Herald replied, draining his glass and standing up, "let me show you."

Using his bar stool as a ladder, he stepped up on it, then up to the bar. Standing straight, he looked down at the floor and around the room. A quiet settled as everyone looked up to see what was going on.

Checkers started to grab Herald but wasn't quick enough. He jumped off the bar and, as with any good parachute landing fall, rotated his body just as the balls of his feet touched the floor. His turning body formed an arc. The momentum of the jump carried him through the arc, and Herald was returned to standing up, looking at Checkers. The bar rocked with applause and cries of "More, more, more!"

Herald gave everyone a big, boozy grin and resumed his position standing on the bar. He yelled, "How much for me to do it again?"

Two older women sitting at the bar wearing their prom dresses from the late 1950s screamed, "Twenty-five bucks says you're toast!"

Three guys, still wearing their construction tool belts, stood up. "We got fifty between us that says you can't!"

Checkers grabbed a pad. "I'll be taking all bets, so talk to the Checkman." After ten minutes, all twenty patrons of the bar had placed their bets. Herald, maintaining his regal stance on the bar, smiled and waved at the mob of drinkers, who were gesturing with—and spilling—their beer and hard liquor, while crying, "Jump, you crazy asshole paratrooper, jump!"

Surveying the crowd, Herald laughed as he pointed from left to right, shouting, "OK, but we had a cheer in the Airborne. When I nod, you say, 'Airborne,' then I jump off the bar and yell, 'All the way!' Got it?"

"Got it!" they all shouted back, raising their glasses in salute.

The crowd waited for Herald to nod. He paused, attempting to focus on the floor, which now seemed to be undulating beneath him. The room grew quiet. Feeling ready, he nodded. The crowd erupted, "Airborne!" Herald shouted, "All the way!" and jumped.

As the balls of his feet touched the floor, he rotated his body perfectly, to form the curve redirecting his momentum. The movement was smooth. All was flawless as his body turned and he started to rise back to a standing position. It was wonderful—except for the table the crowd had moved in closer for the show that he had not factored into his jump. During the rotation, his head came up fast under the table and, with a loud thump, he was out cold.

Everyone gasped. Grabbing the bar telephone, Checkers called information for Herald's home number and dialed.

"Hello?" Thea answered.

"Mrs. Lloyd?"

"Yes. Who's calling?"

"Hi, Mrs. Lloyd, it's Checkers—from the Mustang Ranch down the street from your office?"

There was a brief pause, Thea rolling her eyes. "Yes. What is it?"

"Well, there's been kind of an accident. See, Herald was jumping off the bar and trying to do a ... "

"Wait. Let me guess: a damn parachute landing fall, right?"

"Uh, yeah, and, uh ... "

"The idiot! Is he all right?"

"Well, yeah, sorta, but he's been drinking a bit, and when he hit his head ... uh ... I think you need to come get him. He's pretty disoriented and ... "

"Christ!" she shot back. "OK, thanks. I'll be right down."

The last thing Checkers heard from the other end was a very loud "CLICK!"

CHAPTER 18

FREE-FIRE ZONE OF CIVILIAN LIFE

WITH HERALD'S VW VAN ABANDONED the night before outside Mustang Ranch, the next morning Thea drove him to the office. The silence during the ride was deafening. Thea was furious with Herald, and he had a knot on top of his head the size of a golf ball. His brain pulsed with the fire of an intense hangover, coupled with the physical ache of a battered skull.

The first thing Herald did at the office was to make a pot of coffee for the staff and then poured himself a cup. It went down, rumbling around in his stomach for a moment, then started backing up. Knowing the danger signs, Herald ran to the bathroom and threw up. It had been a hard night. And today was Wednesday, MD 23.

Come on, Herald, you need to get this mother done!

He headed for the Parrot Room to finish the motion. After completing that onerous task, he sat back and sighed.

Today, after I file the motion, will be the long statutory wait, MD 22 to MD7, when the defendant's opposition is due to be filed.

Looking for a distraction, Herald took out his wallet, opened it, and pulled out the historic, mini-pocket-sized notebook paper, now yellowed and tattered, and unfolded it. There was Pearlman's telephone number. Herald looked at it and promised himself that if he won, the first thing he'd do was fulfill his promise.

I don't need any goddamn counseling! I can handle this!

Maybe.

Once the motion was filed, Herald walked to Mustang Ranch to retrieve his VW, without going inside for a drink, and drove home, entering the front door with his usual "Hola, family!" The house was starkly quiet, an abnormal phenomenon, and unnerving to Herald.

Thea walked out from the bedroom, glaring at him. She flicked her hair back, in her angry, dramatic manner, and snapped at him, "Parachute landing fall? Honestly, Herald! You're lucky you didn't kill yourself, causing the same pain and hardship to your wife and children that you suffered when your father was killed in that airplane tragedy!"

"I was so upset by our conversation and your threat to leave me, I went to the bar and got drunk." Giving her a sheepish grin, he added, "The rest, as they say, is parachute history."

"Don't get cute with me. Not in the mood for it."

Thea flicked her hair again, walked back toward the bedroom, and then spun around. "You have to promise never to do the parachute landing fall drunk again. I will not tolerate such dangerous behavior at your age and with your responsibilities. Look, Herald, it's time for us to see a couples counselor. Your Vietnam nightmares, abuse of alcohol, and carelessness at the office are all related and are a massive strain on our marriage. If you lose the motion, don't expect me to hang around. Perhaps a separation would do us both good. You're starting to lose it."

"Well, I definitely lost part of something last night."

Thea scowled and walked back to the bedroom as Herald walked to the refrigerator and grabbed his bottle of bourbon. After rubbing the bottle's coolness over his sweating forehead, he poured a glassful, shook his head and returned to the living room, where he sat on the couch in the dark, focusing on his breath to calm himself, and fell asleep.

Waking up in the wee hours of the night, he tiptoed into the bedroom and crawled into bed without waking Thea. At least she did not acknowledge his presence; she didn't even move.

BACK AT THE OFFICE on MD 7, seven days before the malpractice hearing, the postman rotated the old doorbell knob as he always did before entering the front door. The bell gave off a metallic *ting-a-ling, ting-a-ling* that resounded throughout the office. Herald jumped up from his desk chair, in his haste splashing some coffee-flavored bourbon on his desk. He ignored the spill.

The postman entered the foyer, took a left, and moved to Deborah's desk. While eyeing her low-cut neckline—and its underpinnings—he chirped, "Good day, beautiful. How are you?"

"Terrific! How are you doing?" Never giving the postman as much as a glance, Deborah remained focused on her computer screen, discouraging him from further inquiries. She was in a serious relationship with her new boyfriend and cared not for additional suitors. Winking at her, he left a bundle of mail on her desk.

Before she could look away from her computer screen, Herald, speeding around the corner from the Parrot Room like an Indy 500 racer, burst through the foyer and into her office. He grabbed the bundle, peeled off the rubber band, flipped through the mail, seized a large envelope, and handed the rest to Deborah.

"Wait!" she advised him, "Let me calendar that before you forget!"

"No chance of me forgetting this puppy," he quipped, sprinting off to the office library at the same feverish pace, kicking up one corner of the foyer's Oriental rug.

First, he read each argument and noted the important points; second, he read the entire case cited by his opponent, noting where he could differentiate the facts or law to his favor. It was his favorite methodology. He found nothing more satisfying than taking a case cited by an opponent in support of their argument, and showing why, instead, that case supported his own argument, making his opponent lose credibility with the court. Herald made the necessary notes and wrote his Reply to the Opposition statement.

Finishing the task in just two hours, he strode to Sarah's desk in the renovated kitchen. "Fire up your computer, please. This must go out today."

Sarah, rocking back and forth in her office swivel chair, pointed to the computer to show the case caption was already on the screen, the cursor poised for the opening sentence. From her throne she nodded and whispered for effect, "At your command, Sire. I could see you were just a little worked up over this. I'm good to go ... just been sitting here, rocking, for five minutes. If we have to work late again, OK by me."

Glancing up at the ceiling, Herald scratched his chin. "Sorry if I appear a bit agitated."

Sarah's overture to work late ... is like the spider offering to work late with the fly. Does she think I'm already webbed up?

Speaking over her shoulder, he dictated his reply brief from his case-law notes. He never needed to prepare a written draft. Instead, he was always able to develop his legal arguments straight to dictation. Herald watched the computer screen as his secretary magically typed at his rapid pace of speech, gratified to see each of his words form the sentences to communicate his points. The scent of Chanel No. 5 hung in the air.

Completing his six-page draft, he wrapped it up. Sarah printed the document and handed it to him. He took it to the Parrot Room to review and revise but first sat at his desk and contemplated the environment he might lose: the piles of legal papers ... the slanted floor ... parrot-chewed woodwork ... and the pepper tree outside, with its graceful boughs sprouting spindly leaves that filtered the view of the street.

He was consumed with the crushing embarrassment of malpractice and the potential destruction of the world he and Thea had worked so hard to build.

A wave of nausea with a taste of stomach bile irritated his throat. The palms of his hands began to sweat again. His mind triggered the horror that came with facing his fears. Fighting it, he laughed and shook his head. But the stress caused his shoulder muscles to constrict, giving rise to a painful pressure in his chest.

Time for a couple of consultations with Mr. Bourbon and Mr. Ginger Ale.

The tension of the malpractice threat coupled with his war anxieties activated Herald's Vietnam Memory Retrieval slot machine. His mind thrust in a coin and yanked the handle. The wheels began their fiendish, unpredictable spin.

When they stopped, the symbols from his memory had no apparent relationship to the problem at hand. What appeared was his sexual foray in Taiwan with Bright. Perhaps the memory of this erotic experience would bring respite to his tortured mind.

YEAR 1969

HERALD HAD COCOONED, during the first three days in the hotel room, reveling in its safety and the pleasure of Bright's company. But when they had finished a leisurely breakfast in bed on the fourth day, Bright suggested they take a trip. They had been holed up in the hotel like gangsters on the run. She was starting to feel claustrophobic and needed a little light. He was finishing his breakfast in bed, savoring every bite.

Naked, she pranced from the sink in the bathroom to the bedroom and hopped up on the bed, her body weight causing some of his breakfast coffee to spill onto the tray.

"Look, GI," she pouted, "Been here *three day!* Need out or go crazy. Must go home. You come. We back quick."

Mopping the coffee off his tray with an old, worn, stained napkin, he eyed a last bit of bacon. "It's dangerous out there. I'd much rather stay in the hotel where it's quiet and simple. You can order any personal items you need from the hotel store."

"Hey, how you be soldier and such a cat-scare? 'Cat-scare' correct, yes?" she asked and jumped back onto the floor and started pacing, her naked breasts jiggling.

After admiring her body and how it jiggled in just the right places when she moved, he replied, "The word is 'scaredy-cat,' and it's just too busy and noisy outside."

Bright stopped pacing, turned, and looked into Herald's eyes. "I protect. Time *join* world! You like see where Bright lives?"

Herald was curious as to how people lived in Taiwan. She had found the right way to win Herald over, who sighed, "Well ... OK, but it will take me a few minutes to get ready, and you need to dress anyway."

"OK!" Bright beamed. "You Numbah One!" and with that she jumped back on the bed, giving Herald a big kiss on the cheek. Herald's coffee took another dive. Giving up, he put the tray on the floor. Coffee was dripping off the tray's edges.

Bright opened her travel bag and grabbed a tight, black leather skirt. She stepped into it, pulled it up and fastened it with a quick *zzzip;* then she slipped her head into a black silk halter-top and tied the long tassels behind her back. Dressing, Herald kept an eye on her. Something about watching a woman dress fascinated him.

When they were dressed, they left the hotel room and walked down the hallway.

Stopping at the elevator landing, Herald mentally prepared himself for the unnerving ride ahead as Bright pressed the down button. To their surprise, the button popped off the control panel and fell to the floor.

Great! I'd rather take the stairs, anyway. They don't bounce.

Herald started to bolt in the direction of the stairs, but Bright snatched the back of his shirt, pulling him back, as the car arrived and the doors clanked open.

They entered, and his sweaty hand grasped the handrail as if his life depended on it. The car descended, again swaying and skipping off alternate walls.

The promise of the lobby became a reality. When the elevator doors opened, Herald and Bright stepped out. Bright grasped his hand to make sure he did not turn back, and they walked toward the hotel entrance. Bright opened the huge door to the street, and feeling Herald's body become rigid in resistance, she gripped his hand harder, dragging him outside. As before, the chaotic sounds, smells, and people of Taiwan enveloped them. Bright dropped his hand, walked to the street, and hailed a taxi; Herald again watched as it crossed two lanes without signaling and then screeched to a stop under honking protests by the drivers of the vehicles it had cut off. Bright opened the taxi door while looking over her shoulder at Herald, who was leaning on the front wall of the hotel.

Scowling at his shadow on the sidewalk, he muttered, "You did this to me."

Bright left the cab, walked over to Herald, and pulled on his arm. It took several minutes and three cries of "cat-scare" for her to pry him off the hotel wall and into the taxi, but at last they departed amid the gray-white cloud of taxi exhaust.

After an erratic, lane-cutting trip in the cab, making Herald think of a maniacal ride at an amusement park, the old, beaten taxi pulled up in front of a 1950s-style concrete-block apartment building, four stories high. The gray concrete blocks were patterned with light and dark splotches of the mold that thrived in Taiwan's heat and high humidity. Each balcony flaunted a rainbow of colorful clothes hanging on clotheslines crisscrossing the outdoor living spaces, a vain attempt to dry clothes in Taiwan's damp air. Each clothesline strained under the absolute limit of garments it could hold. The colorful, madcap way the different clothes draped the entire building was something Herald had never witnessed in the U.S. It was a way of living the States had long since abandoned with the advent of home clothes dryers.

They exited the taxi, Herald warily eyeing every inch of his surroundings, feeling vulnerable away from the hotel and the other GIs. He'd heard rumors some GIs had been beaten up—or worse—for their money. He comforted himself with the thought that his being killed by a prostitute or her pimp would give his platoon cause for celebration. Murder by prostitute would elevate him to rock-star status with his sick group of comrades.

Yes, values do get a little weird in a war. Soldiers contemplate cool ways to die, often a topic of daily conversation.

Bright and Herald climbed the dark, unlit cement stairs, to the second floor. He was puzzled how anyone could live in such filth and not feel compelled to wash their hands all the time. Leading him by his hand to her apartment, Bright confronted her door. She pulled out a large group of keys from her purse. The steel door had four deadbolt locks.

As she was fumbling for the correct key for each lock, Herald wondered, *After two locks, would the extra two make any difference?*

Bright pushed the door open to a large, sunlit room. A bed with two end tables was to the right, a small kitchen to the left and, continuing left, a door to what Herald assumed was the bathroom. By Taiwanese standards—and considering that most single women lived with their parents in one large room—the apartment was huge.

Bright reached to the right and flicked on a light with a large ceiling fan. The fan began to spin, giving off a *rooot, rooot, rooot, clack, rooot, rooot, rooot, clack.* She walked into the middle of the room and stretched her arms out to her sides, gesturing a welcome to her home.

"My place, Numbah One! Wealthy-man family have place this big. What you think?" Spinning around, she took three strides, turned and plopped onto her king-sized bed with a bounce. Seated, her miniskirt hiked up to the top of her thighs. Crossing her legs in an exaggerated manner, she reached down with her right hand and loosened the back strap of each shoe. As each strap dropped, she kicked off the sparkling acrylic high heel. The process offered Herald quite a peep show, even from the doorway, as she never wore panties.

With his eyes glued to her most private part, he responded, "Well, Bright, what's important is that you are happy living here." He then stepped in and closed the door. With no concept of her lifestyle but understanding she was proud of her success to afford an apartment like this by herself, there was no reason for him not to be polite. Besides, his view of Bright sitting exposed on the bed was more than OK.

Leaning back onto her elbows while rubbing her legs together and shifting her pelvis, she teased. "Me want be scratched. After you make love to me all week, Bright need be scratched even more. Want to scratch me in my house, yes? Let me touch you, my GI. See how you jump."

As much as he tried to be cool, he flinched when she leapt off the bed and, after two hops, wrapped one arm around his neck and grabbed his manhood with the other.

Herald looked into her dark eyes and solicited, "I want to experiment with something I've never tried. Yeah, how about we try anal sex? After all, do I want to go back to 'Nam without trying everything sexual I ever wanted to attempt?"

"Cost you more, bad boy, much, much more." Quick as lightning she turned and with one large stride jumped onto her bed, landing on all fours like a cat. As she bounced from the impact, she arched her back and opened her legs in a way that the hem of her leather skirt eased up over her buttocks, leaving her tantalizingly exposed. Turning her head around and looking over her shoulder, she taunted him. "Scratch me, bad boy GI. Yes, please, touch me. You very bad."

Just as Herald was about to enter a new world, he noticed a framed eight-by-ten photograph on one of the end tables. Smiling at him through a glossy finish was a U.S. Marine Corps Gunny Sergeant. Scanning the apartment, he saw he had missed about twenty more smaller pictures of this same GI with her. Feeling supervised by her Marine Corps boyfriend, he closed his eyes to block out the intrusion, but the moment was gone; he'd lost his sexual focus.

This new frontier will have to wait. I can't get it all in one trip.

CHAPTER 19
INTO THE LEGAL
VALLEY OF DEATH

YEAR 1988

ON MD I, THE AFTERNOON prior to Herald's desperate
motion hearing to correct his malpractice, he had to navigate the bizarre
procedures of the Law and Motion Court's tentative-rulings system. He
had always been of the opinion that some psychopath had dreamed up
this convoluted system to prevent unnecessary appearances on the Law
and Motion calendar.

This court is the place to resolve procedural disagreements between
parties prior to full trial. The ruling for a pending motion is available by
telephone, usually by 2:00 p.m *the day before* the actual hearing. An attorney wishing to contest a tentative ruling is required to notify the court and
opposing counsel that they request an appearance before the judge in the
actual hearing the next day. All of this must be completed between 2:00
and 4:00 p.m.; on top of this, with Herald's workload of thirty-five litigation cases, one or more always demanded last-minute attention.

Planning ahead, two weeks before, Herald had already cancelled everything or arranged for other counsel to appear in his stead on the firm's other

cases for the day before and the day of his malpractice correction motion. Sitting in the Parrot Room, looking out the window at the pepper tree's gnarled trunk, he contemplated his own knotty problem. A mistake in the tentative-ruling process could forfeit any appeal. The pressure of the process once again triggered anxiety muscle contractions in his chest and shoulders, sharp stabs of pain he did not need.

It was 2:04 p.m. Time to face his fear. Herald needed some help with the stress. Jumping up from his chair, he hurried to the break room and poured himself a coffee cup of bourbon.

The hell with the coffee.

Returning to his desk, he dialed the telephone number for the court's tentative rulings and sipped on his drink. For the first three minutes, he listened to a recording giving instruction on what his options were if the ruling were for or against him. After so many years, he could recite the entire informational recording from memory.

The recorded voice on the line started down the list of cases. With each separate case announcement, Herald took a swig, and a new part of his body started to perspire. Dampness started in his armpits and moved to his forehead; the palms of his hands and the skin behind his ears became moist as well. He waited and waited.

At last his case was announced. Tentative rulings were prepared by the judge's research attorney. As luck would have it, Herald knew the judge personally. Their children had played together at the same preschool.

If there is ever a time for just the tiniest advantage to play a role, this is it.

Should the tentative ruling be in his favor, he promised to call Pearlman's parents immediately.

But the fates had something else in store: *the ruling was against him.* As he heard the monotone voice announce the ruling, Herald thought his head would explode. He felt as if a bolt of lightning had shot through his body, and his mouth had that old metallic taste of blood. Jerking to a standing position with the cup still in hand, he splashed bourbon on the window. Shaking his head "no," he replaced the receiver. It clung briefly to his moist hand before dropping back into its cradle. Using his left hand for support on the desk, he slowly sat back down. A wave of nausea came over him, and he threw up in the trash can. His mind burned with the same fear he'd felt in Vietnam. It was time to drag out the same tactics that had served him so well there.

Herald went to the Vietnam-memory war chest in the basement of his mind, opened the lid, and pulled out Pearlman's advice: "Put yourself in the hurricane's eye." That was it! He would make the malpractice case his hurricane.

His left shoulder pulled toward his rigid chest muscles; the pain was becoming intense. Biting his finger Harvard-hard, he lapsed into a sort of trance to focus on the problem. The taste of blood in his mouth prompted the answer, flashing in his mind: he must call the court and opposing counsel to request an oral argument. Herald's clammy hand reached for the receiver. He made the calls.

To be dead sure of the elements of the ruling, he redialed the tentative-ruling line, enduring the required informational recording, and noted each point made in the ruling.

The sweat beading on his forehead was now rolling down his nose and dripping onto the desk. He had not experienced such fear since Vietnam.

Over and over, Herald repeated the chant that had kept him alive there. "Ride it!"

Next, he researched the points detailed in the recorded ruling so he could persuade the court to change its mind. He knew all too well that judges almost never change their tentative rulings; too many reversals of the rulings would foster too many appearances by desperate attorneys hoping for one last grasp at the merry-go-round's free-ride ring. The orderly conduct of court led to some flawed rulings, but to the court, law was a business of processing as many cases as possible with the least number of mistakes. This was especially true in litigious California.

Before beginning the arduous job, Herald had to regain his strategic mind-set. Just thinking about this enormous task sent a coin dropping into his slot machine of random Vietnam memories. The echo of the noisy, rolling, mechanical journey through the machinery reverberated in his mind and, as always, he pulled the fateful handle.

YEAR 1969

THE SLOT MACHINE'S random flashback took Herald back to the firebase after he'd disobeyed the direct orders of the battalion commander and was relieved of his command. Herald was certain he would be court-martialed that afternoon.

It looks real bad when a battalion commander gives an order relieving you of command, takes charge himself, and is blown up. It matters little that the order you directly disobeyed was stupid and dangerous. As far as the Army is concerned, nobody mars the reputation of a wounded war BC. The blame is filtered down to the next in command, the lieutenant.

It was the day after the battalion commander had lost his foot to Mr. Charlie's trap. Herald was sitting on his bunker, cleaning his weapon for the next day's "follies." The battalion second-in-command, the XO, came up to him and told him to put on a clean shirt and report to the battalion headquarters.

Color my ass court-martialed, he thought, shaking his head.

There was the color reference again. Herald summoned the coloring book's luck to protect him as he approached the command tent, where the XO saw him and ushered him to a line of nine men.

Goddamn, these guys are going to dispense with the trial and just shoot me! Goodbye, Mom. I'm really sorry it ended this way. Your boy was just another foolish casualty of a war for which he volunteered. Poetic justice.

A new commanding officer was in charge, sent down from corps headquarters that day. He stood in front of the line in his tailored, starched uniform and announced, "Men, it is my honor to be here to award you medals for heroism in ground combat. It is a cherished accomplishment to hold your mental state in a firefight—something to be proud of for the rest of your life. Remember, once you have faced your fear in combat, nobody can take that away from you." He looked down at his notes and said, "Will First Lieutenant Herald Lloyd step forward."

Hearing the order, Herald took one step forward and, out of the corner of his left eye, noticed there was a photographer present. While stepping forward, he debated whether to do just that or break into a run, for the absurd incongruity of it all.

They're going to decorate me? For what? Or is this a trap to make me an easy target? It's too weird! Visions of madcap cartoon characters danced through his mind.

The XO moved in front of him and then turned to his aide, who was carrying a black felt display board, about one foot square, with rows of small, rectangular, one-and-a-half-inch long by half-inch wide colored service ribbons. He removed one of the awards with a red-and-blue service ribbon, a Bronze Star, bearing a quarter-inch letter "V" for valor, identifying heroism in ground combat.

The XO looked Herald in the eye, covered his mouth, coughed, and in a forceful tone said, "The Red Cross has notified me that your mother, with her Litchfield political friends, contacted her congressman. It seems you have not been writing home. Also it appears your letters to home, about being safe in the rear, differ from the Army's press release. You should understand that military awards are first approved at a higher command level, and when approved, an immediate press release is sent to the media before the orders for the award trickle back to your level. The Army needs all the good press it can get."

Pinning the Bronze Star on Herald's shirt, he continued. "*The Litchfield Enquirer* published the story of the decoration along with your picture. This is an order: you will immediately go to your bunker, write to your mother, and tell her the truth. Got it?"

"Yes, sir," Herald responded with a salute. Both turned to the photographer, and the camera flashed, confirming his feeling of living in a twisted cartoon.

Man—I was sure I was going to be shot for disobeying an order. Instead, they give me a medal? In 'Nam they don't tell you if you're even being considered for a medal.

He speculated one of the deserted men from the other company who'd ended up abandoned the night of the day's firefight had nominated him for an award—the fight in which Pearlman had died and military order descended into pandemonium. Herald recollected the new recruit, Little Timmy, who was kicked in the face by his squad leader, preventing him from climbing on the already-overcrowded helicopter. Smiling, Herald recalled telling him the story of the frogs croaking *re-up* and the lizards responding *fuk-youuu.*

Hmm … I wonder what Little Timmy did to his squad leader who kicked him off the helicopter?

The ceremony ended, and the band of nine men dispersed. Herald walked back to his bunker scratching his head. He was now positive of the coloring book's power.

Back at the bunker, AckMan approached him. "How bad—*ack*—was it, LT?"

"I have been ordered to write my mother—*and they gave me a Bronze Star with a 'V' insignia.* Is that wacko enough for you?"

"Welcome to—*ack*—'Nam, baby."

YEAR 1988

THE TENTATIVE RULING appeared in his mind like a huge red STOP sign and hauled him back to the present. It also brought him another visual he had cultivated in Vietnam. He imagined his conscious mind was sitting in a race car. On the dashboard to the left and right of the speedometer were his control gauges. Instead of tachometer, temperature, oil and pressure gauges, his gauges registered levels of fear and mental pressure. Checking his current stress-o-meter gauges forming in his imagination, he visualized the pain levels brought about by this motion to rescue him from his malpractice. All gauges were in the red—a sure sign his mental engine was going to blow if he did not take control and calm himself down.

Shit! Wouldn't it be nice to have a simple life rather than this civilian warrior role as an attorney?

The problem with this warrior life are the risks the soldiers must take.

Well, if I were disbarred, I could always start a new career. Working as a librarian in Kansas would be nice.

After reviewing the moving and opposing papers again, he left the office and headed home. Rushing through the door, he retreated to the kitchen. He was sweating profusely and vibrating like a tuning fork.

While he prepared dinner, Thea and the kids walked in and out of the kitchen to retrieve snacks and drinks, but Herald was not his usual talkative self. Instead, he was quiet, concentrating on cooking, to calm himself down. It's an old Buddhist trick to focus the mind away from a problem onto a completely different task with an immediate reward. In this case, the spotlight was preparing the meal. Resting his mind would give Herald the perspective to view the problem another way; to find a better argument. But the reward of gaining a better perspective was not in the cards tonight. He took more of Pearlman's advice and bit his index finger again. The taste of his blood barely made a dent in his anxiety levels. Tomorrow was his Wild West, O.K. Corral showdown.

Thea entered the kitchen. She flicked her hair.

Uh–oh ...

"You know the old saying, 'The attorney who represents himself has a fool for a client?' You should have brought in our malpractice carrier, or at least another attorney, who could be more objective. Remember, this is my life and the kids' also."

"Let me guess," he responded. "This is a legal-partner question."

"Have you reported this to the malpractice carrier?"

"First, the malpractice carrier will not even start to represent me unless the malpractice has occurred and caused economic damage. Second, and more important, we lost our malpractice coverage last year when I objected to the attorney they assigned to represent us on the foreclosure case. They wanted to throw money at the problem to avoid my malpractice suit against our malpractice company for retaining counsel not knowledgeable about notes and deeds of trust. I went along with our insurance company settling, so long as they put a letter of non-liability in our file. Next thing I knew, they canceled our coverage, and there are no other malpractice carriers in the field now."

"As we both found out when we were law clerks with law firms who defended insurance companies, they can be quite unfair, but I'm still waiting for you to answer my riddle about an attorney representing himself."

"Finally, rather than feeling overwhelmed by the prospect of mounting my own defense, I feel calm and organized, as if I were representing someone else.

"I'm working to be calm and directed. It must be a carryover from the war and being in command. When you're in charge, you must face your fear by yourself to survive. If it *is* to be my loss, I prefer it be under *my* control. I can handle this."

"So you think, but I would really appreciate it if you would've taken my advice—just slowed down and been more careful to begin with. After all, what could be simpler than including the names of *both* your clients in the agreement? You criticize *me* for being slow or unable to make decisions. Well, here *we* are, smack dab in the middle of *your* fast decision, which jeopardizes me *and* the children. Damn you!"

She turned briskly, "I'm going to check on the girls to see how they are faring with the tension between their parents."

Remaining silent, Herald slid the onions out of the bowl into the pan. *That was a wife/mother comment.* Forcing his attention back to the task at hand, he served the family a fine dinner.

When everyone was finished with dinner, the girls went back to their bedroom to play, and Herald started clearing the dishes from the table. Thea rose to help and gave him a hug and kiss on the cheek. "No matter how it turns out, we need to go to counseling. Think about how we used to feel about each other. Think of what we have built together. Who's to say a worse malpractice mistake won't happen in the future? I just cannot get my mind around your carelessness with our children's lives. It says very little—actually, it says a lot—about how you feel about us. You may not like the idea of counseling, but you can start and then quit later if you believe it's not doing any good. How about just trying it?"

Pausing, Herald furrowed his brow in disapproval, spitting out, "Don't need any help from someone who has not seen combat and doesn't under-stand." He felt so angry and frustrated he bit his index finger. Pulling his finger out and eyeballing the area of broken skin, he saw there was not much room left for future bites.

Resigned, Thea shook her head and returned to the children to get them ready for bed.

After finishing the dishes and several glasses of wine, Herald studied all twenty pages of the case. It was his final search for flaws in his legal analysis. He read the opposition's arguments and contrasted their points against his own reply brief. To slow his mind, he treated himself to a final glass of wine and afterward went to bed.

How can I get a good night's sleep with the Pearlman curse over my head?

It's difficult to stop a mind going 120 miles an hour; no need for an alarm clock. In Vietnam it was the ever-present threat to his physical safety that kept Herald on edge all night. Now the economic threat was so overwhelming he never really went to sleep. At 3:00 a.m. another finger bite did nothing to abate his anxiety. Not even his mantra of riding the hurricane's eye would let him sleep.

Bored from looking at the clock every ten minutes for the last seven hours, Herald jumped out of bed at 6:00 a.m. and hit the shower.

MD 0: SHOWTIME!

The hot water invigorated his foggy mind.

Wake up or drown!

He brushed his teeth and attempted to shave without removing too much skin. Still facing himself in the mirror, he promised himself, *I will make the call, Pearlman, honest. Just get me out of this!*

With luck, he nicked himself just twice. Both wounds were minor; he was able to stop the bleeding with small bits of toilet paper applied as bandages.

As he dressed, Thea turned over in bed and propped herself up on one arm. "Good luck. And, oh, don't forget to remove the toilet paper from your face before court."

Embarrassed, he smiled. "Thank you, Dear, I promise. If the gods decree that we get out of this, I think it's time for me to investigate the Veterans' services and for us to discover where we lost each other. Do you know where my keys are?"

Rolling over to sleep some more, she replied, "No, you didn't tell me where you put them. Check the mantle."

He went to the fireplace mantle, looked beside and behind his treasured, brass shell-casing vases, and then moved the other items. No keys.

He went to the kitchen and searched everywhere. Still, no keys.

Now a feeling of panic started to grip him. He rushed back into the bedroom and saw Thea standing in the bathroom door spinning the keys on her finger. Flicking her hair back, in silence she tossed the keys to him as he approached.

"Thanks," he sighed as he caught them. "Now nothing else can happen on the way to court."

Nothing! If I miss this appearance with the tentative ruling against me, there's no makeup session.

"Good luck, Herald."

He kissed her right cheek, turned, and walked to the front door. Grabbing the door knob, he went into the cool, dark morning, wondering what his fate would be.

This is like boarding a helicopter on the way to a firefight; you just never know, never ever know how things will turn out.

The VW van's door was a little stiff as Herald opened it. He made a mental note to oil it. After placing the key in the ignition, he pushed the starter button. The engine failed to turn over. Frantic, he eyed the dashboard—and saw the headlight knob was still on.

Damn! The jinx is toying with my van, mocking my stupidity to leave the lights on. Looks like I'm gonna hafta jump-start this baby.

Herald released the parking brake, jumped out of the van, and, leaving the driver's door open, put his shoulder to the doorframe, pushing for a rolling jump-start. The old van hesitated and then began to roll.

Ah yes, there are some advantages to living on a hill.

As he continued to push, he tripped over his front foot and fell. The van continued—true to the rules of gravity—rolling across the street, where it hit the neighbor's hedge and stopped. Sweat started to bead on his forehead, and his chest muscles tightened as he realized the act of leaving for court seemed to be jinxed.

Jumping up, he ran to the van, opening the door, which had swung closed, and grabbed the steering wheel. He turned the wheel toward the steep incline of the street, leaving his neighborhood. Shouldering again into the door frame, he coached himself.

OK, now, just a slight push, and the van should be on its way.

Leaping in, he pumped the gas pedal twice, put in the clutch, and slid the van into second gear. When it gained sufficient momentum, he released the clutch. The van sputtered, sputtered again, and then stopped.

"What's going on? Damn it!" Herald exploded, sending spittle onto the dashboard and windshield.

Coasting halfway down the hill, there was only a short distance until the street leveled and he would lose a final chance to start the engine. He pressed the clutch to the floor and let the van gather more momentum before releasing the clutch. The van sputtered and sputtered; then, thank God, one cylinder fired, and then another—and he was off!

What the hell else can happen?

Herald continued to El Camino Real and waited at the traffic light behind a station wagon loaded with four children, jumping around, distracting their mother. When the light turned green, the car in front entered the intersection, and an old truck ran the red-light signal, hitting the station wagon dead in the middle. The sounds of rending steel and breaking glass reminded Herald of a chilling accident he had seen in Vietnam. Another stress coin dropped in his Vietnam-memory slot machine.

YEAR 1969

AS THE PLATOON APPROACHED the main road, Route One, Herald saw two military deuce-and-a-half trucks barreling down the road in opposite directions. Both were traveling at excessive speeds, overloaded with soldiers from the South Vietnamese Army. These two-and-a-half-ton off-road vehicles had three axles, six wheels, an enclosed cab, and a canvas-covered truck bed but were open at the sides. A normal load would be eight to ten soldiers seated in the pull-down benches on each side of the bed, with equipment stacked in the middle.

But the South Vietnamese loved to pack the beds of their trucks with equipment and have soldiers standing on the benches, others lying on top of the equipment, many hanging from the side support struts, and the rest riding on the canvas roof. With forty-plus men on each, the trucks looked like chicken transporters seen on U.S. highways: big chicken trucks with wooden boxes stacked ten high on top of each other, feathers flying off.

"*Dio cane!*" Ferlinghetti hollered. "I'm-a bet cinque dollari dese-a gooks-a dey collide."

"You got my bet!" Jones called out. "I'm going for they miss each other—with the road as wide as it is here."

"I'm with—*ack*—Ferlinghetti," AckMan added. "Odds—*ack*—two to—*ack*—one."

The entire platoon started to group together as Herald screamed, "Everyone back off! AckMan, you have to know better now; you are platoon sergeant! We ended up popping a Charles within ten yards of us last month when we were grouped up to talk to the college idiot, for God's sake! Place your bets, but keep away from each other! Jones, you write them down."

Herald had his back to the road when he heard the *SCREEEECH* of tires and, almost instantly after, *KEEEERASH!* The sound of steel pounding steel, greased by human flesh, was horrifying. Death was in the noise itself.

Herald spun around to see the two trucks still moving in the final throes of their deadly collision. From his view at 300 yards away, it appeared the truck engines and cabs had vanished, leaving only the two truck beds glued together by a blob of something in the middle. The impact was so severe, the back sets of dual rear wheels of both trucks were off the ground, forming a large set of open wings.

Herald grabbed the radio hook and keyed the mic. "Bandleader, this is Piper One. We have a major accident out here on Route One. Send out medical personnel and tow trucks. This is a bad one. I will call back on a casualty count."

"Piper One," the CC replied, "Bandleader, wilco out."

Turning to his platoon, Herald gave swift emergency orders. "AckMan, take overall security—Jones, the right flank, and Ferlinghetti, the left. Dog, you and the medic see what you can do to help these people."

The closer they moved to the accident, the more surreal the scene became. There were bodies and body parts strewn more than 100 yards from where the trucks were fused together. Herald wondered where both enormous engines had disappeared to. Weapons, grenades, and equipment were scattered in every direction. Counting twenty-five dead, many more were dying or mangled. After two hours, helicopters and road equipment arrived with their own contingent of soldiers for protection while they cleaned up the mess.

YEAR 1988

HERALD STOPPED, YANKED his emergency brake and jumped out of the van. Rushing to the station wagon, he saw that everyone was injured.

What the hell else is the scourge going to throw at me to prevent my court appearance?

Spotting a pay phone on the corner, he ran over to call in the accident. Just as he arrived at the phone booth, a police car pulled up behind his VW. He walked back over as the policeman was calling for an ambulance.

Seeing Herald approach in an expensive-looking, tailored suit, the officer was cordial, figuring him to be an attorney. "Did you see the accident?"

"Yes, but I'm hurrying to a critical court appearance. I have to be there in forty-five minutes. Could I leave you my card and contact you later?"

"Sorry, sir, but you're a material witness. I need your statement now."

Annoyed, Herald pulled out his business card. "Look, I am an attorney and an officer of the court. I will freely go to the station after court, but I have to leave *now*. Do you want me to explain to the judge why I was late after I gave you my contact information and you refused to let me go to court?"

The officer radioed the station about letting his attorney witness leave.

Goddamn it. If I don't get out of here now …

Herald watched the policeman check for serious injuries. He thought about helping but discarded the idea. After ten long minutes, the officer received an OK for Herald to leave and give his witness statement later. Herald glanced at the clock on the police vehicle's dashboard. His hearing would start in thirty-five minutes. He ran to his van, backed it up, and took a side road around the accident just as the ambulance pulled up, its siren screaming.

Herald drove to court as fast as his VW could handle—almost causing his own accident as he swerved around a stalled car, horn blasting. Time was running out.

Twenty-five minutes to go.

He parked the van at the courthouse in a no-parking zone; a parking ticket was the least of his problems. His chest muscles pulled at his left shoulder, giving off stabbing pains. His breathing became labored. He ran into the courthouse.

Twenty minutes to go.

He checked the Law and Motion calendar for his case, to make sure it hadn't been reassigned. *My motion is not on any court calendar for the hearing!* Icy fear chilled him. *Where did I go wrong? Oh, God! Did the curse cause me to make a mistake when I scheduled my motion with the court?*

He bit his finger to calm himself down, remembering there was an opposition filed and he'd paid the fee for the motion to be calendared.

It must be just a small clerical problem, but ... Herald, old buddy, if you f'ed this one up, the last day to file the motion to solve the problem has passed, and you are out—doubly out—of luck.

Fifteen minutes to go.

He approached the civil clerk's counter to ascertain why his motion was not on the calendar. His mind was ablaze with fear. His hands trembling, he gave the clerk a courteous "Hello." He always made it a point to be nice to the clerks; they had real power where it counted.

He recalled a lesson he'd learned as a law clerk, seventeen years earlier. He'd been standing third in line to file court documents behind an attorney at the clerk's window who was yelling at her in a demeaning fashion. The verbal abuse went on and on until the attorney second in line interrupted and tried to calm the situation by pointing out, "Look, the clerk is only trying to do her job. If you have a valid objection, take it to the judge." The clerk had given an exasperated sigh and addressed her irritated customer. "Give me the papers, and I'll see what I can do for you, sir." As the obnoxious attorney left, the clerk, with a Mona Lisa smile and the practiced hand of a pro who handles papers all day long, grasped the top left corner where the document was stapled. She flipped the papers in a practiced manner over her shoulder. The condescending counsel's papers leveled off in flight toward the wastepaper basket and, with a muted rush, like a Ruffed Grouse in flight, descended into the "circular file." No one noticed but Herald, standing at an angle where he could see the trash can behind her.

Well, Herald remembered thinking at the time, *she kept her word; she did what she could with his papers. Moral: If you want your papers to be handled with respect, then treat the clerk with respect.*

It was Herald's turn at the window. The clerk, who remembered his friendly nature, was eager to help, and confirmed his motion was in fact on the calendar. "Mr. Lloyd, it's odd your matter wasn't posted on the written calendar in the hall, but here it is on the computer's calendar, and that's what counts. The clerk who typed up the printed calendar must have omitted your matter by mistake. Sorry." Then, raising her eyes from the computer screen, she said, "You look a little gray today, Mr. Lloyd. Are you ill?"

"No, but thank you for asking, and I appreciate your help finding my motion."

Ten minutes to go. Phew!

Walking to the elevator, Herald thought he'd heard her also say something about tissue on his face, but he was too preoccupied with getting into the courtroom. As he hustled, he recalled a line of dialogue from a movie. The scene flashed in his mind: a jail guard opening the cell of a condemned man and shouting, "Dead man … walking."

Herald had known the judge appointed to his case for years, a man who held to a strict interpretation of the law. It was going to be a long walk off a short pier, a real pirate's-plank scene.

Eight minutes to go.

He entered the crowded elevator. It started to climb the eight floors. With each floor, Herald's stress rose higher. He envisioned a clock on the elevator wall, with its fast-moving second hand ticking away precious moments.

As if on cue, Herald could almost feel the cerebral stress coin dropping in his Vietnam-flashback slot machine and the thump of its handle releasing. When the reels behind his eyes stopped, his slot symbol returned him to an elevator ride he had taken with Bright in Taiwan.

Moron! Now is not the time for a stupid sex fantasy.

But fight it as he might, his subconscious mind had taken control. He was back in Taiwan on an elevator with Bright.

"OK," he angrily whispered to his rebellious mind, "have it your way, but only for a minute. We must get with the program and stop arguing about this in public."

When he stopped whispering, he noticed the woman behind him was staring at him like he was crazy. Herald smiled and said, "Sorry, just a little preoccupied with the day's events." She huffed and turned her head. His devilish, slot-machine mind shot directly to the most outrageous act he had ever committed in an elevator.

YEAR 1969

HERALD AND BRIGHT had just entered the hotel elevator alone on their way down to the restaurant on his fourth day of R&R.

Herald kicked the one door when it jammed halfway from closing. The door responded with a *squeeek, thump,* and the doors rumbled together, making Bright laugh.

Bright, standing at the control panel, looked over her right shoulder, giving him an impish grin as she pressed the button to the lobby. After the elevator started its descent, with its bouncing-off-the-walls movement, she moved her back up against him and started pressing and rotating her rear clockwise against his pelvis. Putting her right hand behind her back with the inside of her palm turned to touch him, she rubbed him up and down. After a short time, with the rise of his hunger, she started unzipping his fly.

This woman knows elevator magic.

The naughty fantasy of public sex conquered his elevator paranoia. Bright, standing next to the big, red, emergency shut-off switch, reached over and placed her index finger just above it. Her hand hesitated for a second; then she triggered the emergency system, bringing the elevator to a jolting stop and causing the car to swing back and forth.

His left hand inched down to catch Bright's miniskirt hem between his fingers and raise it over her waist. He slid his right hand down the outside of her thigh and moved it over her rear and in between her thighs. She opened her legs, shifted her weight to her toes, and raised her heels off the floor, giving him easy access to her. He cupped her in his slow, gentle way.

After several minutes, still with her back to him, she moved her hand inside his pants and maneuvered him out. Holding him hard, she raised her right leg to her chest and pressed her knee into the elevator door for support. Now she was wide open. She cocked her pelvis rearward and slid him all the way into her.

Herald imagined they were in a huge department store in New York City, with an elevator operator announcing the floors.

Going down, third floor, ladies' wear; second floor, domestics; first floor, sexual intercourse.

Bright reached back with her left hand, grabbed his shirt collar, and, with a pulling motion, set the tempo of their passion; alternating pulling hard, then harder, at her pace, increasing the speed of the motion. As she lowered her head, placing her hand on the elevator door to brace herself, she hissed, "Scratch me, GI, scratch me hard, like no tomorrow."

Herald, absorbed in his first-floor sexual adventure, left all thoughts of Vietnam far behind. Bright's softness evoked in him a warm sensation of melting. In the next instant, pent-up anger from suffering the war's day-to-day fear of the unknown—being shot or blown up—swept over him. He pounded her to the beat of her hand pulling on his shirt as she laughed into the elevator wall.

"Fuck me, GI! Fuck me hard!"

The intensity of their lovemaking caused the elevator to bang back and forth in loud protest against the shaft's cement walls. Feeling his involuntary shudder into her, Herald placed his hand on the elevator control panel above her head to steady himself. With his shuddering, Bright's body shivered. She shook her head and purred "OH-ehh, ehh." After the last "ehh," she lifted her head to his forearm and bit hard, but Herald's labored breathing, tears, and the sweat dripping off his face evidenced his compulsion to get away from the war: he did not feel her teeth on his skin.

Still clinging to each other, the elevator alarm began blaring, and shouts of "Stop holding up the elevator and get a room, you assholes!"

Herald rushed to zip up his pants and help Bright pull down her skirt. She switched the "Off" lever to "On" and pressed the button for the lobby. The elevator started up with a clunk and descended one more floor to the lobby; the doors opened.

Luck was on their side. The would-be greeting party had left the lobby, and they exited the elevator without harassment.

YEAR 1988

SIX MINUTES TO GO.

The courthouse elevator stopped on the eighth floor, and the doors rumbled open.

Five minutes …

Herald shot out of the elevator like a racehorse. The hall had a nice overview of the city, but today Herald wasn't interested in panorama. His only thought was that, if he lost the plea, the jump down would be sufficient to end the pain. His life insurance would be enough for the family.

Four minutes …

He reached the doors to his courtroom. Opening one side of the regal, large, oak double doors and one side of the second set of interior double doors, he entered the room.

Three minutes …

He proceeded to the judge's clerk to check in. As he approached the clerk, whom he knew from many other appearances, she greeted him. "Hello, Mr. Lloyd. Having a nice day?"

Herald, feeling the blood rushing in his ears, attempted a smile while searching her face for any clue to his fate. "Nice so far, but the day is young. I have the case listed on line twenty-one."

As Herald walked away deep in thought, the clerk called out. "Mr. Lloyd, your face ... " But lost in space, he did not catch the importance of her remark.

One minute and countdown ...

He moved back to the gallery, where he took a seat; his face flushed, heart pounding, and right leg slightly twitching.

The courtroom, seventy-five by fifty feet, was evenly divided: half for the gallery, half for the orderly process of law. There were two large tables for the attorneys. Off to the right was the separate box of raised seating for the jury. On the front-left wall in the corner was the clerk's desk, connected to the judge's bench. The witness chair was in the middle of the front wall, with the court reporter's chair in front of it. This was his civilian battlefield.

As Herald sat down, Opposing Counsel Dan Duddroff entered the courtroom. He nodded at Herald in a manner suggesting he hated screwing over another attorney, but this was for his client and his job. Winning would be a prize plum for Duddroff, a ticket to promotion and prestige.

Herald imagined what Duddroff was thinking: *Sad that this is a brother attorney, but there's blood in the water—and it's not mine. The thrill of the kill ... and the tentative ruling is in my favor. Lloyd might just as well hang up his carcass. Let's see, I always enjoy my opponent charbroiled, yeah, well done.*

The malpractice judgment against Herald would be for $2.4 million, and liability was clear. Herald would not be entitled to contest the merits of the case, as his mistake had forfeited the opportunity. The case law surrounding the issue of leaving a name out of a multi-page document was usually fatal to the attorney who made the error, even when it was clear all parties to the agreement intended to relieve his client and the client's corporation from default.

Thea would be right, of course. She always told him his bad habit of speed-reading these important documents would one day be his downfall. The day of reckoning was at hand, and the opposition was preparing burnt crow for his lunch. Herald prayed and once again promised himself that he would call Pearlman's parents if the curse was lifted and he won.

Mr. Duddroff was a good trial attorney who lived for the kill in litigation. Today Herald was in his sniper-scope crosshairs. Upholding a tentative ruling at oral argument was only a formality; the win was in the bag for him.

Watching him, Herald let his mind wander, appalled by his opponent's ill-fitting suit and cheap tie.

He looks awful! His clothes are wrinkled and untailored, and his shirttail protrudes below his coat. This is the man who is kicking my ass? Shame, Herald, shame on you!

Herald's case was number twenty-one. For forty-five minutes, he witnessed all the rulings on line items one through twenty. Each tentative ruling was upheld. With each decision, Herald felt colder; the fear in his bones increased. It was pathetic; each attorney requesting oral argument was like a lamb going to slaughter. The attorney would argue "BAAH—BAAH—BAAH," and the next sound was the sweet hiss of the metal blade of the judge's guillotine as the tentative ruling was upheld.

Herald jolted upright when the clerk called the abbreviated caption, "Buck v. Thall, Rogers and Associates, Inc., line item twenty-one." Grabbing the seat in front of him, to help himself stand, he rose, coughed, and then walked slowly to the counsel table. There was the distinct metallic taste of blood in his mouth, just like the day Pearlman was killed. *Must be the taste of fear*, he thought as he announced, "Herald Lloyd for the defendant and moving party."

Dead man ... standing.

Opposing counsel laid his briefcase on the plaintiff's table. "Dan Duddroff for the plaintiff and opposing party."

The judge turned to look at Herald. As he did so, he hesitated as if witnessing something very odd. He cocked his head and addressed both attorneys. "Counsel, please approach the bench."

Surprised, Duddroff and Herald looked at each other and walked around the respective ends of their large counsel tables to the judge's bench. They stopped at the edge of the bench. The judge whispered, "Mr. Lloyd, do you want me to take your arguments seriously?"

Herald could not believe what he just heard, the parameters of the question were so great. He had to do what every trial attorney dreads—answer an ambiguous question. In the most deferential tone, Herald responded, "Yes, Your Honor, as I made what I thought was a well-founded and serious motion, even if the tentative ruling was against me."

The judge read Herald's face and realized he was not being insulting to the court. "Mr. Lloyd, if you want me to take you seriously, please take a moment and remove the bits of toilet paper from your face."

Herald stepped back, and it came to him. The filing and court clerks were not engaging in idle chatter; they were trying to tell him to remove the toilet paper from his face before he went before the judge. He gave a feeble smile. "Yes, Your Honor. I was just a little bit excited about today and forgot to remove my shaving bandages. They'll be off by the time I am back to the counsel table."

He felt like a schoolboy who had been caught picking his nose and reprimanded himself.

Great way to start one of the most important court days of my life, while rubbing the toilet paper off his face. Now he was worried that his rubbing might cause the cuts to bleed again. *Great, my choices are either toilet paper decoration or hemorrhaging before the court.*

After counsel were seated at their respective tables, the judge looked to Herald. "Mr. Lloyd, as the disadvantaged party, you requested this hearing. You may proceed."

Herald rose and faced the judge, no longer afraid. He realized his own insignificance when he weighed his feelings against what was truly important: his family and his client. A bead of sweat rolled off his forehead, down past his left eyebrow, and onto his cheek. And he began.

"The court's tentative ruling emphasized relief from default was time-barred; more importantly, this reasoning centered on the relief being material. Ordinarily, this would be correct. However, in the matter at hand, there are factors by which the court may determine the relief requested is only ministerial in nature.

"Here we have the admission by plaintiff's counsel that both my clients were to be included in the release, and the only missing part is the name of one client. No material terms of the agreement are to change, just the addition of one party's name," he pleaded.

"This renders the error ministerial, not material. I submit, under these facts, the name missing from this document can be likened to a court clerk recording a judgment where one name is missing. There is no substantive change. Adding a name omitted by the court is considered ministerial and not subject to any of the time-barred substantive issues."

The judge looked at opposing counsel. Duddroff, who had been so sure of himself with the tentative ruling in his favor, now looked as if he'd been hit with a sledgehammer. He had failed to consider Herald's analogy of a court clerk leaving off the name of a judgment debtor. Looking down at his papers, he shuffled them a bit while clearing his throat with a slight, "Ehh, ehh."

"Counsel, any comments to Mr. Lloyd's argument?" the judge asked Duddroff.

"Your Honor," Duddroff began, his mind spinning for a solution, "I feel the court's tentative-ruling analysis as to altering any aspect of the settlement agreement is more on point. How could the addition of a name not ever be a critical and material aspect of any agreement?" Sweat now formed on Duddroff's brow; his hands rubbed each other over and over as his confidence wavered. He knew this motion was up for grabs.

The judge looked up at the ceiling and back to Herald. "Anything else, Mr. Lloyd?"

"Your Honor, Mr. Duddroff's argument would be correct if the change or addition of a name were at odds with the intent of all counsel and parties to the agreement. Here, the agreement was to relieve all of my client's corporation and himself individually from default. More important, plaintiff would obtain a windfall profit from what may end up a defense verdict, when litigated against my corporate defendant. This would lead to an inconsistent judicial result as the individual client, who carries the engineering license, and his corporation stand in the same legal shoes.

"In addition, since my mistake caused this motion to be set with plaintiff's counsel to prepare the opposing brief and appear in court, it is appropriate I pay sanctions, if the court grants my motion for relief, in the sum of $750."

The judge rubbed his face with both his hands. "Is the matter submitted?"

"Submitted," they both answered in unison.

There was a pause, which, to Herald, felt like an entire night in Vietnam. During this time, the judge looked down at his papers while rubbing his temples.

As the judge appraised the case, Herald prayed; he was sweating so profusely he felt like he was in the tropics. The noise of blood gushing from his pounding heart grew so loud he felt Duddroff must be able to hear it. In addition, that metallic taste was still present.

At last the judge spoke. "I have to agree that only adding a name to a settlement agreement, for which all the terms and parties remain the same and had been agreed to previously by all parties, would be more akin to a court clerk mistakenly omitting a party's name from a judgment. If all the parties agreed to the relief from default for all defendants, adding the omitted defendant is not material. The intent of the parties was to include all defendants. With that, I grant the motion and reverse the tentative ruling.

"Furthermore, Mr. Lloyd, your offer to pay sanctions for the economic cost of your mistake is well taken. Sanctions are awarded to Plaintiff and against you in the sum you suggested of $750. Mr. Lloyd, you will prepare the order and pay the sanctions forthwith. I trust I will never see you here again on this type of error. Any questions?"

"No, Your Honor," both replied. Herald looked at Duddroff and saw his confusion, thinking the ruling was a slam-dunk but which had somehow slipped through his fingers.

This was far too much excitement for Herald—right up there with hearing the familiar *snap-snap* of Mr. AK-47 over his head. He turned and offered his hand to Duddroff. "Good job, Counsel."

Duddroff shook Herald's hand, uttering, "Thank you" in a voice betraying his disappointment. How was he going to explain to his client that what he had represented as a no-brainer motion had gone south at the last moment?

Herald followed the advice of the first attorney for whom he'd law clerked: "After you win, don't just walk; *flee* the courtroom to be sure the judge does not reconsider." Jumping up and down, or other childish acts of victory, such as those demonstrated in the world of professional sports, were the kinds of behavior Herald had seen aggravate the court and cause a change of ruling.

CHAPTER 20
THE LONG ROAD HOME

HERALD HURRIED TO THE ELEVATORS but didn't stop to push the call button; instead, he continued to the emergency stairs. Pain jabbed at his chest muscles as he opened the door to the stairwell. Panting, he placed his hand on the wall to steady himself for a few moments. The thought that he could still be brought back for the judge to change his ruling flashed in his mind. Herald flew down the eight floors, two stairs at a time, giddy about dodging the fatal legal bullet.

Taking a moment to catch his breath on the first floor, he eyed the bank of pay phones near the men's room.

Have to call Thea.

Pulling out his wallet, he removed his telephone credit card and dialed home.

Thea answered on the second ring. "How bad is it?"

"We won! Christ, out of the frying pan!"

"Is there any appeal or something else that could bite us?"

"Nope, this decision is well within the judge's discretion, so we're good on appeal, and there are no new facts that would support a Motion for Reconsideration, so this is it. We're in the clear; back to where we were!"

"Not so fast, lieutenant! Don't you understand what your family has gone through? Who wants to raise a family clinging to a stormy litigation cliff? Even now you can't convince me this will not happen again, you, with your alcohol and careless attitude. I need to hear you're going to undertake some program to deal with your nightmares and flashbacks. Time for you to go to the Veterans Affairs, mister!"

"Listen! I'm sooo sorry to have put you through this and taken several years off both our lives. I have to hit the office on a few matters, so, be home later. Thanks for hanging in there—this entire mess has sucked us dry. I'll consider the VA, but indulge me with enjoying a brief respite from this disaster."

"I'm sticking it out, as I do love you, Herald, which is why this is so hard. See you tonight. What are you making for dinner?"

"How 'bout liver and onions?"

"Uhh ... right. You know I hate liver and onions!"

"Right-o. Just teasing. How about shrimp scampi?"

"Fine. See you soon."

"Love you," he squeezed in before they hung up.

Letting go a sigh of relief, Herald wiped a thin sweat from his forehead. *Whew. Ducked that bullet ... but am still under the gun.*

As he opened his wallet to replace the telephone card, the old, tattered piece of paper with Pearlman's telephone number popped out, fluttering to the polished stone floor. Picking it up, he unfolded the paper. The faded numbers were hard to read after all these years. Tears welled up in his eyes.

I promised, and now I'm going to do it.

Herald dialed the same number he'd called on the date of his discharge. Just as in the past, his guilt flared up, threatening to overwhelm him. During the series of long-distance telephone-connection clicks, his guilt grew to gigantic proportions.

The first ring sounded so loud, he nearly dropped the receiver. The second followed so quickly that it startled him; his body flinched. Not to be deterred this time, he reflected upon the Serenity Prayer to give him strength, giving way to an epiphany: Pearlman's death had been a random incident of war beyond his control.

On the third ring, a woman's voice answered. "Hello, Pearlman residence."

"Hello," Herald stammered back, "is this Mrs. Pearlman?"

"Yes," the voice responded, "but I do not accept telephone solicitations."

"Mrs. Pearlman, my name is Herald Lloyd. Did you have a son who died in Vietnam?"

There was a long pause and then a question. "Why would you want to know?"

"I was your … your son's platoon leader when he died. We … we had a promise to call the other's parents if one of us, if … the other did not make it back. I tried to call you many years ago but … I just didn't have the courage. I'm so sorry. But just today, something has happened to give me that courage. Is there anything you would like to ask me?"

There was a longer pause. At last Mrs. Pearlman spoke. Her voice was bitter. "What kind of selfish, non-caring, self-absorbed person are you? Without notice, you raise my dead son after eighteen years! Have you ever experienced the loss of a close relative?"

Ashamed, he blushed, "Yes, my father was killed in an airplane crash when I was ten."

"Well, what if a survivor of your father's plane crash telephoned you eighteen years later totally out of the blue and asked you the same sort of question you're asking me? How would you feel?"

"I feel ashamed that my only focus was to free me from my promise. I wasn't considering your feelings."

"There must be some reason for your guilt. Did you cause his death in some way, by maybe … what is the term … oh yes, friendly fire?"

"No! Oh my God, no! But I was with him when it happened."

"Was he in any pain when he died?"

"No, Mrs. Pearlman, it was instantaneous. He never felt a thing."

"Are you lying to me to make me feel better? If you have any decency, you will tell me the truth."

"I *am* telling the truth; he did not feel any pain. You should be very proud of him. He was a great platoon sergeant."

"Did my son want you to say anything to us?"

"Yes, he wanted … he wanted me to tell you two things. First, he was … was sorry to quit Harvard and disappoint you. Second, he loved you and his … his father very much."

Mrs. Pearlman took a moment to reflect; then, in a low, quavering voice, she replied, "I am so sorry any of you were mixed up in that dreadful war. God, there is not a day goes by I do not miss my only child. I can only wonder if our pressure on him to go to Harvard was the cause of him joining the Army. Why him and not you? The only answer is God chose Johnny to be with him first. Thank you for the call. I feel ill and need to hang up now."

Yes, the burden of failing to keep his promise to Pearlman was lifted; but now a different type of guilt replaced it. How selfish he'd been in failing to consider the parents' feelings. Perhaps they just wanted to forget the pain of their son's death? Perhaps a more subtle inquiry, to find out if they even wanted to have a conversation, would have been more thoughtful?

Why couldn't I get past the promise and consider the consequences?

Herald lowered his head, guilt flooding his mind.

Where does it stop? The pain of Vietnam is doomed to repeat itself in a myriad of ways. Even so … I felt I did the honorable thing making the call to Pearlman's parents no matter how his mom reacted.

The phone conversation did not give Herald the total relief he had expected. However, being able to answer Mrs. Pearlman's inquiry as to how her son died and to tell her of his respect for him almost justified the pain he'd caused her. He let his forehead rest on the pay phone as his breathing relaxed and his heart resumed its normal rhythm.

Leaving the granite building, Herald leapt down the twelve stone courthouse steps in three strides. He had fulfilled his promise to Pearlman after being haunted by it all these years.

Striding through the courthouse's cement path, he noticed, adjacent to the courthouse, a filthy man with debris tangled in his matted hair and a mangy beard. He was kneeling on a small area of grass resembling a minipark with a stone bench and fountain, wearing worn Army fatigue pants, and no shirt. Next to him staked in the grass at a 45-degree angle was a sign with a scribbled message: "My name is Louis. I am Homeless Vietnam Vet. Give What You Can. I Did For You."

An instantaneous sense of déjà vu gave Herald an alarming feeling of affinity with the man; he saw himself kneeling there in the grass shirtless. Herald paused, his brow furrowed.

How do you even spell "déjà vu?"

Then he remembered himself kneeling at Travis Air Force Base while performing his uniform-burning ritual after his discharge from Vietnam.

Of all the ironies Herald had experienced in the military, the cruelest was the Army's idea of out-processing. There was no discharge program. The only notice a soldier received that indicated their change of status from soldier to civilian was a twenty-five-hour flight out of Vietnam and a sign at the stateside clinic door reading, "Out-Processing Station, Exit."

When you walked out the exit door—blink—you were a civilian. Good luck! And don't let the door hit you on the way out!

In Vietnam Herald had promised himself that if he ever made it back, he would maintain a permanent good attitude, a pledge that would remain timeless, no matter what happened. He had kept his commitment, albeit flawed in his execution.

This vet in front of him had fought the same war but now was homeless and destitute. He had suffered a bad roll of the dice and could not make the transition to civilian life. Begging and seeming unable to care for himself, he didn't even have it together enough to plant his sign upright.

Herald pondered what had saved him from the same fate as this shirtless vet. His own difficulty in getting past his Vietnam service had kept him mired in the experience, as manifested by the persistent pounding of his suppressed war memories.

He was fortunate to have had a few special friends and circumstances—just a different destiny from this homeless man's. However, both their lives were in shambles—thanks to alcohol and uncontrollable war flashbacks. Maybe he couldn't handle it, either?

As Herald walked closer, the vet turned and looked him directly in the eye. Startled, Herald stopped and jumped back, envisioning his own face superimposed on the angry visage of the homeless vet. It was his own face! The homeless vet, wearing Herald's face, begged to pose a question. *Was it all really worth it?*

"Yes," Herald muttered aloud. "I have something nobody can take away from me."

The homeless man's weathered face hardened into a scowl of anger; this conversation was at him, not with him. Seeing no one else around, the vet yelled back, "Who you talking to, Mr. La-a-awyer? What'cha looking at, buddy? Ain't you never seen a homeless vet before? Hey, how 'bout some change?"

Herald snapped out of the vision, reached into his pocket and drew out a twenty-dollar bill. Placing it in the homeless veteran's hand, he whispered, "Remember, in Vietnam you faced your fear every day, even when you walked out on patrol. Nobody can take that away from you. Under incredible stress, you retained *the ability to make decisions*. It's the best foundation to deal with the civilian world. Go to the VA and get cleaned up. If you beat your fear once, there is no reason you can't do it again."

A feeling of euphoria flooded Herald. He walked up the street past the Small Claims Court, with its small area of grass where two streets intersected. On this corner was a food cart under a bright red umbrella reading, "Doggone Good Hot Dogs." Still on a high from his achievements of the day, he approached it, glancing at the four-item menu. Scratching his chin, he gave his order to the vendor. "Polish sausage with kraut and a diet something to drink, please."

Giving a polite smile and nod to Herald, the vendor opened the lid to one of the stainless steel warming trays. He picked up a paper wrapper, opened it, and, with metal tongs, removed a bun from the warmer and placed it in the wrapper. With a deft hand, he opened the steam canopy enveloping the sausages, the steam obscuring his face as he reached in with the tongs, and withdrew a moist sausage from the tray. Plunking the sausage into the bun and handing it to Herald, he said, "Four dollars, please."

He handed the vendor a five. "Keep the change."

Grinning at Herald, the vendor wiped his hands on his apron. "Kraut on the table, soda in the chest to your left ... and thanks for the tip, man."

Herald took the meal-on-a-bun to the condiment table and heaped sauerkraut on the sausage, and topped it with spicy mustard. Leaning over the soda ice chest, he trolled through the frigid ice water. His hand began to ache from the cold; he yanked out the closest diet root beer.

There was a four-seat wooden bench steps away. Herald sauntered over to it, savoring the blue sky and his world.

As he sat down, he thought he'd finally conquered his nightmares, what with the hearing and the phone call over, but the intense stress of the motion hearing was not fully released. The pounding on his mental metal doors grew in volume, blocking out any noise of the day. He concentrated on the chill of the root beer; it reminded him of the young Vietnamese soda peddlers who followed his patrols. Once more a coin was plunked into Herald's Vietnam-memory slot machine. The chrome handle was pulled, sending the wheels spinning.

YEAR 1969

HERALD'S PLATOON WAS SEARCHING for buried bombs on both sides of Highway One leading to Firebase Jackson. As the platoon advanced, Dog walked point and every few seconds jerked his head and shoulders to the left or right, betraying his nervousness with "Yip, yip, yip."

Charles, to safeguard himself from being discovered by Americans in the concealed spider holes, devised a preemptive strike to shield himself from being uncovered. When threatened, he had a nasty habit of detonating a bomb buried nearby; this custom tended to get on the GIs' nerves.

LeMaire, positioned in the middle of the platoon for fire support, grumbled, "*Mon Dieu, merde.*"

Hollywood raised his sunglasses and rested them on his knotted forehead muscles to stave off Herald yelling at him. Like some sort of double-eyed insect, he surveyed the area for anything dangerous. Jones, walking in the rear, alternated examining the ground and writing in his notebook.

Ferlinghetti, after scanning all directions, offered to read another poem.

"*Ack*—That's a negatron on the poem, Ferlin. We need to—*ack*—be focused on booby traps and bombs for now."

Switching gears, AckMan laughed as he saw several approaching vehicles. "Hey, guys—*ack*—here come four cyclos. Let's spread out the—*ack*—platoon and ride home."

Herald waved to the drivers to halt and nodded to AckMan in agreement. "Good idea, why not? The map says we've finished our booby trap patrol. Rather than walk down the road, we can become the first Wolfhound mechanized platoon to ride the commute."

A small cheer rose from the men as Herald placed twenty dollars in military scrip in the lead cyclo driver's hand. He raised four fingers, pointed to the other three cyclos, and motioned all drivers to go west to the firebase.

The first driver grinned and nodded, "You Numbah One, GI. Take you home."

Herald motioned for LeMaire to take the lead cyclo with two 40 mm blooper men. LeMaire jumped on the cyclo, causing it to rock wildly under his weight. Standing in the truck bed, he set up his machine gun on one of the exposed roof staves, ready to fire. The men who carried 40 mm grenade launchers knelt on either side of the bed, their weapons ready to give support for LeMaire's gunfire. The strategy: LeMaire would pin down any enemy force, and the blooper men would drop 40 mm grenades on them. The rest of the men spread out among the other vehicles, with Herald choosing the second cyclo to maintain command, and AckMan as platoon sergeant assigned to the fourth cyclo as cleanup.

Herald jumped on the second cyclo's bed. Steadying himself from the rocking, he rested his M-16 on a roof stave with his right hand, holding its pistol grip, and pitched his left arm signaling forward, calling out, "Wagons Ho-o-o!"

The four small two-cycle engines revved to a high-pitched *wheee-wheee-wheee* and belched clouds of bluish smoke as the little force started down the road. Ferlinghetti, in the second cyclo with his squad, and Herald started singing the first phrase of their theme song, "We Gotta Get Out of This Place." Jones, in the third cyclo with part of his squad, joined in. AckMan, in the fourth cyclo, started singing with part of Jones's squad; Jones was too busy chewing on his filthy left thumbnail and writing in his notebook.

The entire platoon was singing loudly—and way off-key. When singing the same line became boring, the second cyclo started singing in a round. Men in the third cyclo started the refrain, "We Gotta Get Out of This Place." When they reached "of this place," the fourth cyclo chorus started their round, and when they neared the end of the musical phrase, the first cyclo singers raised their voices. The entire progression sounded like a multiple layered chant of an ancient tribe, with the men in each cyclo attempting to hit the correct timing of lyrics and tones while alternating starting points. Whereas the sound was chaotic, it was a fine example of camaraderie and playfulness to release stress.

They went two klicks down the road singing at the tops of their lungs as they approached a small village of ten huts.

KABLAAAM! A rocket-propelled, antitank weapon blast was followed by the old *snap-snap* of Mr. AK-47.

"AAAUGH!" The windshield shattered; LeMaire's driver was hit. His arms flew up into the air as he screamed. Large clumps of his bloody flesh splattered the interior of the cyclo. His body lurched back in his seat, flopping onto the steering wheel, abruptly turning the cyclo to the right. It bounced off the road into a ditch bordering a field adjacent to the road, tossing the men.

LeMaire, thrown to the ground, checked his machine gun and rubbed his head. *"Mon Dieu, merde!"* The only good thing about cyclos was their maximum speed of 20 mph, so the abrupt stop just shook them up; there were no bodily injuries.

The other three cyclos stopped, and the platoon dispersed, spreading themselves three to four yards apart, married to the ground, facing the village in a line.

"Jones!" Herald yelled. "Form up on either side of LeMaire. LeMaire! Open up to keep them busy while I radio our CC for artillery and armor support. AckMan, you and Ferlinghetti's squad cover our flank and rear."

LeMaire opened up with measured five-to-six-round machine-gun bursts. Charles's returned fire slowed and became sporadic. The blooper men with their 40 mm grenade launchers started firing. After a couple of rounds, they honed in on the target area where the snipers were believed to be located. When the 40 mm grenades started exploding, all enemy fire ceased.

While Herald was calling in enemy contact, one of the routine U.S. armored patrol units assigned to keep Route One open pulled up next to the fighting line. The patrol was comprised of four American M-48 heavy battle tanks and four armored personnel carriers. Herald crawled from the fighting line to the cover of the tank's huge metal carriage.

The tank commander, also a lieutenant, yelled out over the deafening sounds of the idling diesel engines. "What's going on? Why are you in the ditch?"

Herald leaned on the tank's track guard as far as he could, shouting back, "Snipers were in the village!"

Before he could say another word, the tank commander spoke into his microphone. The huge tank turrets, with their 90 mm cannons, slowly rotated in the direction of the village.

Herald covered his ears with his hands and fell to the ground, roaring, "Everyone stay down and cover your ears!" just as the four main cannons began to thunder.

KAABLAAAM! KAABLAAAM! KAABLAAAM! KAABLAAAM!
The village was lost in the smoke of the large tank-gun explosions, accented

by walls of red-colored machine-gun tracers raking every inch of the grass houses back and forth. The smell of expended gunpowder and cordite filled the air. The ground trembled with the thatched huts vanishing as if scraped from the earth by a giant hand. Herald felt the explosions as a hollow tremor in his chest and his ears ached from the main gun blasts.

Attempting to stop the madness, Herald beat on the tank with his rifle butt, to no avail.

After what seemed like hours but in reality was only two or three minutes, the onslaught stopped. The little village was gone—leveled flat—there were no more targets.

The tank commander turned his body in his turret and faced Herald. "Well, we got the snipers, didn't we?"

"What kind of monster are you?" Herald blared while adjusting his helmet. "Did it ever occur to you that a few snipers are not worth an entire village? How in God's name are we going to cut a deal with the Vietnamese if they're all dead? Hearts and minds of dead people do not make a country democratic. It's very hard to get dead people to vote—or haven't you noticed?"

The tank commander looked at Herald, paused, and spit over his shoulder. He turned in his turret, surveyed the smoking destruction of the village and blasted back, "Gooks are Slopes. They were most likely hiding Charles, anyway. With the village dead, there's one less Charles motel and restaurant—and we do not leave the light on for them; we put their lights *out*. Besides, this is the first time I've had a chance to really open up this baby. Fun! After all, you told me you were in contact. We'll be going now, so check the body count, and call it in later. Also, don't bother to 'tank' us for saving your ass. Hahaha!" He continued laughing at his pun as he signaled his tanks and armored personnel carriers to move out. In a cloud of diesel smoke, the vehicles moved down the road.

Herald grouped his platoon together and bid adieu to the cyclos. He was still stunned and angry, overlooking a blackened wound on the earth

348   CURSE OF THE COLORING BOOK

that had been a small village minutes ago. His platoon moved through the smoldering ashes. There were no weapons—only four old men, seven women, three children, twenty-five chickens, three dogs, and four water buffalo, all very dead. Herald had his men cover the bodies out of respect. Calling in to his CC, he reported the slaughter. The CC called in the local politician to take control of the village situation. It took two hours for the CC to find the local politician and arrange for an American and South Vietnamese combat patrol to accompany them to the site.

The platoon proceeded to walk home in silence; mechanized travel made the men too vulnerable. Being even two feet above ground in a vehicle was too far away from Mother Earth.

Much later, with the platoon having just cleared the wire and now within the safety of the firebase, a relieved Herald called out to his troops. "That was one hell of a walk back, huh, guys?"

As they cleaned up and massaged each other's shoulders, the company CC strode over and yelled, "Lieutenant, over here!"

Herald jumped up and walked to the CC. "At your command."

"Cut the 'command' shit. The local politician just left. It just cost the U.S. Army ten dollars a person, five dollars a chicken, two dollars a dog, and forty dollars a water buffalo, all because you called a fire mission without my permission! I may take this out of your pay, and God help you if you call in a fire mission again without first consulting me. It was you who pointed out the village to those tanks, right? What the hell did you think would happen?"

With a dazed look on his face, Herald turned and looked back toward his platoon as the CC walked away.

A water buffalo was worth more than a person? Another bizarre cartoon twist to this twisted war.

Ferlinghetti, always on watch, came over. "'Ey, LT, I 'ave una bella poema. Wan-a to 'ear?"

"Sure. Why not? Could the day get any stranger?"

Ferlinghetti opened the worn, dirty pages and started.

In Goya's greatest scenes we seem to see
                                    the people of the world
            exactly at the moment when
                    they first attained the title of
                                    'suffering humanity'
            They writhe upon the page
                            in a veritable rage
                                    of adversity
            Heaped up
                    groaning with babies and bayonets
                                    under cement skies
            in an abstract landscape of blasted trees
                    bent statues bats wings and beaks
                            slippery gibbets
                    cadavers and carnivorous cocks
            and all the final hollering monsters
                    of the
                            'imagination of disaster'
            they are so bloody real
                            it is as if they really still existed

        And they do

            Only the landscape has changed

        They still are ranged along the roads
                    plagued by legionnaires
                            false windmills and demented roosters

        We are the same people
                            only further from home
                on freeways fifty lanes wide
                        on a concrete continent
                            spaced with bland billboards
                    illustrating imbecile illusions of happiness ...

                                    (A Coney Island of the Mind: Poems, page 9)

        "W'at-a you t'ink-a dees-a one, e'?"

        Herald scratched the back of his head. "Well, the events of today seem
to bear out the poem's sordid imagery of suffering humanity, especially
when a water buffalo is worth more than a human life."

YEAR 1988

HERALD SAT ON THE BENCH, immobilized by his thoughts, hand raised, ready to take the next bite of his sausage, when a Brewer's Blackbird with iridescent colors of black, midnight blue, metallic green and piercing yellow eyes, alighted on his hand. Sensing no objection, the bird picked at the hot-dog roll, bringing him back from his trance. Herald flicked his wrist, surprising the bird, which for a moment clung to his wrist and glared at him. When Herald moved the left hand holding the soda, the bird thought better of the face-off, flapping off with a *chirp*!

Eyeing the sausage in his right hand and the soda in his left, Herald pondered his situation. His reliance on his cornerstone war experience had not failed him in his civilian contest; it had given him the foundation to face his problem and maneuver out of his own legal puzzle. Yet something was missing. There was still another piece of unfinished business.

Finishing the sausage, Herald stood up and walked back to the homeless vet. As he approached, the vet recognized him and shoved Herald's twenty-dollar bill in his shoe, leery he was coming back to retrieve it.

Herald dropped to the infantry's "one knee down" position. The suspicious vet peered into his eyes. Looking squarely back at him, Herald said, "I need you to help me go to the Veterans Hospital. Will you show me the way?"

The vet's eyes narrowed as his body cringed at the offer. "Whatta *you* gonna get outta this? Feeling better 'bout your leech-lawyer guilt, leaving those you sent to war in the lurch? You never left the U.S., motherfucker!"

Herald raised his head and laughed; then he resumed eye contact. "I was a combat infantry lieutenant in 'Nam with the Wolfhounds in the 25th Infantry Division on the Cambodian border. I received two bronze stars, one for heroism in ground combat.

"Yes, I'm an attorney, but I'm not looking for anything other than a way to quiet my own fears that now haunt me. You and I have a bond. Will you go with me? By the way, my name is Herald; what's yours?"

Pointing to the sign the vet countered, "So you're a vet, too? Think that makes us related? Louis ... my name is Louis, and drinking is my game. Look—can handle this by myself. Don't need no counseling from some war motherfucker!"

"Yeah, thought I didn't need any help, either, and could handle it by myself, too, but now I realize I need professional help. Need someone to help me go to the VA Center. I've got whiskey in my car. Will you help me?"

The vet beamed. "Whiskey? Hey, now you're talkin'. As for takin' you to the VA, sure! They have good food there. I'll help you, even if you are a damned officer-lawyer. Hey, pick up my sign, but be careful—it was a lot of work—then help me up, and color us gone."

Laughing as he took the vet's extended right arm, helping him to his feet, Herald said, "Louis, I think this could be the beginning of a be-au-ti-ful re-hab friendship."

Standing, Louis glanced over to Herald with his bloodshot eyes. "Hey, ain't that a line from some old war movie?"

"Different war. This storm is on the home front. There ought to be a law against allowing susceptible assholes like me being exposed to John Wayne stereotypes."

Louis looked into Herald's eyes. Herald caught a glimpse of understanding in the receding darkness of Louis's alcohol-impaired mind as Louis agreed. "Fuckin' A, man."

The two of them traipsed over to Herald's VW. Louis directing the way, they headed for the VA Center, disregarding the parking ticket waving at Herald all the way there, flapping in the wind under the windshield wiper, just like a page from the *GI Joe Coloring Book*.

The metallic taste in Herald's mouth was gone.

GLOSSARY

As Remembered by the Author

air cav   air cavalry helicopter gunship assault teams

AK-47   assault rifle; the basic weapon of the communist forces, character-
ized by an explosive popping sound

AO   area of operations for a military unit

arty   abbreviation for artillery

bandolier   cloth strap, two-to-three feet long, formed into circle and
placed over the head to wear on chest with numerous pouches to hold
M-16 ammunition

BC   battalion commander, usually a Lt. Colonel with four companies

blooper man   soldier whose weapon is the M-79, 40 mm grenade launcher;
shotgun-like weapon that shoots spin-armed "balls" or small grenades

boo-coo   English bastardized-French word "beaucoup" meaning "much"
or "many"

boot   soldier just out of boot camp, inexperienced and untested, also
called a "newbie"

buck sergeant   a rank nickname distinguishing from other senior grades
of sergeants; can be used in different contexts, good or demeaning

353

C-ration   combat rations for meals in the field, consisting of several different menus, including the main course (ham, corned beef hash, beans, and the like); can of fruit, packet of dessert, cigarettes, and chewing gum

CC   company commander, usually a captain in rank

catch one   being hit by a bullet

Charles / Charlie / Sir Charles   slang for communist soldiers, including Viet Cong (VC), and North Vietnamese Army (NVA)

Chieu Hoi   Vietnamese for "open arms," refers to clemency program and financial aid to encourage Viet Cong and NVA soldiers to surrender, defect, stop fighting for the communists, and switch sides to work and fight for the Western forces

chop chop   slang for food

chopper   helicopter

claymore   an antipersonnel mine carried by the infantry which, when detonated, propelled small steel cubes in a sixty-degree, fan-shaped pattern to a maximum distance of 100 meters

comics   topographic map

concertina wire   coiled barbed wire used as a protective obstacle typically around the perimeter of the firebase or building

cyclo   motorized rickshaw

dance   term for one squad in position to provide fire cover for another squad to maneuver

deuce-and-a-half   two-and-a-half ton truck, diesel powered; drives very fast for a large truck

didi   slang for Vietnamese word "di," meaning to leave, go

dinky dau   Vietnamese slang for crazy

eagle flights   large air assault of helicopters

FAC   forward air controller, who is the liaison between the Air Force and Army and coordinates air strikes

fragging   assassination of an officer by his own troops, usually by a grenade

golden BB   single bullet from a Viet Cong's small-arms fire which critically disables a Western aircraft

gook   derogatory word for an Asian enemy soldier, derived from Korea

green brick bullets   Russian and Chinese tracer ammunition that generates green light to focus aim on target

ground-pounder   soldiers who walked the war, as opposed to the Air Force

Gunny   nickname for a Gunnery Sergeant in the U.S. Marines

Heli / helo   helicopter

hook   radio handset

horn   radio microphone

in or out of country   being in or out of Vietnam

Jody   person who wins the affection of your spouse or lover while you are in Vietnam

jungle utilities   lightweight tropical fatigues

kill / killing zone   designated area of an ambush where weapons fire either kills or wounds everyone

klick   military term for distance of 1,000 meters (one kilometer, or .62 miles)

lieutenant   a commissioned officer in the U.S. Army

lit up   fired upon by the enemy

little people   slang for the enemy

LOH   light observation helicopter, pronounced "loach," used for observation, unarmed, seats pilot and three others

LOP   light observation plane, unarmed propeller plane used for observation

looky-loo   brief aerial reconnaissance

LZ   landing zone

mic   microphone to the portable radio used by infantry to communicate

muzzle flash   visible sight of a muzzle blast; expels high-temp, high-pressure gases from muzzle of a firearm

'Nam   abbreviation for Vietnam, used by those who served in Vietnam War

newbie   soldier just out of boot camp newly arrived in Vietnam, inexperienced and untested, also called a "boot"

NVA   North Vietnamese Army, communist soldiers

oak leaf cluster   a ribbon device in the shape of a miniature bronze or silver twig of four oak leaves with three acorns on the stem, awarded for a specific set of decorations and awards to denote subsequent decorations and awards

OCS   Officer Candidate School

Phos   white phosphorus; a shell containing a chemical that is detonated from the combat firebase that creates a white cloud of smoke in the air above the soldiers in the field, confirming the firebase's coordinates to target their artillery if requested; burns very hot, dangerous if it touches human flesh

platoon   a subdivision of a company-sized military unit, normally consisting of two or more squads or sections

platoon leader   officer in command of a platoon, usually a junior officer—a second or first lieutenant or an equivalent rank, usually assisted by a platoon sergeant

pop smoke   to ignite a smoke grenade to signal an aircraft, or mark a soldier's position for another soldier to know and follow his location. Smoke comes in different colors, green, yellow, or red, to let the soldiers know whether it's a smoke signal from their Army or from the enemy's

PTSD   post-traumatic stress disorder. Described by the Mayo Clinic as a mental health condition that's triggered by a terrifying event—either experiencing it or witnessing it. Symptoms may include flashbacks, nightmares and severe anxiety, uncontrollable thoughts re-experiencing the traumatic event. Other symptoms include exaggerated startle response; stressed or frightened even when no longer in danger; numbing of responsiveness to, or involvement with, the external world; difficulty in concentrating; memory impairment; guilt feelings and sleep difficulties. Getting effective treatment after PTSD symptoms develop can be critical to reduce symptoms and improve function

R&R   rest and recreation (or recuperation), a three- to seven-day vacation from the war for a soldier. For Vietnam, the Army's R&R destinations offered were to Bangkok, Hawaii, Hong Kong, Sydney or Taipei

redoubt   stronghold for defense

REMF   abbreviation for Rear Echelon Mother Fucker, a derogatory reference to a soldier in a support service job to the soldiers in the field, providing supplies and administration at a protected base, far from the front lines, generally not exposed to combat danger

riki tik   act rapidly, hastily, move fast

rucksack   backpack issued to infantry in Vietnam; cloth sack carried over one's back

sapper   a Viet Cong or NVA infiltrator armed with an explosive device

sergeant   a noncommissioned officer ranking in the Army above a corporal or specialist 4

shooter   nickname used to identify enemy fire delivering a good shot, usually a sniper

shrap   abbreviation for shrapnel; pieces of metal sent flying by an explosion

Sky Raider   name of Air Force ground support propeller aircraft

slick   Bell UH-1 Iroquois (unofficially Huey), military helicopter used for transporting troops in air assault operations. The helicopter did not have protruding armaments and was, therefore, "slick"

slope   derogatory term for an Asian enemy soldier

Snake   Cobra helicopter gunship with two pilots, rockets, grenade launcher, and mini gun; not for passengers

tracer   ammunition chemically treated so, when ignited by firing a machine gun, every fifth round delivers a bright light to allow the gunner to see his line of fire

VC / Viet Cong   Vietnamese communist soldiers

wilco   used especially in radio messages to indicate that a message received will be complied with

W/V Device   with Valor device, also called "V" Device, Combat Distinguishing Device or Combat "V," is a miniature bronze or gold ¼-inch letter medal and ribbon device awarded for valor or meritorious service in combat

WP / Willie Peter   white phosphorus; a shell containing a chemical that is detonated from the combat firebase that creates a white cloud of smoke in the air above the soldiers in the field, confirming the firebase's coordinates to target their artillery if requested; burns very hot, dangerous if it touches human flesh

XO   executive officer, who is second in command of a unit

GLOSSARY

Grrh = Disgusting
GRRrrrr = This could be dangerous
Hur-roh = Hello
Rah-ROU! = Careful!
Rah-TA-RATH = Serves you right
Rarh = Yeah
Rarh-re-ROOH = Here we go
Roh-RAH = OK
Roh-ra-Roh! = Oh My God!
Rooh-rooh-rooh = Crying
Ror—ro—RRH! = Make Room
ROUH-rah-HA-HA = Laughing
RrrrOH! = Wow!
Rr-rr-*ruff* = Absolutely
Ruff = Approval
RUGGH = Gross
RUH-Roh = Uh-oh
Ur Rat = You're right
WRRRrr Rot! = Immediate danger!
Yipping = Nervous

ACKNOWLEDGMENTS

Special thanks goes to Jenifer Behling, my wife and partner, who tirelessly worked on this novel, along with family and friends' feedback, to make *Curse of the Coloring Book* the novel it is today. Thanks to Brenda Krauss for the original book cover design, Photos by Craig Burleigh/BurleighPhoto.com, and 1106 Design for book interior design and much more.

EDITORS

A huge thank you to editors Sue Reynolds, Ken Malucelli, and Wyn Cooper

EARLY DRAFT READERS

The Lit Sisters Book Club	**In Order of Reading**
Karin Cordell	David Hibbard
Ana Lisa Hedstorm	Tom Hibbard
Susan Krauss	John Vileisis
Esther San Miguel	Doug Gauvreau
Rebecca Schnier	Tom Bailey
Diana Wayne	Jeff McKay
	Peggy Payne
Honorary Lit Sisters Book Club	Rick Newkold
Victor Cordell	Dave Mandelkern
Bill Sorich	Sue Uccelli

Lauren Hibbard

Brenda Krauss

Sam Steyer

Lisa Kehe

Elizabeth Williams

Ann Nejasmich

Ken Foster

Lori Foster

Chris Wolfenden, "Wolfy"

Corrin Trowbridge

Virginia Trowbridge

Loretta Seabrook

Polly Taylor

Peninsula Veteran Center

Ann Marie Fisher

Sam Torres

Linda Fernandez

HOWARD L. HIBBARD'S
VIETNAM WOLFHOUNDS

2nd Platoon, Charlie Company
2/27 Wolfhounds, 25th Infantry Division

"Big John" Quintrell

James L. Brandau, "Jim"

William I. Calhoun, MD

James Calvert, MD, "Jim"

Tommy Clack

Cyrus Jay Creveling, "Cy"

Larry Austin Dasher

Bruce R. Deisinger

Robert E. Mollenhauer, "Moose"

John P. Mulvaney

Paul R. Naso, "Nase"

Richard D. Schimmoeller, "Smokes"

Bob Segers

Scott Mollberg, Son of Wolfhound

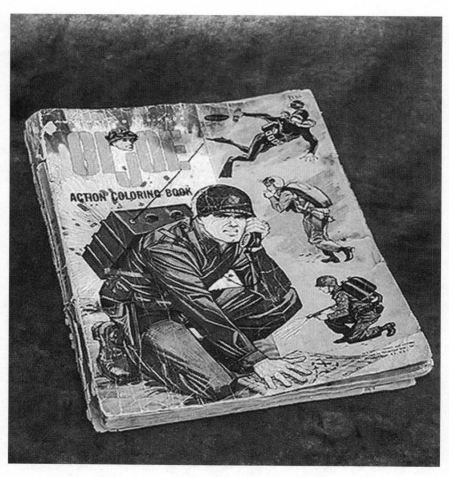

GI Joe Action Coloring Book © 1965 Hassenfeled Bros., Inc.
*All rights reserv*ed. Whitman Publishing Company

U.S. 105 mm brass artillery shell casing, handcrafted by Vietnamese peasant into flower vases with etching of deer and landscape. Shell primer appears on base.

VETERANS RESOURCES

U.S. Department of Veterans Affairs, www.va.gov

Operation SAVE

Veterans Crisis Line, 1.800.273.8255, press 1.

Confidential chat at **VeteransCrisisLine.net** or **text to 838255**. Remember **Operation SAVE** if you encounter a veteran who is in suicidal crisis.

1. Signs of suicidal thinking should be recognized
2. Ask the question: "Are you thinking of killing yourself?"
3. Validate the veteran's experience
4. Encourage treatment and expedite getting help

Readjustment Counseling Service, U.S. Department of Veterans Affairs, www.va.gov/rcs/

Combat Call Center, 1.877.WAR.VETS (927.8387)

Around-the-clock, confidential call center where combat veterans and their families can call to talk about their military experience or any other issue they are facing in their readjustment to civilian life. The staff is comprised of combat veterans from several eras, as well as family members of combat veterans. This benefit is prepaid through the veteran's military service.

Vet Center, www.vetcenter.va.gov
Readjustment Counseling Services

The Vet Center is focused on a wide range of psycho-social services offered to eligible veterans and their families in the effort to make a successful transition from military to civilian life. Examples include:

- Individual and group counseling for veterans and their families relating to a wide variety of issues from: Post-Traumatic Stress Disorder (PTSD); Traumatic Brain Injury (TBI); sexual trauma and substance abuse or other mental health issue that stems from military service; employment assessment and referral; Veterans Benefits Administration (VBA) benefits explanation and more.

"Peter the PTSD Awareness Penguin" is a non-profit organization founded to bring soldiers together to talk about mutual PTSD issues and raise awareness about the things they deal with day to day.

Originally started for infantrymen, the group has expanded to include all military, their family, and supporters, to express themselves freely without judgment, share humor and laughter, and be a part of a meaningful community. This is not a medical professional site, just veterans helping veterans.

http://us-infantry.com/peter-the-ptsd-awareness-penguin

Donations ~ Please consider donating to your local Vet Center or another association you see doing good work for our veterans. Thank you!

HOWARD L. HIBBARD

BORN IN DELAWARE, HOWARD quit college in 1967 to volunteer for the Army during the escalation of the Vietnam War. He rose through the ranks, and was discharged at age twenty-two. By then he was a paratrooper, a first lieutenant combat platoon leader, and briefly a company commander. Among the medals he received were two Bronze Stars, one W/V Device for heroism in ground combat, one Oak Leaf Cluster, and an Army Commendation Medal. After the Army, he graduated from college and law school, and practiced as an attorney for thirty-four years.

Curse of the Coloring Book is based on his combat and legal experiences, along with his Post-Traumatic Stress Disorder. It was with the help of his spouse, and veteran services, that this first novel was completed.

Currently he's adapting this book into a screenplay, and working on the sequel novel, *Revenge of The Coloring Book*. Howard lives in the San Francisco area with his wife, and is a grandfather to his two daughters' children. Cooking is his daily meditation; his handle is Chef PTSD.

I hope you enjoyed **Curse of the Coloring Book**, and would enjoy hearing from you. Please post a review on your favorite book website.

The Hearing Is Over, But the Battle Has Just Begun.

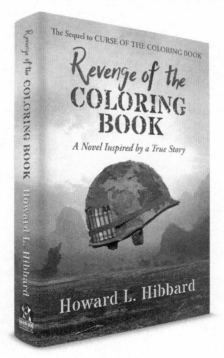

Visit www.HowardLHibbard.com

- To find out when the sequel, **Revenge of the Coloring Book**, will be published.
- Follow "Chef PTSD" to get easy, healthy, flavorful recipes.
- Read and engage with Howard on his provocative social commentary blogs on current news events.

369

54933256R00236

Made in the USA
San Bernardino, CA
26 October 2017